grand Guignol orchestra

2

STORY AND ART BY

KAORI
YUKI

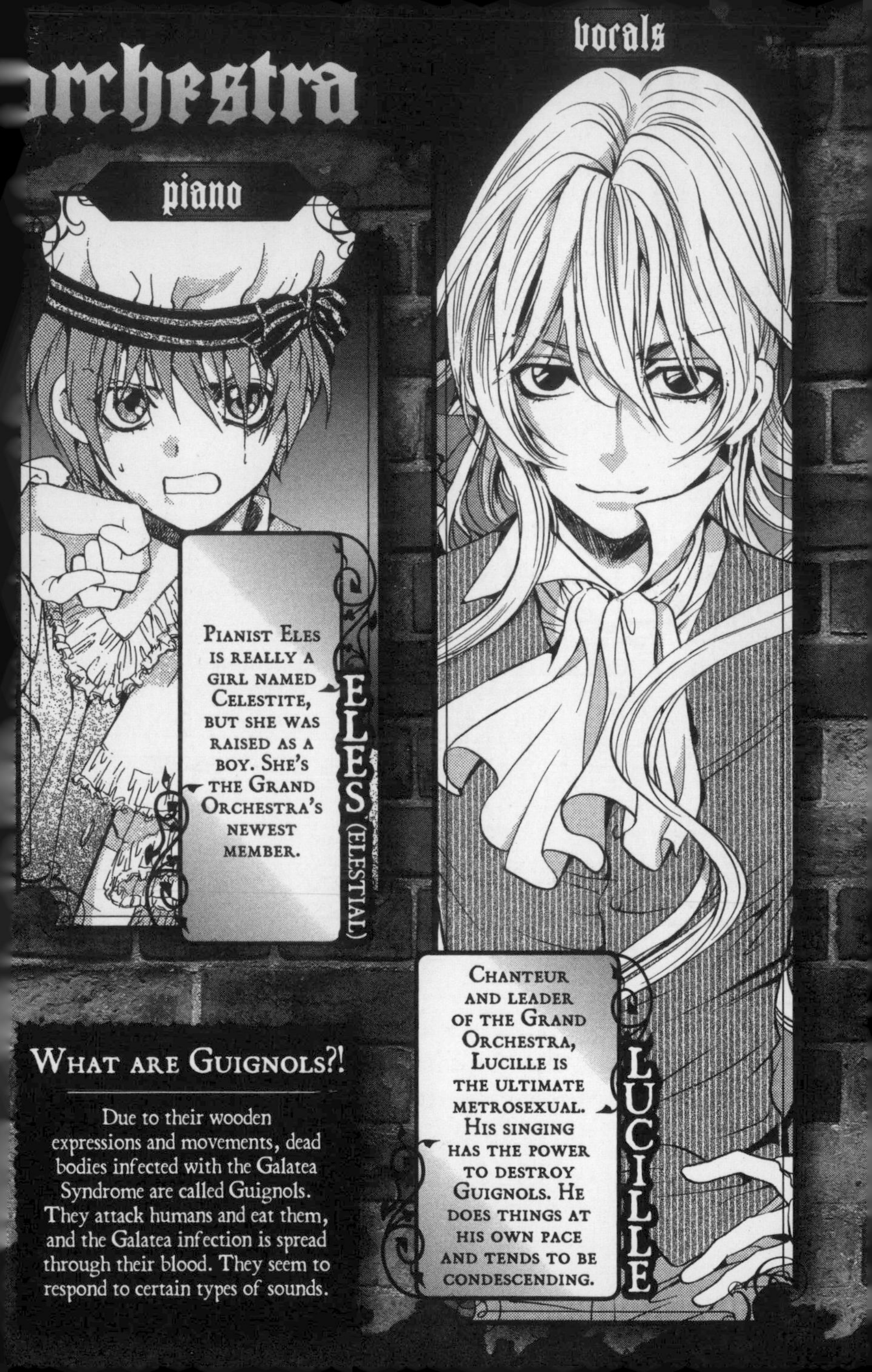
vocals
LUCILLE
Chanteur and leader of the Grand Orchestra, Lucille is the ultimate metrosexual. His singing has the power to destroy Guignols. He does things at his own pace and tends to be condescending.
rchestra
piano
ELES (ELESTIAL)
Pianist Eles is really a girl named Celestite, but she was raised as a boy. She's the Grand Orchestra's newest member.

What are Guignols?!

Due to their wooden expressions and movements, dead bodies infected with the Galatea Syndrome are called Guignols. They attack humans and eat them, and the Galatea infection is spread through their blood. They seem to respond to certain types of sounds.

grand Guignol

Member Introductions

cello

violin

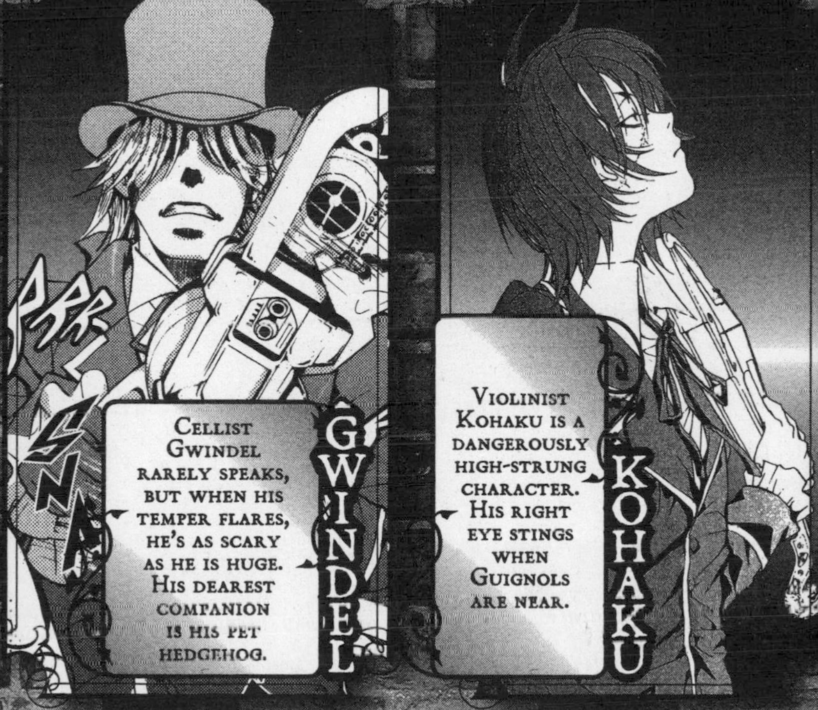
Cellist Gwindel rarely speaks, but when his temper flares, he's as scary as he is huge. His dearest companion is his pet hedgehog.
GWINDEL
Violinist Kohaku is a dangerously high-strung character. His right eye stings when Guignols are near.
KOHAKU

The world is infested by a bizarre plague that gives rise to man-eating zombies known as Guignols. Lucille and his gang are the "unofficial" Grand Orchestra, willing to perform any piece of music for the right price. Lucille's *Black Hymnal* contains songs that can perform all sorts of miracles. What awaits this Guignol-hating group of traveling musicians?

grand Guignol orchestra

2

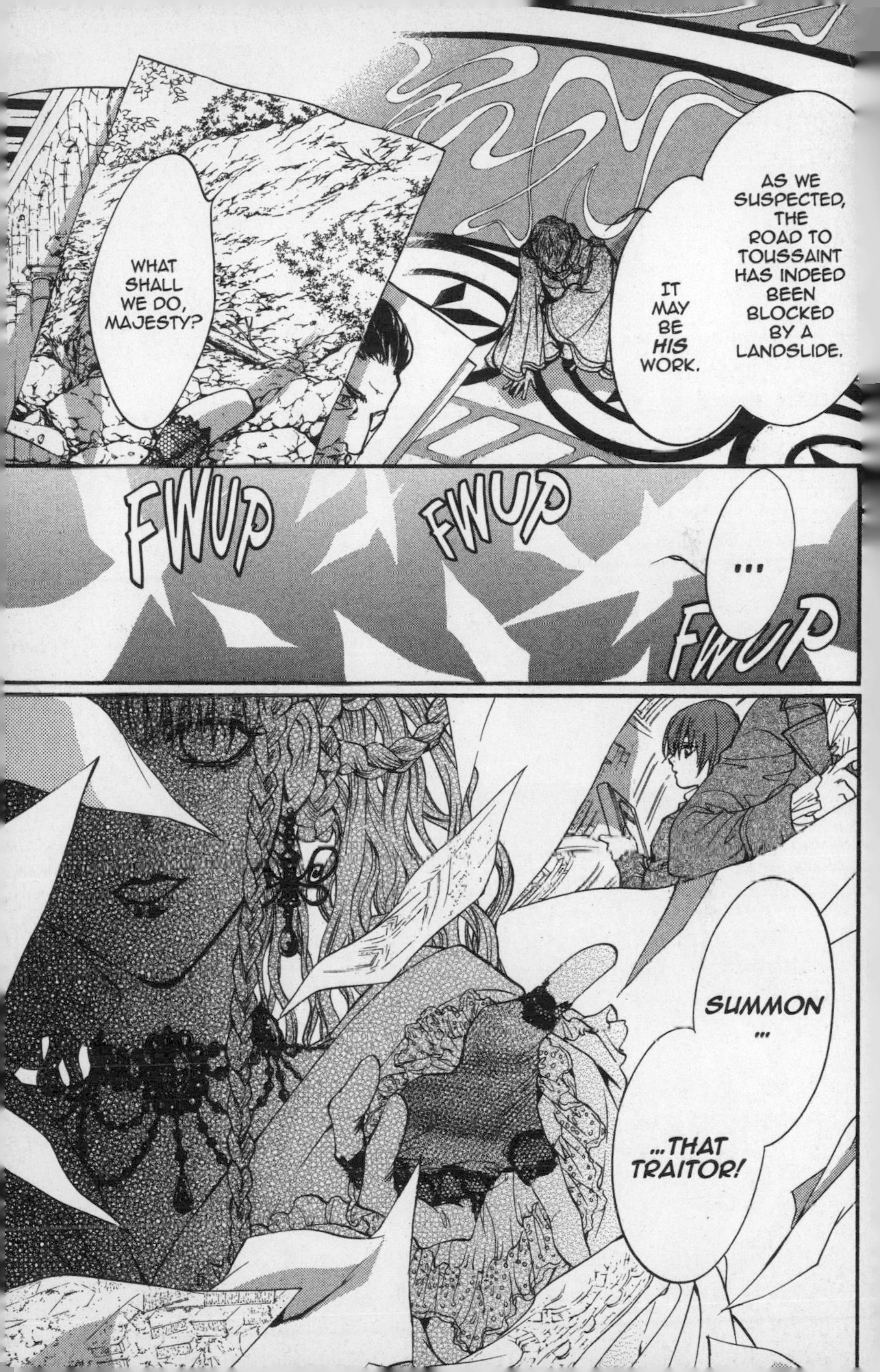
AS WE SUSPECTED, THE ROAD TO TOUSSAINT HAS INDEED BEEN BLOCKED BY A LANDSLIDE.
IT MAY BE HIS WORK.
WHAT SHALL WE DO, MAJESTY?
...
FWUP
FWUP
FWUP
SUMMON ...
...THAT TRAITOR!

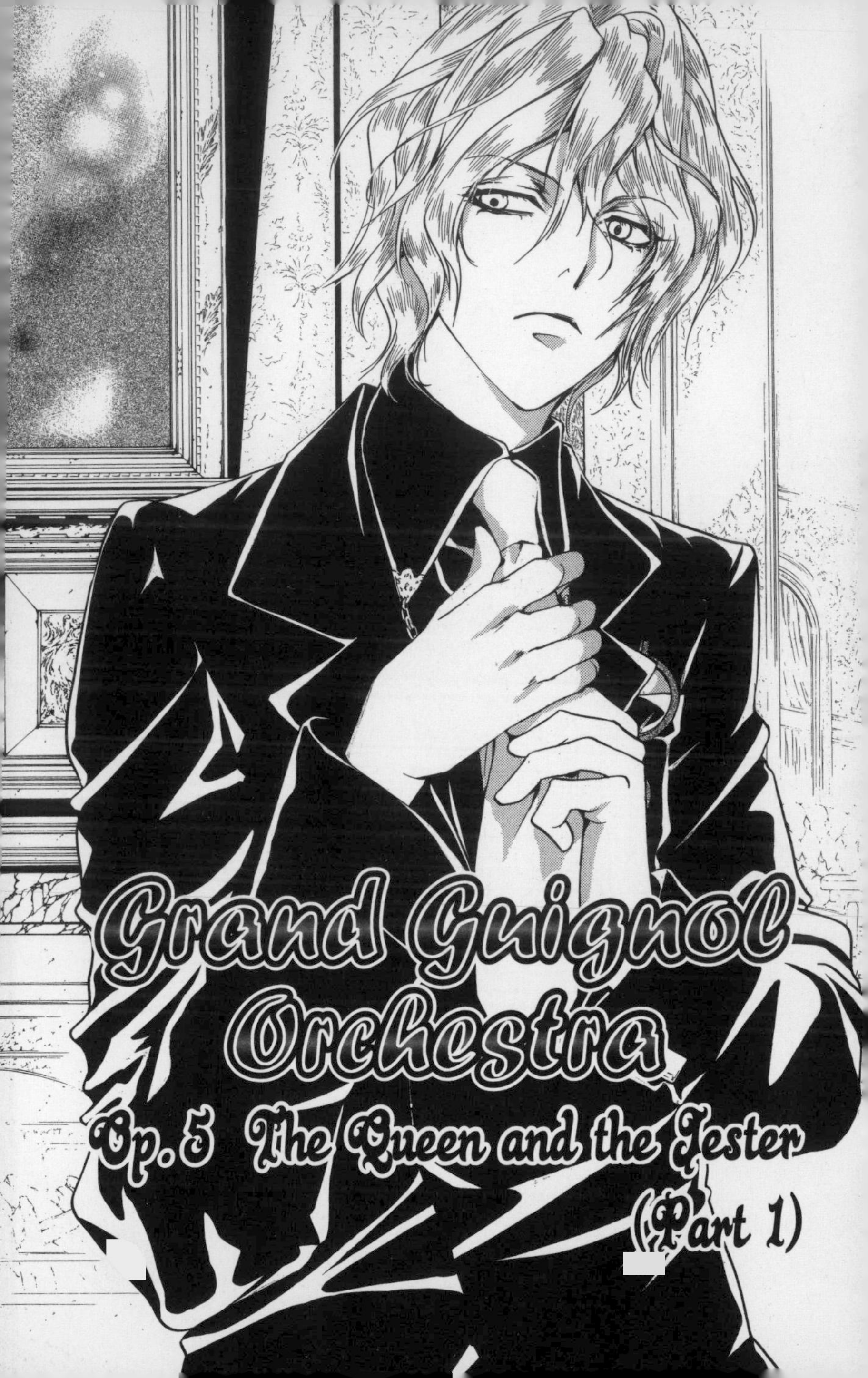
Grand Guignol Orchestra
Op. 5 The Queen and the Jester
(Part 1)

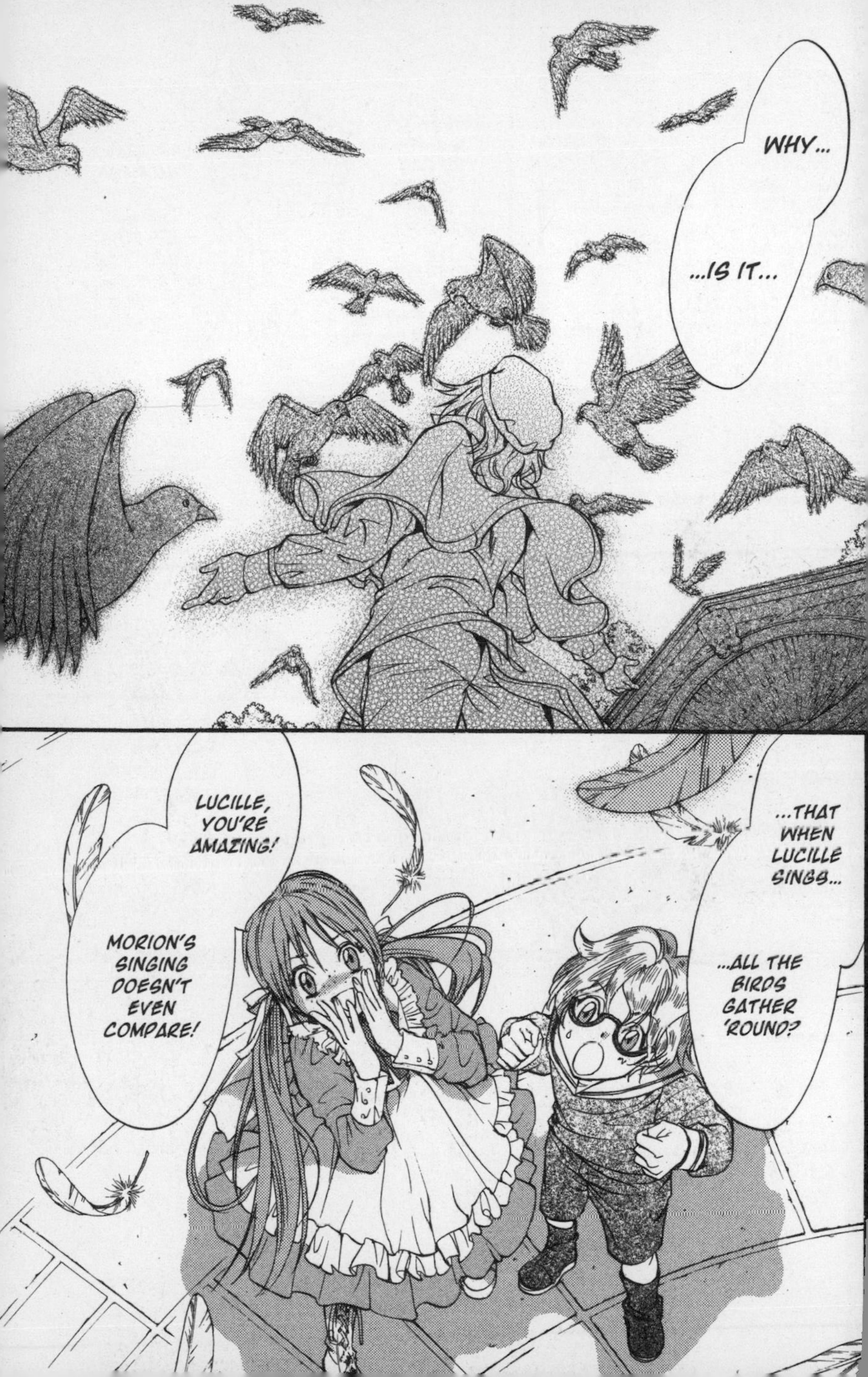
WHY...
...IS IT...
...THAT WHEN LUCILLE SINGS...
...ALL THE BIRDS GATHER 'ROUND?
LUCILLE, YOU'RE AMAZING!
MORION'S SINGING DOESN'T EVEN COMPARE!

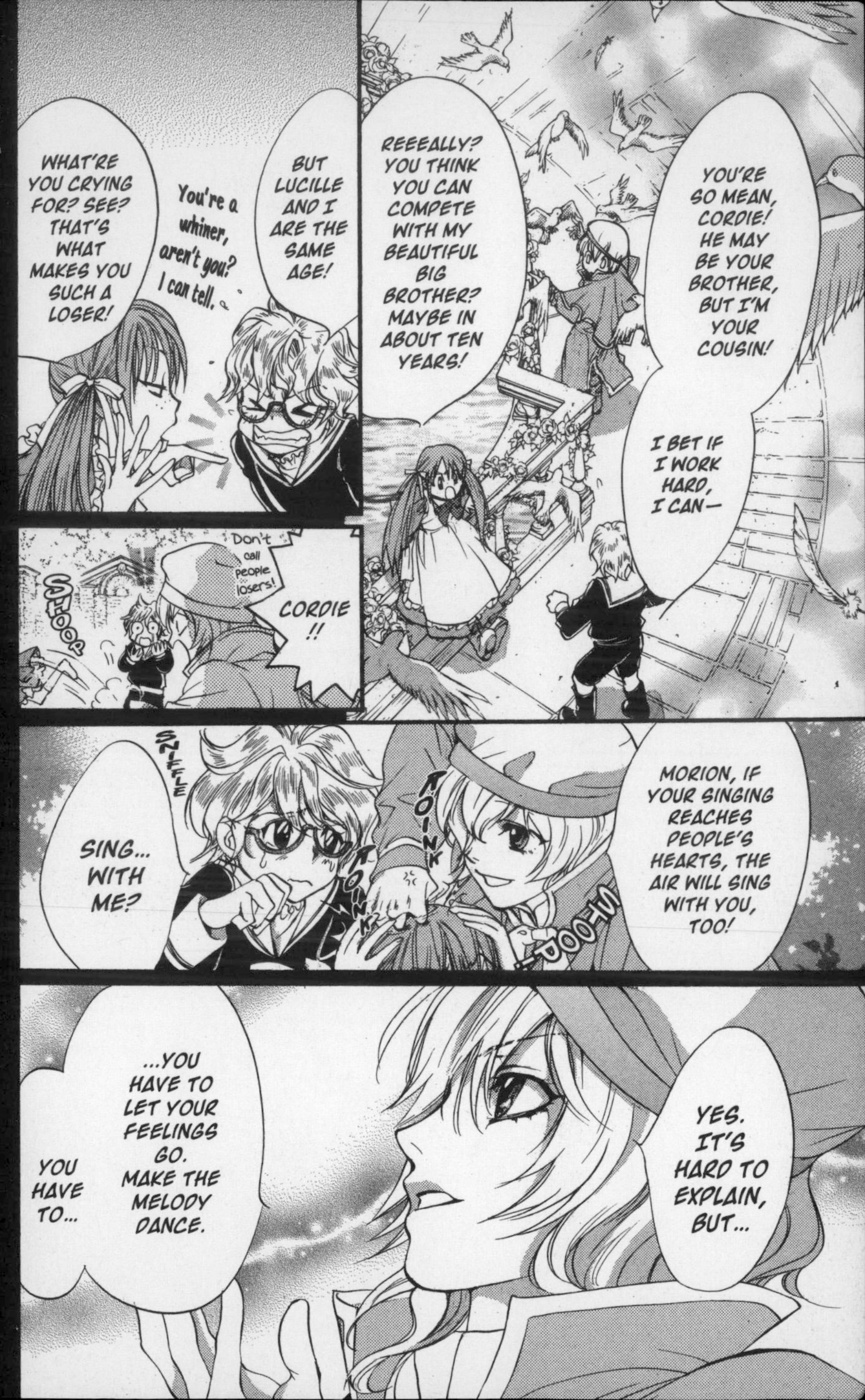
YOU'RE SO MEAN, CORDIE! HE MAY BE YOUR BROTHER, BUT I'M YOUR COUSIN!
I BET IF I WORK HARD, I CAN—
REEEALLY? YOU THINK YOU CAN COMPETE WITH MY BEAUTIFUL BIG BROTHER? MAYBE IN ABOUT TEN YEARS!
BUT LUCILLE AND I ARE THE SAME AGE!
You're a whiner, aren't you? I can tell.
WHAT'RE YOU CRYING FOR? SEE? THAT'S WHAT MAKES YOU SUCH A LOSER!
Don't call people losers!
CORDIE !!
SHOOP
MORION, IF YOUR SINGING REACHES PEOPLE'S HEARTS, THE AIR WILL SING WITH YOU, TOO!
BOINK
BOINK
SNIFFLE
SING... WITH ME?
YES. IT'S HARD TO EXPLAIN, BUT...
...YOU HAVE TO LET YOUR FEELINGS GO. MAKE THE MELODY DANCE.
YOU HAVE TO...

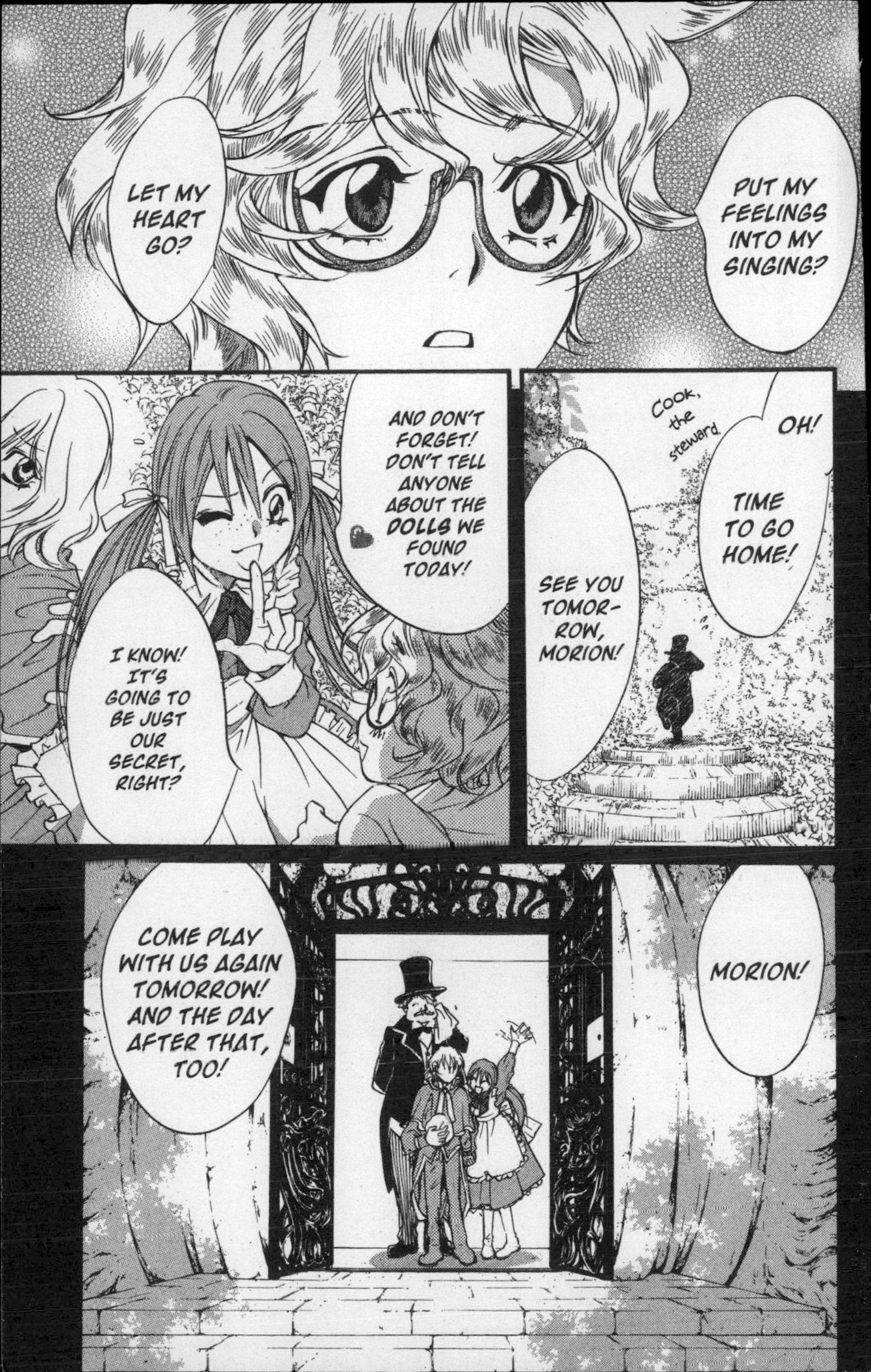
PUT MY FEELINGS INTO MY SINGING?
LET MY HEART GO?
OH!
Cook, the steward
TIME TO GO HOME!
SEE YOU TOMOR-ROW, MORION!
AND DON'T FORGET! DON'T TELL ANYONE ABOUT THE DOLLS WE FOUND TODAY!
I KNOW! IT'S GOING TO BE JUST OUR SECRET, RIGHT?
MORION!
COME PLAY WITH US AGAIN TOMORROW! AND THE DAY AFTER THAT, TOO!

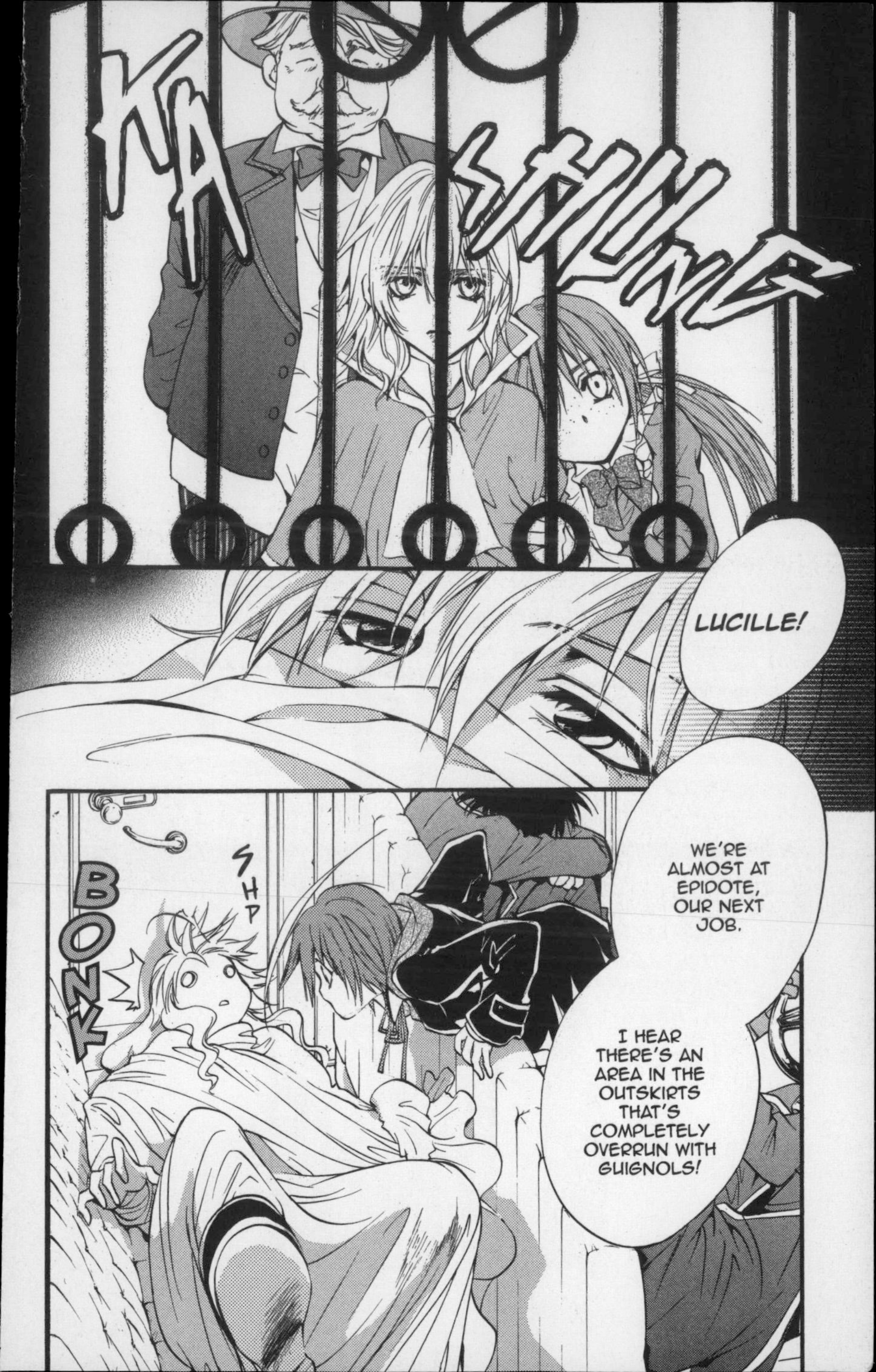
KA-SHING
LUCILLE!
WE'RE ALMOST AT EPIDOTE, OUR NEXT JOB.
I HEAR THERE'S AN AREA IN THE OUTSKIRTS THAT'S COMPLETELY OVERRUN WITH GUIGNOLS!
SHP
BONK

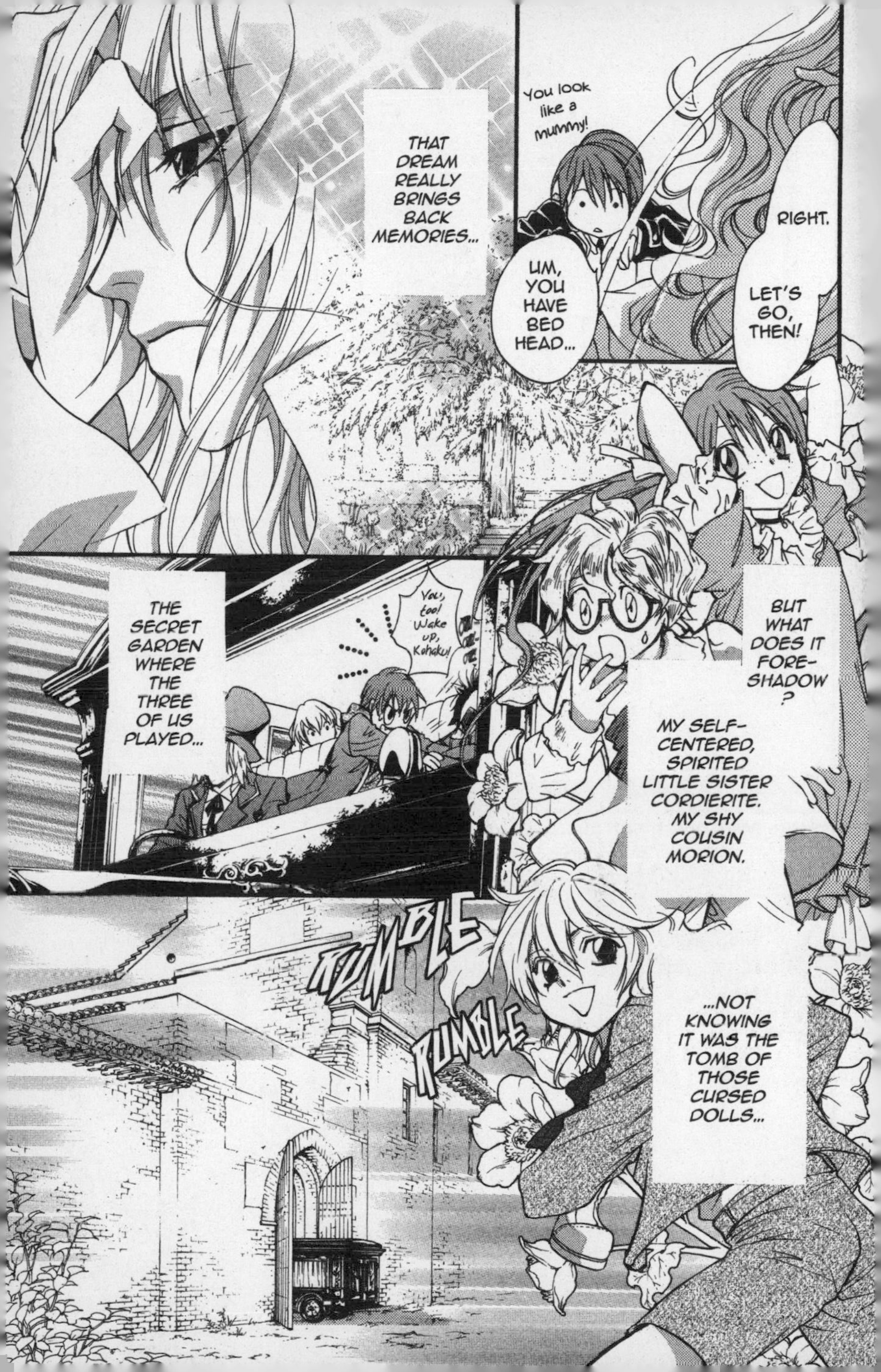
RIGHT.
LET'S GO, THEN!
You look like a mummy!
UM, YOU HAVE BED HEAD...
THAT DREAM REALLY BRINGS BACK MEMORIES...
BUT WHAT DOES IT FORE-SHADOW?
MY SELF-CENTERED, SPIRITED LITTLE SISTER CORDIERITE. MY SHY COUSIN MORION.
You, too! Wake up, Kohaku!
...
THE SECRET GARDEN WHERE THE THREE OF US PLAYED...
...NOT KNOWING IT WAS THE TOMB OF THOSE CURSED DOLLS...
RUMBLE
RUMBLE

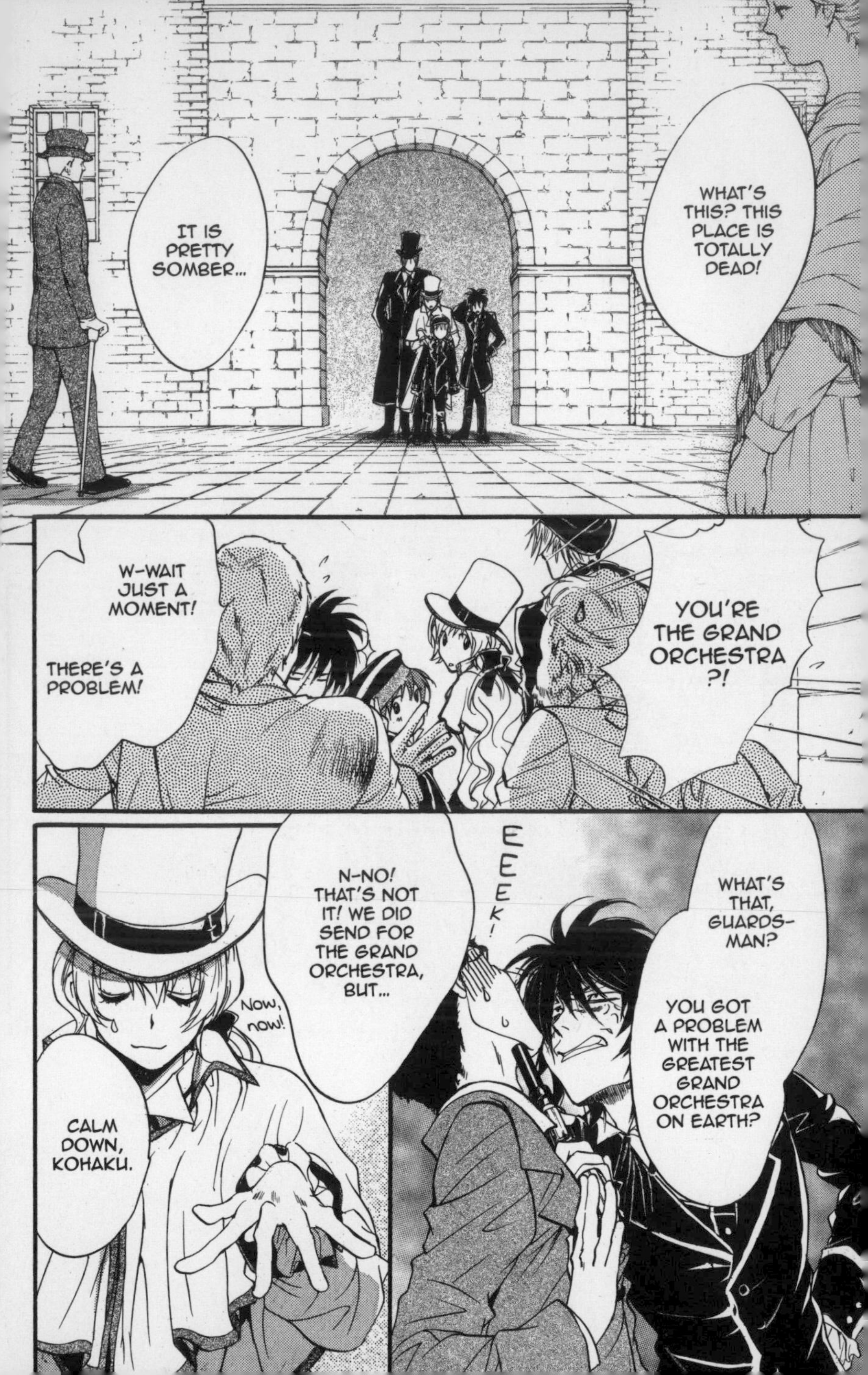
WHAT'S THIS? THIS PLACE IS TOTALLY DEAD!
IT IS PRETTY SOMBER...
YOU'RE THE GRAND ORCHESTRA?!
W-WAIT JUST A MOMENT!
THERE'S A PROBLEM!
WHAT'S THAT, GUARDS-MAN?
YOU GOT A PROBLEM WITH THE GREATEST GRAND ORCHESTRA ON EARTH?
EEEEK!
N-NO! THAT'S NOT IT! WE DID SEND FOR THE GRAND ORCHESTRA, BUT...
Now, now!
CALM DOWN, KOHAKU.

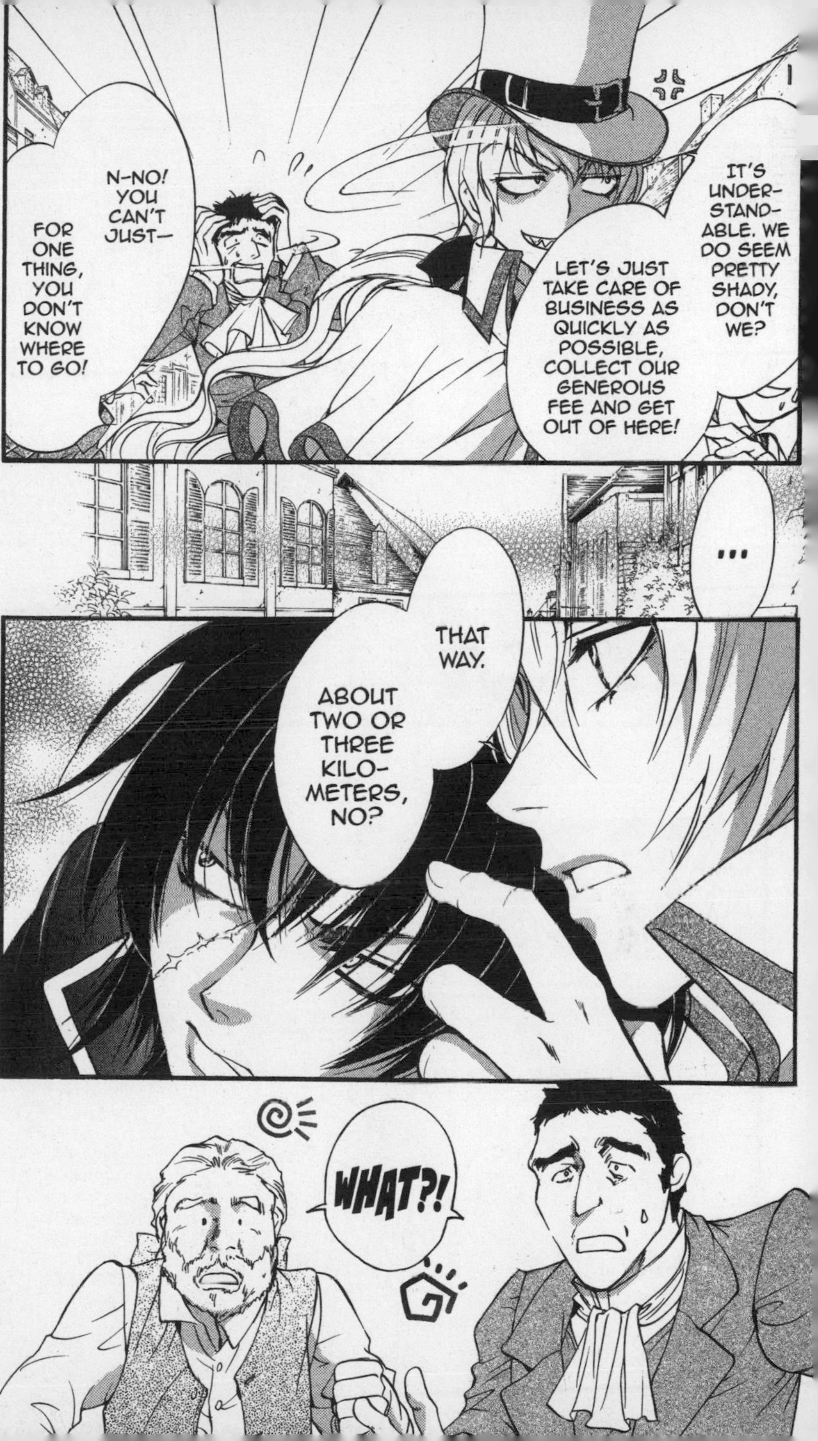
IT'S UNDERSTANDABLE. WE DO SEEM PRETTY SHADY, DON'T WE?
LET'S JUST TAKE CARE OF BUSINESS AS QUICKLY AS POSSIBLE, COLLECT OUR GENEROUS FEE AND GET OUT OF HERE!
N-NO! YOU CAN'T JUST—
FOR ONE THING, YOU DON'T KNOW WHERE TO GO!
...
THAT WAY.
ABOUT TWO OR THREE KILOMETERS, NO?
WHAT?!

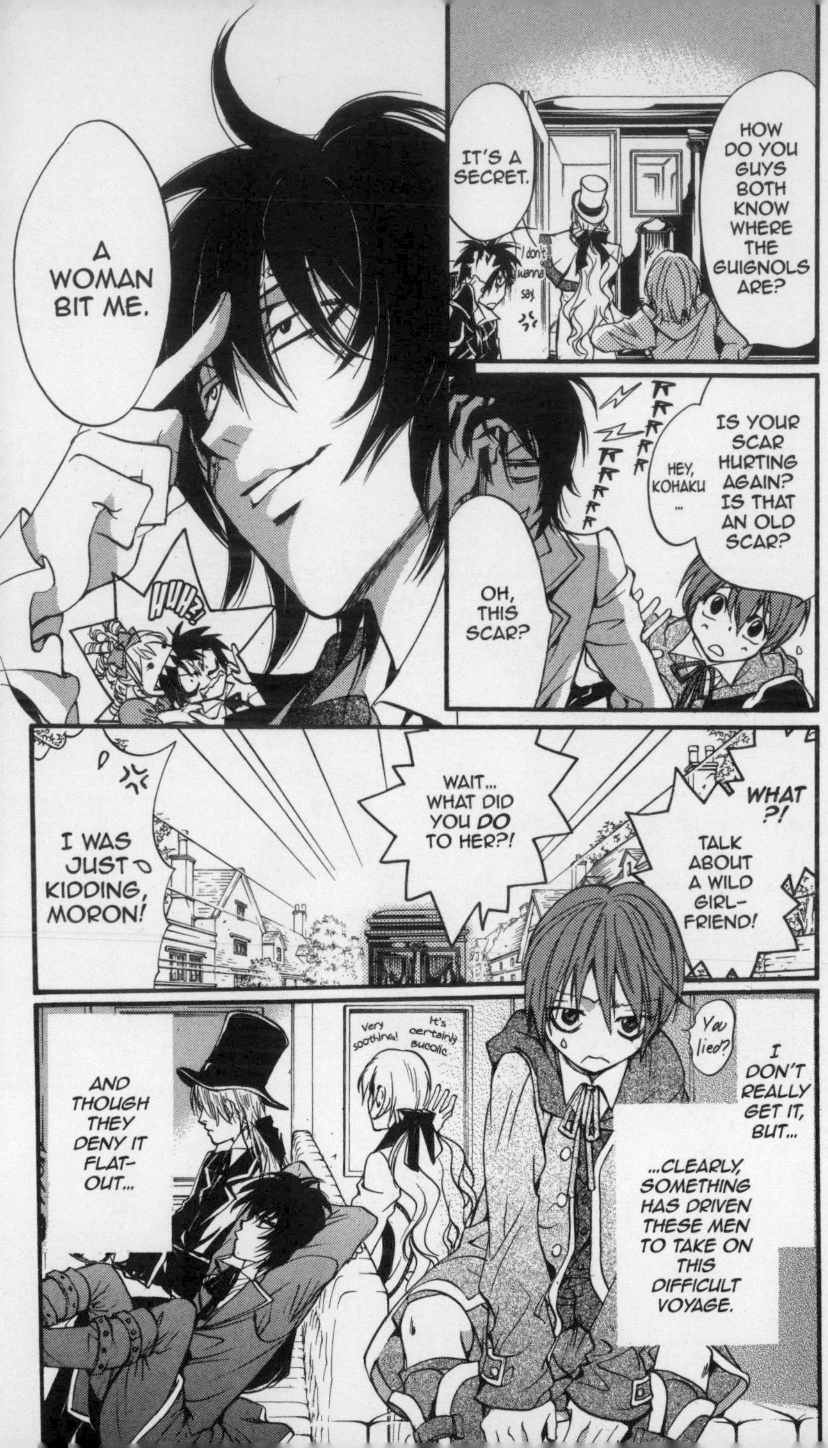
HOW DO YOU GUYS BOTH KNOW WHERE THE GUIGNOLS ARE?
IT'S A SECRET.
I don't wanna say.
IS YOUR SCAR HURTING AGAIN? IS THAT AN OLD SCAR?
HEY, KOHAKU...
RRRRRRRRRRRR
OH, THIS SCAR?
A WOMAN BIT ME.
HUH?!
WHAT?!
TALK ABOUT A WILD GIRL-FRIEND!
WAIT... WHAT DID YOU DO TO HER?!
I WAS JUST KIDDING, MORON!
I DON'T REALLY GET IT, BUT...
You lied?
...CLEARLY, SOMETHING HAS DRIVEN THESE MEN TO TAKE ON THIS DIFFICULT VOYAGE.
It's certainly bucolic
Very soothing!
AND THOUGH THEY DENY IT FLAT-OUT...

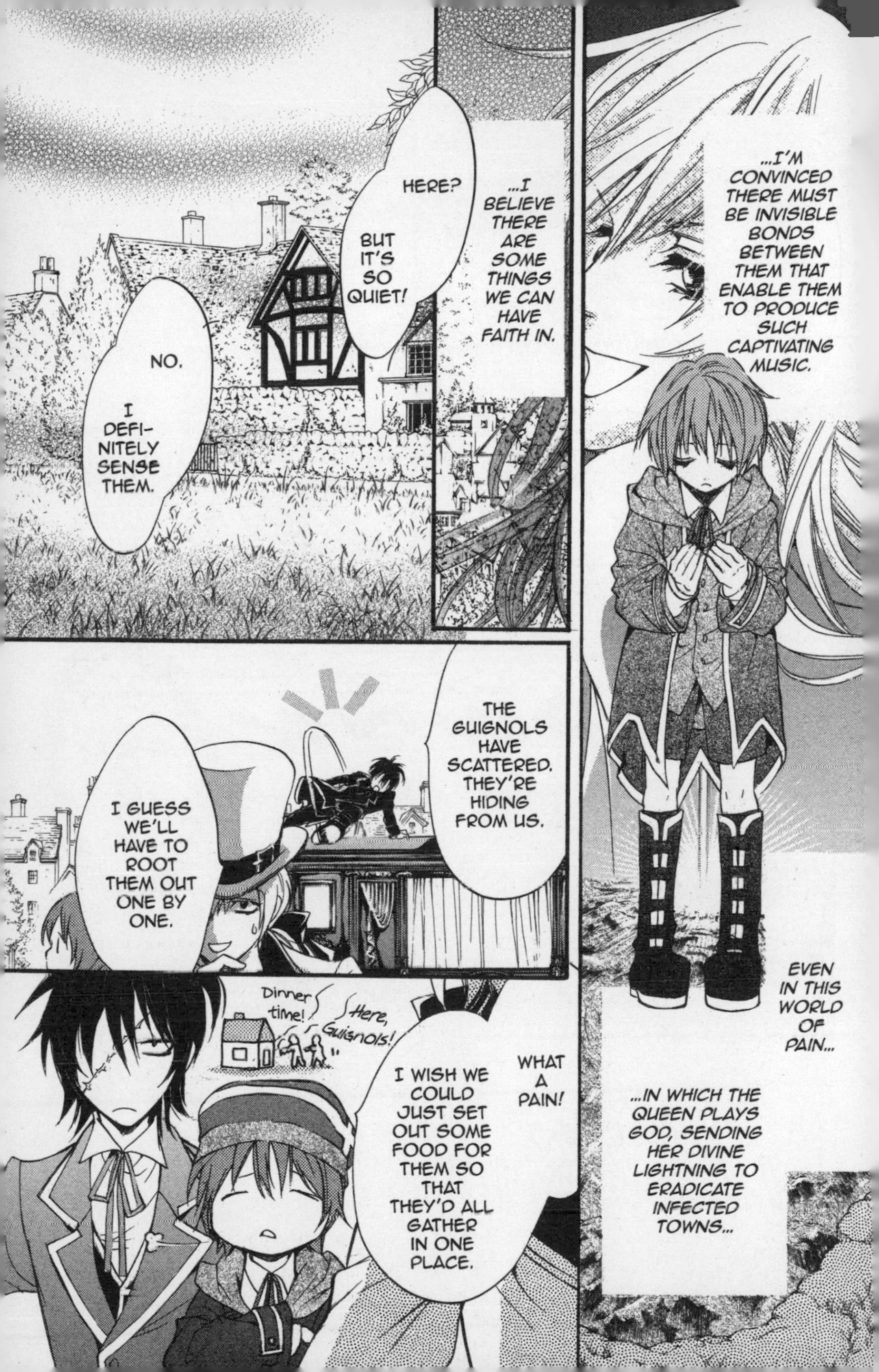
...I'M CONVINCED THERE MUST BE INVISIBLE BONDS BETWEEN THEM THAT ENABLE THEM TO PRODUCE SUCH CAPTIVATING MUSIC.
EVEN IN THIS WORLD OF PAIN...
...IN WHICH THE QUEEN PLAYS GOD, SENDING HER DIVINE LIGHTNING TO ERADICATE INFECTED TOWNS...
...I BELIEVE THERE ARE SOME THINGS WE CAN HAVE FAITH IN.
HERE? BUT IT'S SO QUIET!
NO. I DEFINITELY SENSE THEM.
THE GUIGNOLS HAVE SCATTERED. THEY'RE HIDING FROM US.
I GUESS WE'LL HAVE TO ROOT THEM OUT ONE BY ONE.
WHAT A PAIN!
I WISH WE COULD JUST SET OUT SOME FOOD FOR THEM SO THAT THEY'D ALL GATHER IN ONE PLACE.
Dinner time!
Here, Guignols!

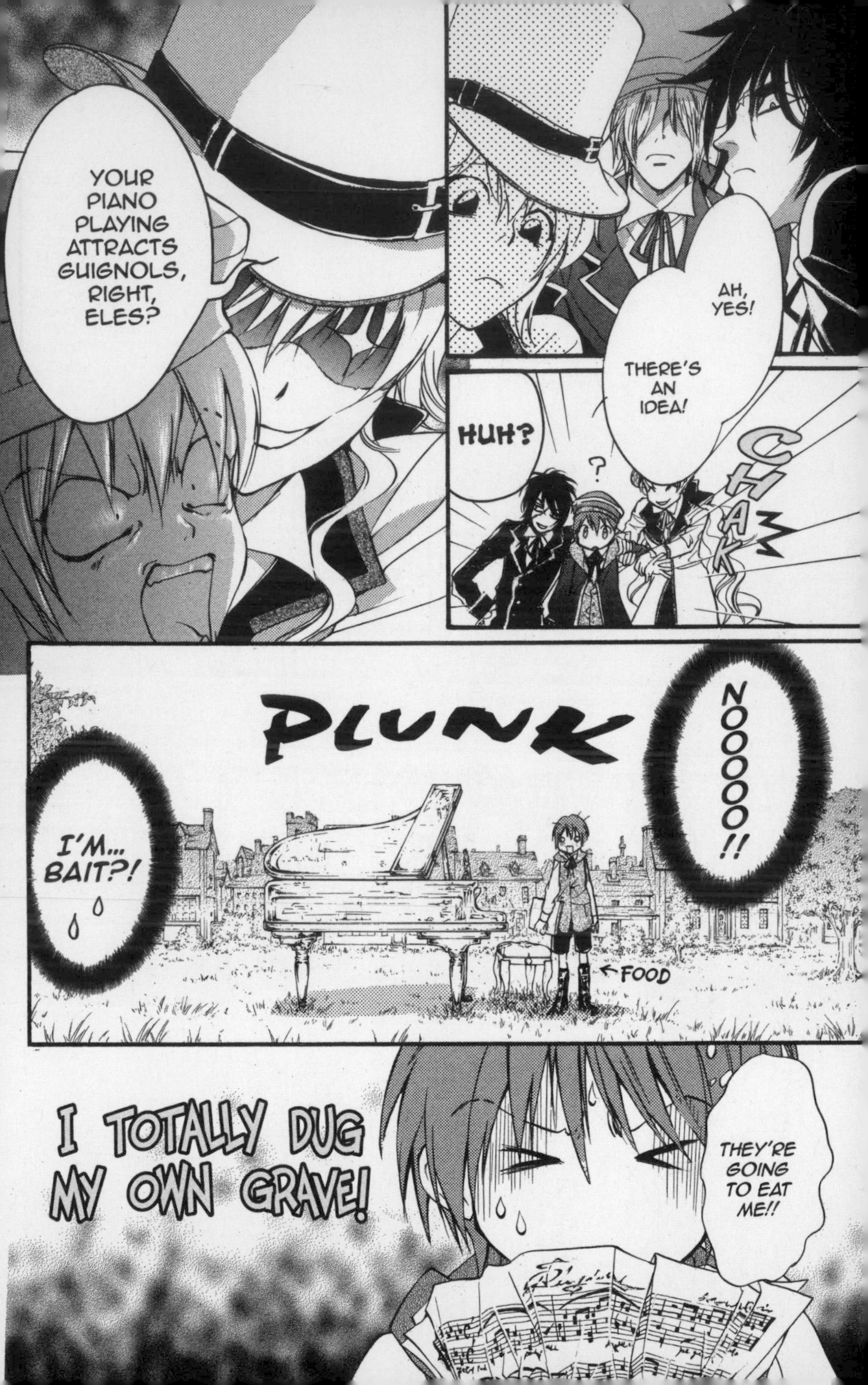
AH, YES!
THERE'S AN IDEA!
HUH?
?
CHAK
YOUR PIANO PLAYING ATTRACTS GUIGNOLS, RIGHT, ELES?
NOOOOOO!!
PLUNK
I'M... BAIT?!
←FOOD
THEY'RE GOING TO EAT ME!!
I TOTALLY DUG MY OWN GRAVE!

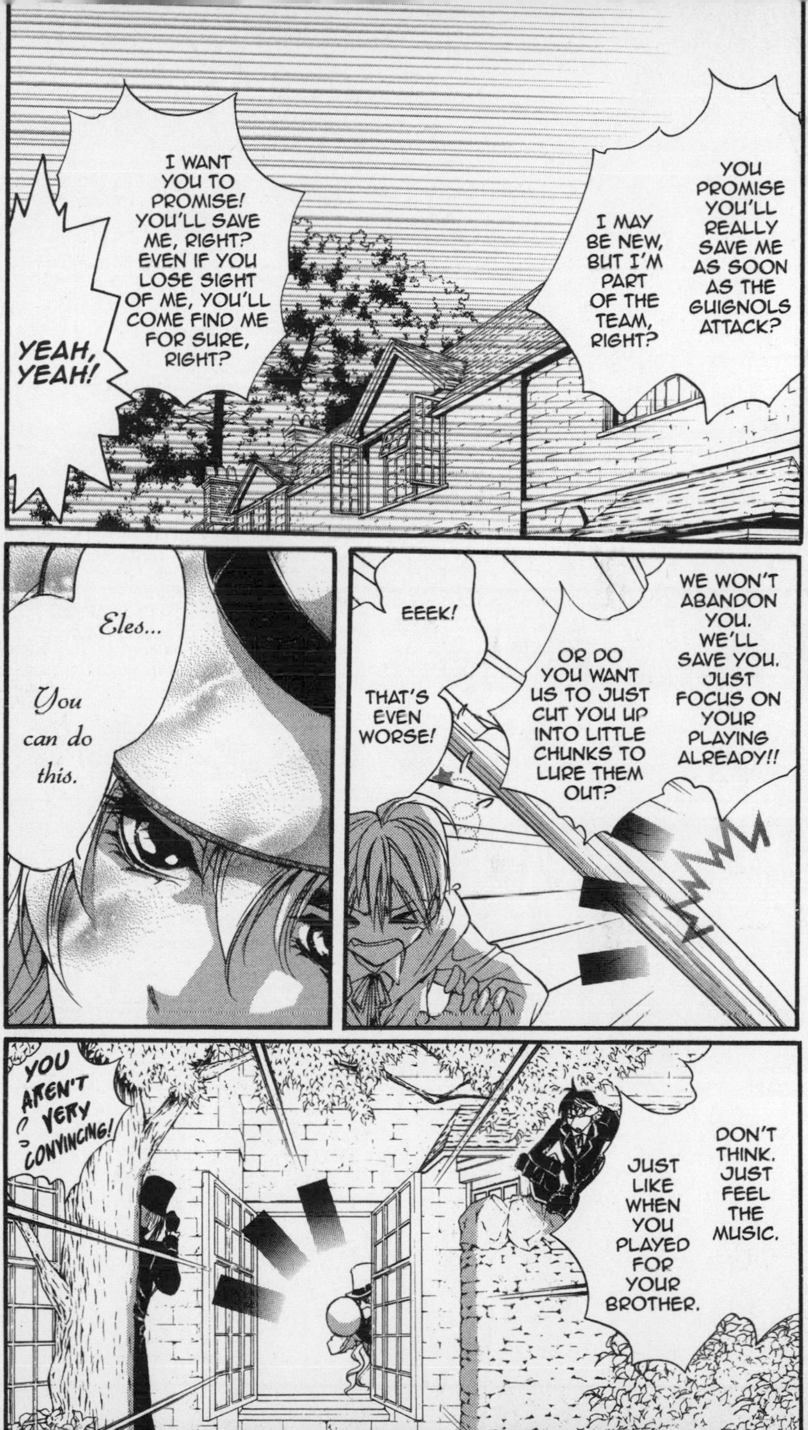
YOU PROMISE YOU'LL REALLY SAVE ME AS SOON AS THE GUIGNOLS ATTACK?
I MAY BE NEW, BUT I'M PART OF THE TEAM, RIGHT?
I WANT YOU TO PROMISE! YOU'LL SAVE ME, RIGHT? EVEN IF YOU LOSE SIGHT OF ME, YOU'LL COME FIND ME FOR SURE, RIGHT?
YEAH, YEAH!
WE WON'T ABANDON YOU. WE'LL SAVE YOU. JUST FOCUS ON YOUR PLAYING ALREADY!!
OR DO YOU WANT US TO JUST CUT YOU UP INTO LITTLE CHUNKS TO LURE THEM OUT?
EEEK!
THAT'S EVEN WORSE!
Eles...
You can do this.
DON'T THINK. JUST FEEL THE MUSIC.
JUST LIKE WHEN YOU PLAYED FOR YOUR BROTHER.
YOU AREN'T VERY CONVINCING!

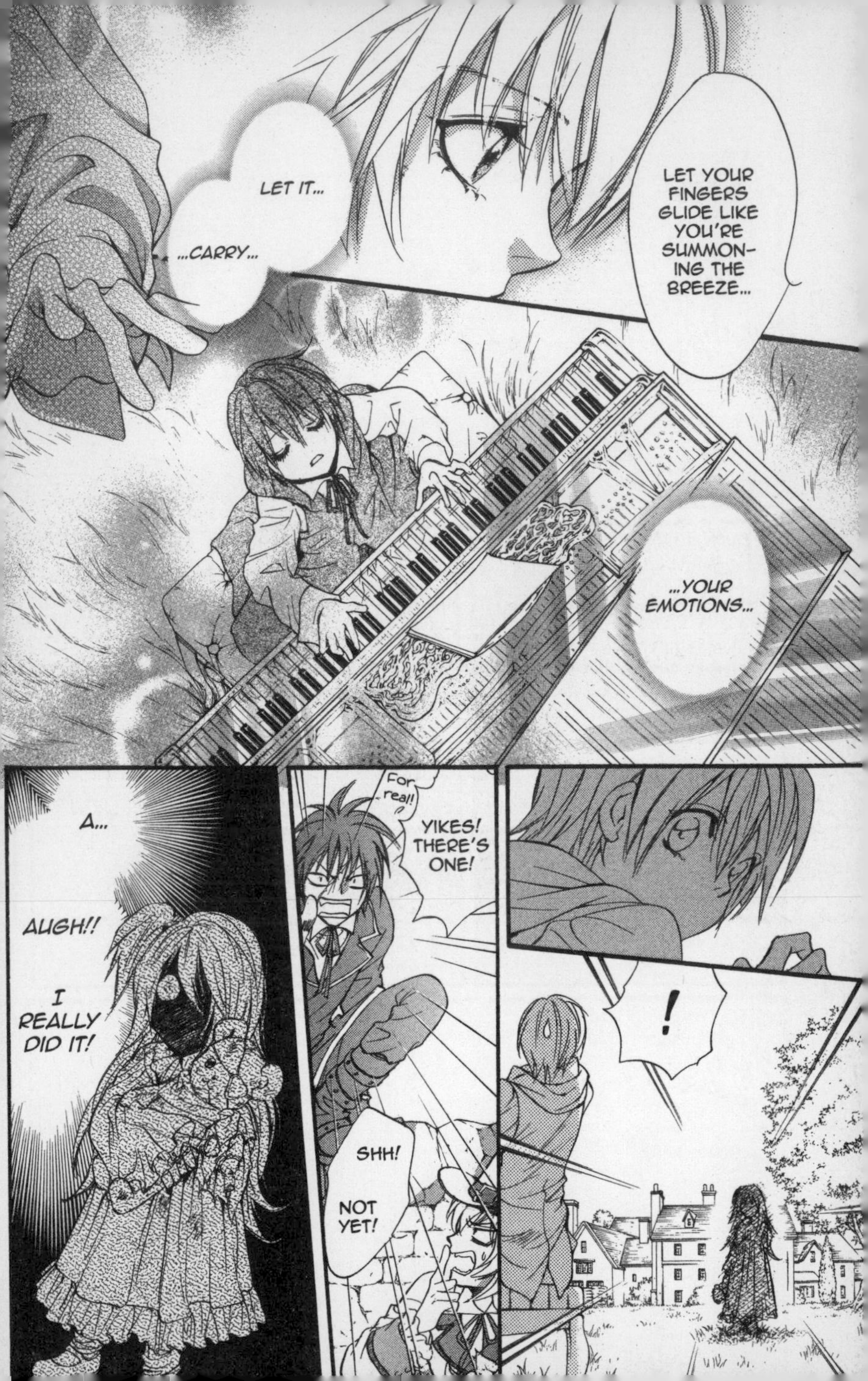
LET YOUR FINGERS GLIDE LIKE YOU'RE SUMMONING THE BREEZE...
LET IT...
...CARRY...
...YOUR EMOTIONS...
!
YIKES! THERE'S ONE!
For real!
SHH!
NOT YET!
A...
AUGH!!
I REALLY DID IT!

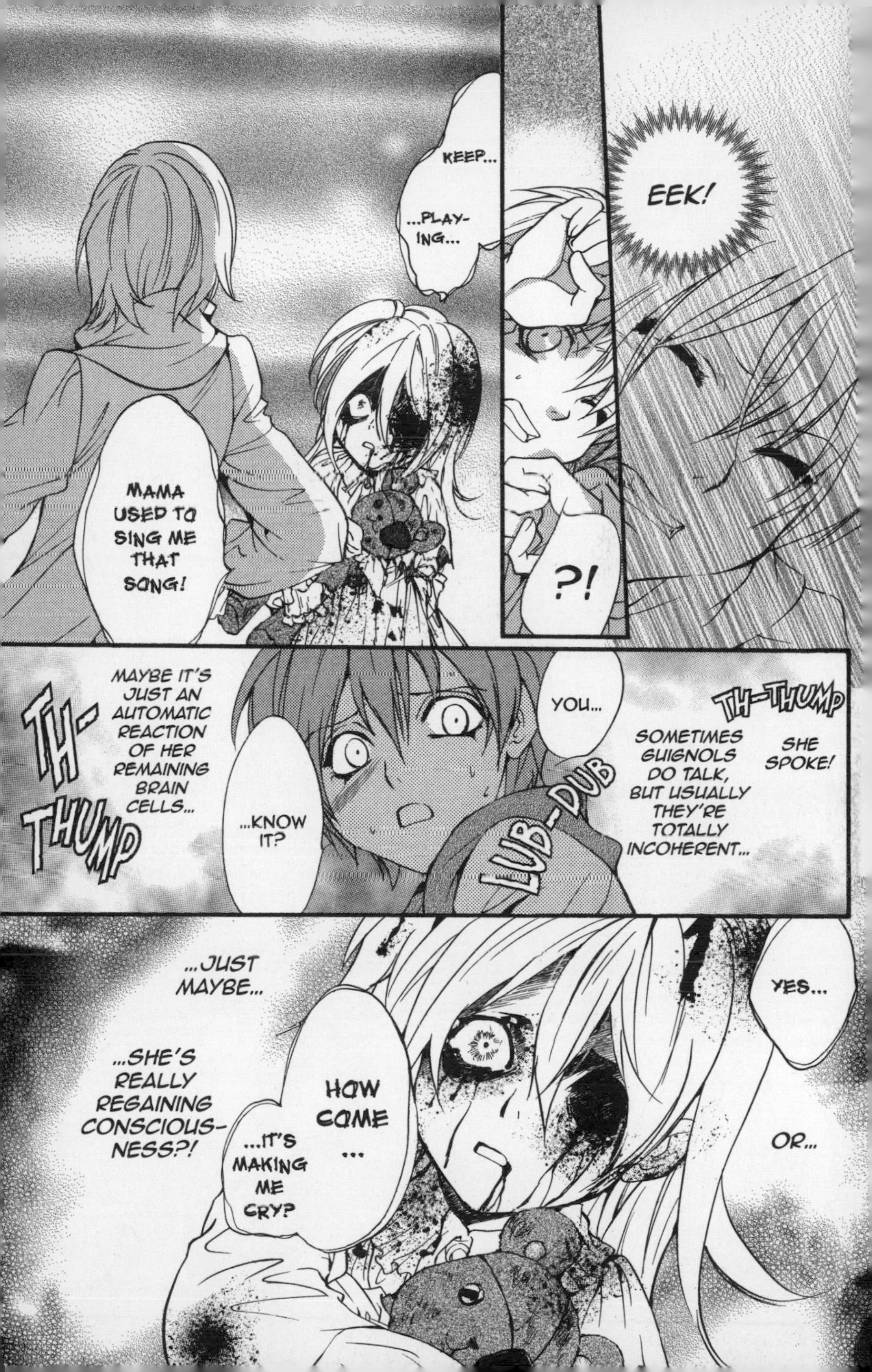
EEK!
?!
KEEP...
...PLAY-ING...
MAMA USED TO SING ME THAT SONG!
TH-THUMP
SHE SPOKE!
SOMETIMES GUIGNOLS DO TALK, BUT USUALLY THEY'RE TOTALLY INCOHERENT...
YOU...
LUB-DUB
...KNOW IT?
MAYBE IT'S JUST AN AUTOMATIC REACTION OF HER REMAINING BRAIN CELLS...
TH-THUMP
YES...
OR...
HOW COME...
...IT'S MAKING ME CRY?
...JUST MAYBE...
...SHE'S REALLY REGAINING CONSCIOUS-NESS?!

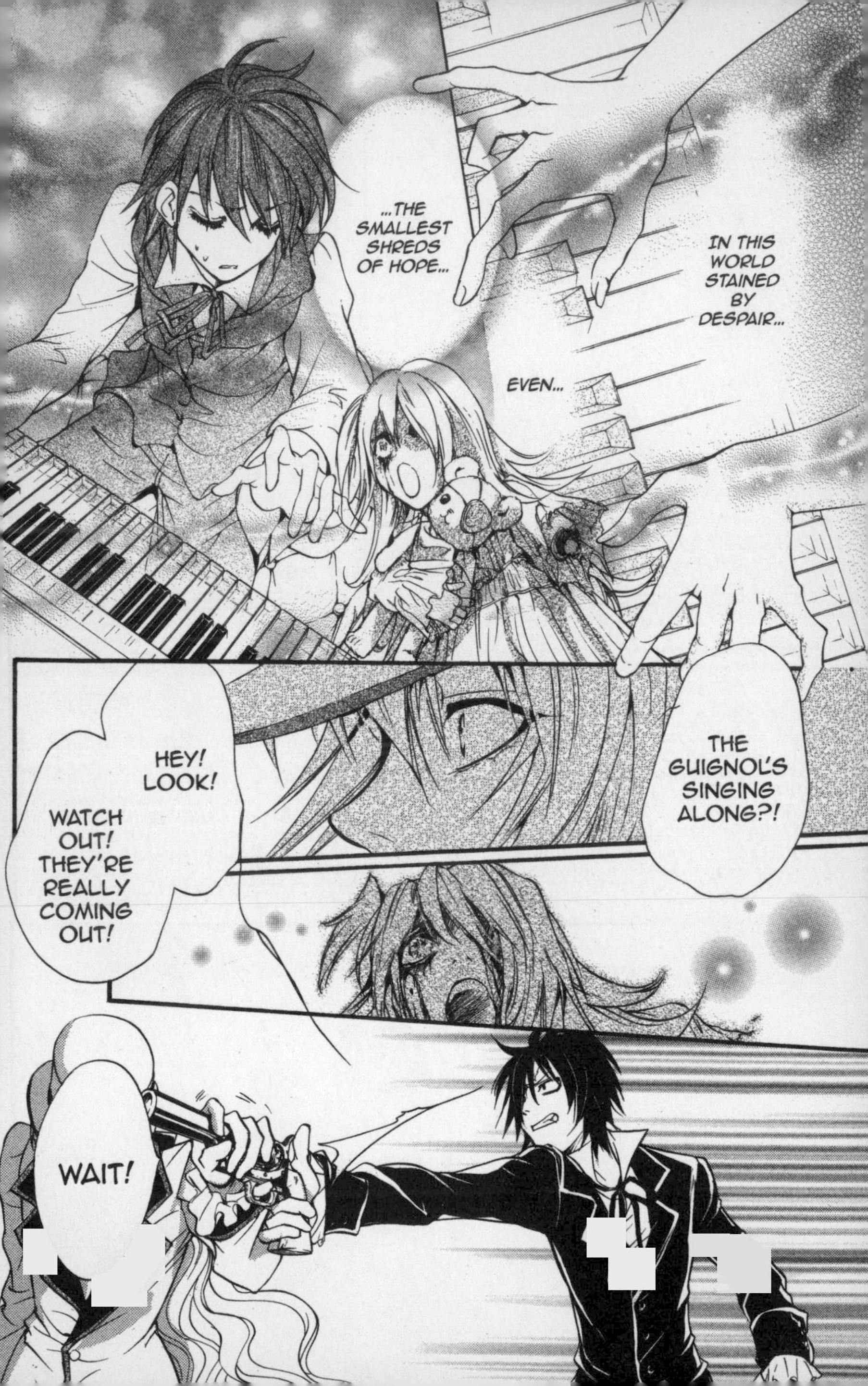
IN THIS WORLD STAINED BY DESPAIR...
EVEN...
...THE SMALLEST SHREDS OF HOPE...
THE GUIGNOL'S SINGING ALONG?!
HEY! LOOK!
WATCH OUT! THEY'RE REALLY COMING OUT!
WAIT!

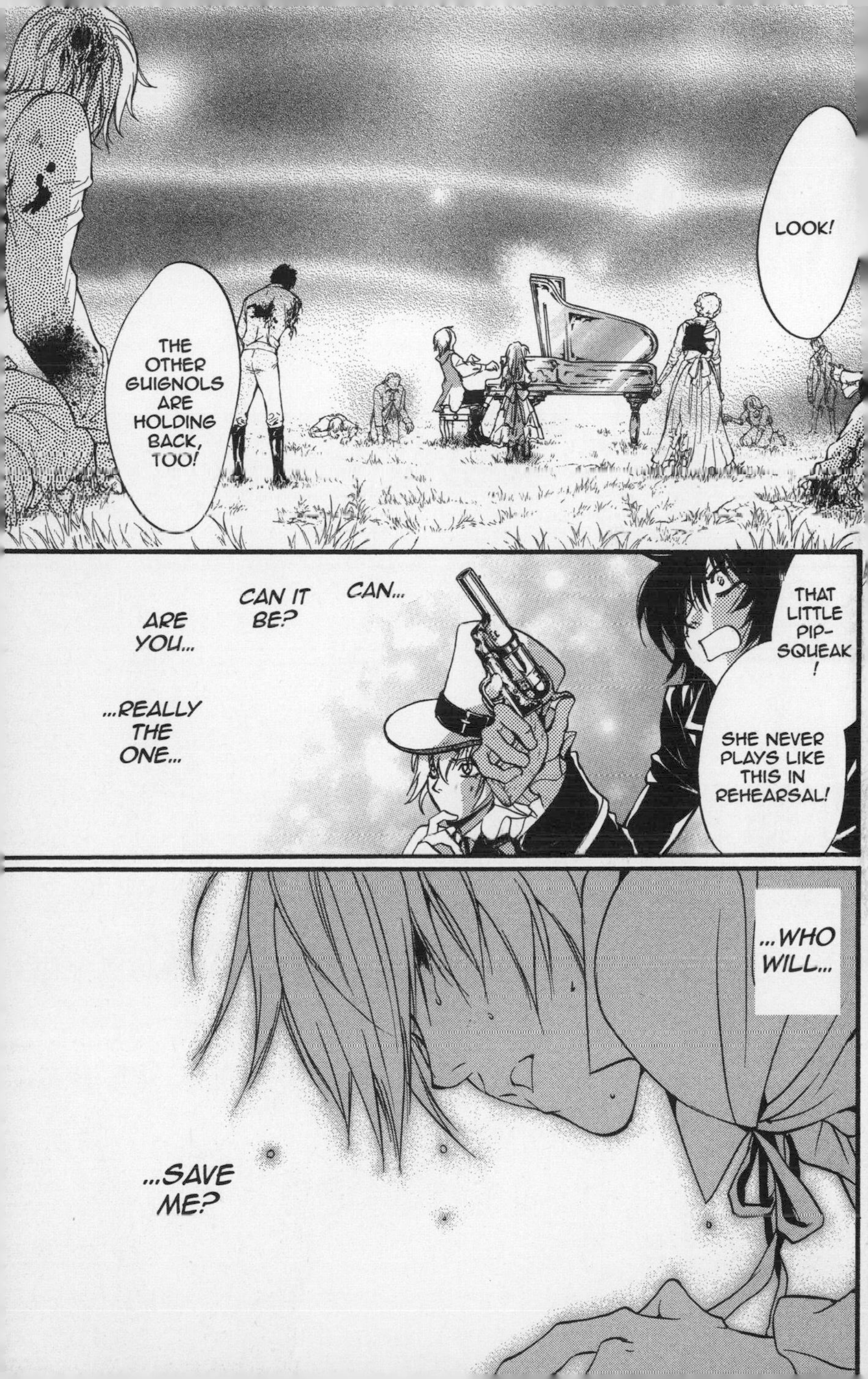
LOOK!
THE OTHER GUIGNOLS ARE HOLDING BACK, TOO!
THAT LITTLE PIP-SQUEAK!
SHE NEVER PLAYS LIKE THIS IN REHEARSAL!
CAN...
CAN IT BE?
ARE YOU...
...REALLY THE ONE...
...WHO WILL...
...SAVE ME?

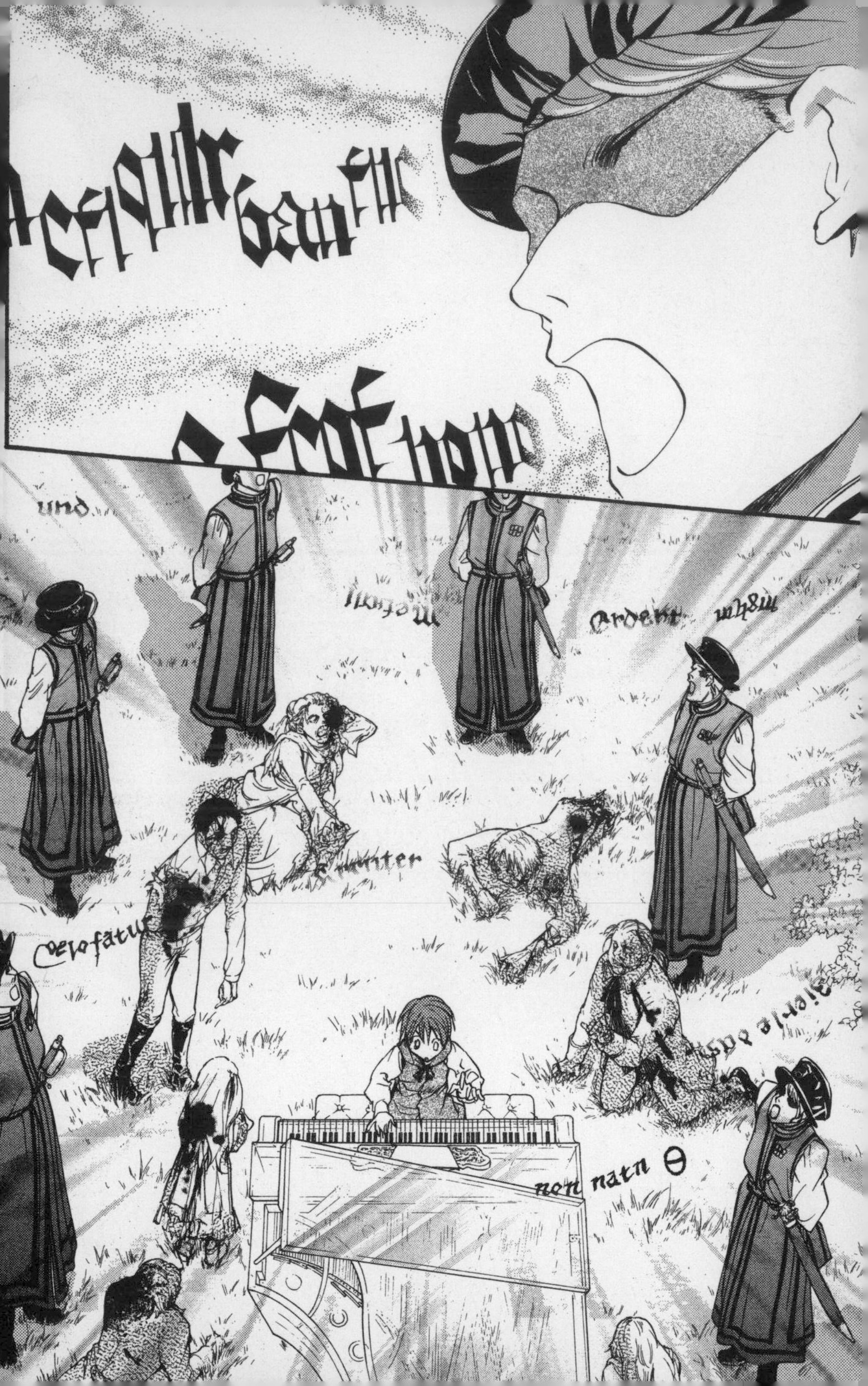
und
non natn

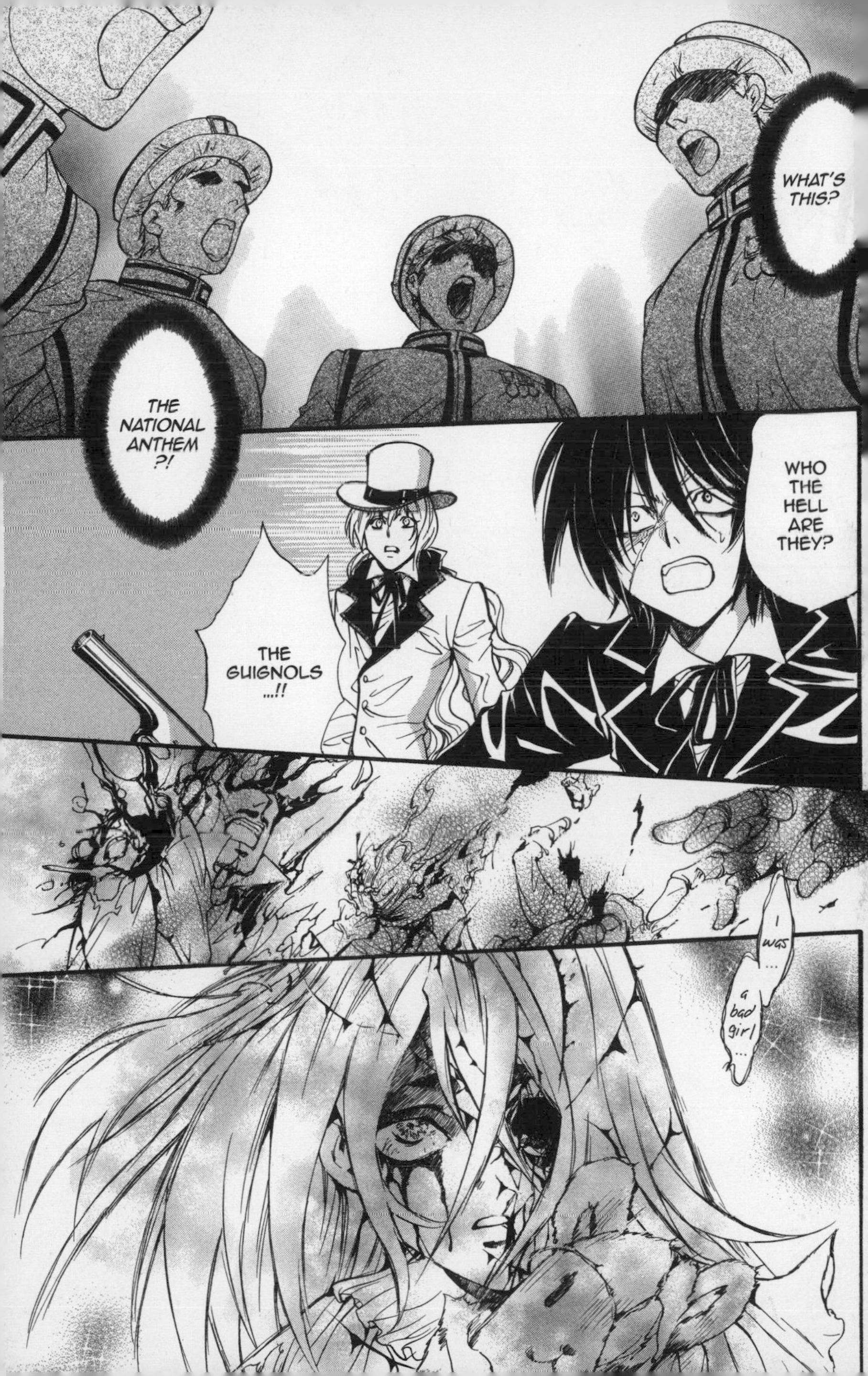
WHAT'S THIS?
THE NATIONAL ANTHEM ?!
WHO THE HELL ARE THEY?
THE GUIGNOLS ...!!
I was ... a bad girl ...

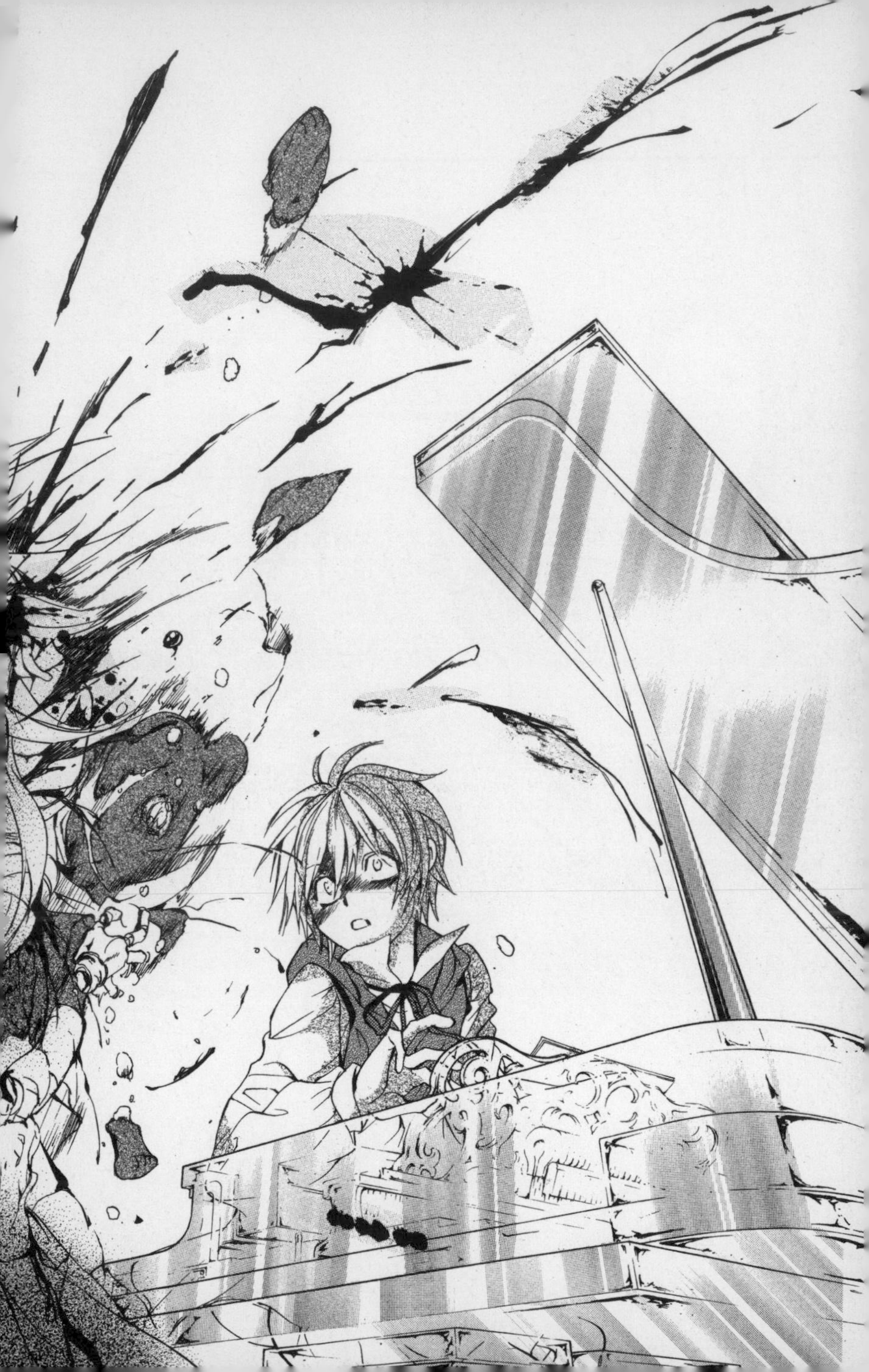

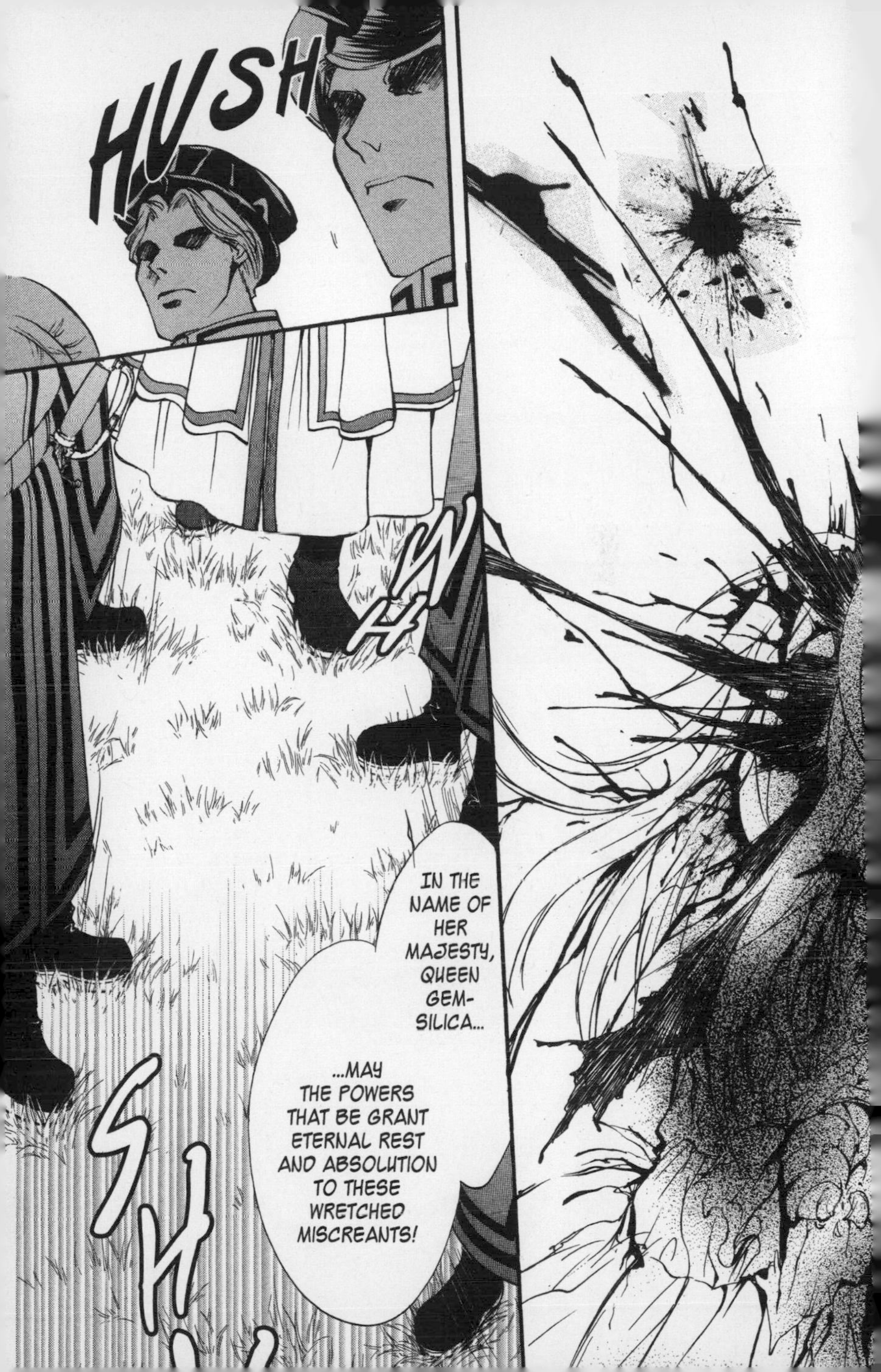
HUSH
IN THE NAME OF HER MAJESTY, QUEEN GEM-SILICA...
...MAY THE POWERS THAT BE GRANT ETERNAL REST AND ABSOLUTION TO THESE WRETCHED MISCREANTS!

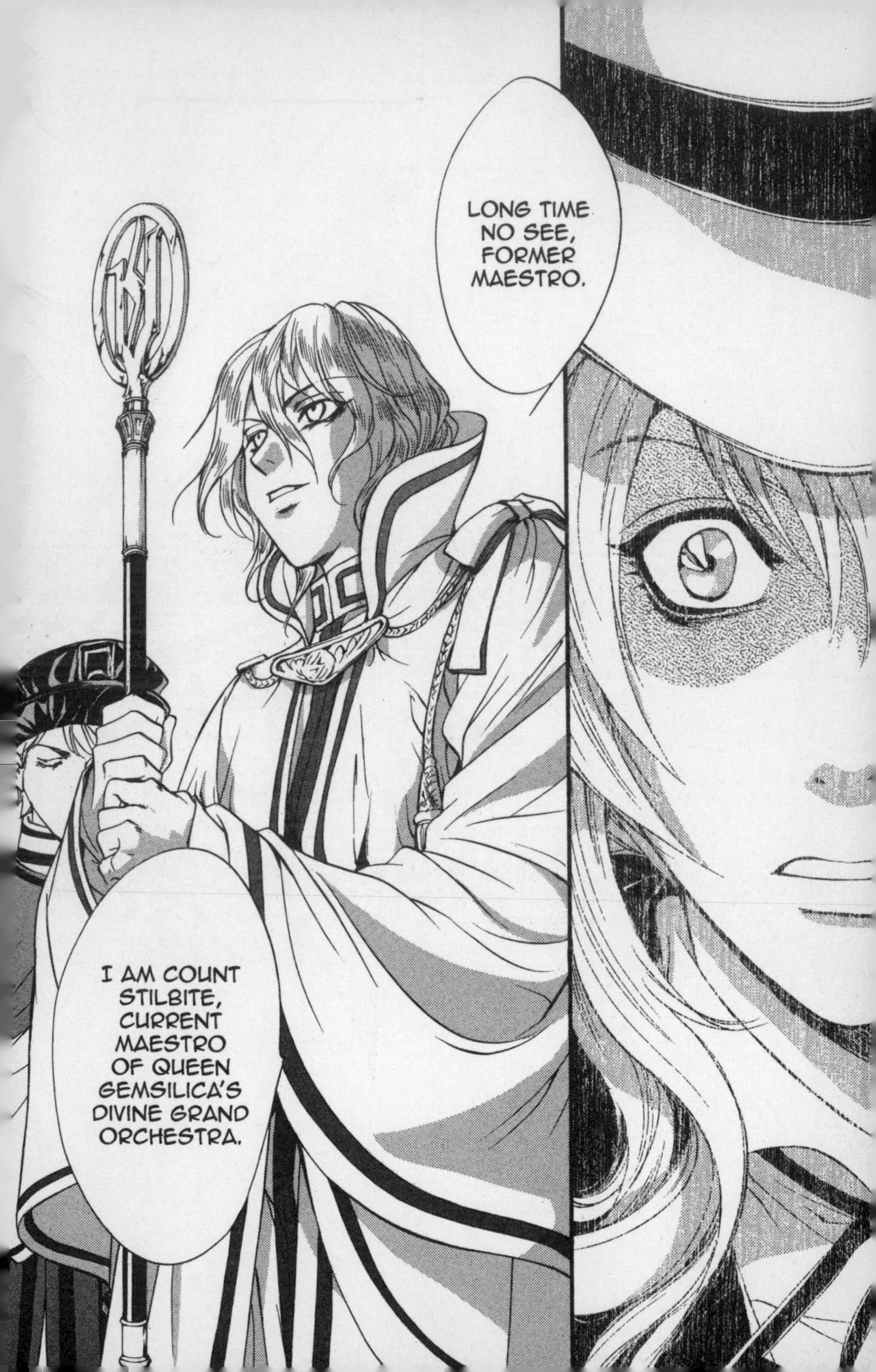
LONG TIME NO SEE, FORMER MAESTRO.
I AM COUNT STILBITE, CURRENT MAESTRO OF QUEEN GEMSILICA'S DIVINE GRAND ORCHESTRA.

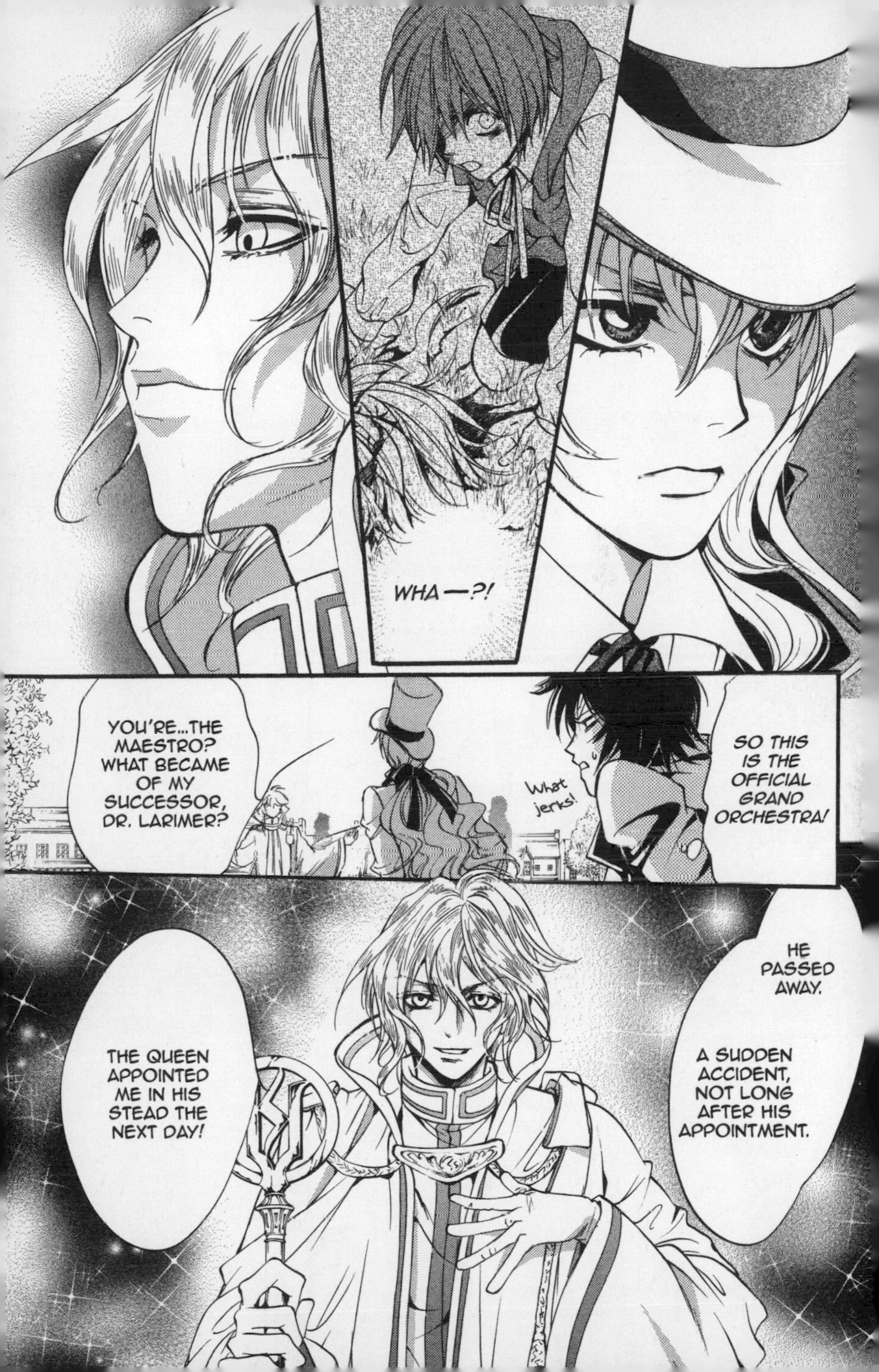
WHA—?!
SO THIS IS THE OFFICIAL GRAND ORCHESTRA!
What jerks!
YOU'RE...THE MAESTRO? WHAT BECAME OF MY SUCCESSOR, DR. LARIMER?
HE PASSED AWAY.
A SUDDEN ACCIDENT, NOT LONG AFTER HIS APPOINTMENT.
THE QUEEN APPOINTED ME IN HIS STEAD THE NEXT DAY!

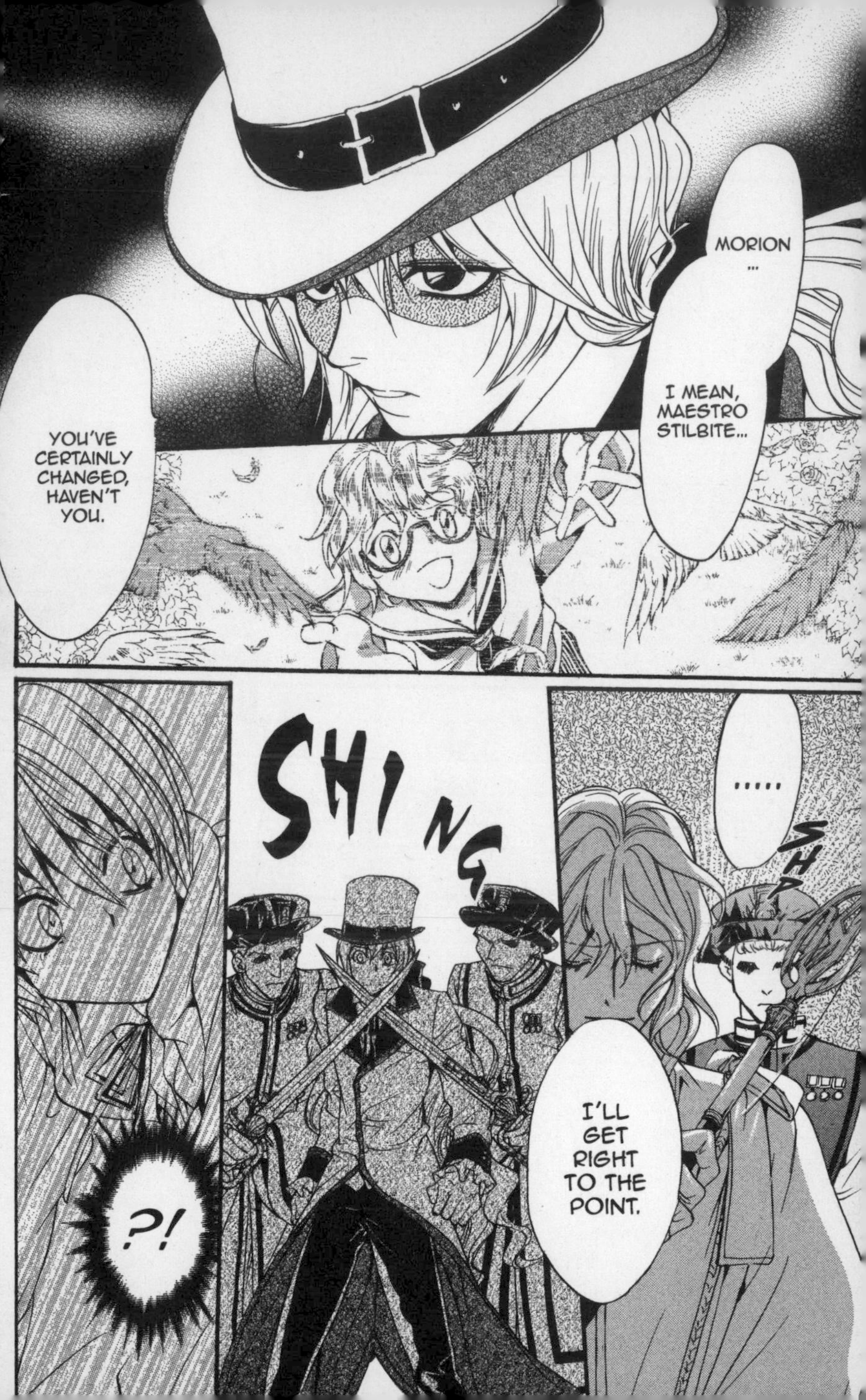
MORION ...
I MEAN, MAESTRO STILBITE...
YOU'VE CERTAINLY CHANGED, HAVEN'T YOU.
.....
SHP
I'LL GET RIGHT TO THE POINT.
SHING
?!

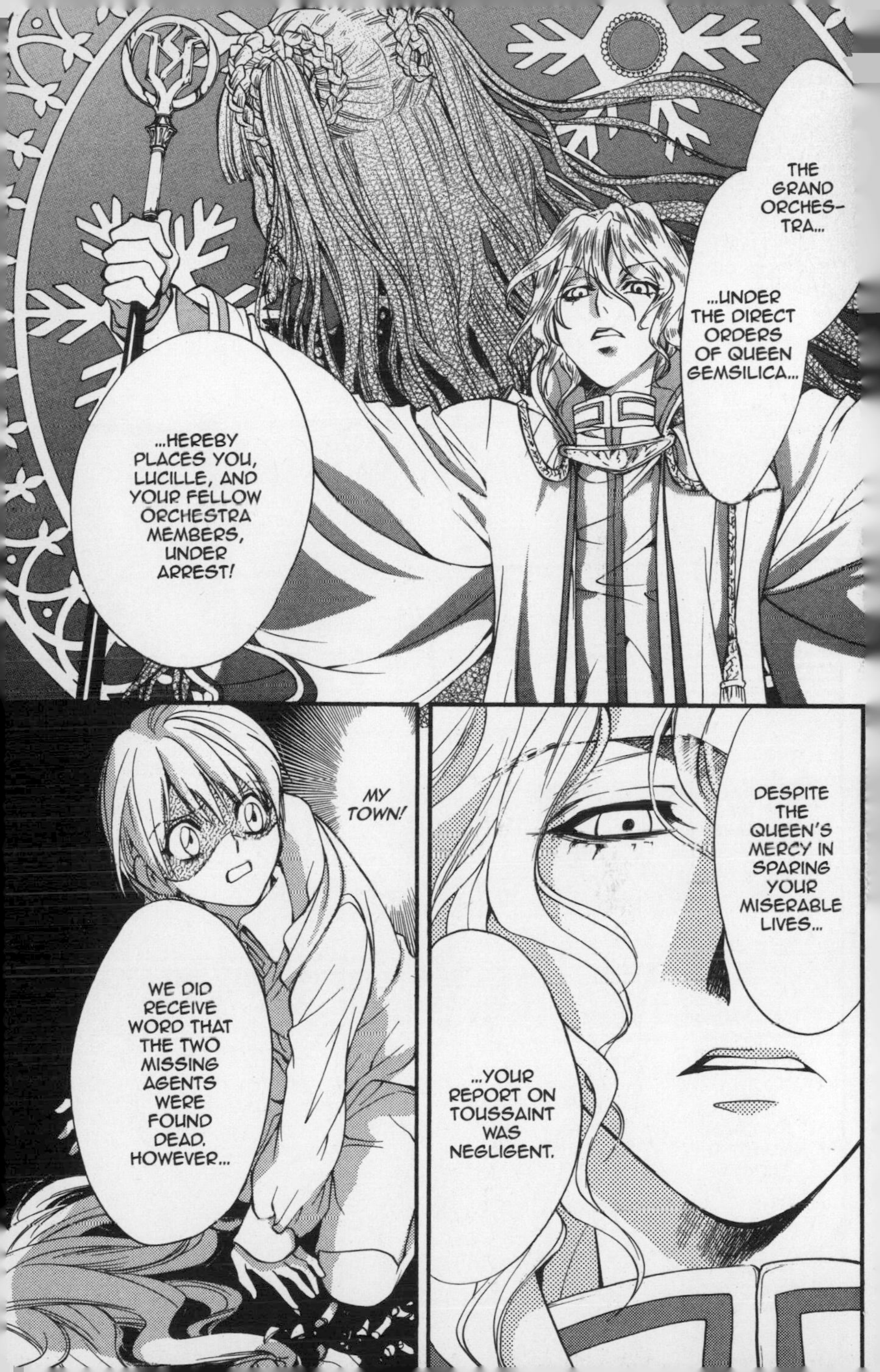
THE GRAND ORCHESTRA...
...UNDER THE DIRECT ORDERS OF QUEEN GEMSILICA...
...HEREBY PLACES YOU, LUCILLE, AND YOUR FELLOW ORCHESTRA MEMBERS, UNDER ARREST!
DESPITE THE QUEEN'S MERCY IN SPARING YOUR MISERABLE LIVES...
...YOUR REPORT ON TOUSSAINT WAS NEGLIGENT.
MY TOWN!
WE DID RECEIVE WORD THAT THE TWO MISSING AGENTS WERE FOUND DEAD. HOWEVER...

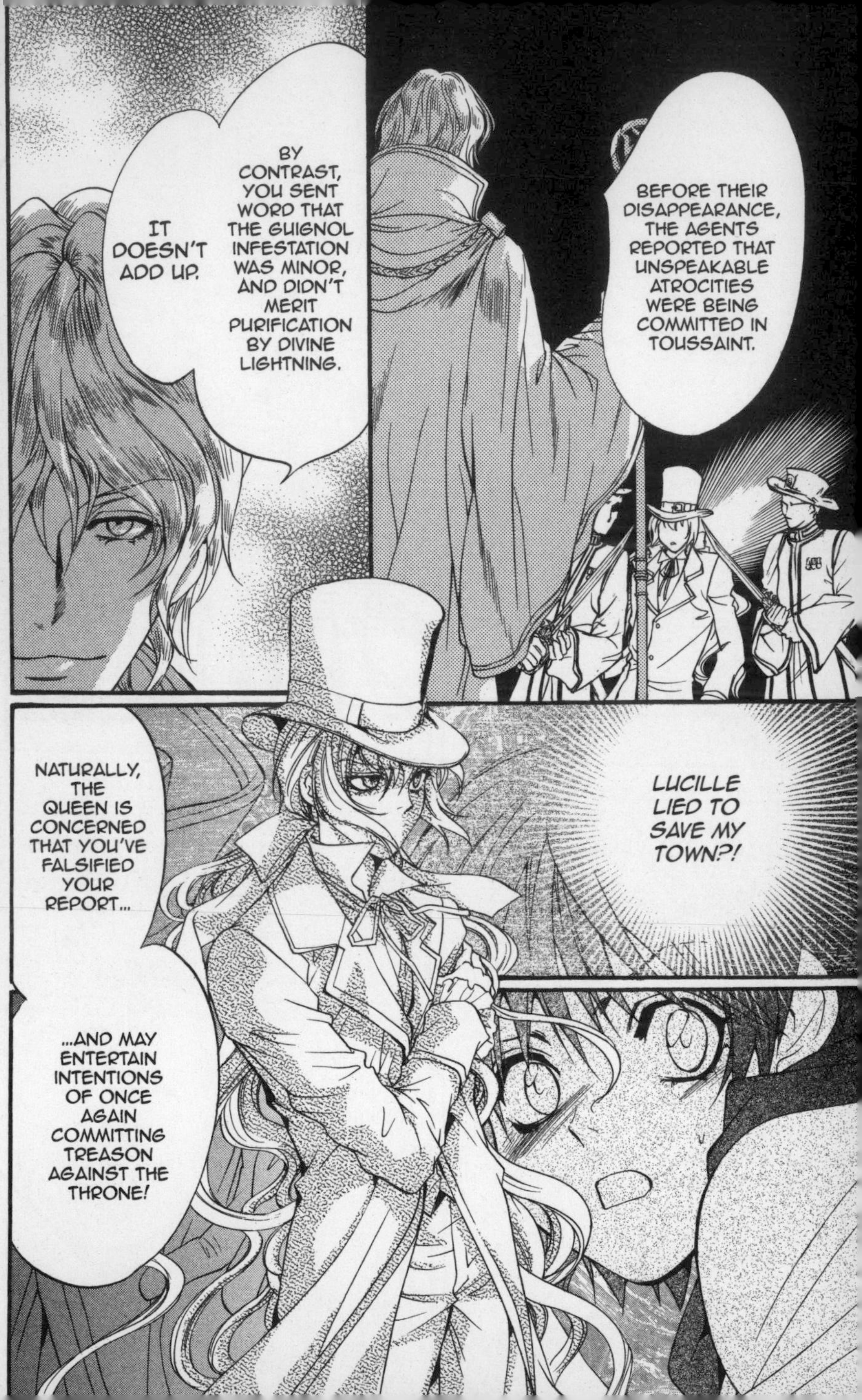
BEFORE THEIR DISAPPEARANCE, THE AGENTS REPORTED THAT UNSPEAKABLE ATROCITIES WERE BEING COMMITTED IN TOUSSAINT.
BY CONTRAST, YOU SENT WORD THAT THE GUIGNOL INFESTATION WAS MINOR, AND DIDN'T MERIT PURIFICATION BY DIVINE LIGHTNING.
IT DOESN'T ADD UP.
LUCILLE LIED TO SAVE MY TOWN?!
NATURALLY, THE QUEEN IS CONCERNED THAT YOU'VE FALSIFIED YOUR REPORT...
...AND MAY ENTERTAIN INTENTIONS OF ONCE AGAIN COMMITTING TREASON AGAINST THE THRONE!

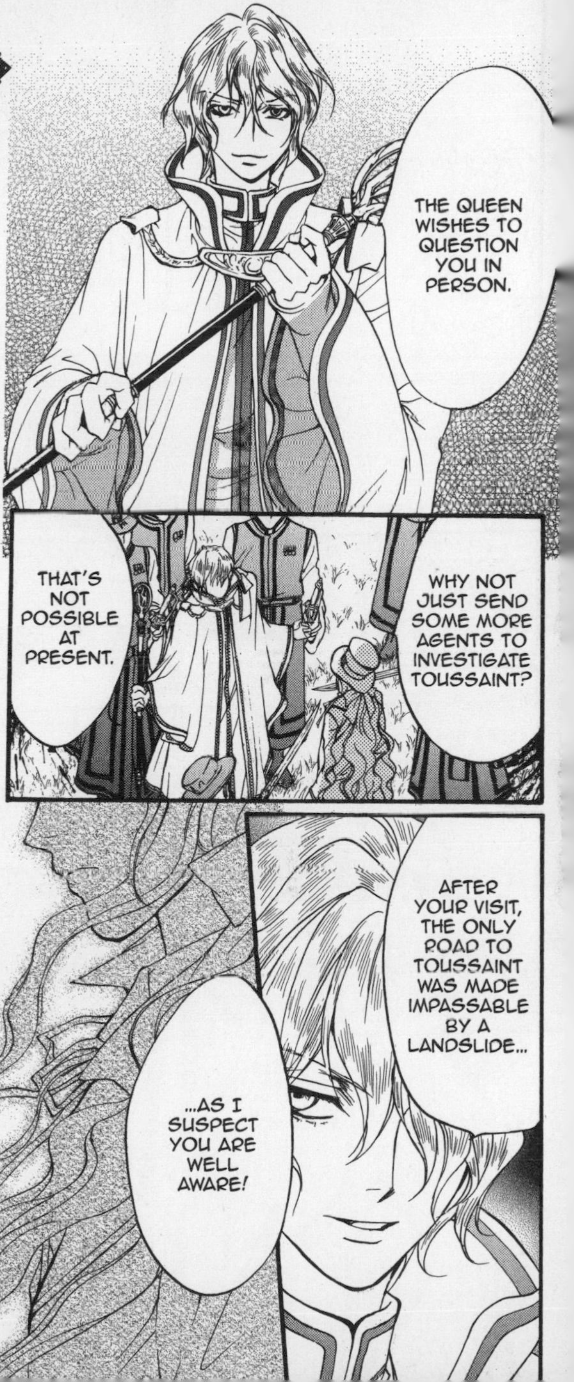
THE QUEEN WISHES TO QUESTION YOU IN PERSON.
WHY NOT JUST SEND SOME MORE AGENTS TO INVESTIGATE TOUSSAINT?
THAT'S NOT POSSIBLE AT PRESENT.
AFTER YOUR VISIT, THE ONLY ROAD TO TOUSSAINT WAS MADE IMPASSABLE BY A LANDSLIDE...
...AS I SUSPECT YOU ARE WELL AWARE!

I'm Kaori Yuki—currently obsessed with *Oni-chan* and *The Bear's School*— and this is Vol. 2 of Grand Guignol Orchestra. Physically, I've been catching colds from my kids and suffering from all kinds of annoying little maladies, like twitching cheeks, nausea, and sore hip muscles. The other day, the arm of the chair I worked in snapped off—now my chair has no left arm. I know I need to hurry up and replace it but there's no time... no time...

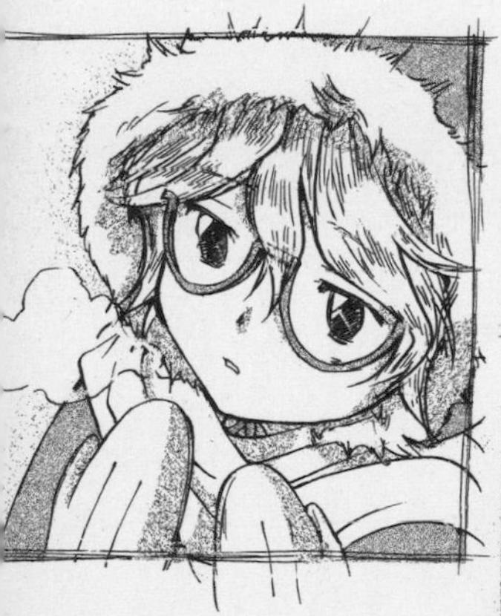

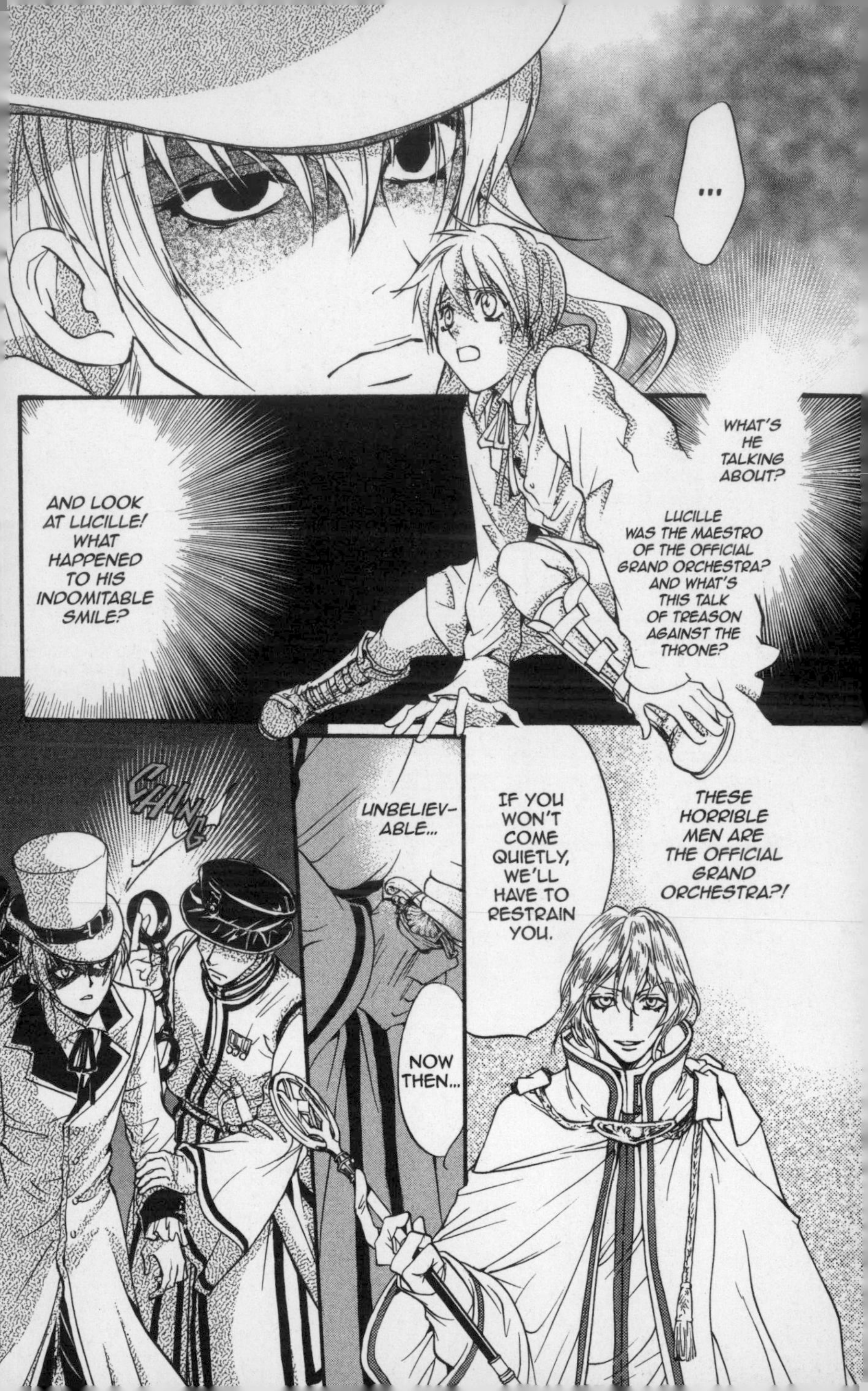
...
WHAT'S HE TALKING ABOUT?
LUCILLE WAS THE MAESTRO OF THE OFFICIAL GRAND ORCHESTRA? AND WHAT'S THIS TALK OF TREASON AGAINST THE THRONE?
AND LOOK AT LUCILLE! WHAT HAPPENED TO HIS INDOMITABLE SMILE?
THESE HORRIBLE MEN ARE THE OFFICIAL GRAND ORCHESTRA?!
IF YOU WON'T COME QUIETLY, WE'LL HAVE TO RESTRAIN YOU.
NOW THEN...
UNBELIEV-ABLE...
CHING

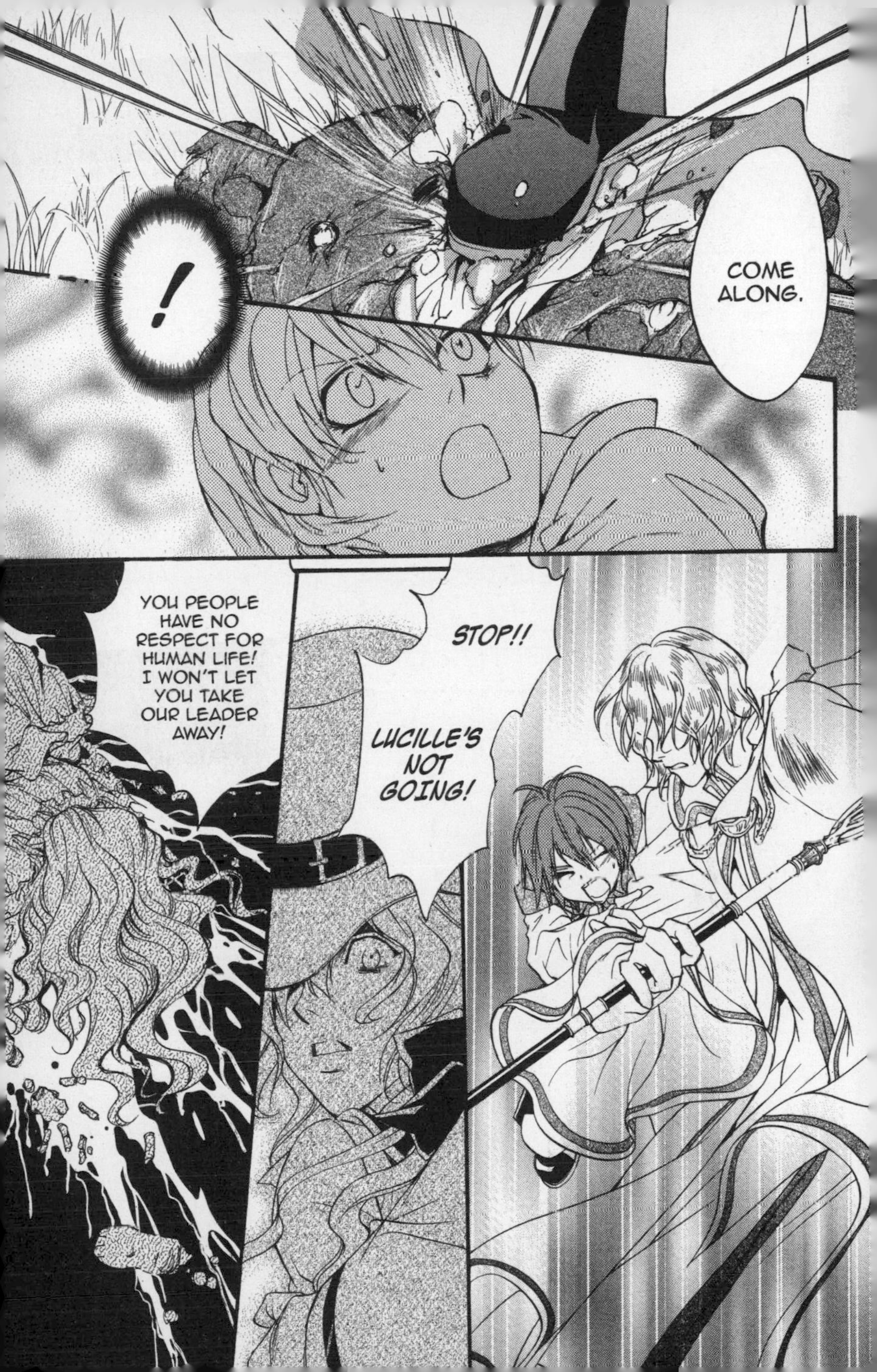
COME ALONG.
!
STOP!!
LUCILLE'S NOT GOING!
YOU PEOPLE HAVE NO RESPECT FOR HUMAN LIFE! I WON'T LET YOU TAKE OUR LEADER AWAY!

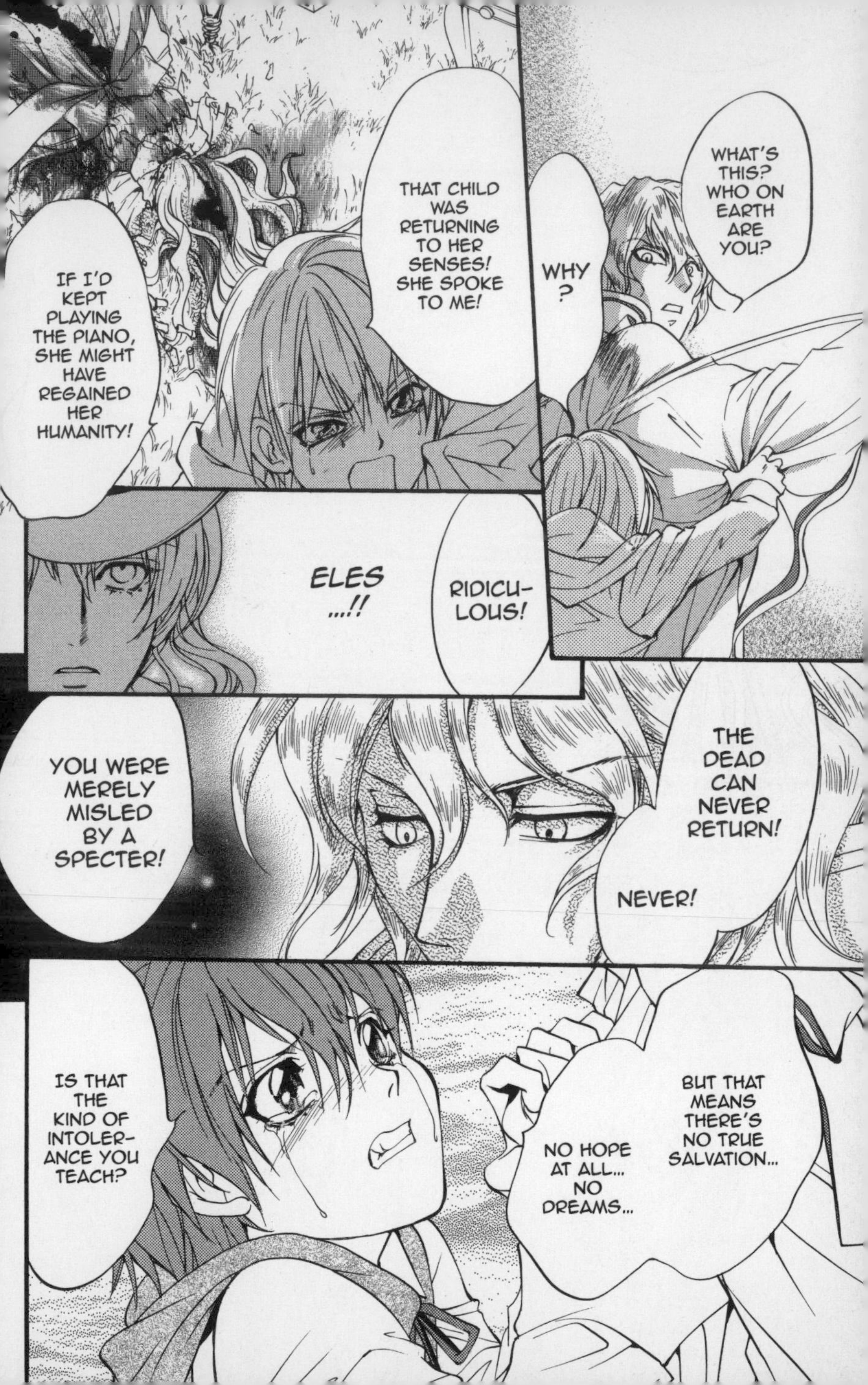
WHAT'S THIS? WHO ON EARTH ARE YOU?
WHY?
THAT CHILD WAS RETURNING TO HER SENSES! SHE SPOKE TO ME!
IF I'D KEPT PLAYING THE PIANO, SHE MIGHT HAVE REGAINED HER HUMANITY!
RIDICU-LOUS!
ELES ...!!
THE DEAD CAN NEVER RETURN!
NEVER!
YOU WERE MERELY MISLED BY A SPECTER!
BUT THAT MEANS THERE'S NO TRUE SALVATION...
NO HOPE AT ALL... NO DREAMS...
IS THAT THE KIND OF INTOLER-ANCE YOU TEACH?

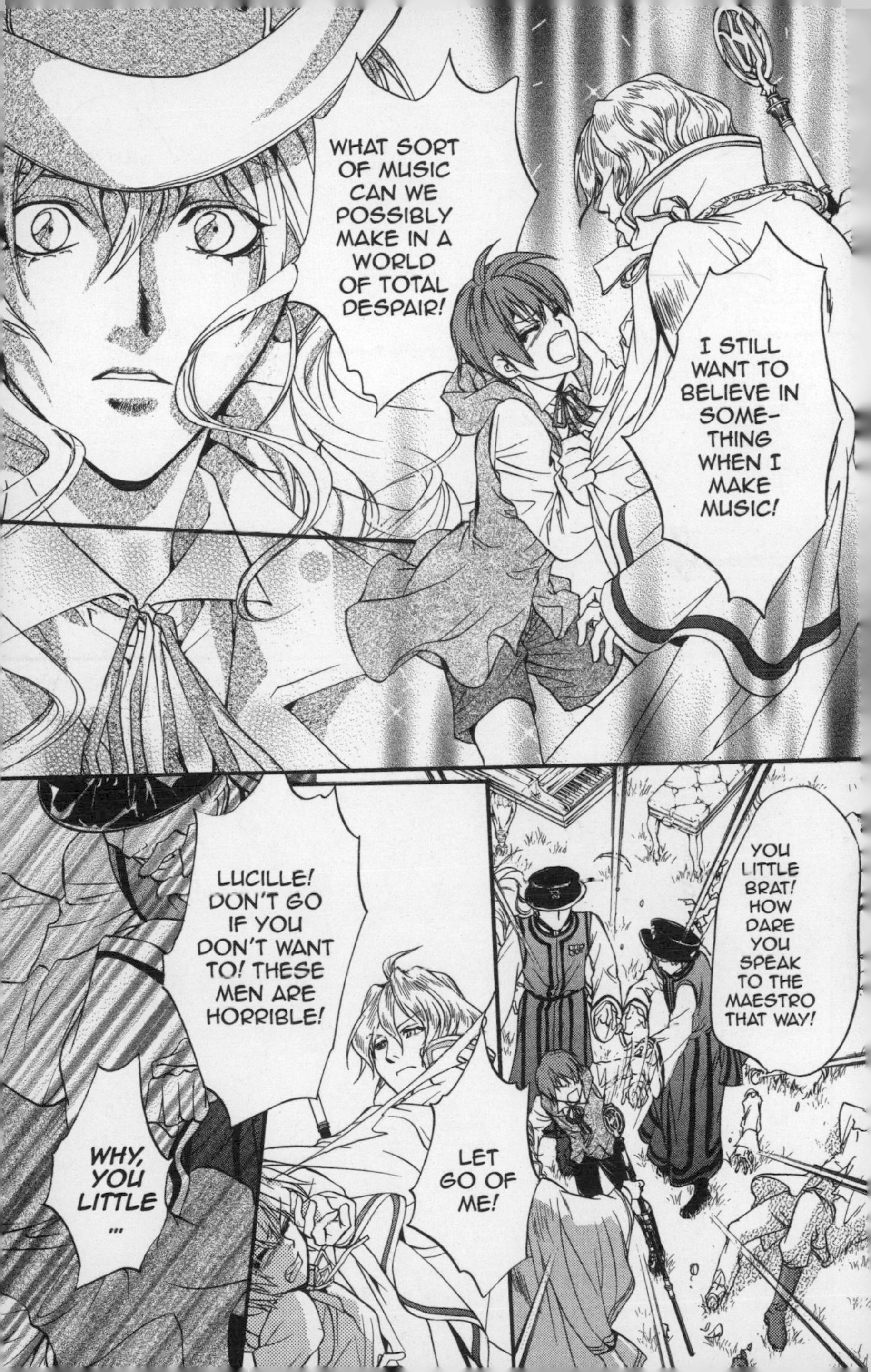
WHAT SORT OF MUSIC CAN WE POSSIBLY MAKE IN A WORLD OF TOTAL DESPAIR!
I STILL WANT TO BELIEVE IN SOME-THING WHEN I MAKE MUSIC!
YOU LITTLE BRAT! HOW DARE YOU SPEAK TO THE MAESTRO THAT WAY!
LUCILLE! DON'T GO IF YOU DON'T WANT TO! THESE MEN ARE HORRIBLE!
LET GO OF ME!
WHY, YOU LITTLE ...

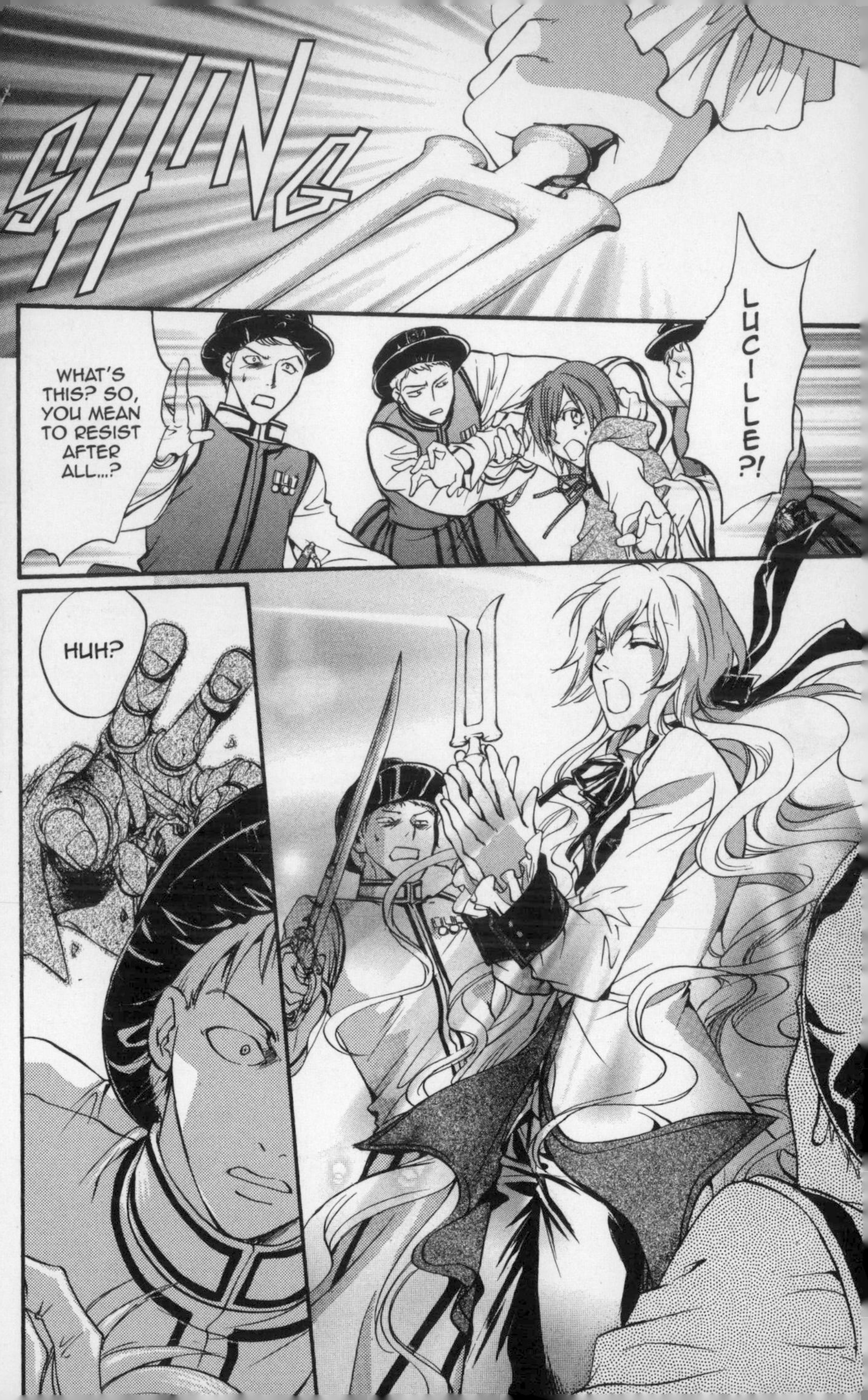
SHING
LUCILLE?!
WHAT'S THIS? SO, YOU MEAN TO RESIST AFTER ALL...?
HUH?

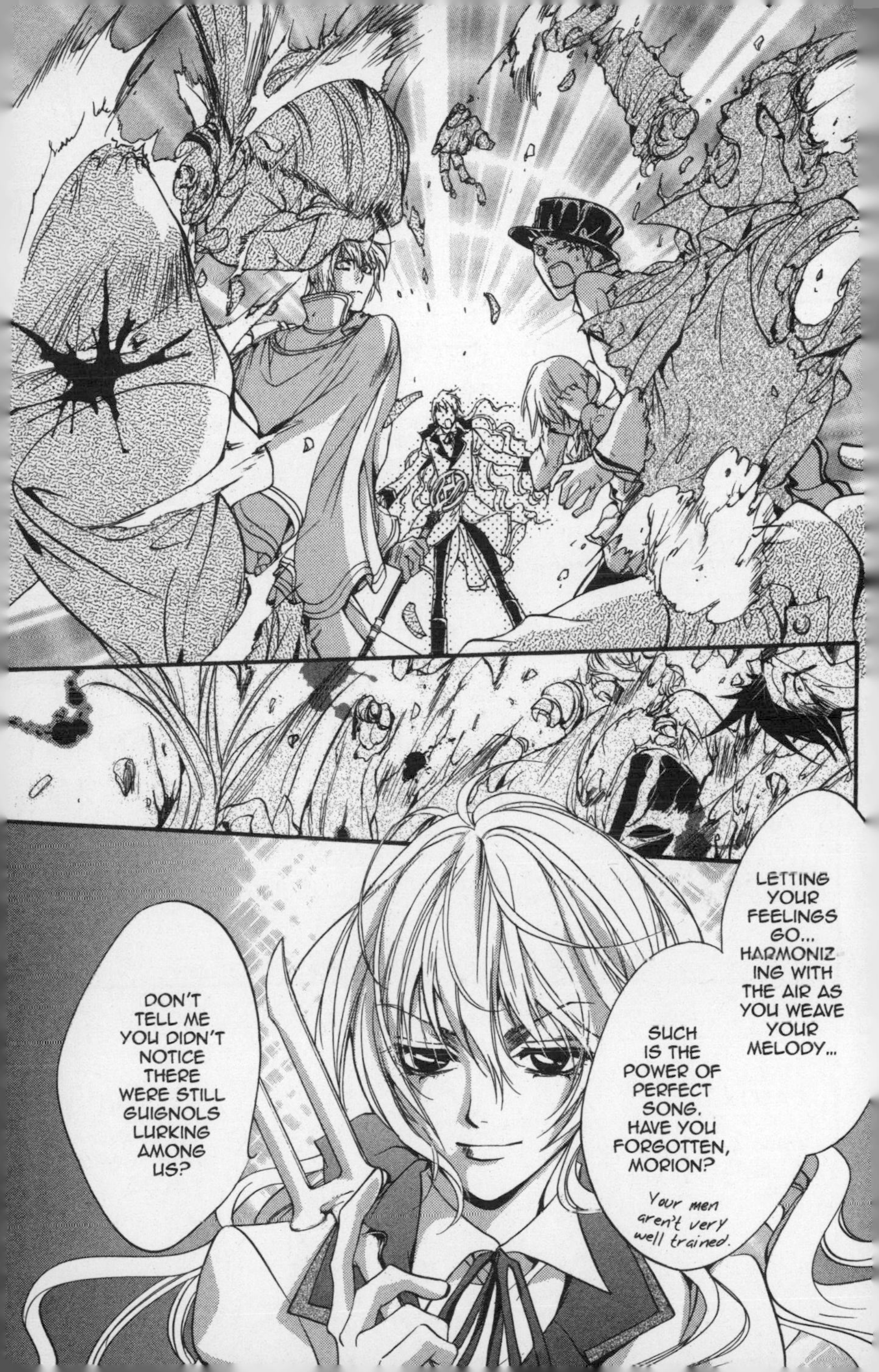
LETTING YOUR FEELINGS GO... HARMONIZING WITH THE AIR AS YOU WEAVE YOUR MELODY...
SUCH IS THE POWER OF PERFECT SONG. HAVE YOU FORGOTTEN, MORION?
DON'T TELL ME YOU DIDN'T NOTICE THERE WERE STILL GUIGNOLS LURKING AMONG US?
Your men aren't very well trained.

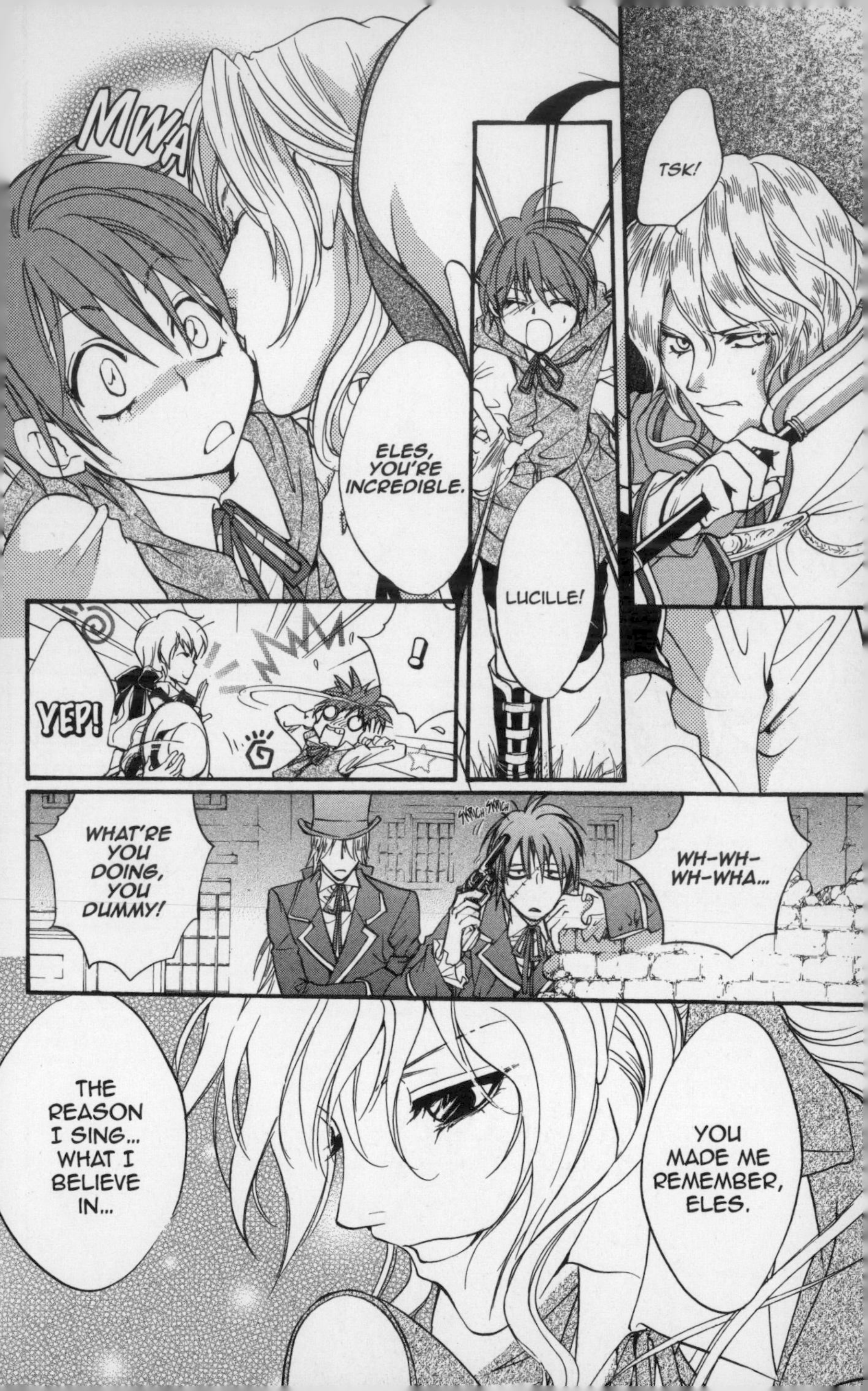
TSK!
LUCILLE!
MWA
ELES, YOU'RE INCREDIBLE.
!
G
YEP!
WH-WH-WH-WHA...
WHAT'RE YOU DOING, YOU DUMMY!
YOU MADE ME REMEMBER, ELES.
THE REASON I SING... WHAT I BELIEVE IN...

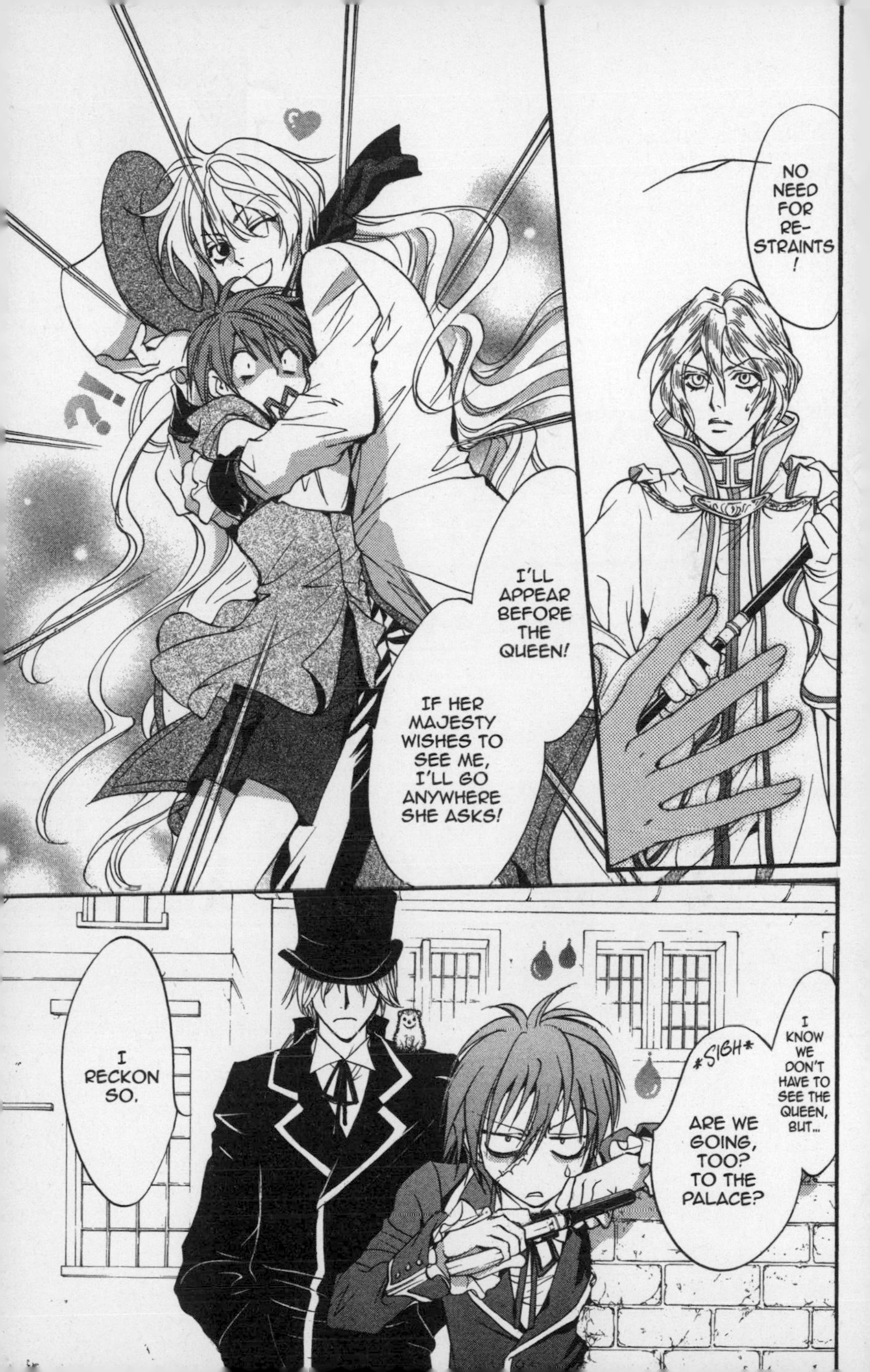
NO NEED FOR RE-STRAINTS!
?!
I'LL APPEAR BEFORE THE QUEEN!
IF HER MAJESTY WISHES TO SEE ME, I'LL GO ANYWHERE SHE ASKS!
SIGH
I KNOW WE DON'T HAVE TO SEE THE QUEEN, BUT...
ARE WE GOING, TOO? TO THE PALACE?
I RECKON SO.

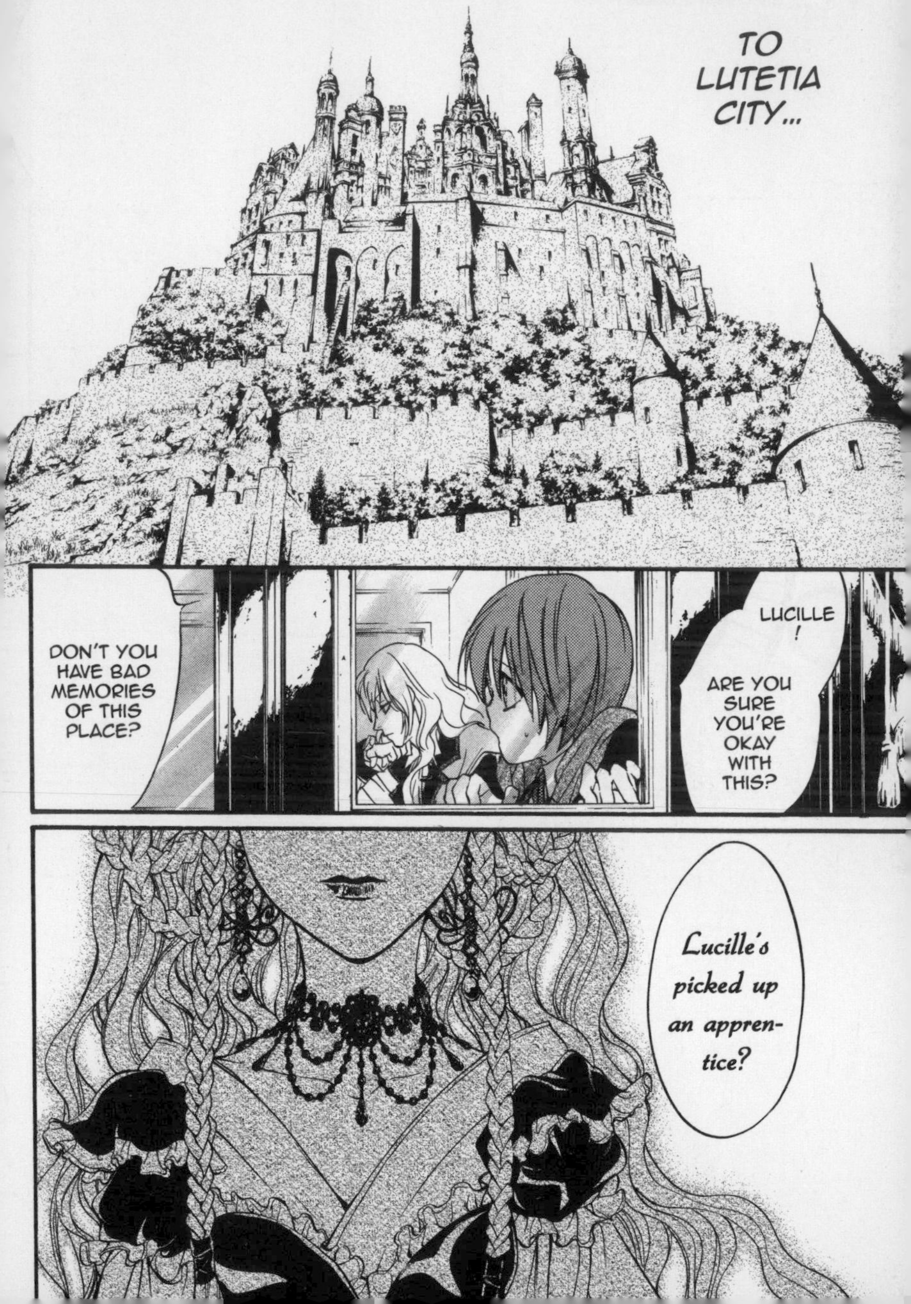
TO LUTETIA CITY...
LUCILLE!
ARE YOU SURE YOU'RE OKAY WITH THIS?
DON'T YOU HAVE BAD MEMORIES OF THIS PLACE?
Lucille's picked up an appren-tice?

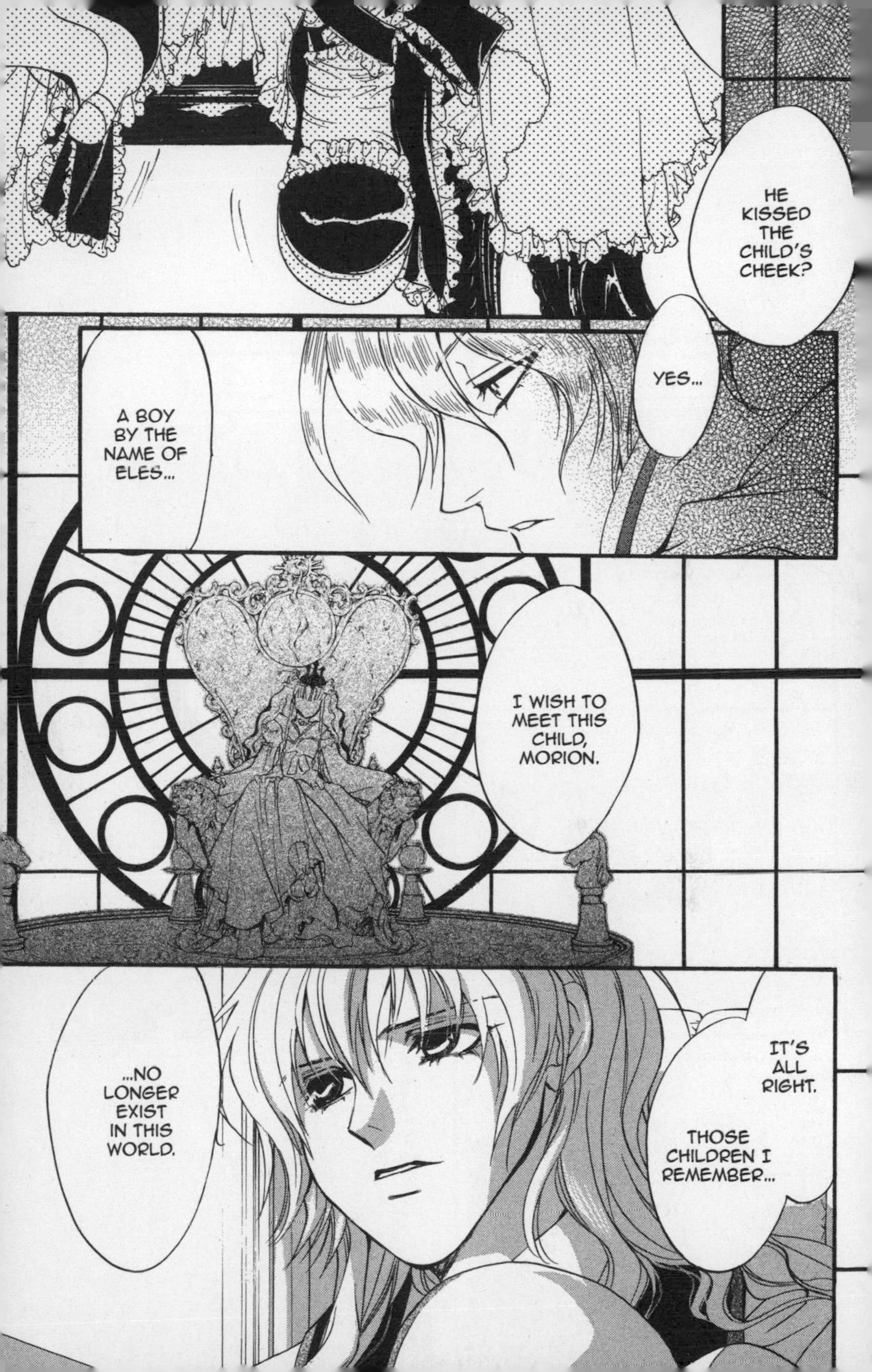
HE KISSED THE CHILD'S CHEEK?
YES...
A BOY BY THE NAME OF ELES...
I WISH TO MEET THIS CHILD, MORION.
IT'S ALL RIGHT.
THOSE CHILDREN I REMEMBER...
...NO LONGER EXIST IN THIS WORLD.

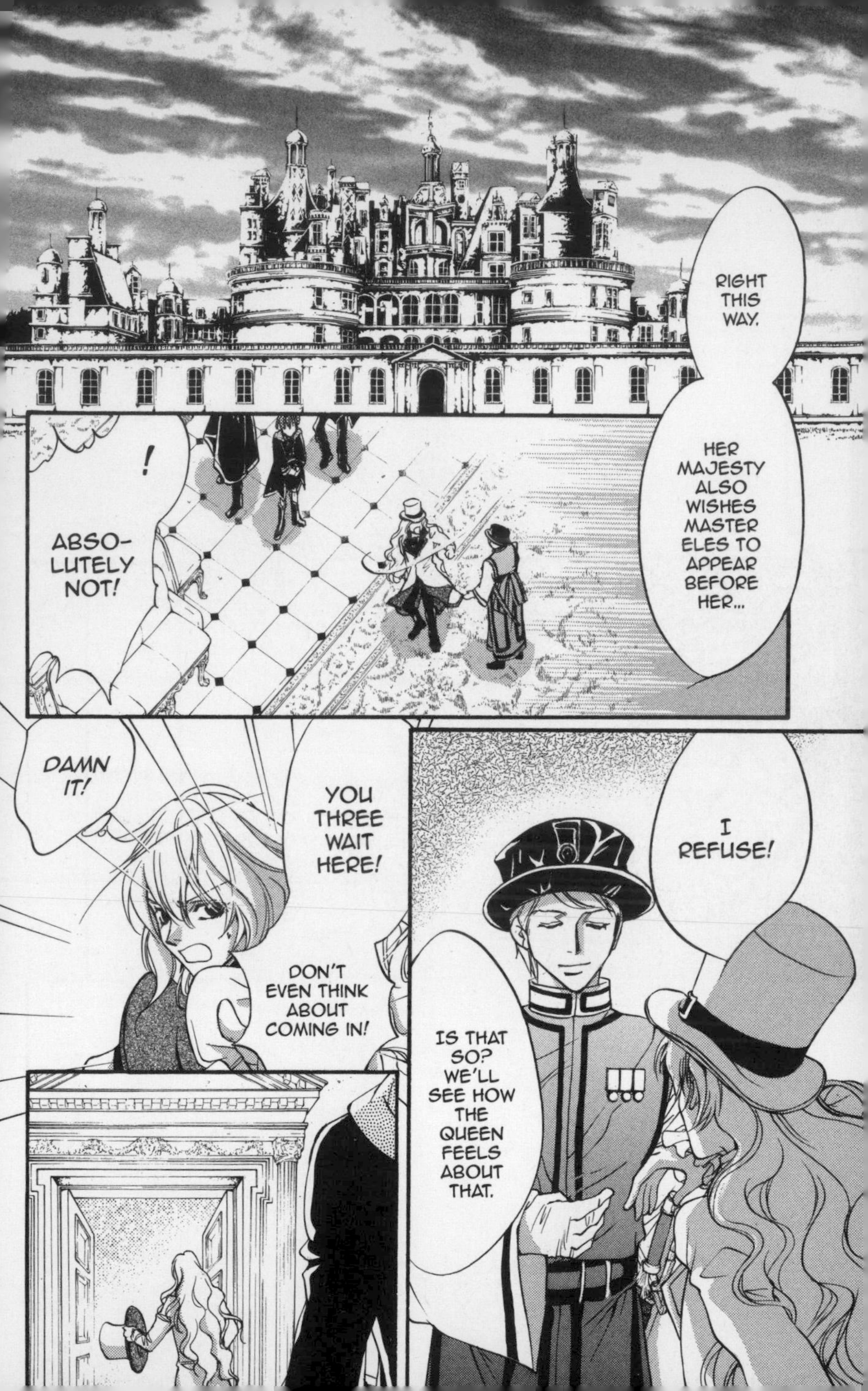
RIGHT THIS WAY.
HER MAJESTY ALSO WISHES MASTER ELES TO APPEAR BEFORE HER...
!
ABSO-LUTELY NOT!
I REFUSE!
IS THAT SO? WE'LL SEE HOW THE QUEEN FEELS ABOUT THAT.
DAMN IT!
YOU THREE WAIT HERE!
DON'T EVEN THINK ABOUT COMING IN!

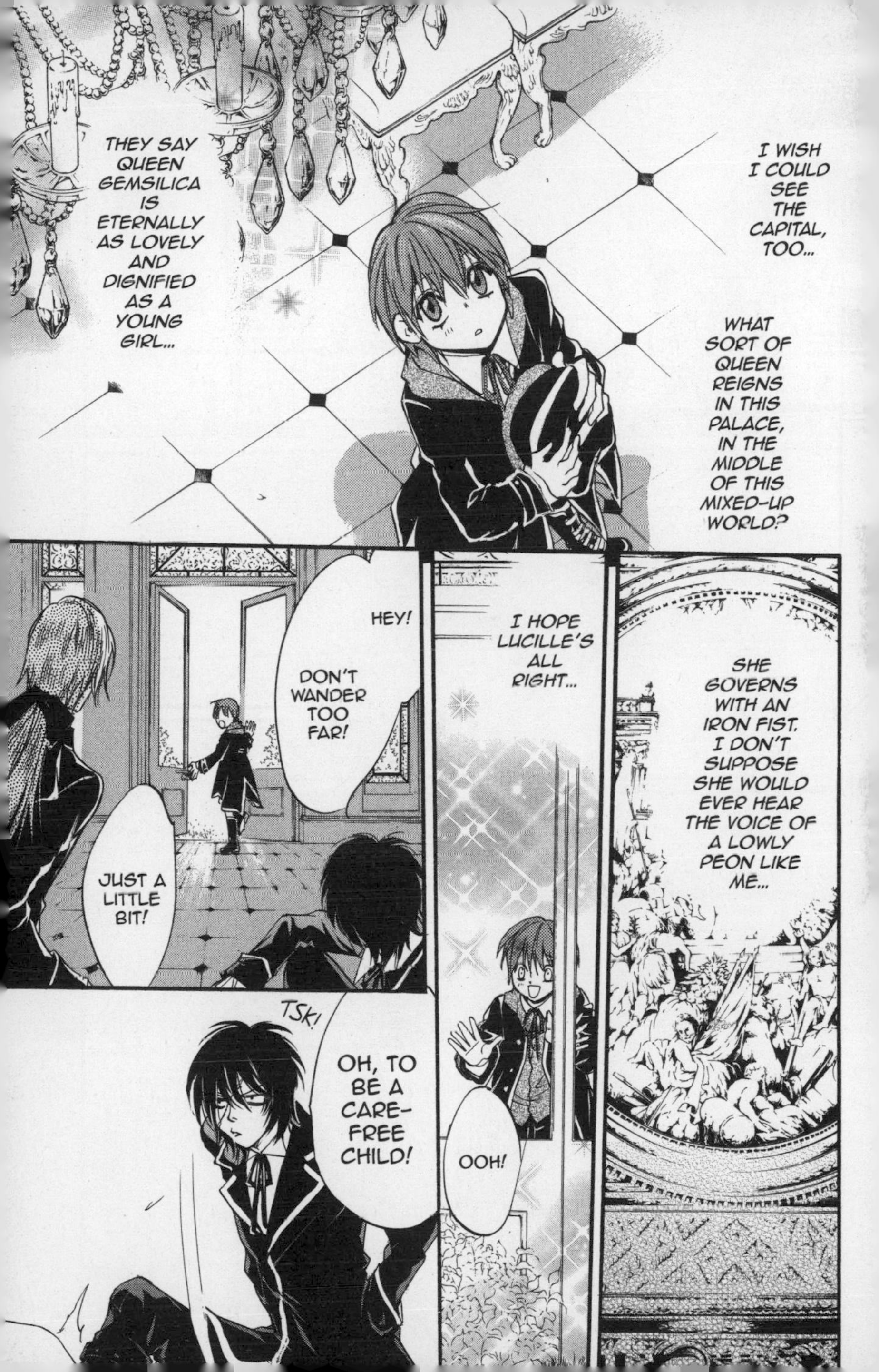
I WISH I COULD SEE THE CAPITAL, TOO...
THEY SAY QUEEN GEMSILICA IS ETERNALLY AS LOVELY AND DIGNIFIED AS A YOUNG GIRL...
WHAT SORT OF QUEEN REIGNS IN THIS PALACE, IN THE MIDDLE OF THIS MIXED-UP WORLD?
SHE GOVERNS WITH AN IRON FIST. I DON'T SUPPOSE SHE WOULD EVER HEAR THE VOICE OF A LOWLY PEON LIKE ME...
I HOPE LUCILLE'S ALL RIGHT...
OOH!
HEY!
DON'T WANDER TOO FAR!
JUST A LITTLE BIT!
TSK!
OH, TO BE A CARE-FREE CHILD!

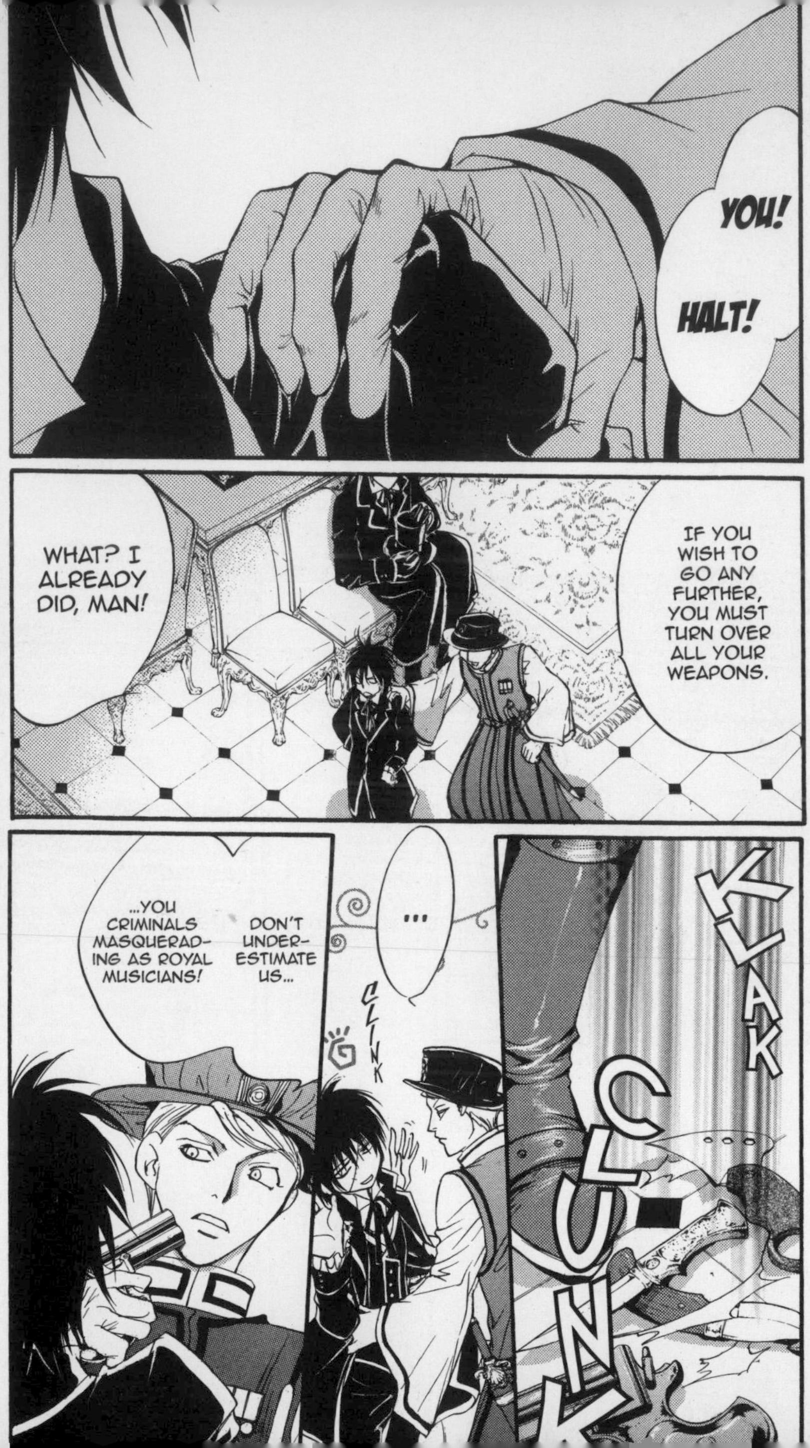
YOU!
HALT!
IF YOU WISH TO GO ANY FURTHER, YOU MUST TURN OVER ALL YOUR WEAPONS.
WHAT? I ALREADY DID, MAN!
KLAK
CLUNK
...
CLINK
DON'T UNDERESTIMATE US...
...YOU CRIMINALS MASQUERADING AS ROYAL MUSICIANS!

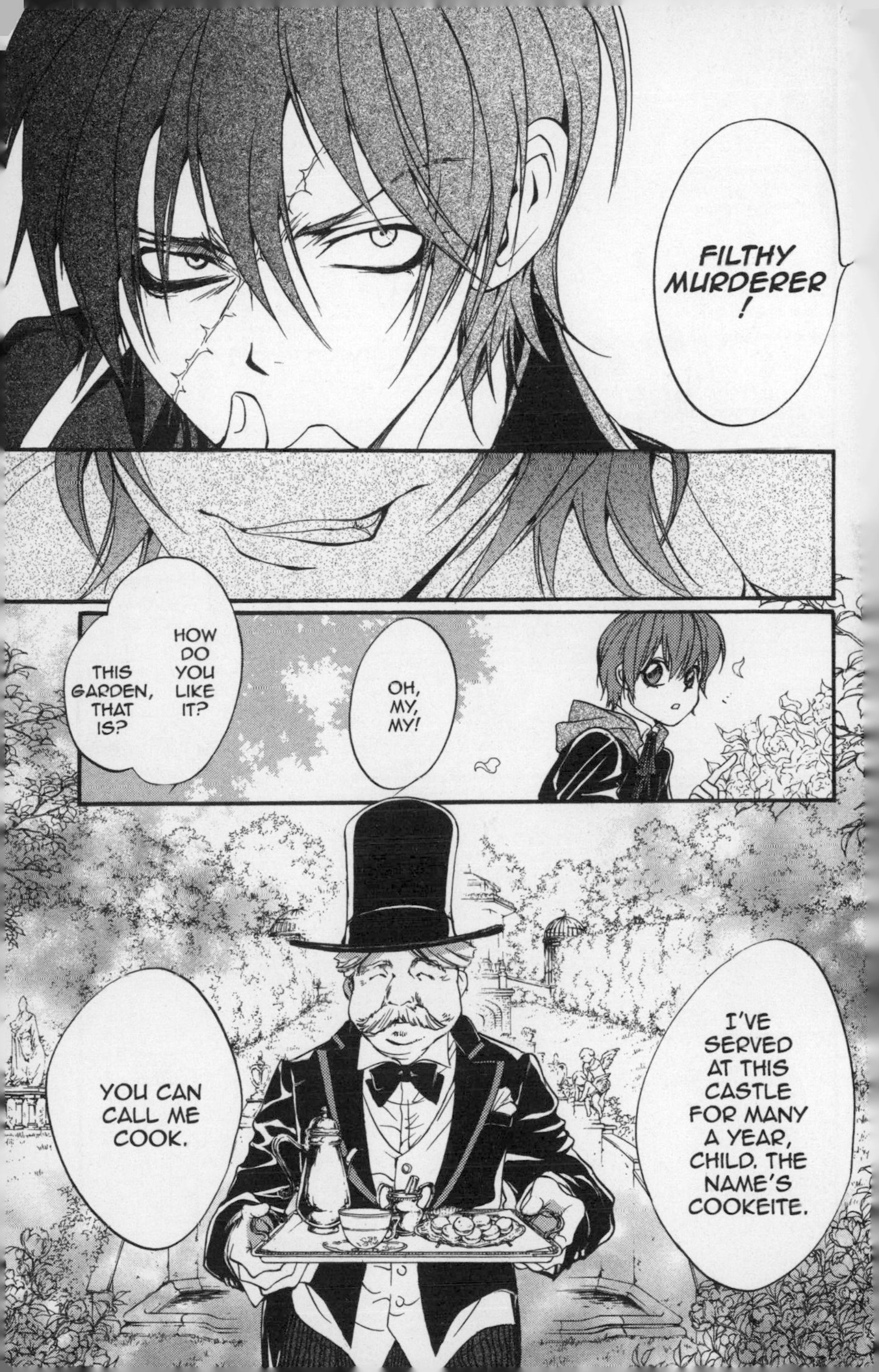
FILTHY MURDERER!
OH, MY, MY!
HOW DO YOU LIKE IT?
THIS GARDEN, THAT IS?
I'VE SERVED AT THIS CASTLE FOR MANY A YEAR, CHILD. THE NAME'S COOKEITE.
YOU CAN CALL ME COOK.

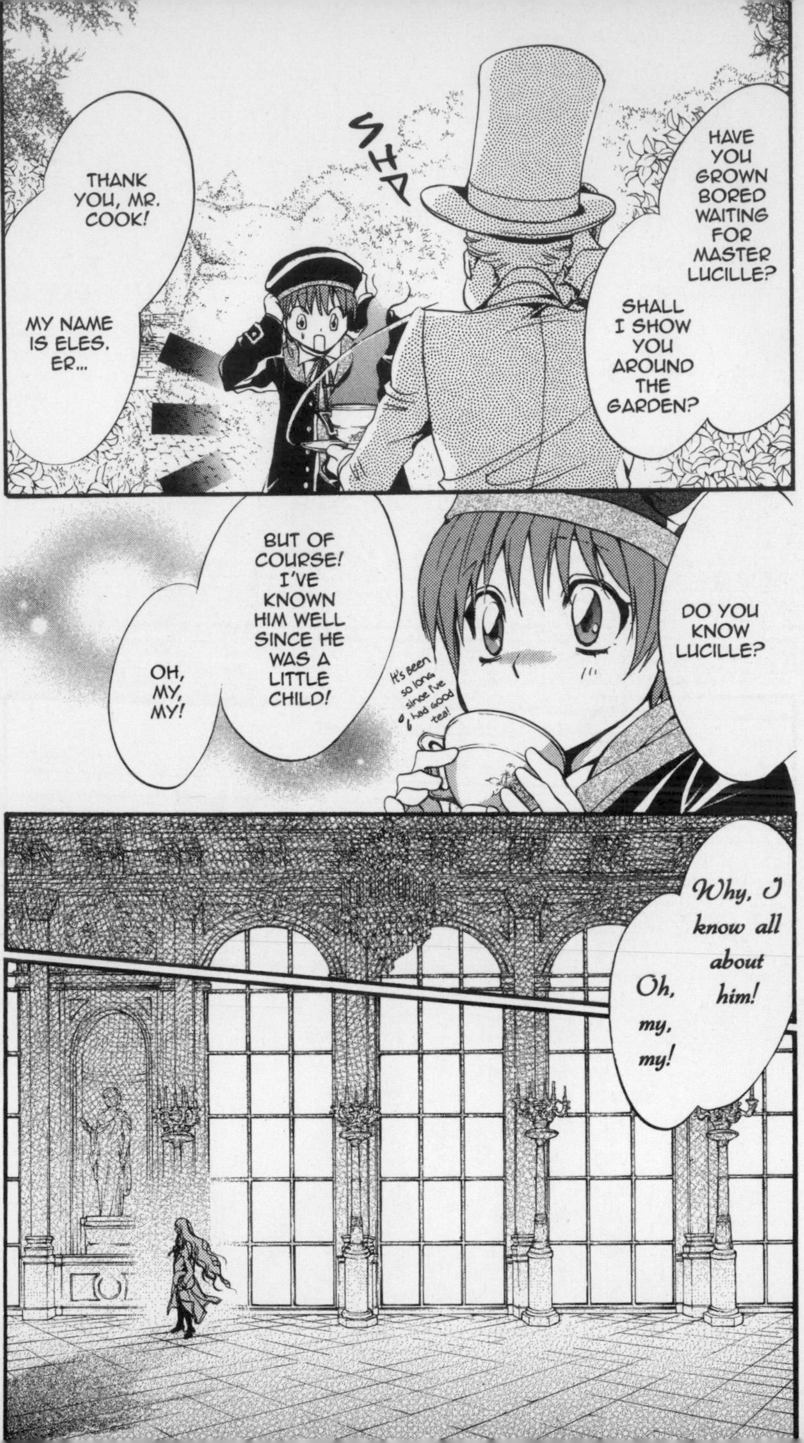
HAVE YOU GROWN BORED WAITING FOR MASTER LUCILLE?
SHALL I SHOW YOU AROUND THE GARDEN?
SHP
THANK YOU, MR. COOK!
MY NAME IS ELES. ER...
DO YOU KNOW LUCILLE?
It's been so long since I've had good tea!
BUT OF COURSE! I'VE KNOWN HIM WELL SINCE HE WAS A LITTLE CHILD!
OH, MY, MY!
Why, I know all about him!
Oh, my, my!

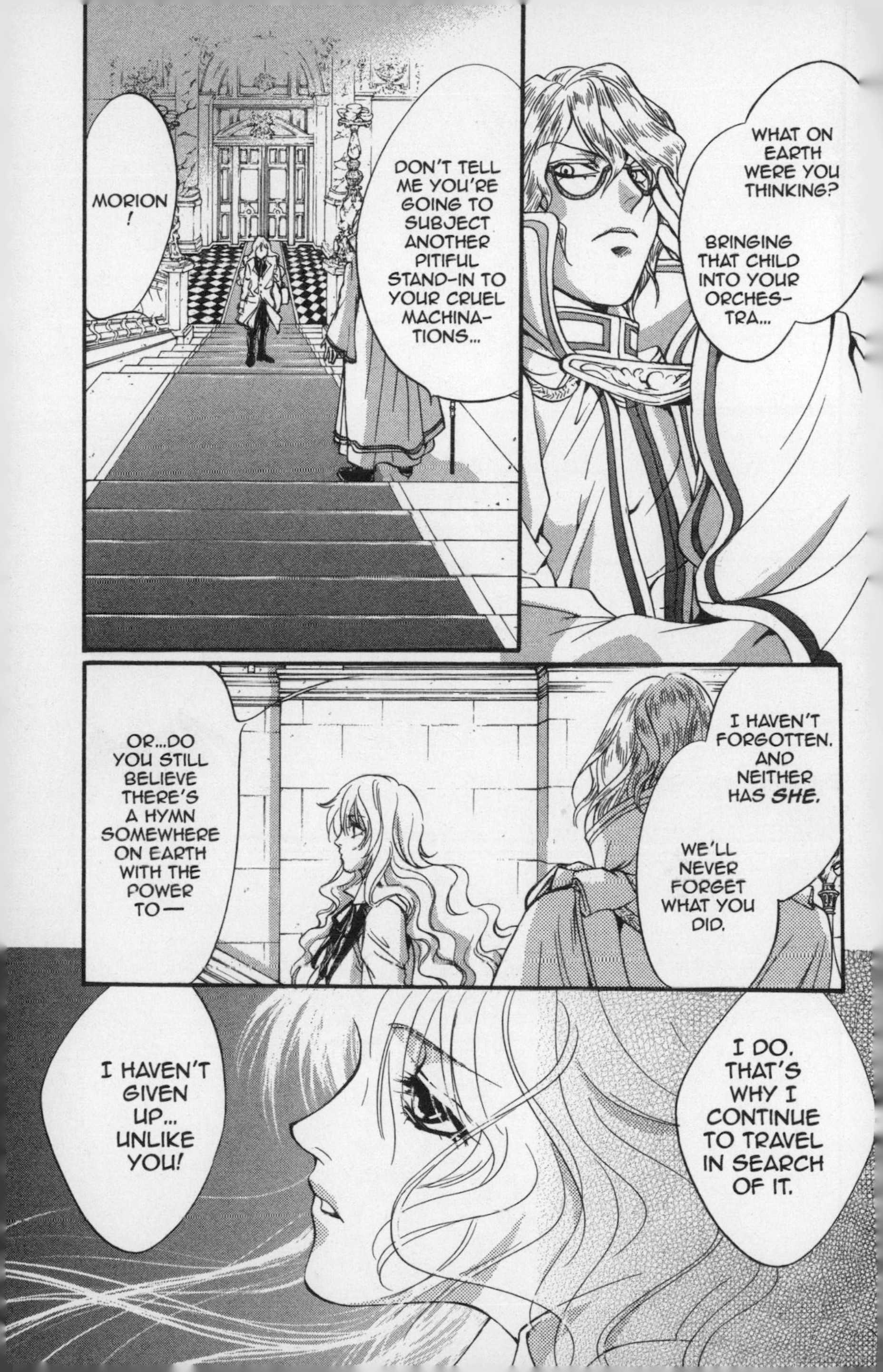
WHAT ON EARTH WERE YOU THINKING?
BRINGING THAT CHILD INTO YOUR ORCHES-TRA...
DON'T TELL ME YOU'RE GOING TO SUBJECT ANOTHER PITIFUL STAND-IN TO YOUR CRUEL MACHINA-TIONS...
MORION!
I HAVEN'T FORGOTTEN. AND NEITHER HAS *SHE*.
WE'LL NEVER FORGET WHAT YOU DID.
OR...DO YOU STILL BELIEVE THERE'S A HYMN SOMEWHERE ON EARTH WITH THE POWER TO—
I DO. THAT'S WHY I CONTINUE TO TRAVEL IN SEARCH OF IT.
I HAVEN'T GIVEN UP... UNLIKE YOU!

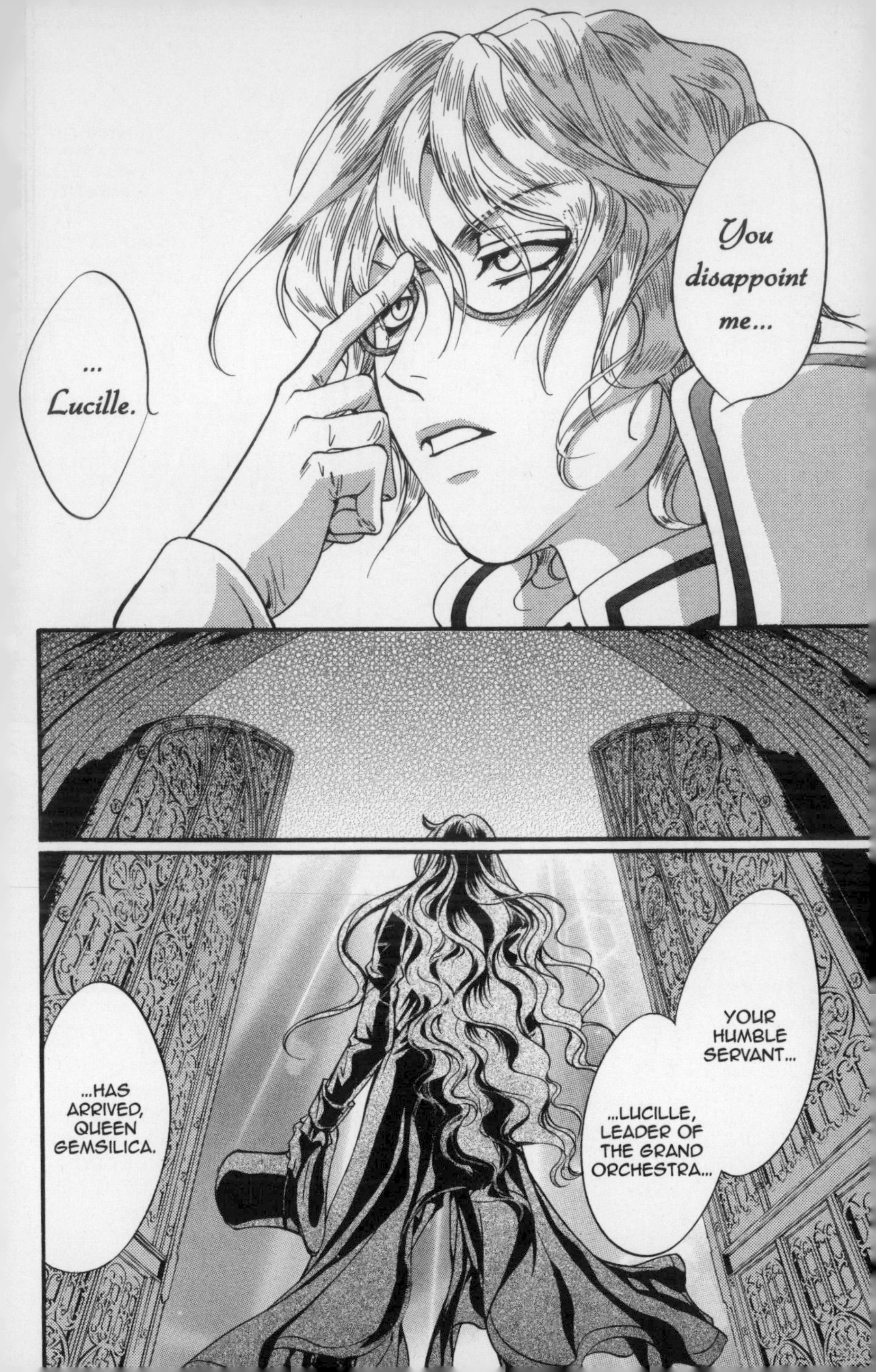
You disappoint me...
... Lucille.
YOUR HUMBLE SERVANT...
...LUCILLE, LEADER OF THE GRAND ORCHESTRA...
...HAS ARRIVED, QUEEN GEMSILICA.

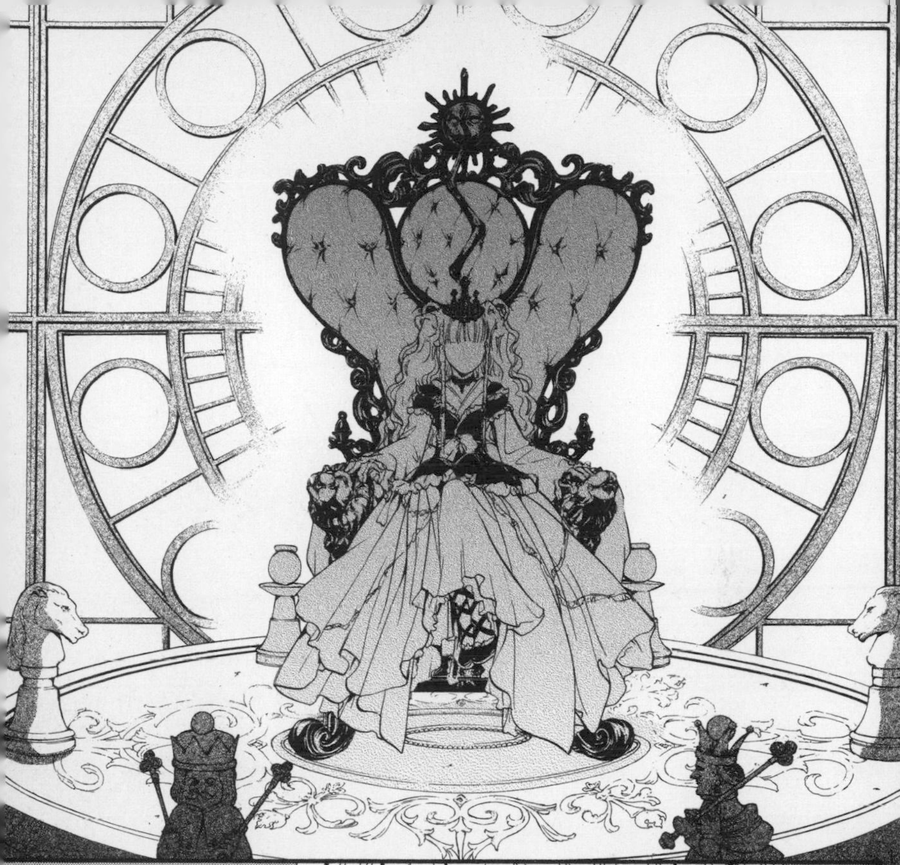

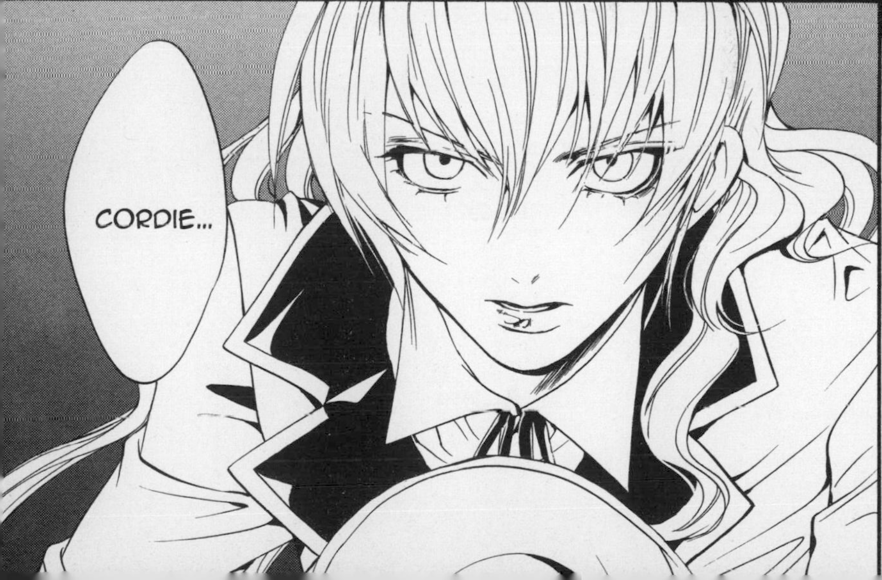
CORDIE...

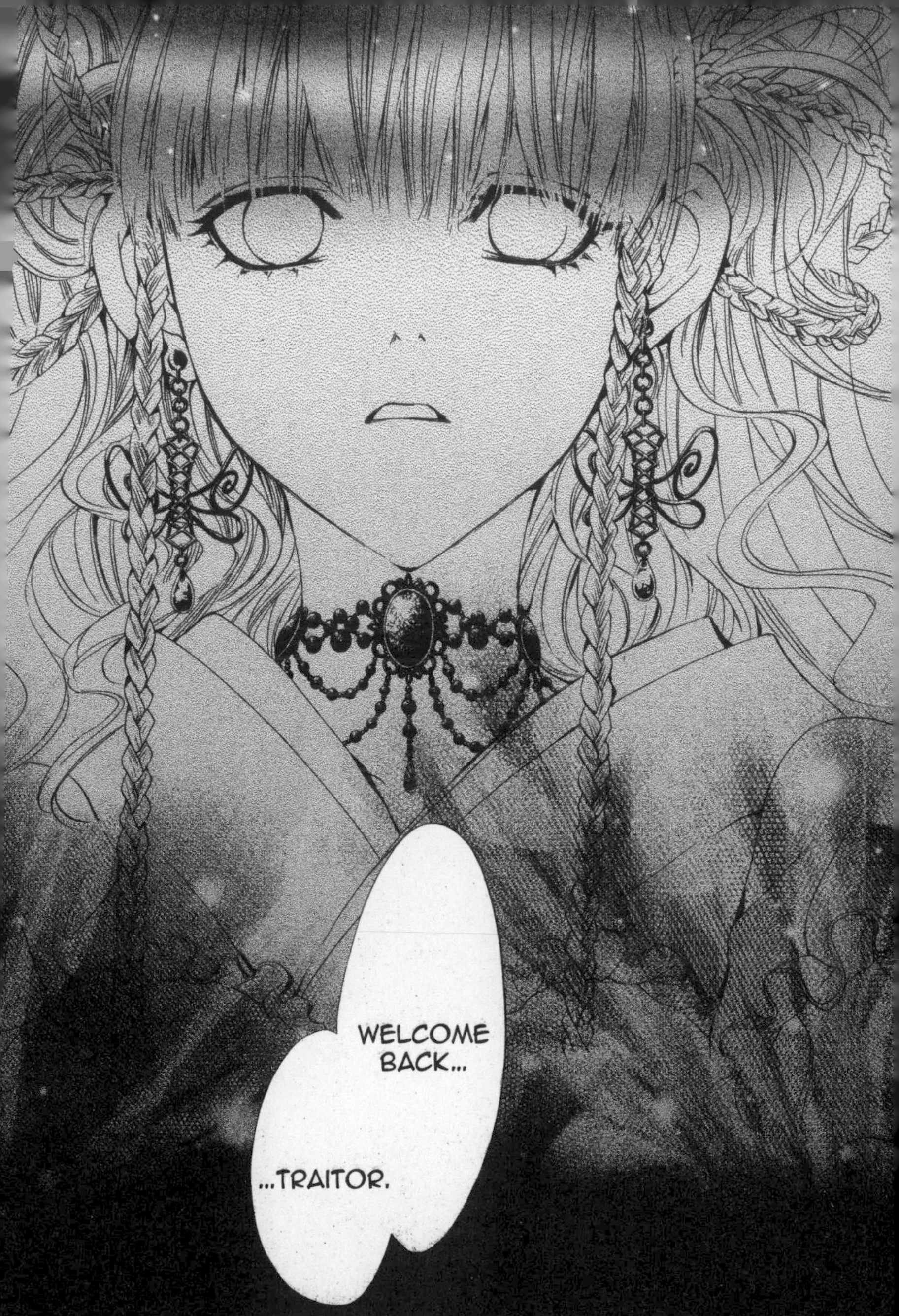
WELCOME BACK...
...TRAITOR.

Op. 5 The Queen and the Jester (Part 1) / End

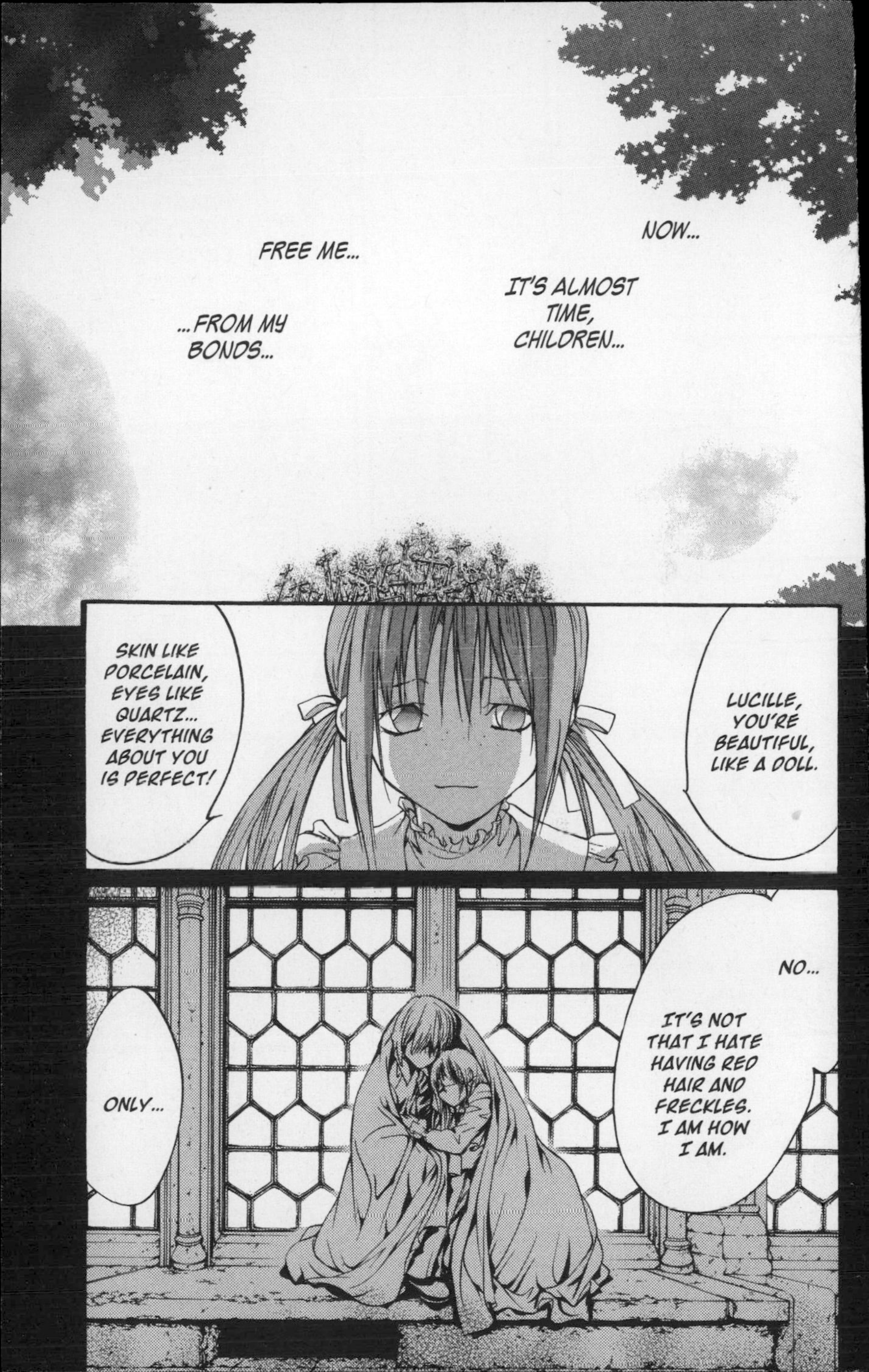
NOW...
IT'S ALMOST TIME, CHILDREN...
FREE ME...
...FROM MY BONDS...
LUCILLE, YOU'RE BEAUTIFUL, LIKE A DOLL.
SKIN LIKE PORCELAIN, EYES LIKE QUARTZ... EVERYTHING ABOUT YOU IS PERFECT!
NO...
IT'S NOT THAT I HATE HAVING RED HAIR AND FRECKLES. I AM HOW I AM.
ONLY...

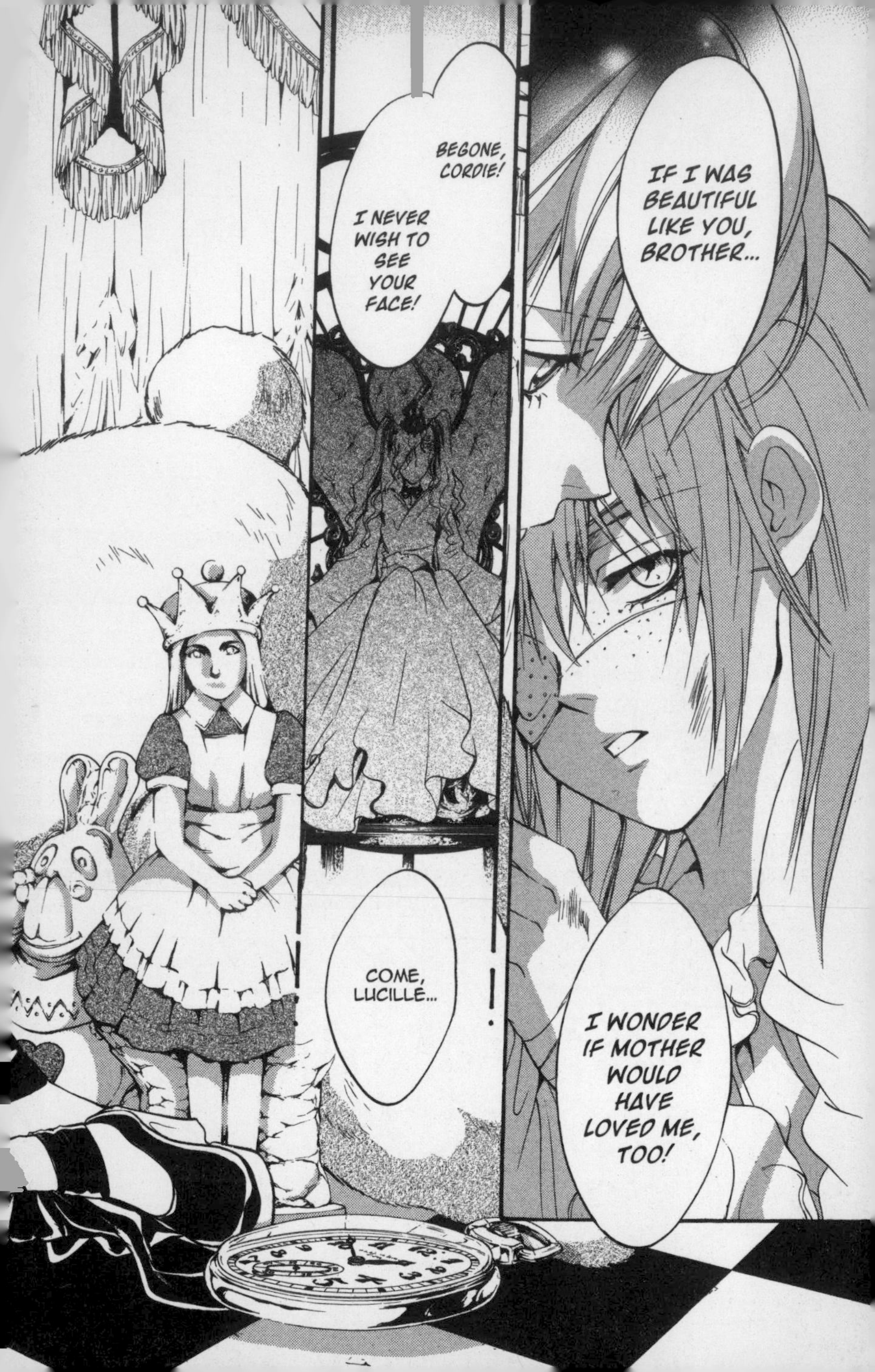
IF I WAS BEAUTIFUL LIKE YOU, BROTHER...
I WONDER IF MOTHER WOULD HAVE LOVED ME, TOO!
BEGONE, CORDIE!
I NEVER WISH TO SEE YOUR FACE!
COME, LUCILLE...

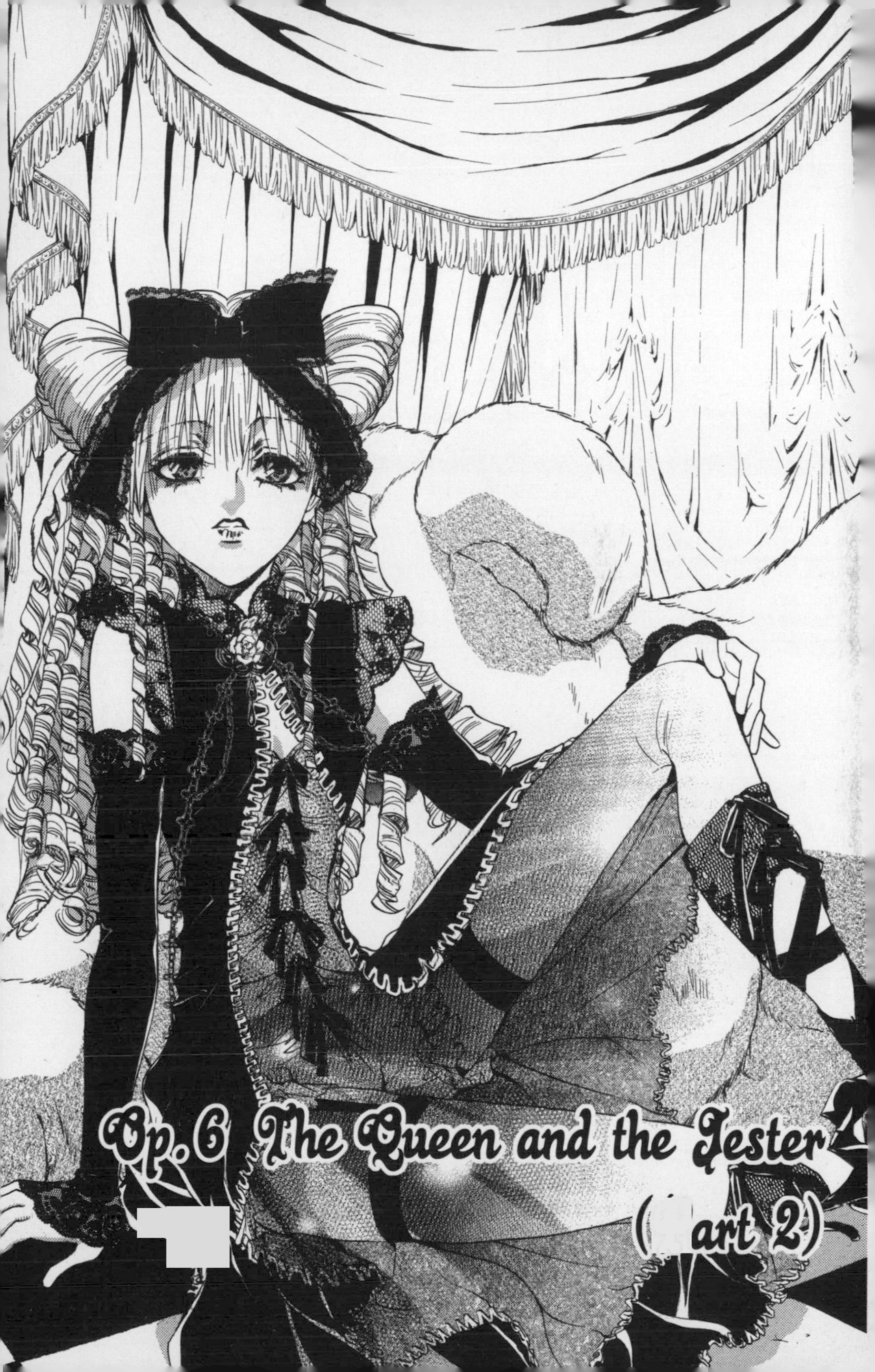
Op.6 The Queen and the Jester
(art 2)

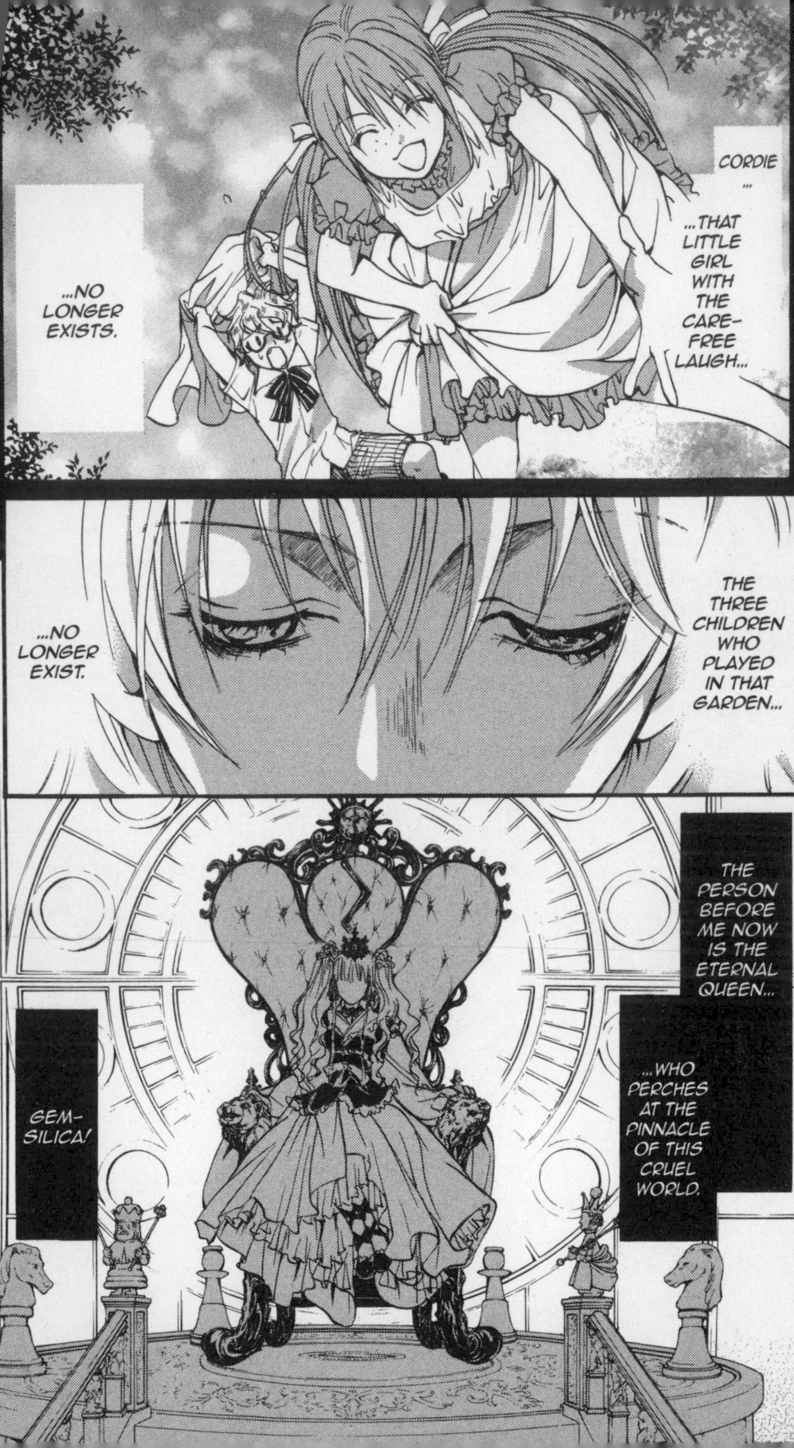
CORDIE ...
...THAT LITTLE GIRL WITH THE CARE-FREE LAUGH...
...NO LONGER EXISTS.
THE THREE CHILDREN WHO PLAYED IN THAT GARDEN...
...NO LONGER EXIST.
THE PERSON BEFORE ME NOW IS THE ETERNAL QUEEN...
...WHO PERCHES AT THE PINNACLE OF THIS CRUEL WORLD.
GEM-SILICA!

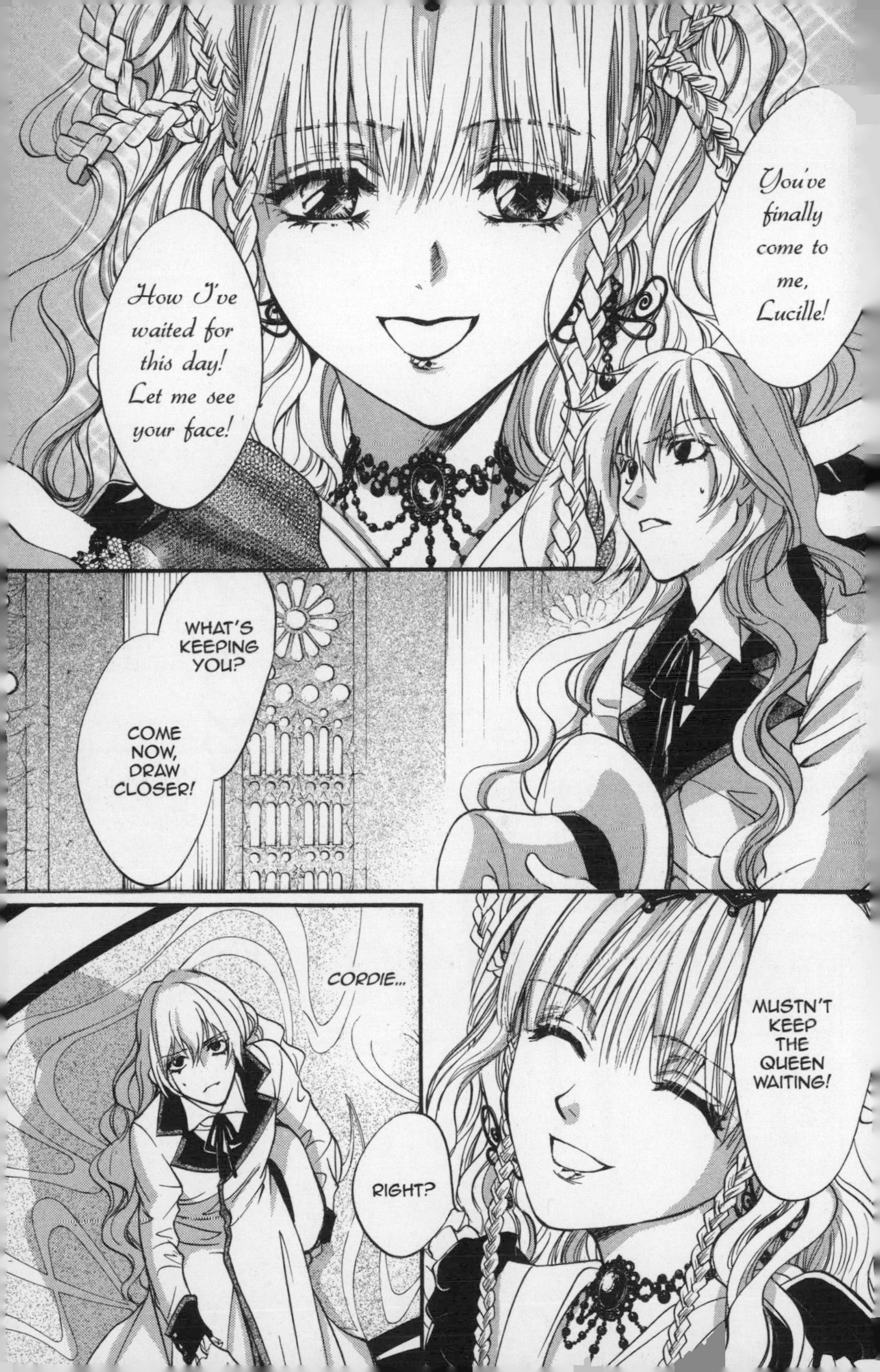
You've finally come to me, Lucille!
How I've waited for this day! Let me see your face!
WHAT'S KEEPING YOU?
COME NOW, DRAW CLOSER!
MUSTN'T KEEP THE QUEEN WAITING!
RIGHT?
CORDIE...

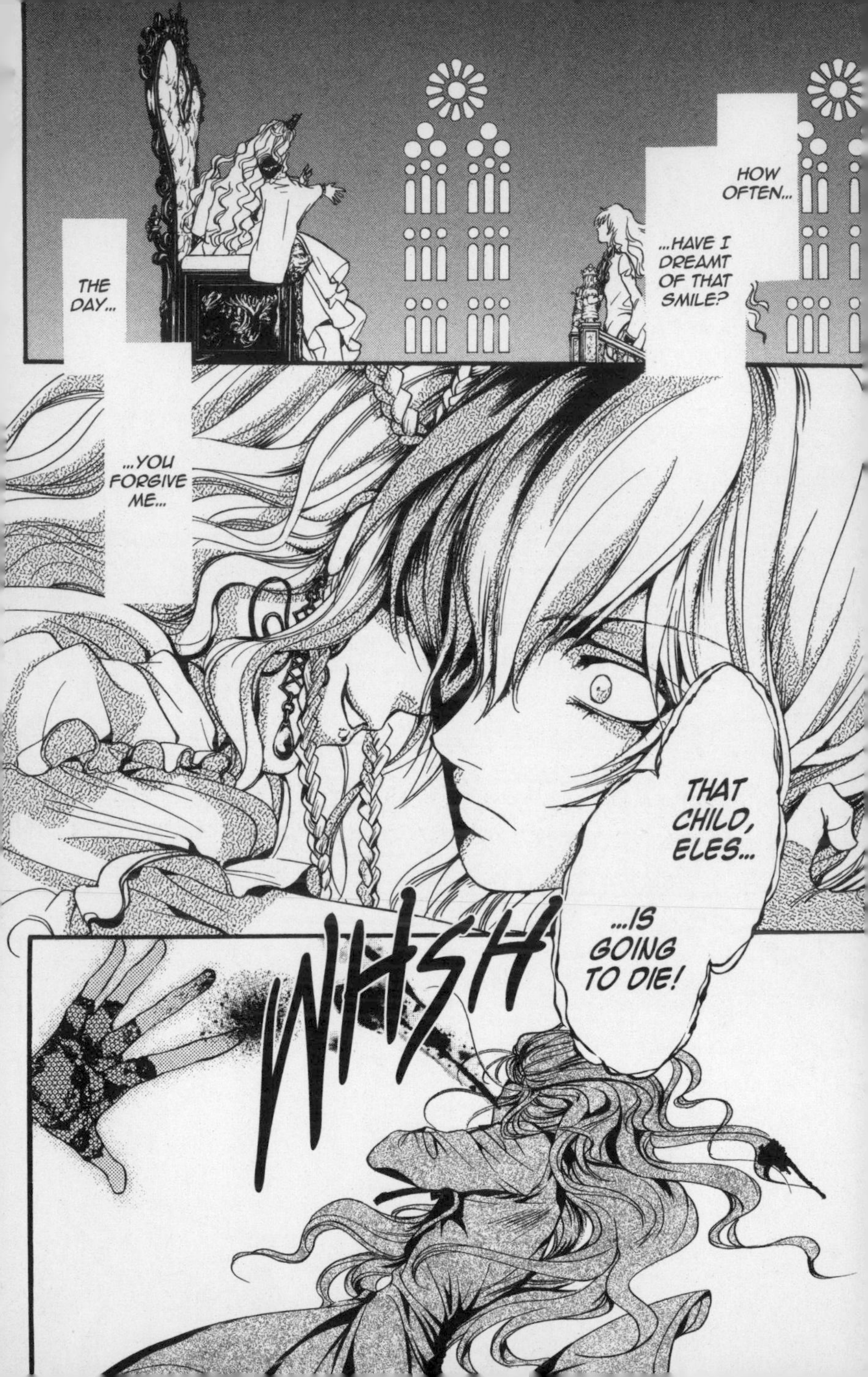
HOW OFTEN...
...HAVE I DREAMT OF THAT SMILE?
THE DAY...
...YOU FORGIVE ME...
THAT CHILD, ELES...
...IS GOING TO DIE!
WHSH

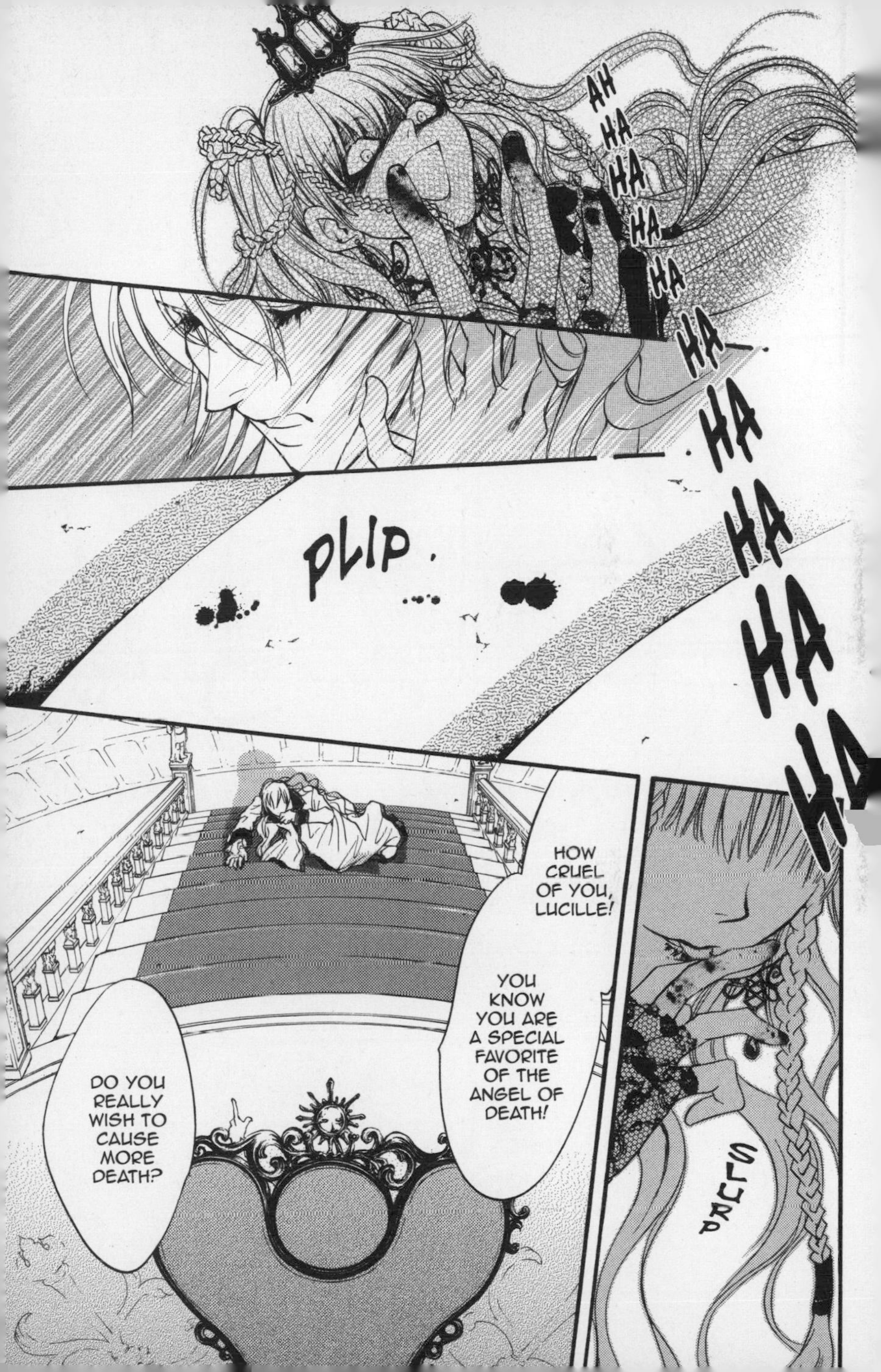
AH HA HA HA HA HA HA HA HA HA HA HA
PLIP
SLURP
HOW CRUEL OF YOU, LUCILLE!
YOU KNOW YOU ARE A SPECIAL FAVORITE OF THE ANGEL OF DEATH!
DO YOU REALLY WISH TO CAUSE MORE DEATH?

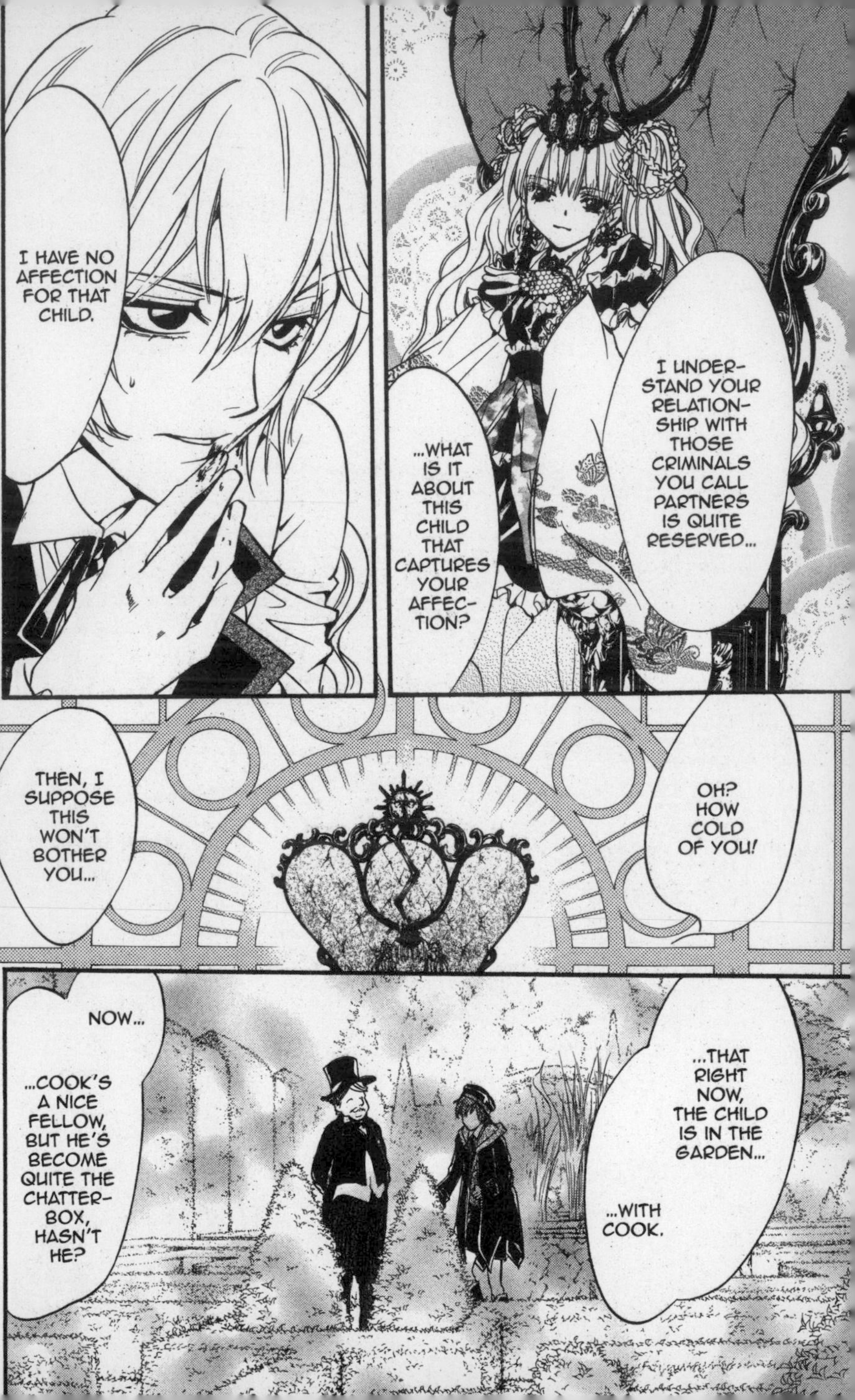
I UNDER-STAND YOUR RELATION-SHIP WITH THOSE CRIMINALS YOU CALL PARTNERS IS QUITE RESERVED...
...WHAT IS IT ABOUT THIS CHILD THAT CAPTURES YOUR AFFEC-TION?
I HAVE NO AFFECTION FOR THAT CHILD.
OH? HOW COLD OF YOU!
THEN, I SUPPOSE THIS WON'T BOTHER YOU...
...THAT RIGHT NOW, THE CHILD IS IN THE GARDEN...
...WITH COOK.
NOW...
...COOK'S A NICE FELLOW, BUT HE'S BECOME QUITE THE CHATTER-BOX, HASN'T HE?

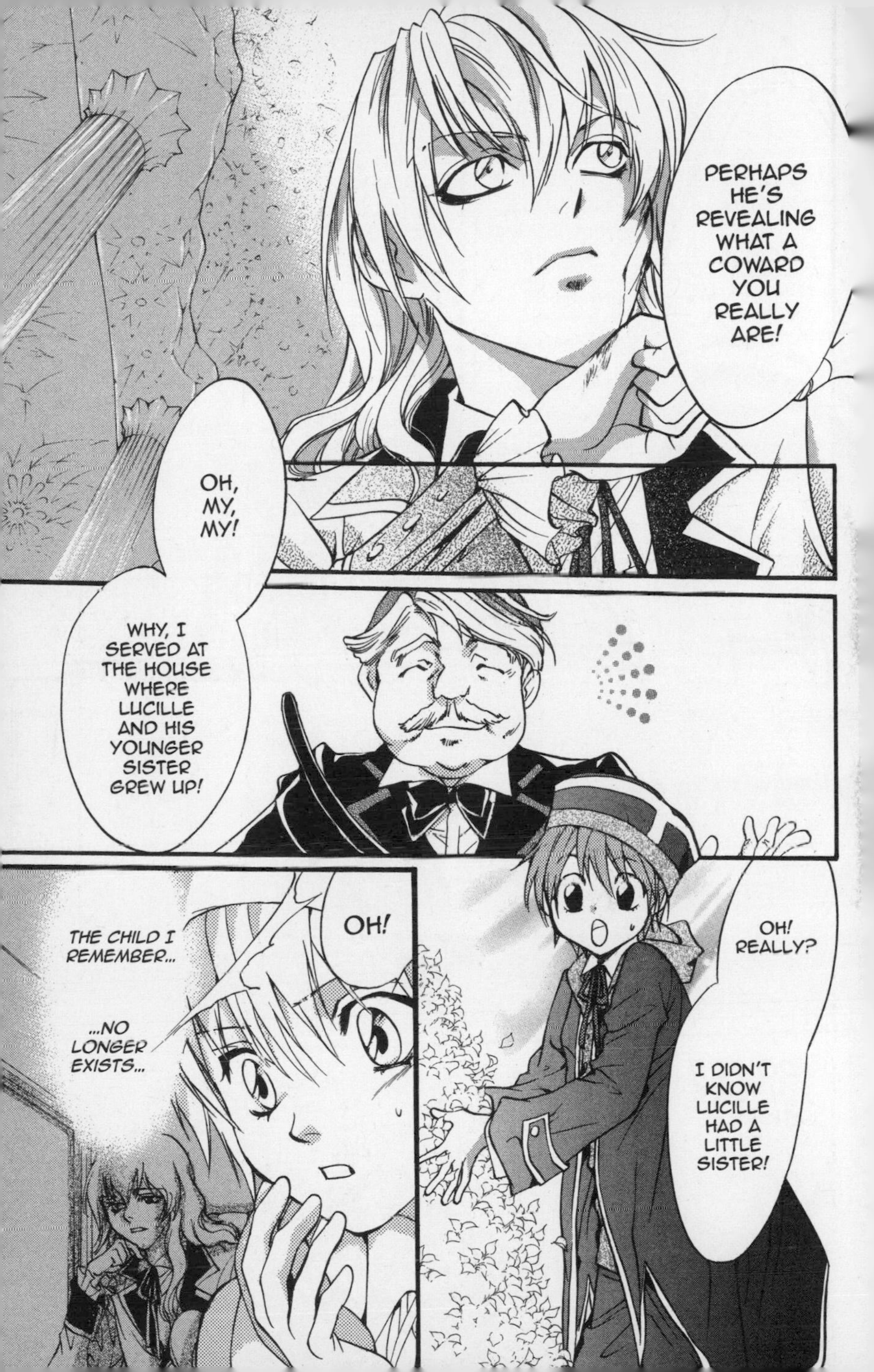
PERHAPS HE'S REVEALING WHAT A COWARD YOU REALLY ARE!
OH, MY, MY!
WHY, I SERVED AT THE HOUSE WHERE LUCILLE AND HIS YOUNGER SISTER GREW UP!
OH! REALLY?
I DIDN'T KNOW LUCILLE HAD A LITTLE SISTER!
OH!
THE CHILD I REMEMBER...
...NO LONGER EXISTS...

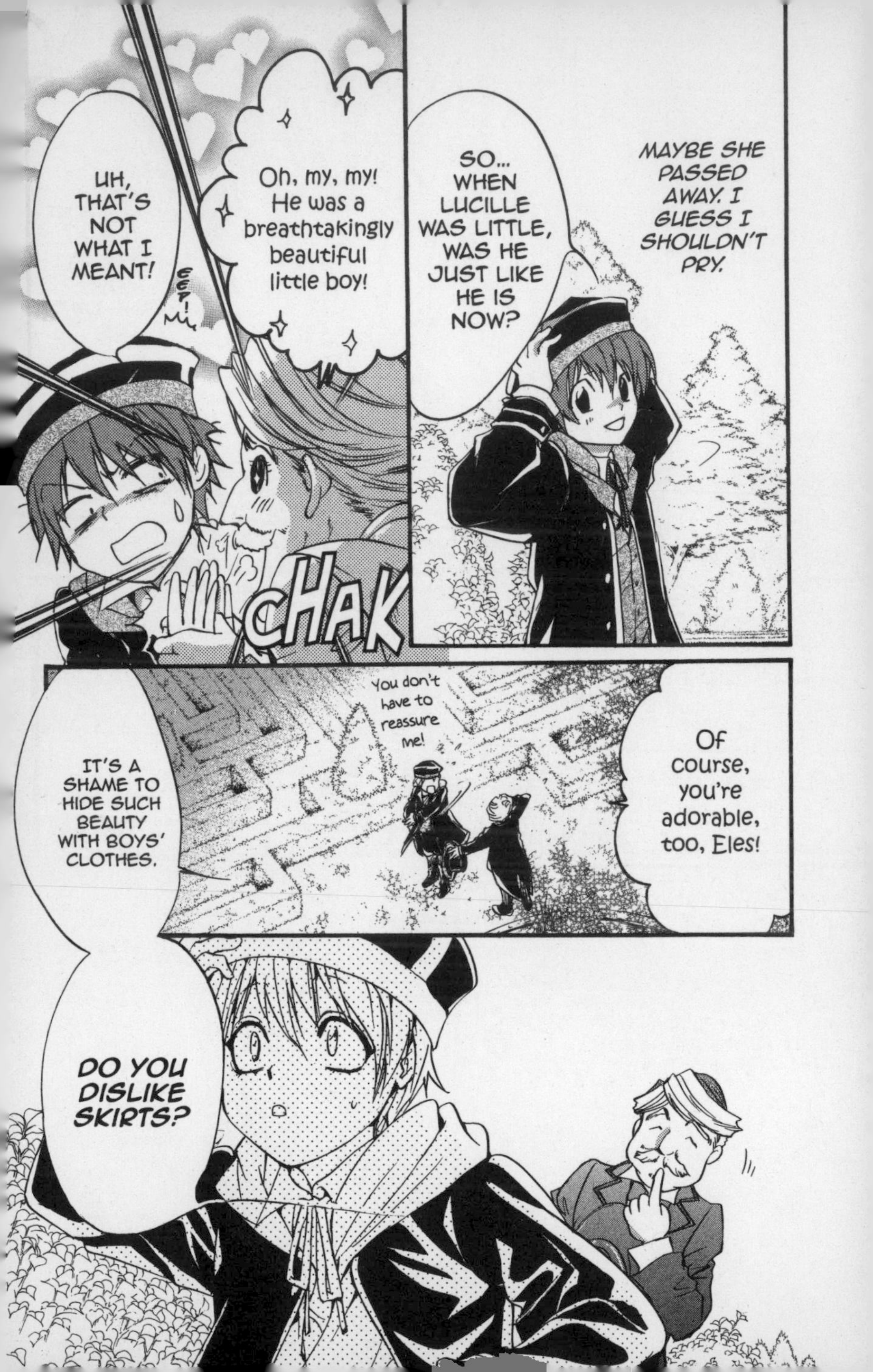
MAYBE SHE PASSED AWAY. I GUESS I SHOULDN'T PRY.
SO... WHEN LUCILLE WAS LITTLE, WAS HE JUST LIKE HE IS NOW?
Oh, my, my! He was a breathtakingly beautiful little boy!
UH, THAT'S NOT WHAT I MEANT!
EEP!
CHAK
Of course, you're adorable, too, Eles!
You don't have to reassure me!
IT'S A SHAME TO HIDE SUCH BEAUTY WITH BOYS' CLOTHES.
DO YOU DISLIKE SKIRTS?

In the story about the queen, the illustrations of the palace were a real challenge. Of course, the throne and the character design were just as hard. Naturally, I like Cordie back in her freckled, plain phase better than how she looks as Queen Gemsilica.
I based the garden in Lucille's childhood memories on the Bomarzo Monster Park in Italy.

I like the Coral Castle, too!

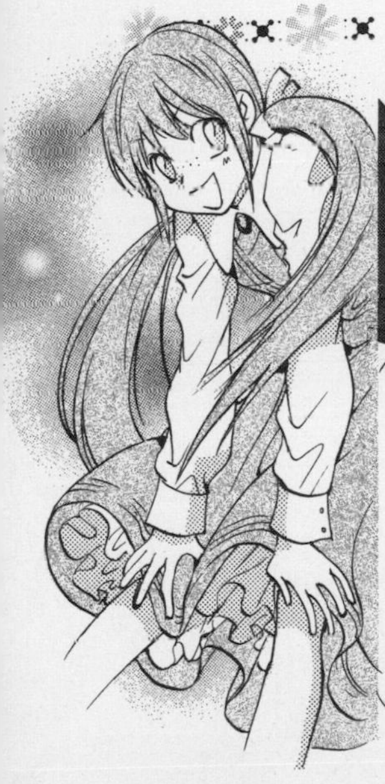

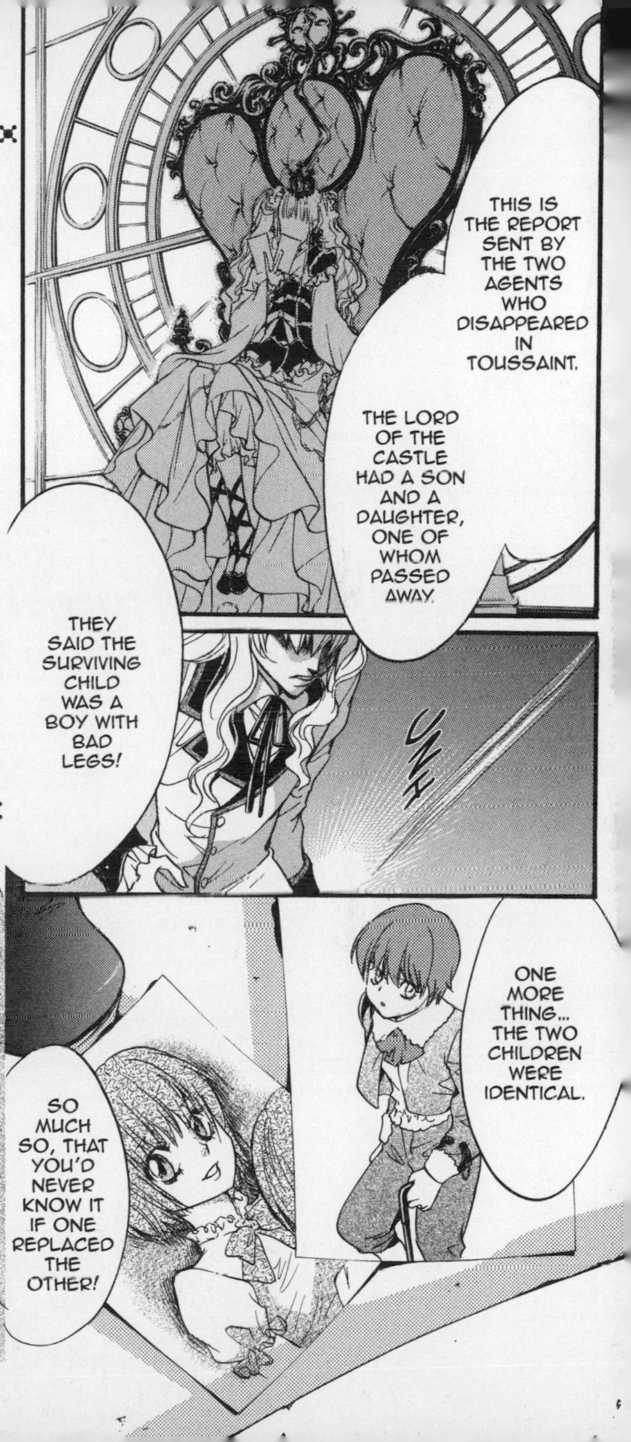
THIS IS THE REPORT SENT BY THE TWO AGENTS WHO DISAPPEARED IN TOUSSAINT.
THE LORD OF THE CASTLE HAD A SON AND A DAUGHTER, ONE OF WHOM PASSED AWAY.
THEY SAID THE SURVIVING CHILD WAS A BOY WITH BAD LEGS!
ONE MORE THING... THE TWO CHILDREN WERE IDENTICAL.
SO MUCH SO, THAT YOU'D NEVER KNOW IT IF ONE REPLACED THE OTHER!

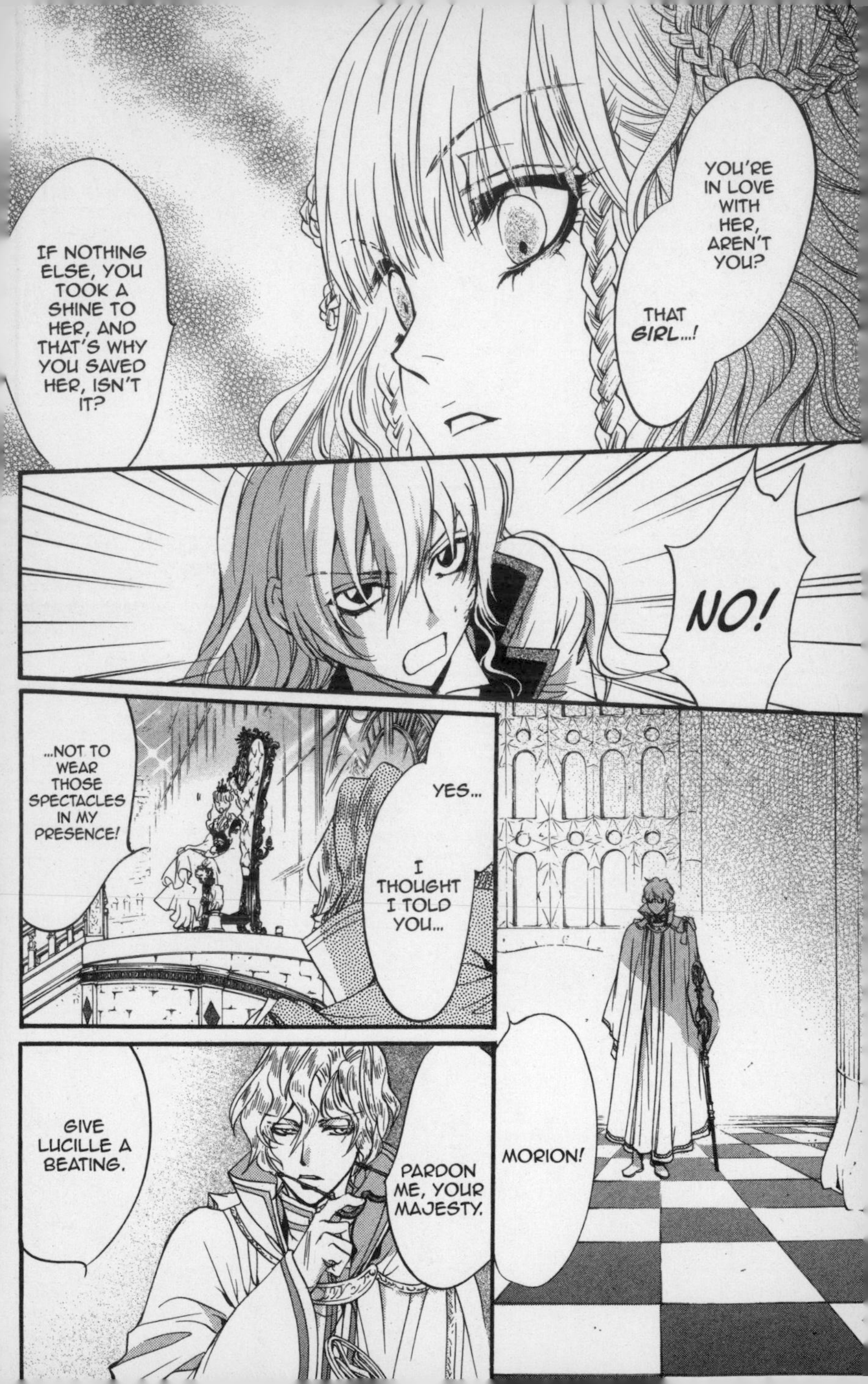
YOU'RE IN LOVE WITH HER, AREN'T YOU?
THAT *GIRL*...!
IF NOTHING ELSE, YOU TOOK A SHINE TO HER, AND THAT'S WHY YOU SAVED HER, ISN'T IT?
NO!
MORION!
YES...
I THOUGHT I TOLD YOU...
...NOT TO WEAR THOSE SPECTACLES IN MY PRESENCE!
PARDON ME, YOUR MAJESTY.
GIVE LUCILLE A BEATING.

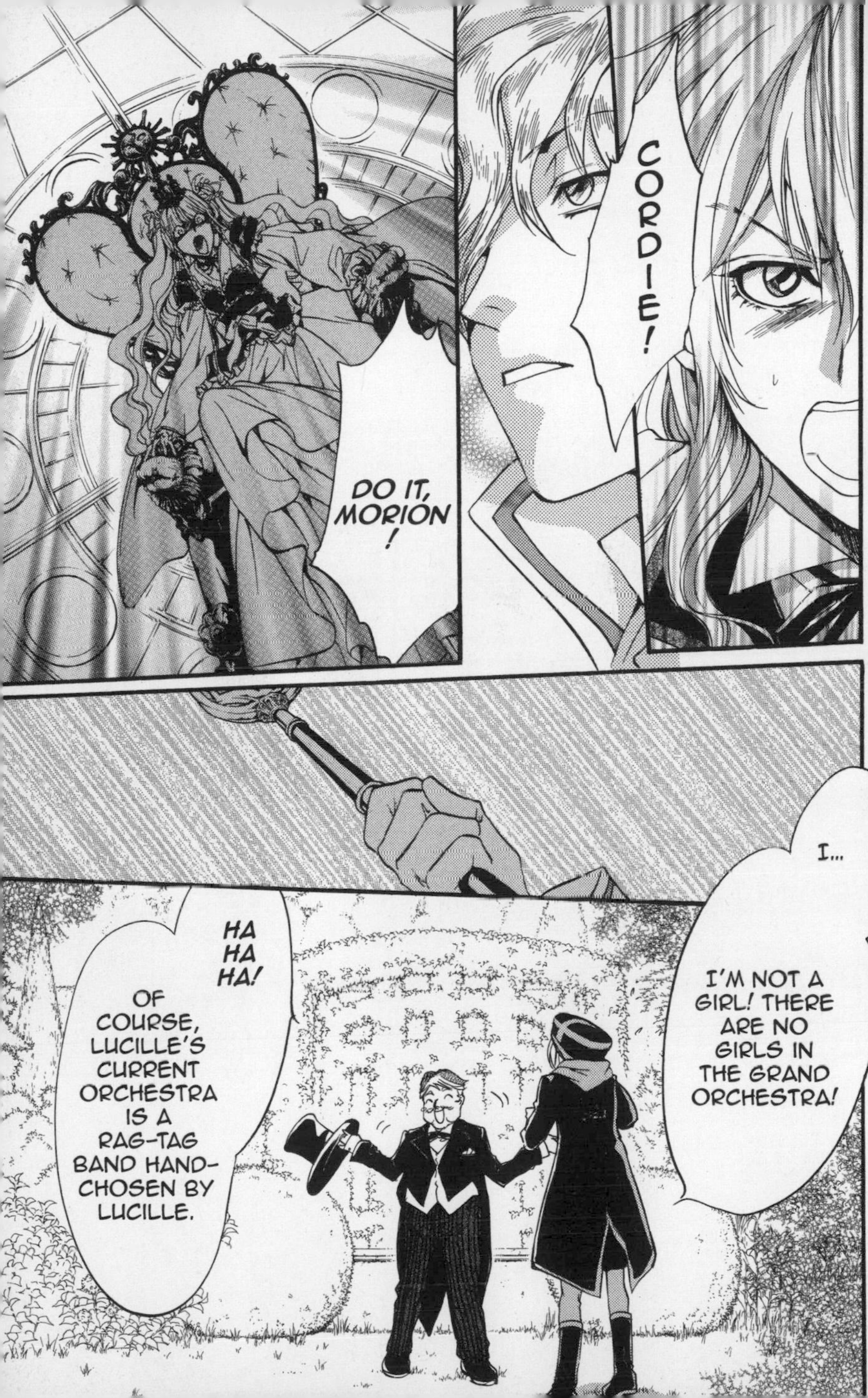
CORDIE!
DO IT, MORION!
I...
I'M NOT A GIRL! THERE ARE NO GIRLS IN THE GRAND ORCHESTRA!
HA HA HA!
OF COURSE, LUCILLE'S CURRENT ORCHESTRA IS A RAG-TAG BAND HAND-CHOSEN BY LUCILLE.

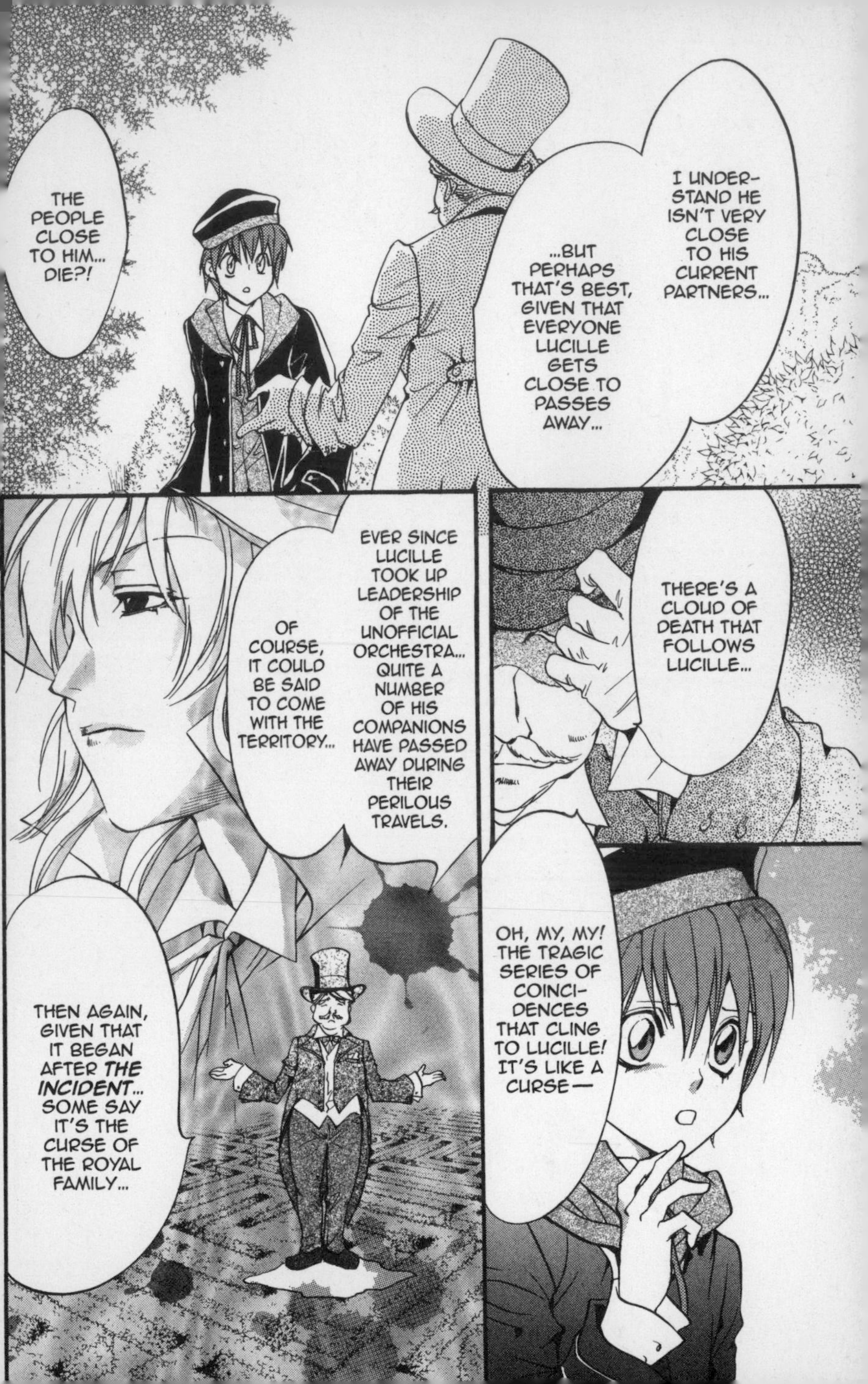
I UNDER-STAND HE ISN'T VERY CLOSE TO HIS CURRENT PARTNERS...
...BUT PERHAPS THAT'S BEST, GIVEN THAT EVERYONE LUCILLE GETS CLOSE TO PASSES AWAY...
THE PEOPLE CLOSE TO HIM... DIE?!
THERE'S A CLOUD OF DEATH THAT FOLLOWS LUCILLE...
OH, MY, MY! THE TRAGIC SERIES OF COINCI-DENCES THAT CLING TO LUCILLE! IT'S LIKE A CURSE—
EVER SINCE LUCILLE TOOK UP LEADERSHIP OF THE UNOFFICIAL ORCHESTRA... QUITE A NUMBER OF HIS COMPANIONS HAVE PASSED AWAY DURING THEIR PERILOUS TRAVELS.
OF COURSE, IT COULD BE SAID TO COME WITH THE TERRITORY...
THEN AGAIN, GIVEN THAT IT BEGAN AFTER ***THE INCIDENT***... SOME SAY IT'S THE CURSE OF THE ROYAL FAMILY...

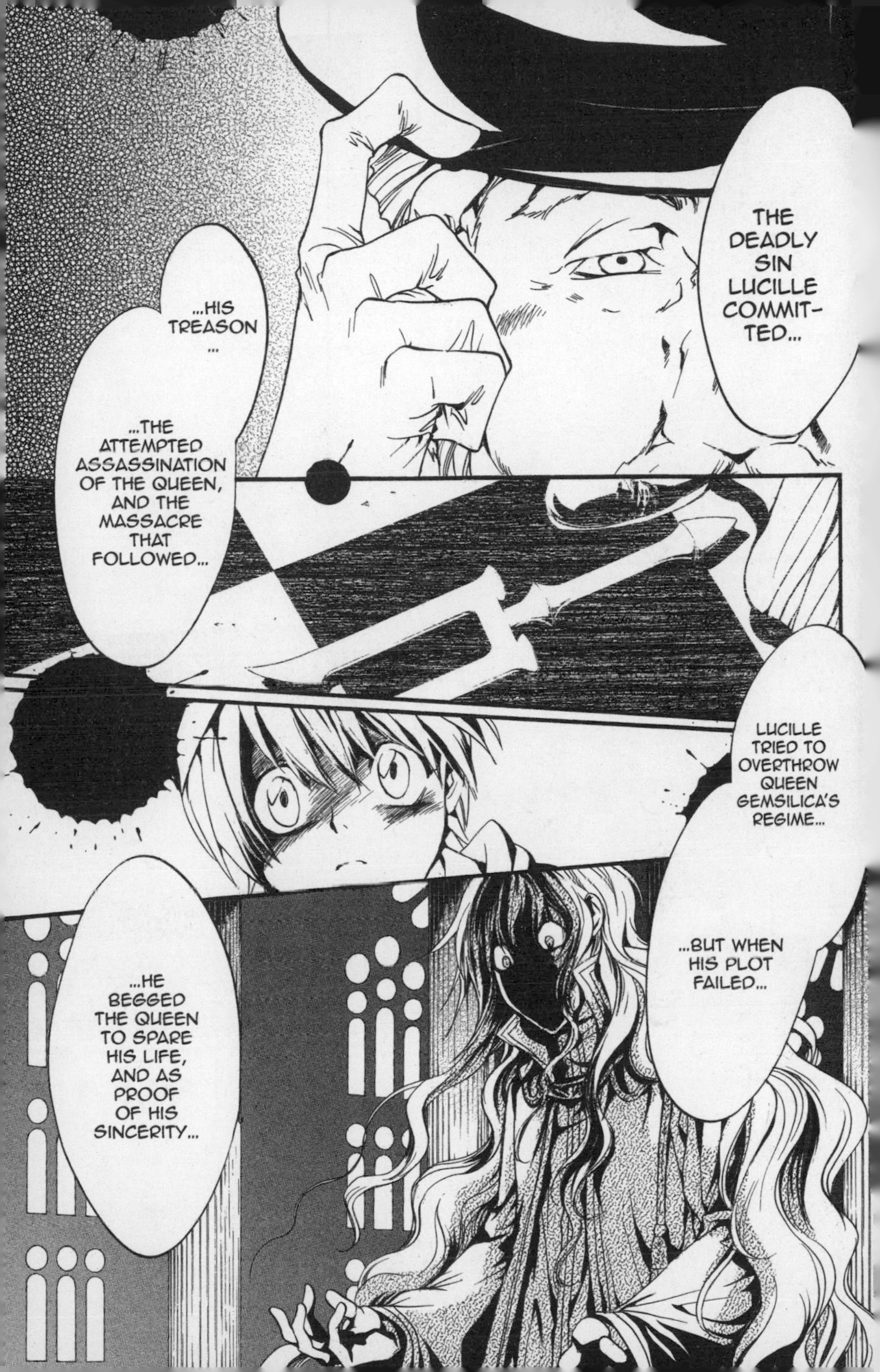
THE DEADLY SIN LUCILLE COMMIT-TED...
...HIS TREASON ...
...THE ATTEMPTED ASSASSINATION OF THE QUEEN, AND THE MASSACRE THAT FOLLOWED...
LUCILLE TRIED TO OVERTHROW QUEEN GEMSILICA'S REGIME...
...BUT WHEN HIS PLOT FAILED...
...HE BEGGED THE QUEEN TO SPARE HIS LIFE, AND AS PROOF OF HIS SINCERITY...

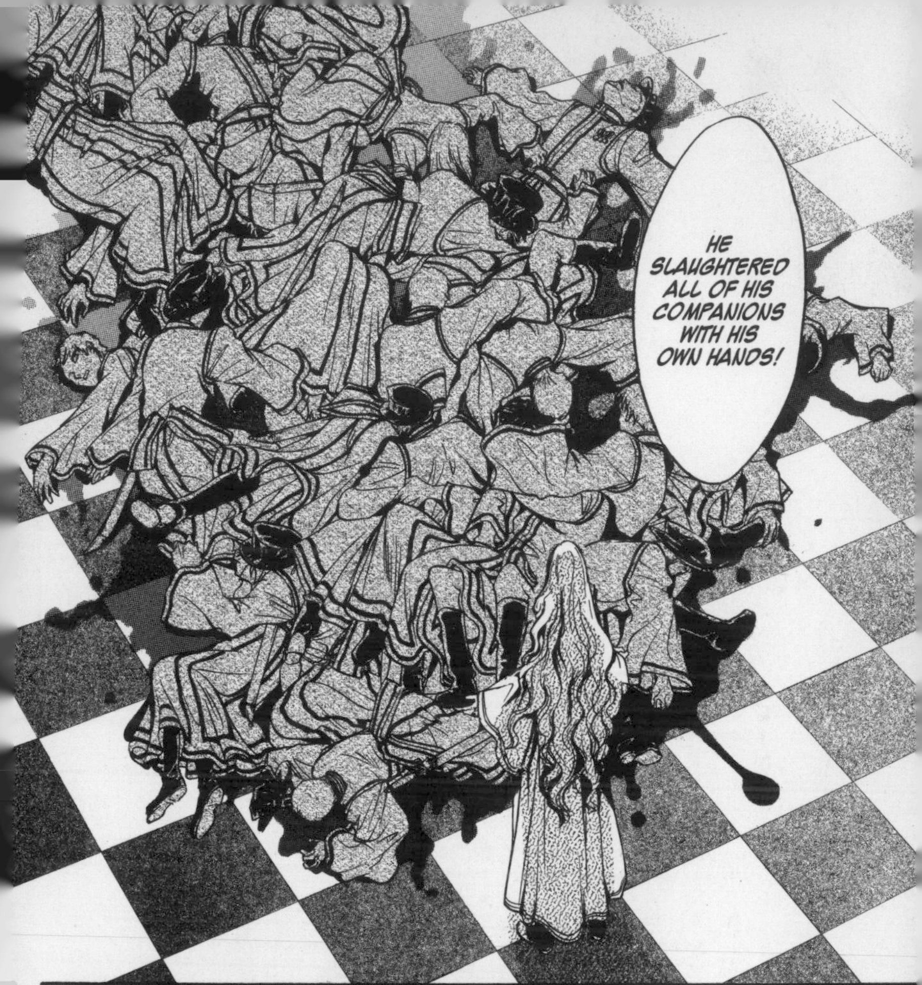
HE SLAUGHTERED ALL OF HIS COMPANIONS WITH HIS OWN HANDS!
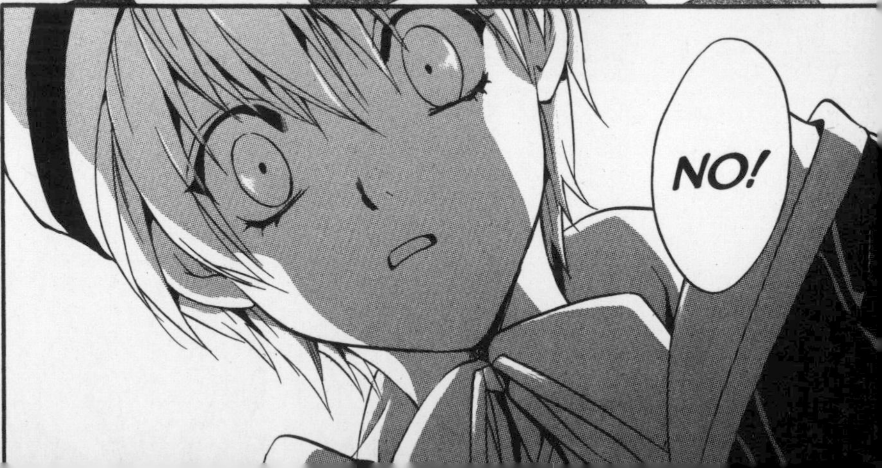
NO!

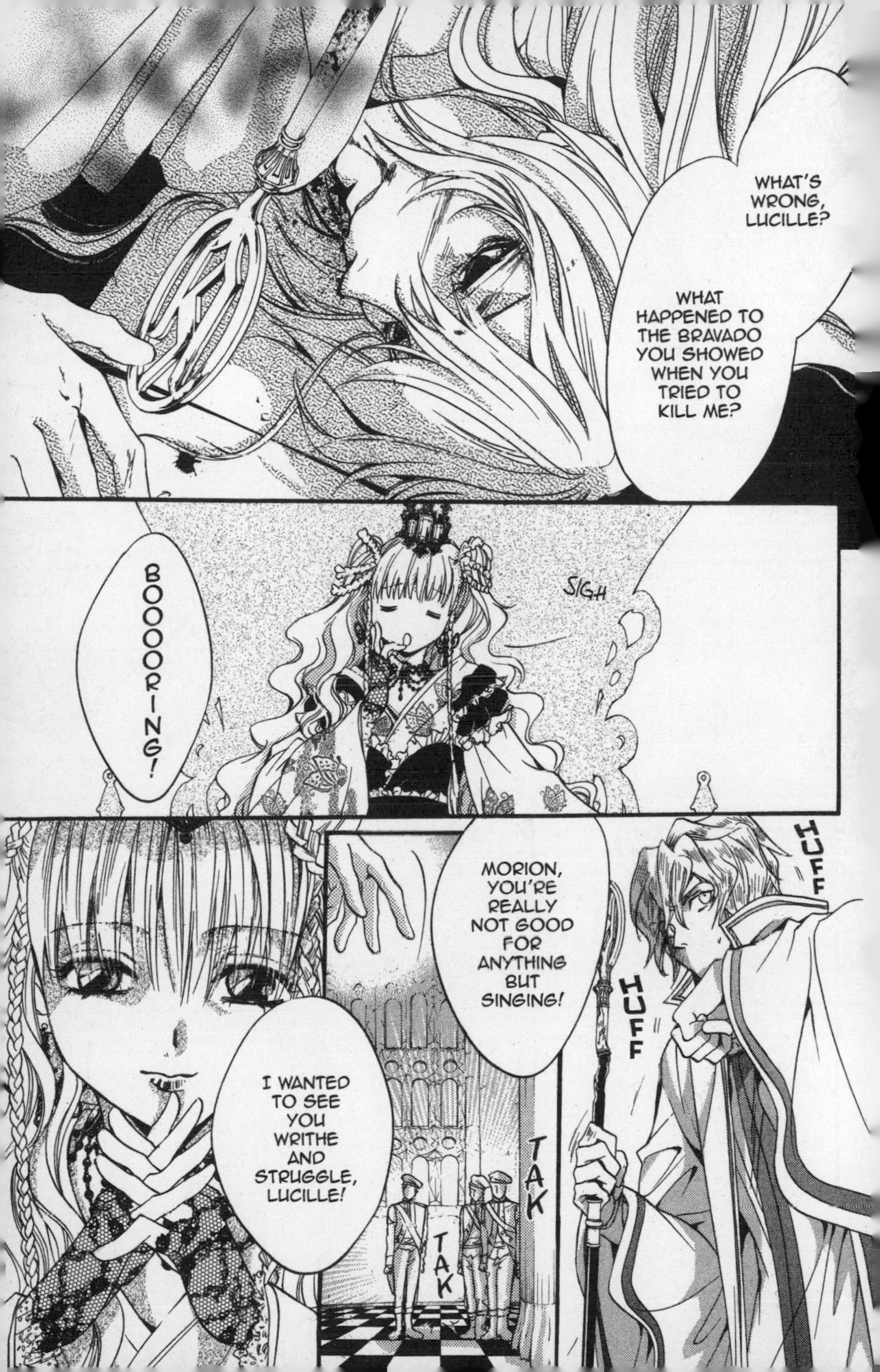
WHAT'S WRONG, LUCILLE?
WHAT HAPPENED TO THE BRAVADO YOU SHOWED WHEN YOU TRIED TO KILL ME?
SIGH
BOOOORING!
HUFF
HUFF
MORION, YOU'RE REALLY NOT GOOD FOR ANYTHING BUT SINGING!
TAK
TAK
I WANTED TO SEE YOU WRITHE AND STRUGGLE, LUCILLE!

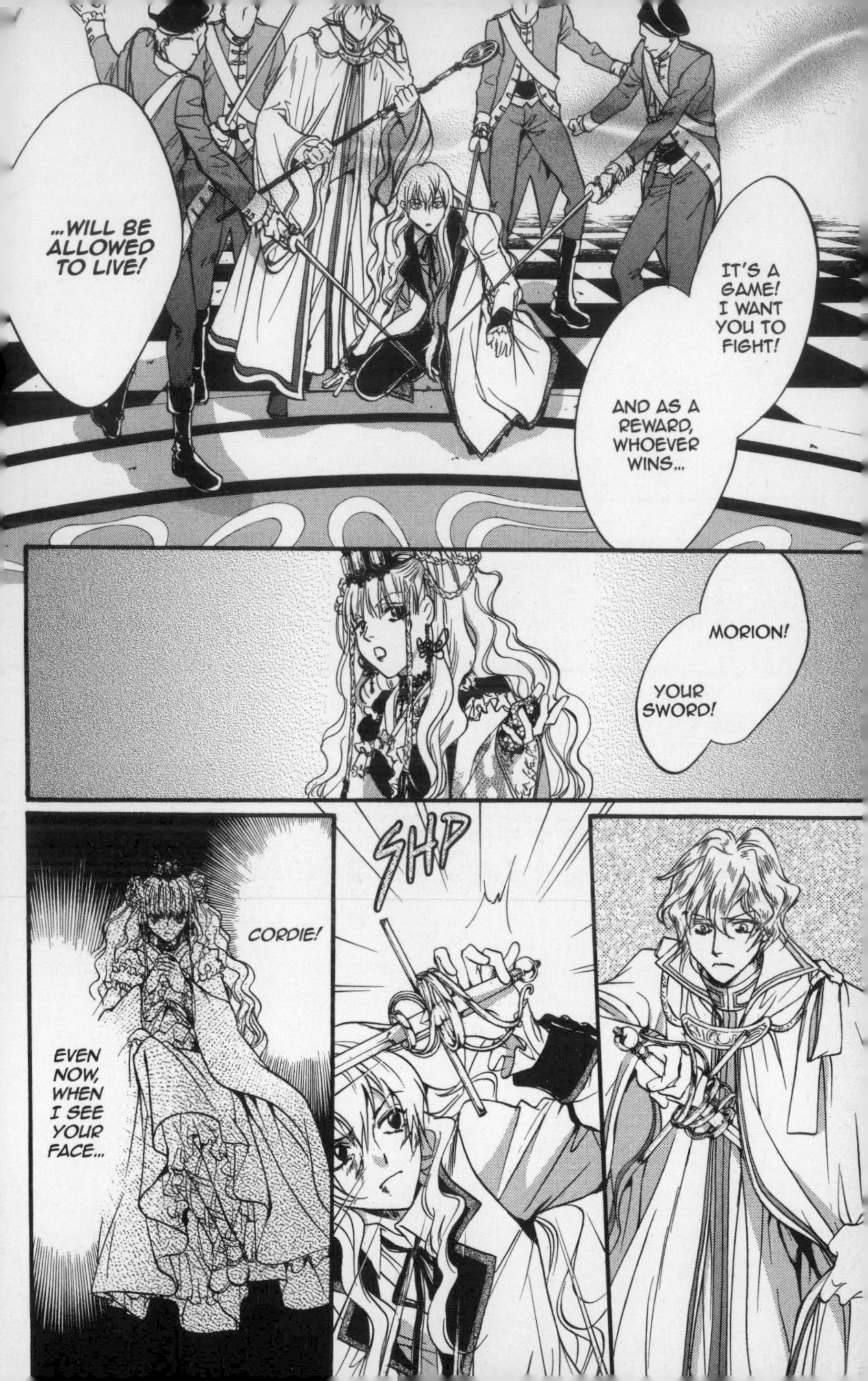
IT'S A GAME! I WANT YOU TO FIGHT!
AND AS A REWARD, WHOEVER WINS...
...WILL BE ALLOWED TO LIVE!
MORION!
YOUR SWORD!
SHP
CORDIE!
EVEN NOW, WHEN I SEE YOUR FACE...

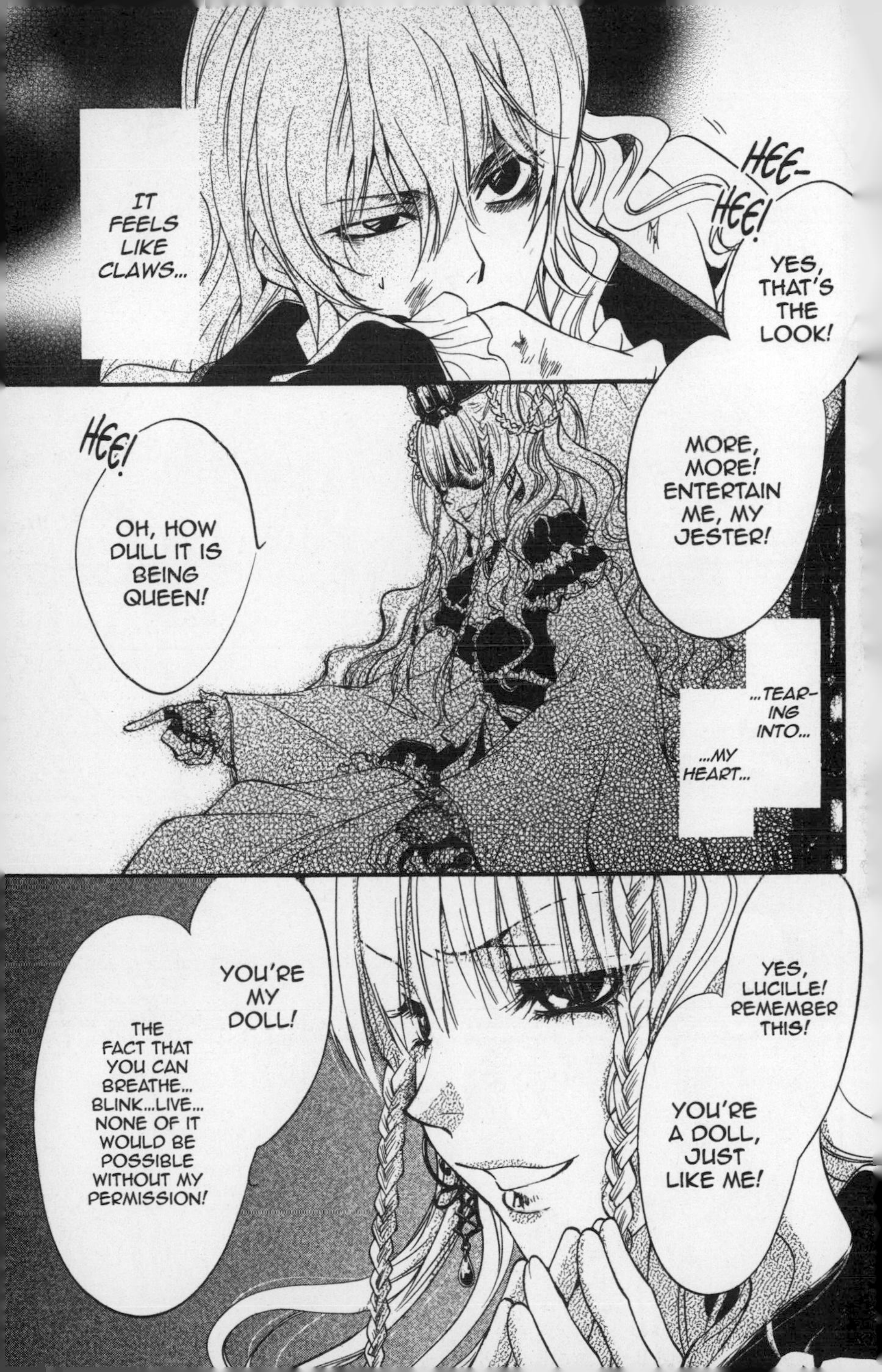
HEE-HEE!
YES, THAT'S THE LOOK!
IT FEELS LIKE CLAWS...
MORE, MORE! ENTERTAIN ME, MY JESTER!
...TEARING INTO...
...MY HEART...
HEE!
OH, HOW DULL IT IS BEING QUEEN!
YES, LUCILLE! REMEMBER THIS!
YOU'RE A DOLL, JUST LIKE ME!
YOU'RE MY DOLL!
THE FACT THAT YOU CAN BREATHE... BLINK...LIVE... NONE OF IT WOULD BE POSSIBLE WITHOUT MY PERMISSION!

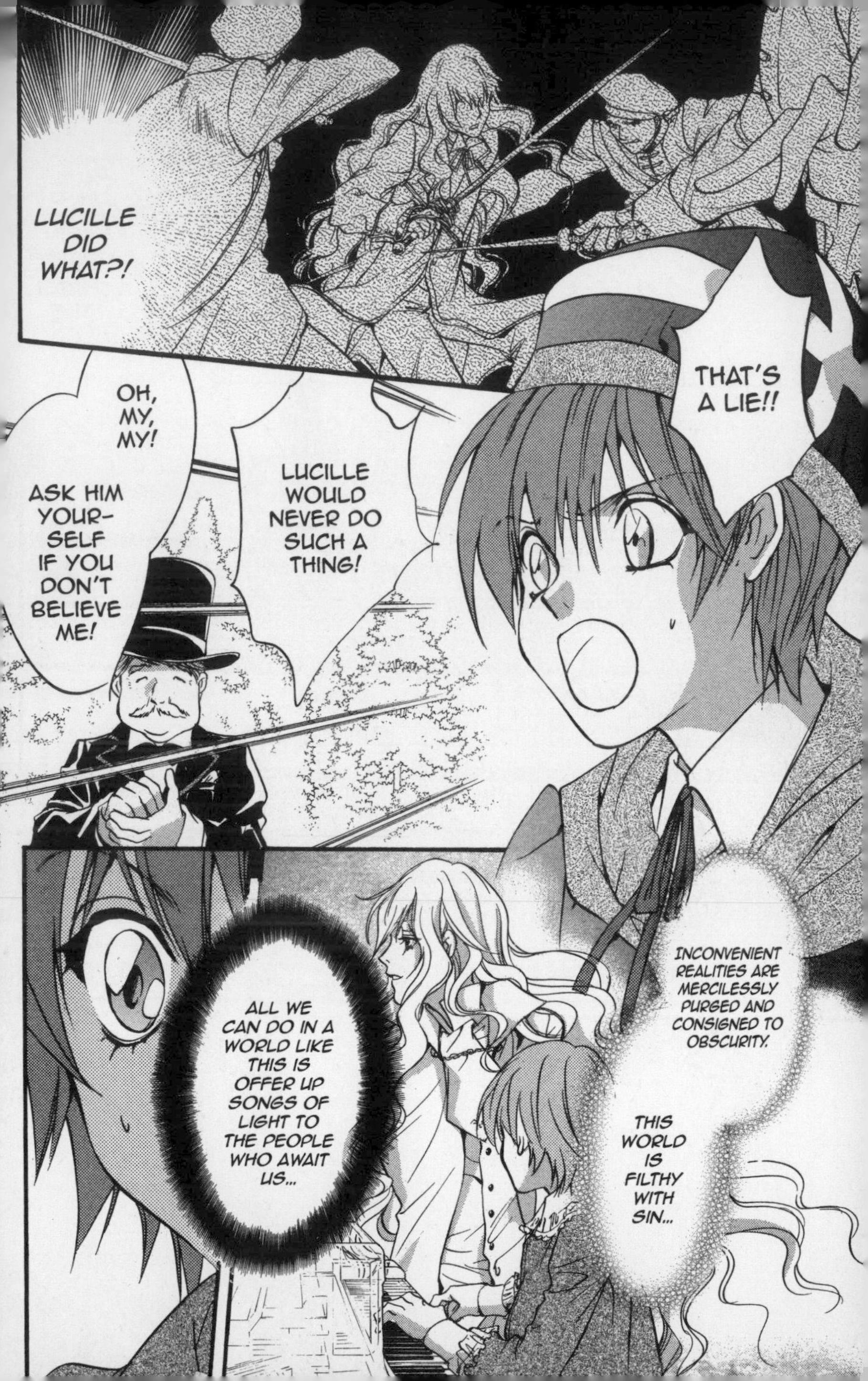
LUCILLE DID WHAT?!
THAT'S A LIE!!
LUCILLE WOULD NEVER DO SUCH A THING!
OH, MY, MY!
ASK HIM YOUR-SELF IF YOU DON'T BELIEVE ME!
INCONVENIENT REALITIES ARE MERCILESSLY PURGED AND CONSIGNED TO OBSCURITY.
THIS WORLD IS FILTHY WITH SIN...
ALL WE CAN DO IN A WORLD LIKE THIS IS OFFER UP SONGS OF LIGHT TO THE PEOPLE WHO AWAIT US...

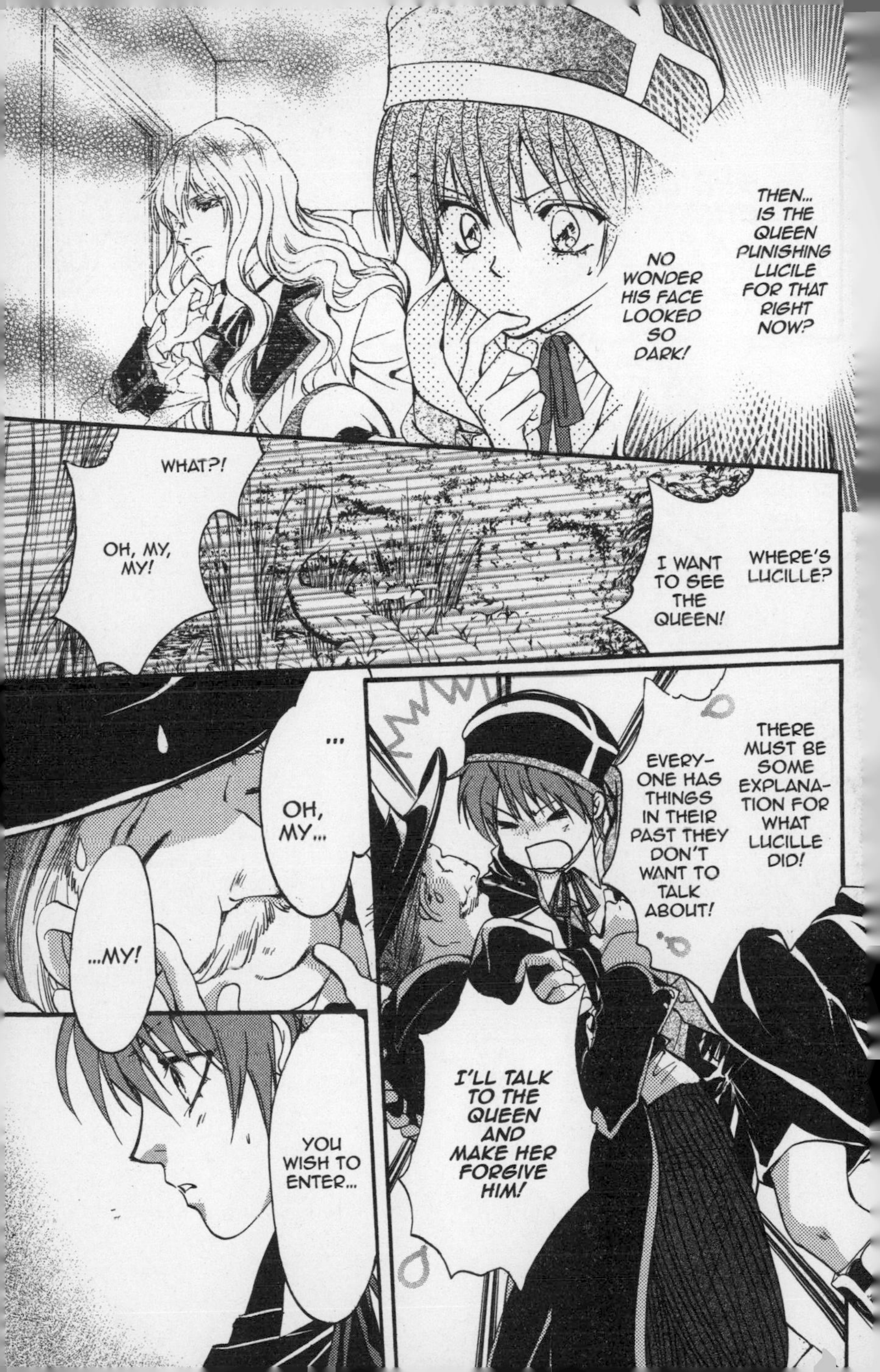
THEN... IS THE QUEEN PUNISHING LUCILE FOR THAT RIGHT NOW?
NO WONDER HIS FACE LOOKED SO DARK!
WHERE'S LUCILLE?
I WANT TO SEE THE QUEEN!
WHAT?!
OH, MY, MY!
THERE MUST BE SOME EXPLANATION FOR WHAT LUCILLE DID!
EVERYONE HAS THINGS IN THEIR PAST THEY DON'T WANT TO TALK ABOUT!
I'LL TALK TO THE QUEEN AND MAKE HER FORGIVE HIM!
...
OH, MY...
...MY!
YOU WISH TO ENTER...

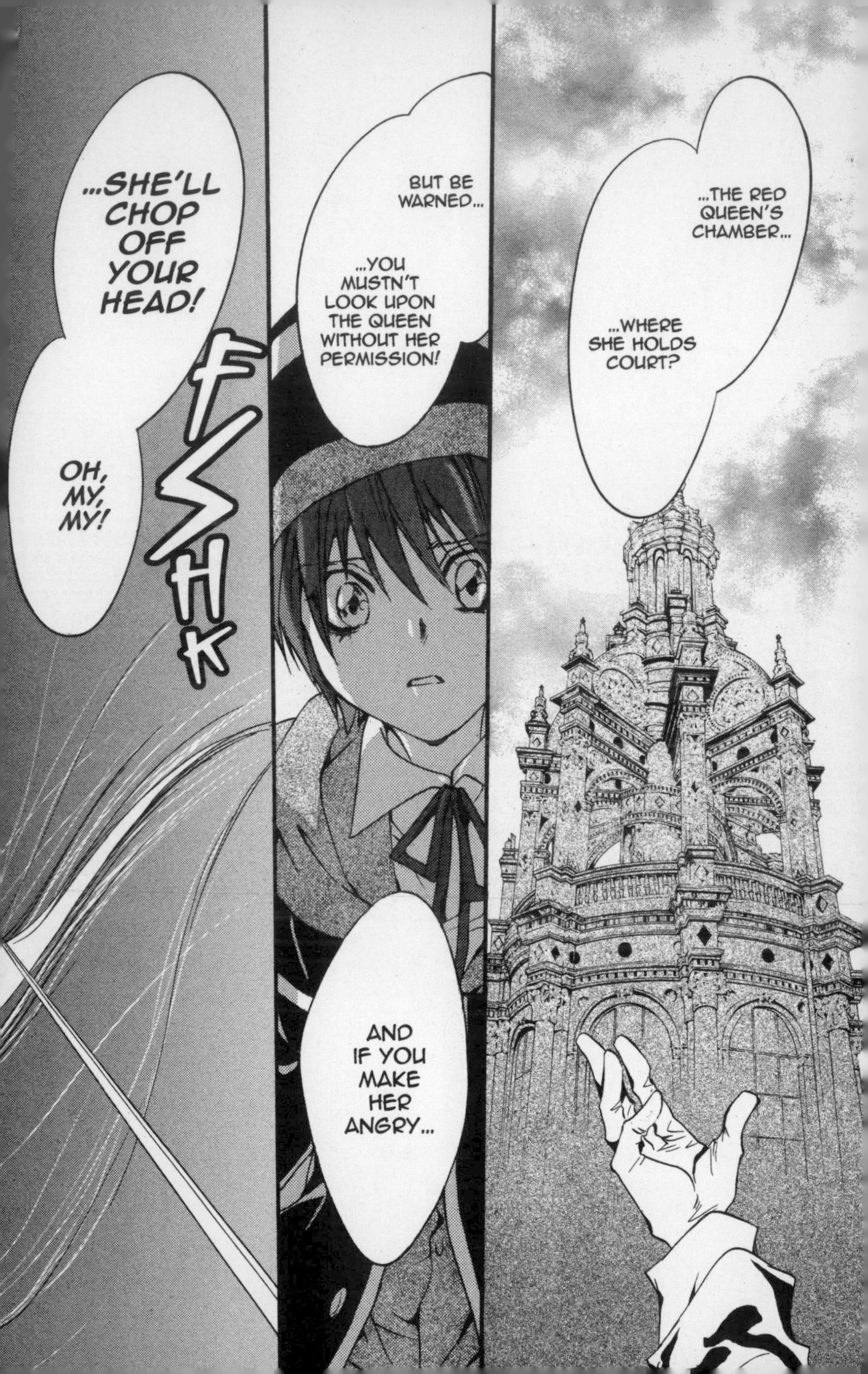
...THE RED QUEEN'S CHAMBER...
...WHERE SHE HOLDS COURT?
BUT BE WARNED...
...YOU MUSTN'T LOOK UPON THE QUEEN WITHOUT HER PERMISSION!
AND IF YOU MAKE HER ANGRY...
...SHE'LL CHOP OFF YOUR HEAD!
FSHK
OH, MY, MY!

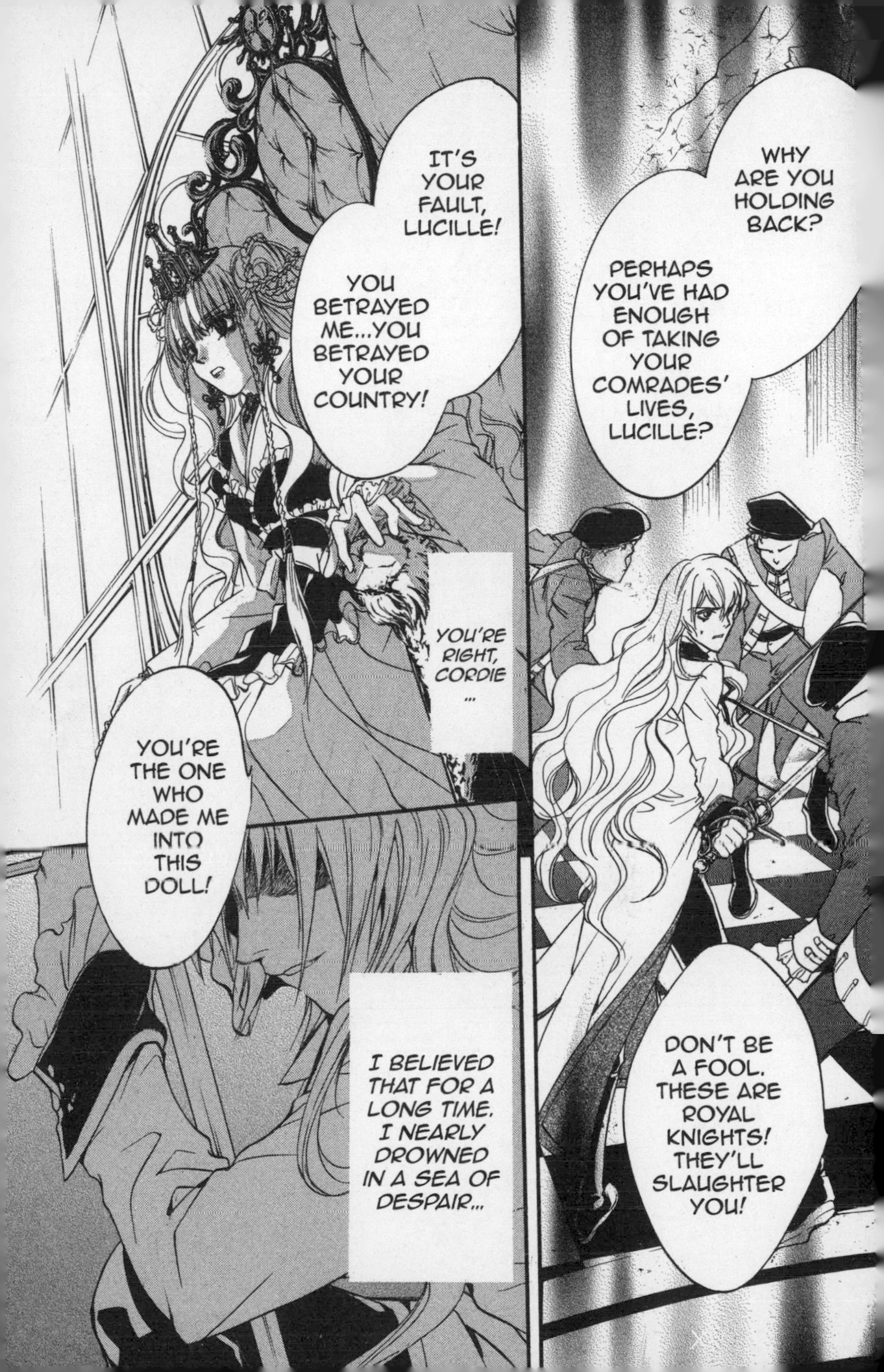
WHY ARE YOU HOLDING BACK?
PERHAPS YOU'VE HAD ENOUGH OF TAKING YOUR COMRADES' LIVES, LUCILLE?
DON'T BE A FOOL. THESE ARE ROYAL KNIGHTS! THEY'LL SLAUGHTER YOU!
IT'S YOUR FAULT, LUCILLE!
YOU BETRAYED ME...YOU BETRAYED YOUR COUNTRY!
YOU'RE THE ONE WHO MADE ME INTO THIS DOLL!
YOU'RE RIGHT, CORDIE...
I BELIEVED THAT FOR A LONG TIME. I NEARLY DROWNED IN A SEA OF DESPAIR...

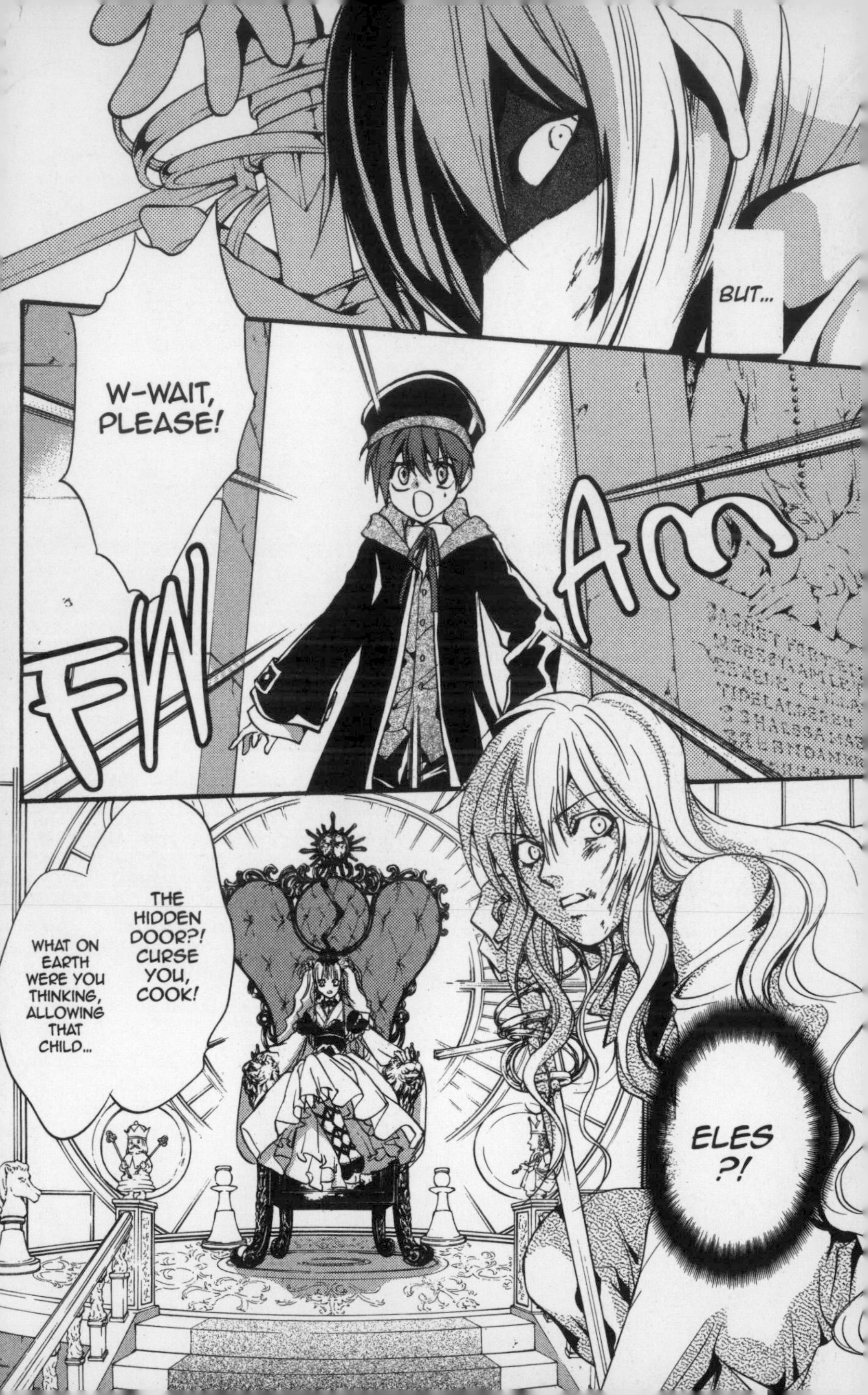
BUT...
W-WAIT, PLEASE!
FWAm
ELES ?!
THE HIDDEN DOOR?! CURSE YOU, COOK!
WHAT ON EARTH WERE YOU THINKING, ALLOWING THAT CHILD...

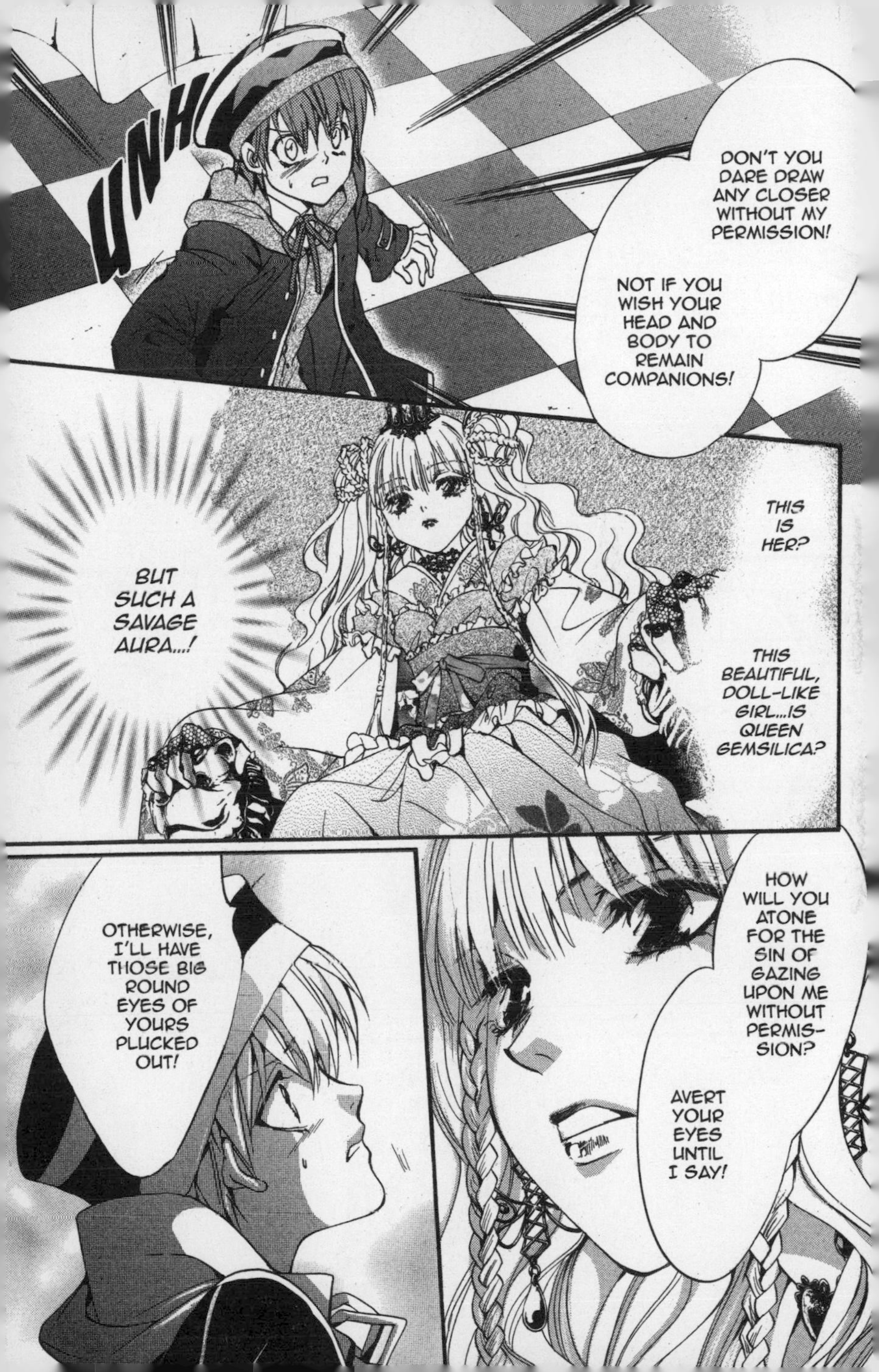
DON'T YOU DARE DRAW ANY CLOSER WITHOUT MY PERMISSION!
NOT IF YOU WISH YOUR HEAD AND BODY TO REMAIN COMPANIONS!
UNH
THIS IS HER?
THIS BEAUTIFUL, DOLL-LIKE GIRL...IS QUEEN GEMSILICA?
BUT SUCH A SAVAGE AURA...!
HOW WILL YOU ATONE FOR THE SIN OF GAZING UPON ME WITHOUT PERMIS-SION?
AVERT YOUR EYES UNTIL I SAY!
OTHERWISE, I'LL HAVE THOSE BIG ROUND EYES OF YOURS PLUCKED OUT!

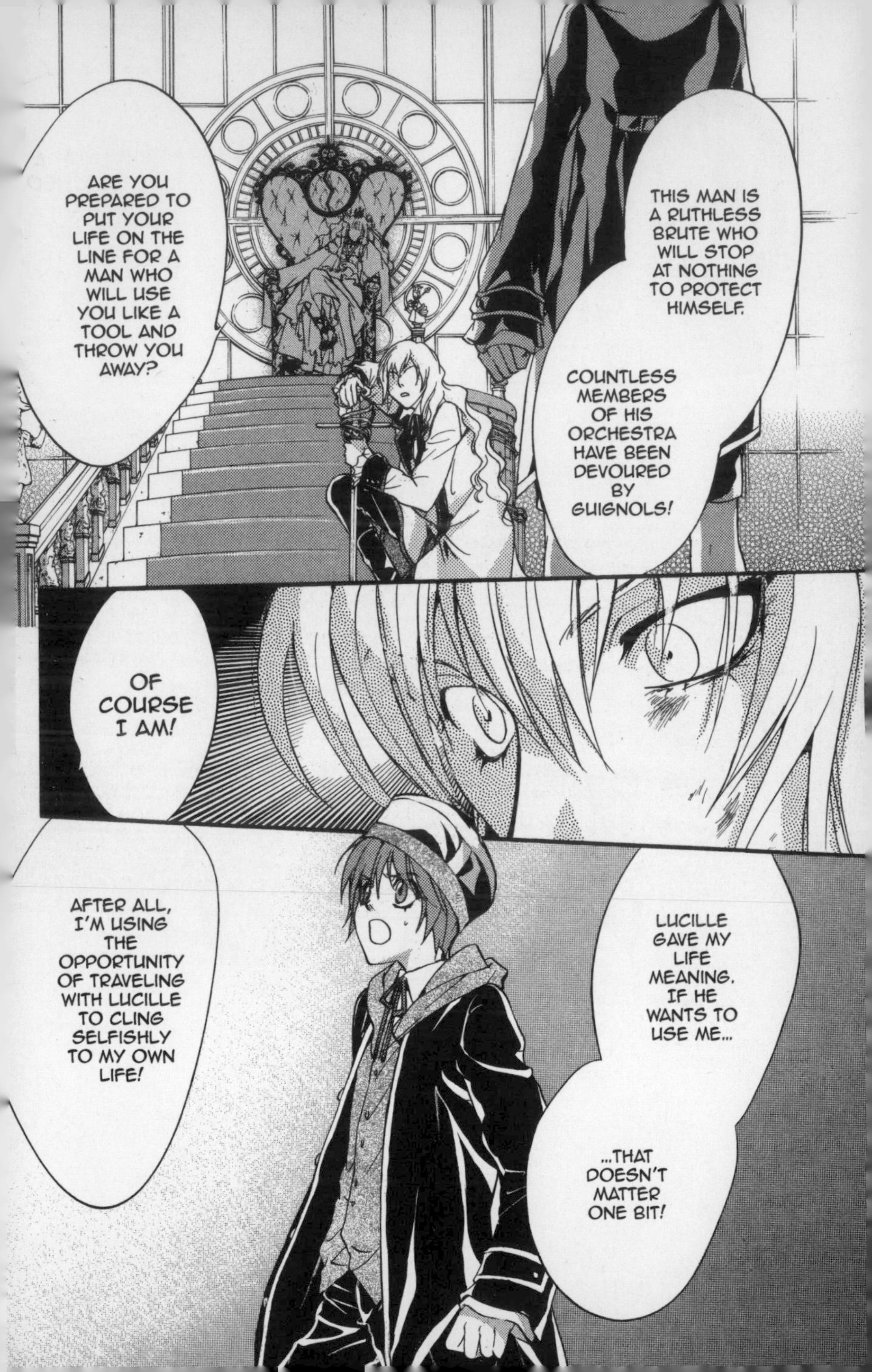
THIS MAN IS A RUTHLESS BRUTE WHO WILL STOP AT NOTHING TO PROTECT HIMSELF.
COUNTLESS MEMBERS OF HIS ORCHESTRA HAVE BEEN DEVOURED BY GUIGNOLS!
ARE YOU PREPARED TO PUT YOUR LIFE ON THE LINE FOR A MAN WHO WILL USE YOU LIKE A TOOL AND THROW YOU AWAY?
OF COURSE I AM!
LUCILLE GAVE MY LIFE MEANING. IF HE WANTS TO USE ME...
...THAT DOESN'T MATTER ONE BIT!
AFTER ALL, I'M USING THE OPPORTUNITY OF TRAVELING WITH LUCILLE TO CLING SELFISHLY TO MY OWN LIFE!

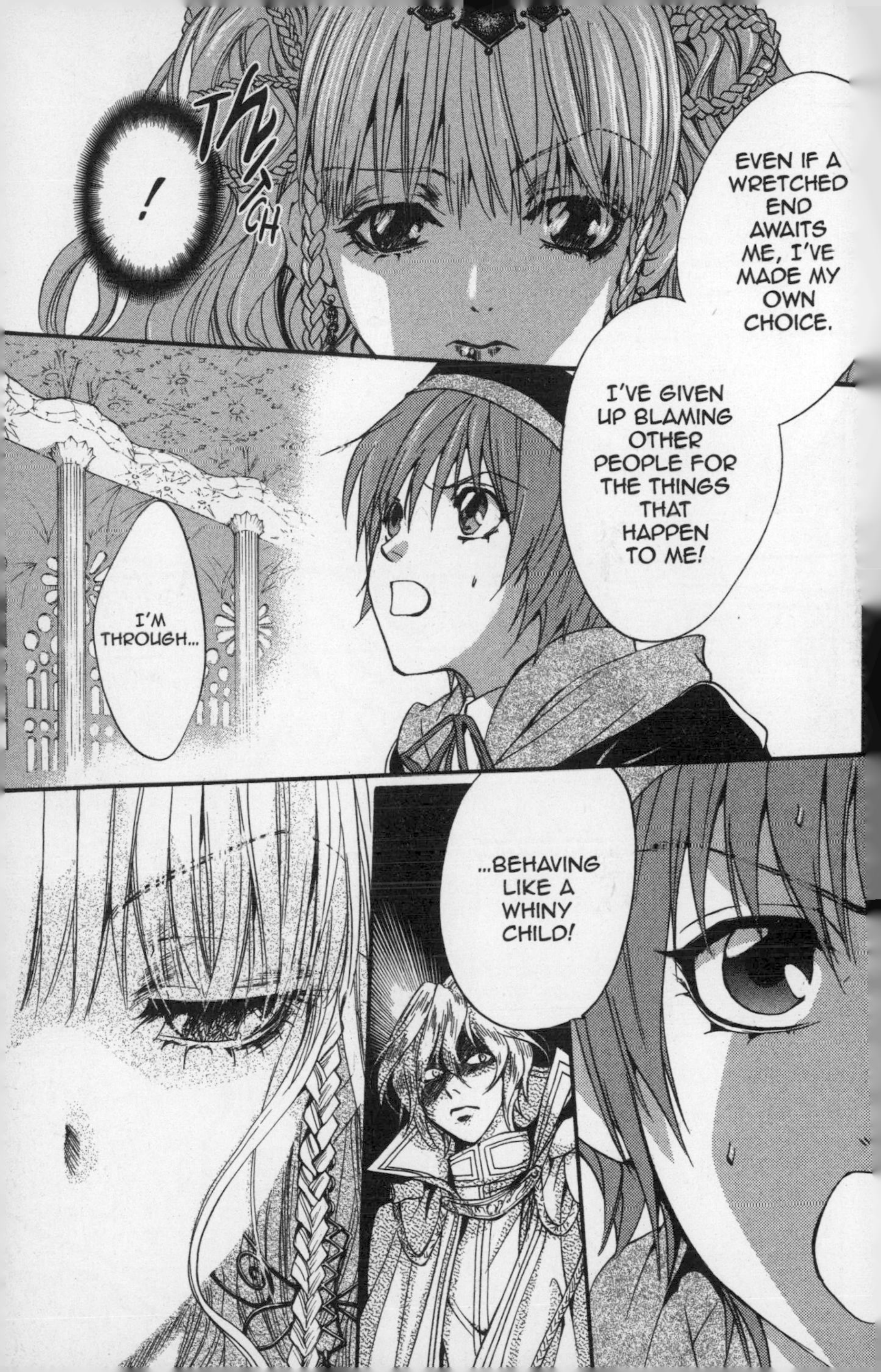
EVEN IF A WRETCHED END AWAITS ME, I'VE MADE MY OWN CHOICE.
TWITCH
!
I'VE GIVEN UP BLAMING OTHER PEOPLE FOR THE THINGS THAT HAPPEN TO ME!
I'M THROUGH...
...BEHAVING LIKE A WHINY CHILD!

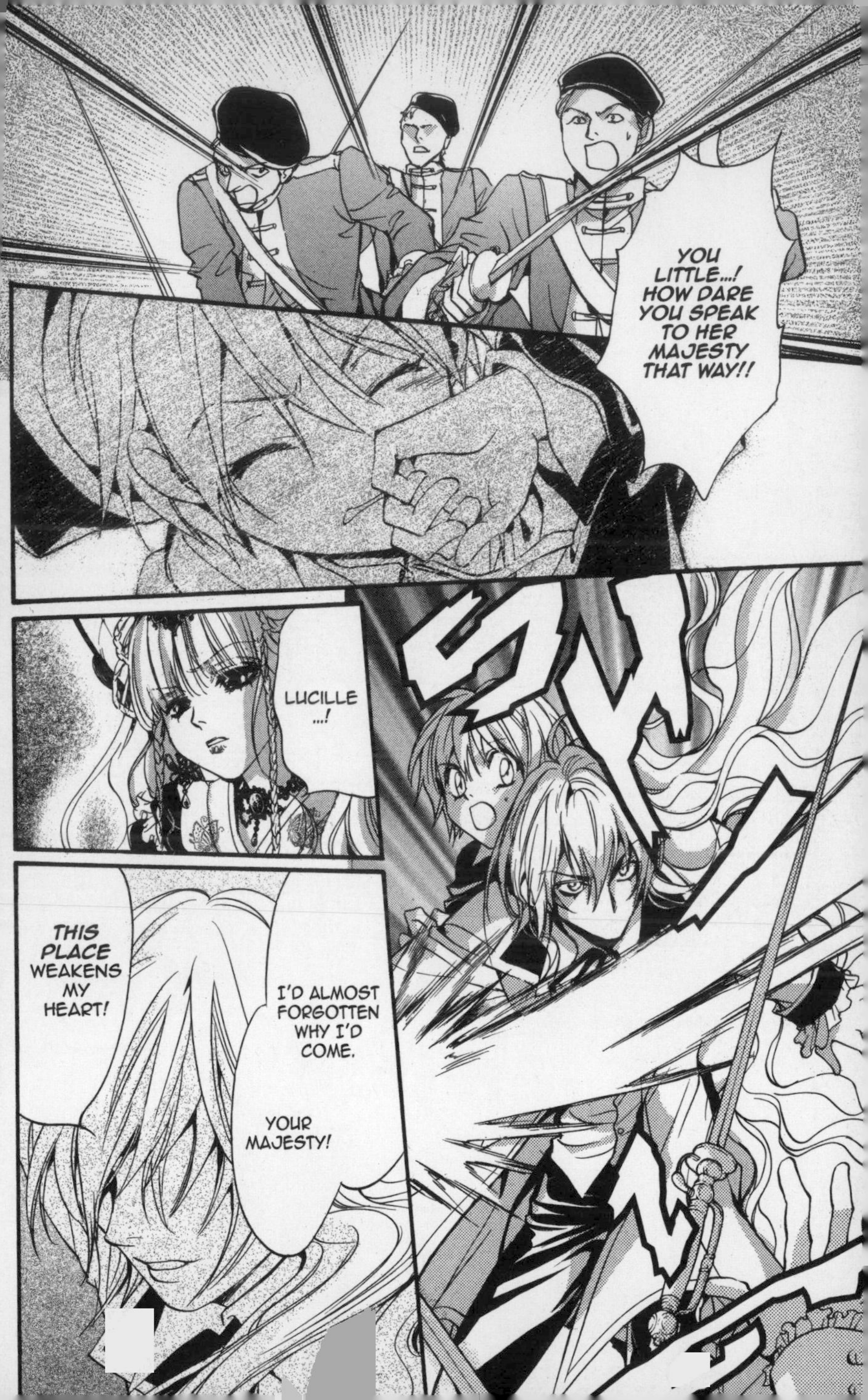
YOU LITTLE...! HOW DARE YOU SPEAK TO HER MAJESTY THAT WAY!!
LUCILLE ...!
I'D ALMOST FORGOTTEN WHY I'D COME.
THIS PLACE WEAKENS MY HEART!
YOUR MAJESTY!

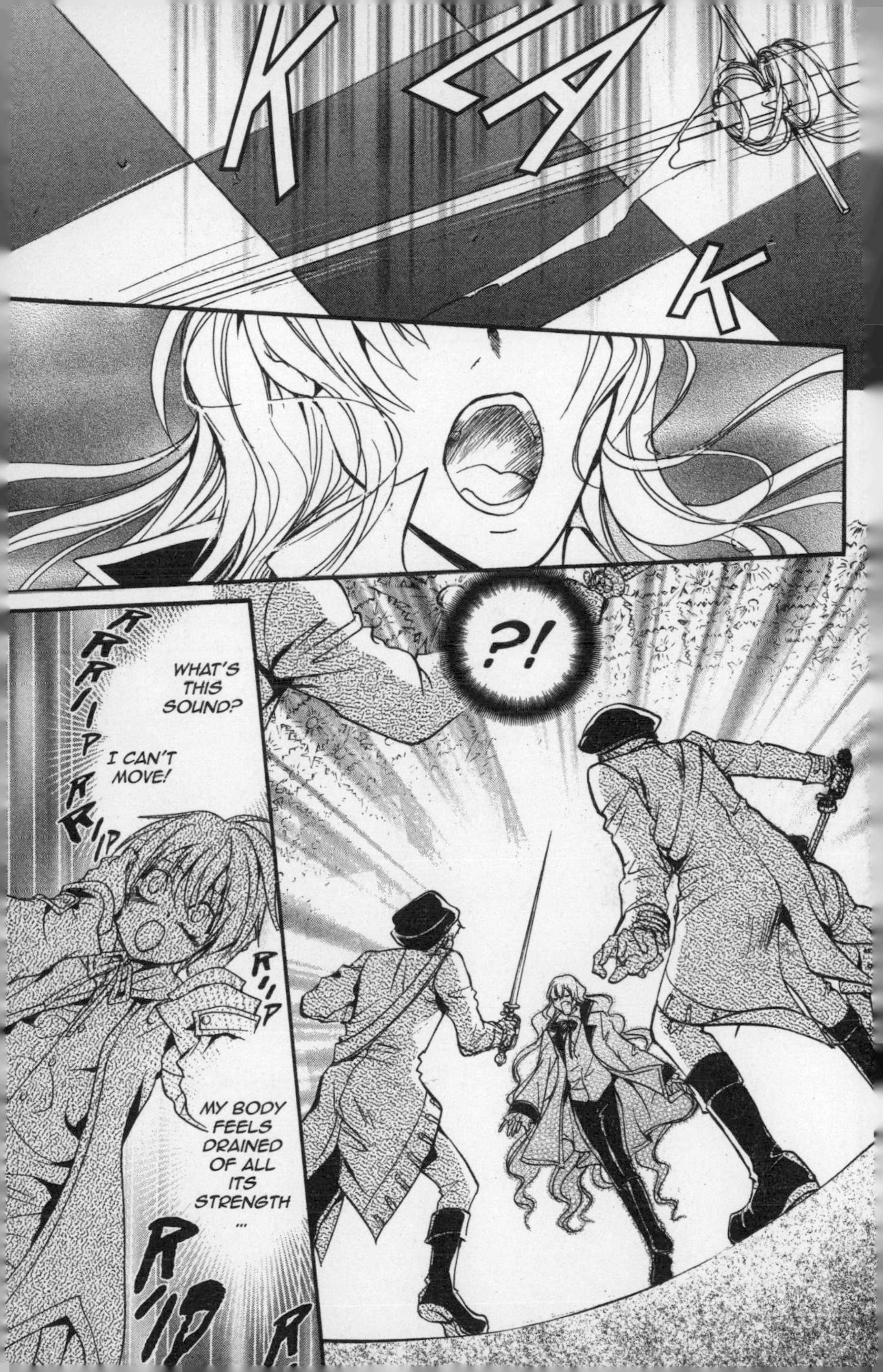
KLAK
?!
WHAT'S THIS SOUND?
I CAN'T MOVE!
RIIP
MY BODY FEELS DRAINED OF ALL ITS STRENGTH ...

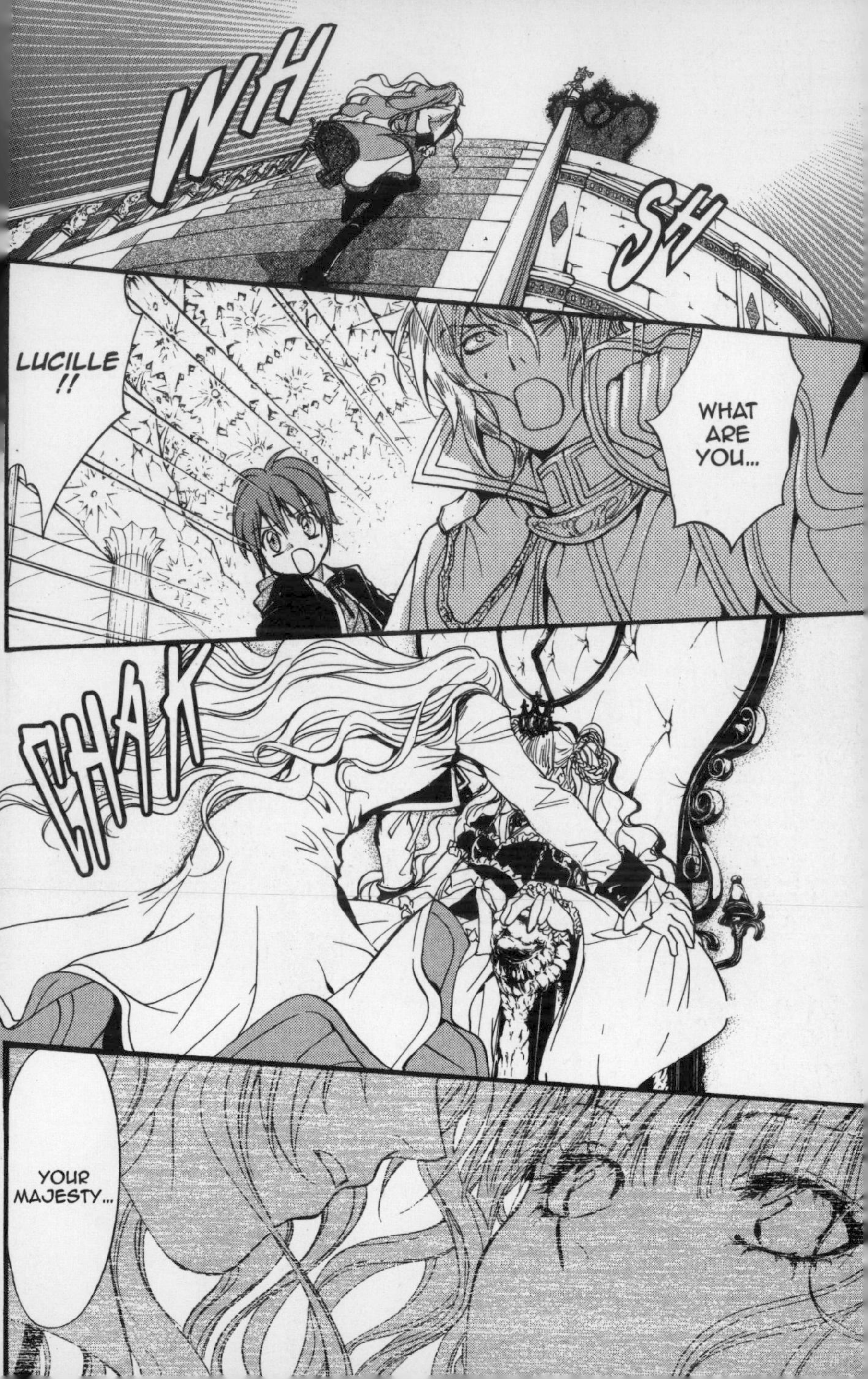
WH
SH
WHAT ARE YOU...
LUCILLE !!
CHAK
YOUR MAJESTY...

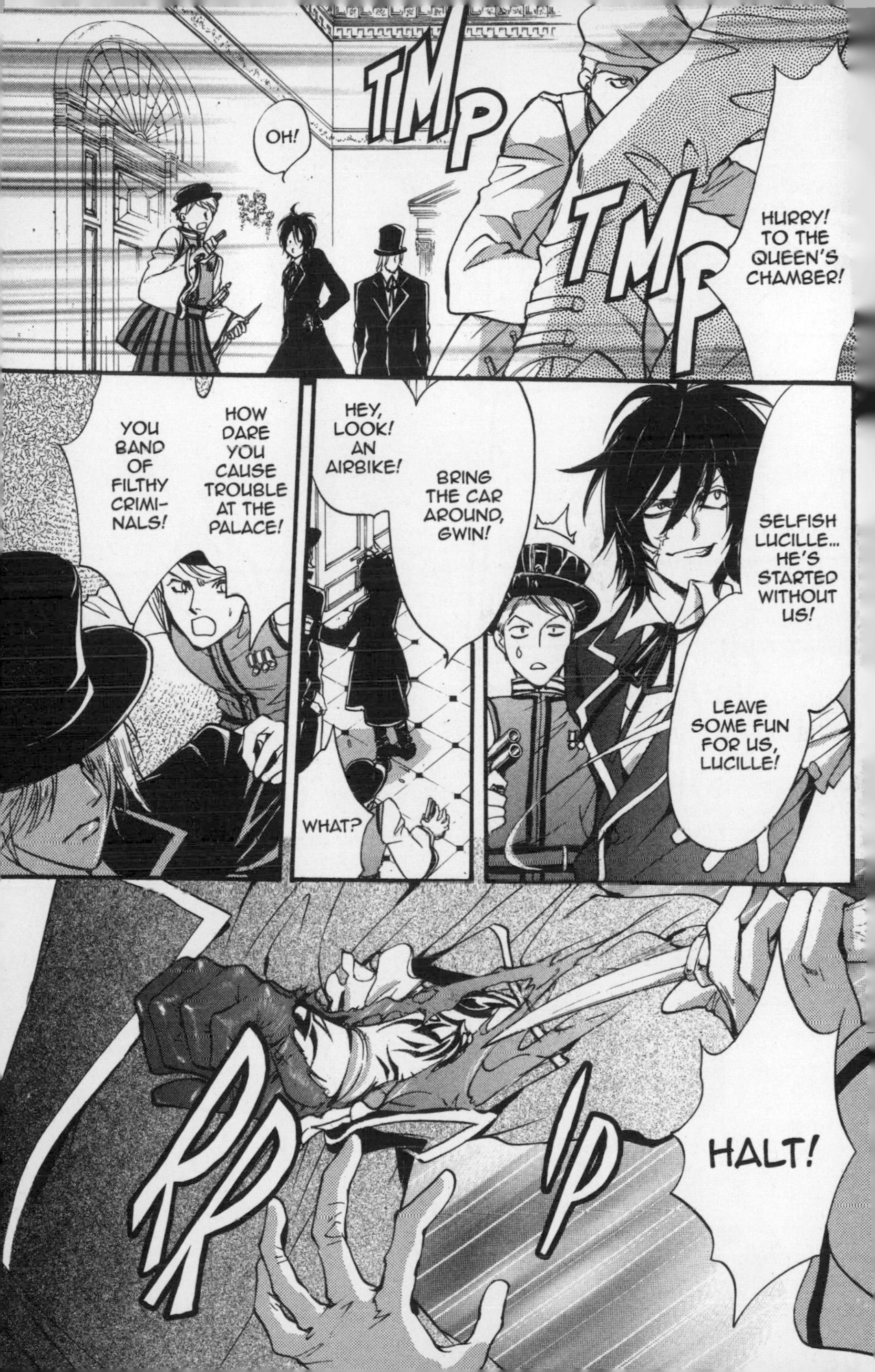
TMP
HURRY! TO THE QUEEN'S CHAMBER!
TMP
OH!
SELFISH LUCILLE... HE'S STARTED WITHOUT US!
LEAVE SOME FUN FOR US, LUCILLE!
HEY, LOOK! AN AIRBIKE!
BRING THE CAR AROUND, GWIN!
WHAT?
HOW DARE YOU CAUSE TROUBLE AT THE PALACE!
YOU BAND OF FILTHY CRIMINALS!
HALT!
RRIP

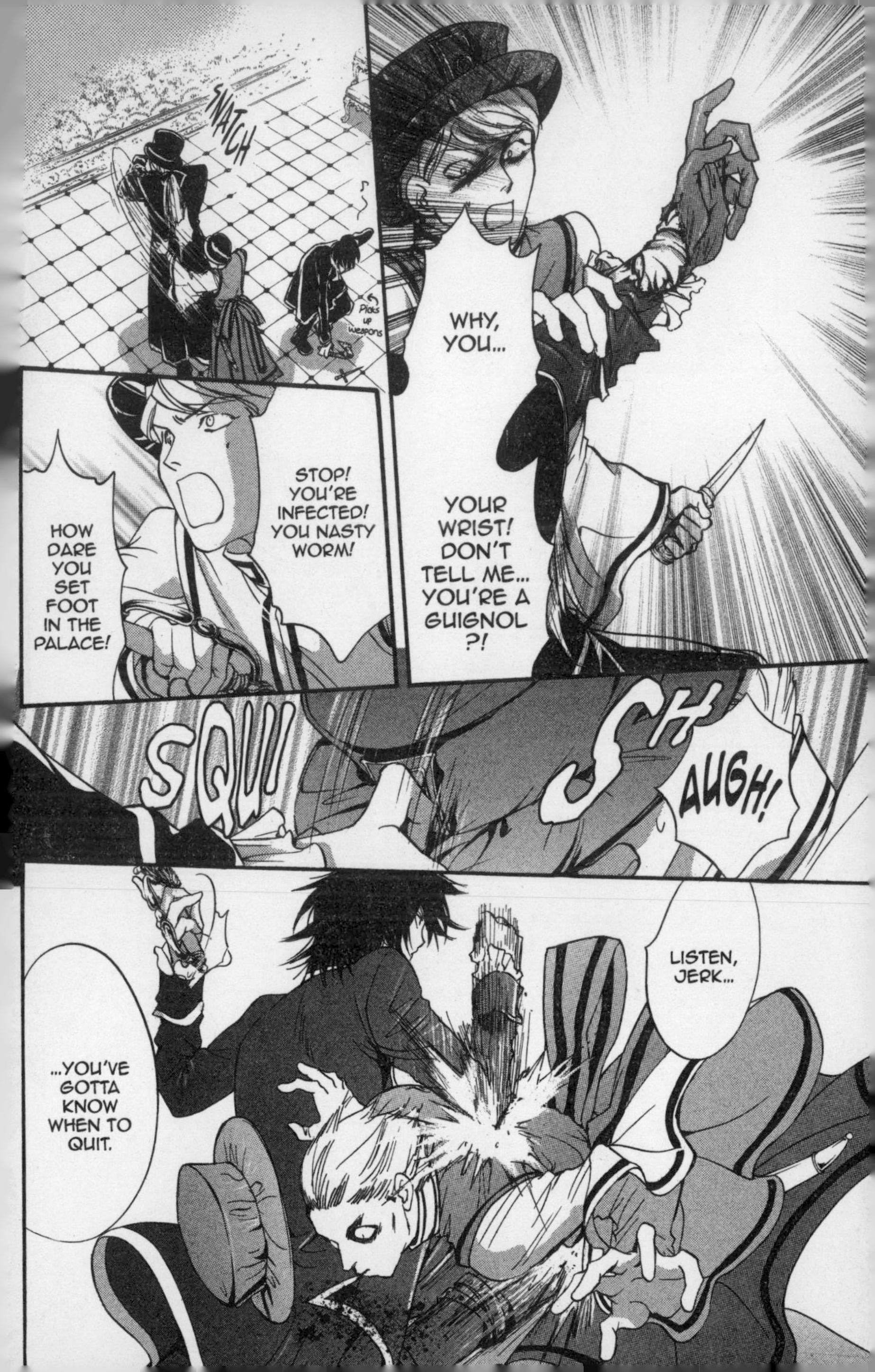
WHY, YOU...
YOUR WRIST! DON'T TELL ME... YOU'RE A GUIGNOL ?!
SNATCH
Picks up weapons
STOP! YOU'RE INFECTED! YOU NASTY WORM!
HOW DARE YOU SET FOOT IN THE PALACE!
AUGH!
SQUISCH
LISTEN, JERK...
...YOU'VE GOTTA KNOW WHEN TO QUIT.

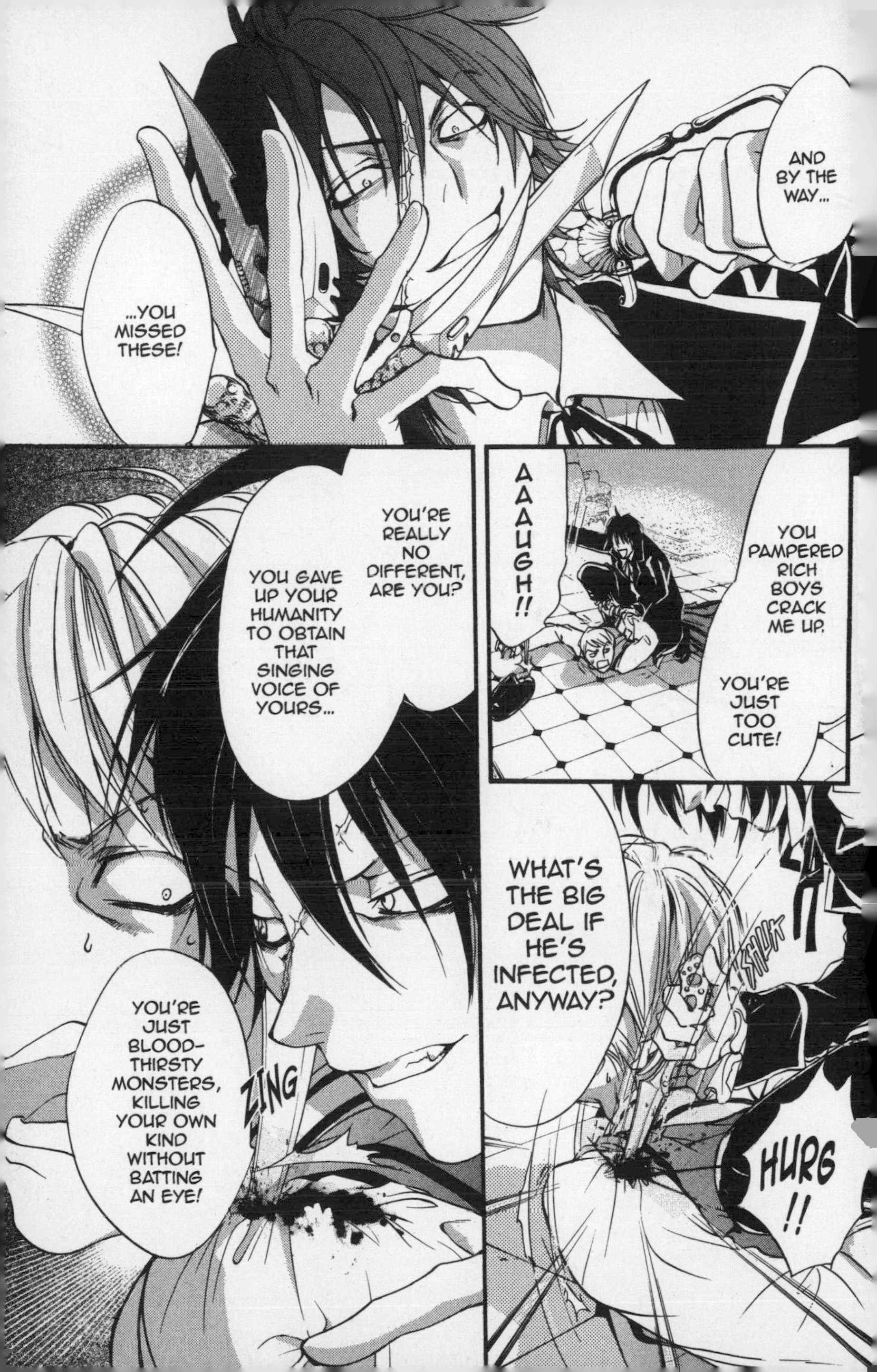
AND BY THE WAY...
...YOU MISSED THESE!
YOU PAMPERED RICH BOYS CRACK ME UP.
YOU'RE JUST TOO CUTE!
AAAUGH!!
WHAT'S THE BIG DEAL IF HE'S INFECTED, ANYWAY?
SHUK
HURG!!
YOU'RE REALLY NO DIFFERENT, ARE YOU?
YOU GAVE UP YOUR HUMANITY TO OBTAIN THAT SINGING VOICE OF YOURS...
YOU'RE JUST BLOOD-THIRSTY MONSTERS, KILLING YOUR OWN KIND WITHOUT BATTING AN EYE!
ZING

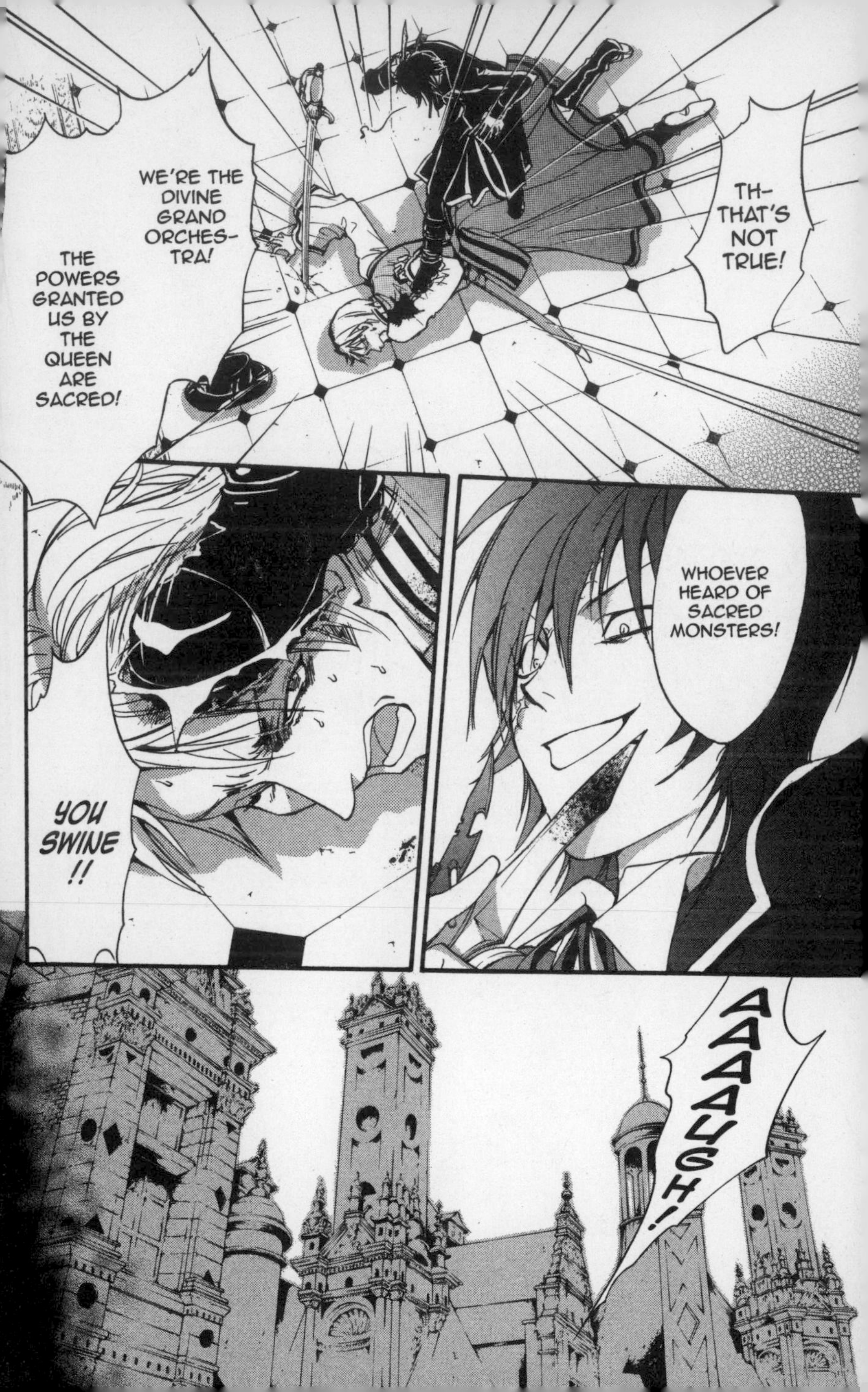
TH-THAT'S NOT TRUE!
WE'RE THE DIVINE GRAND ORCHESTRA!
THE POWERS GRANTED US BY THE QUEEN ARE SACRED!
WHOEVER HEARD OF SACRED MONSTERS!
YOU SWINE!!
AAAAUGH!

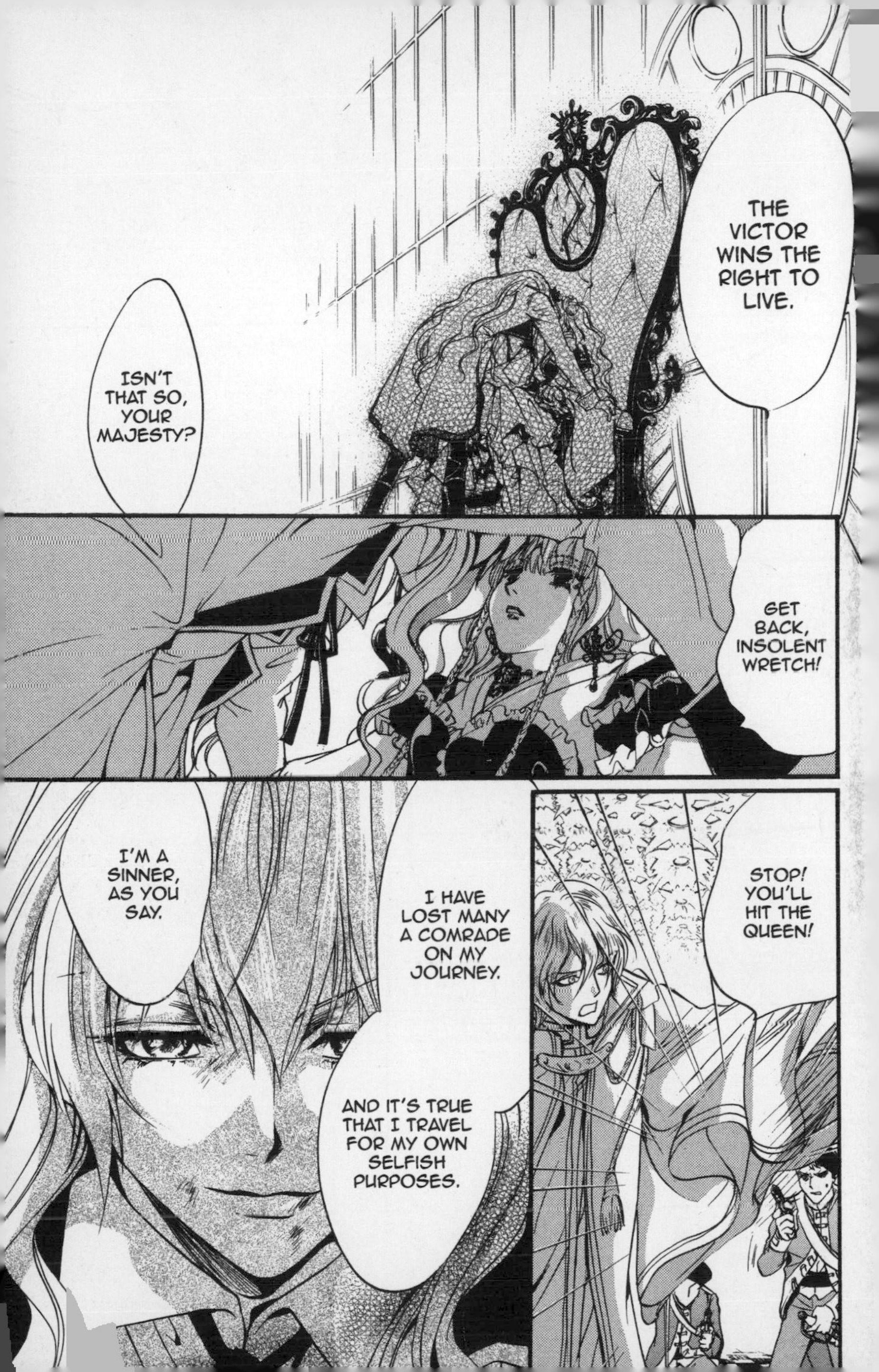
THE VICTOR WINS THE RIGHT TO LIVE.
ISN'T THAT SO, YOUR MAJESTY?
GET BACK, INSOLENT WRETCH!
STOP! YOU'LL HIT THE QUEEN!
I'M A SINNER, AS YOU SAY.
I HAVE LOST MANY A COMRADE ON MY JOURNEY.
AND IT'S TRUE THAT I TRAVEL FOR MY OWN SELFISH PURPOSES.

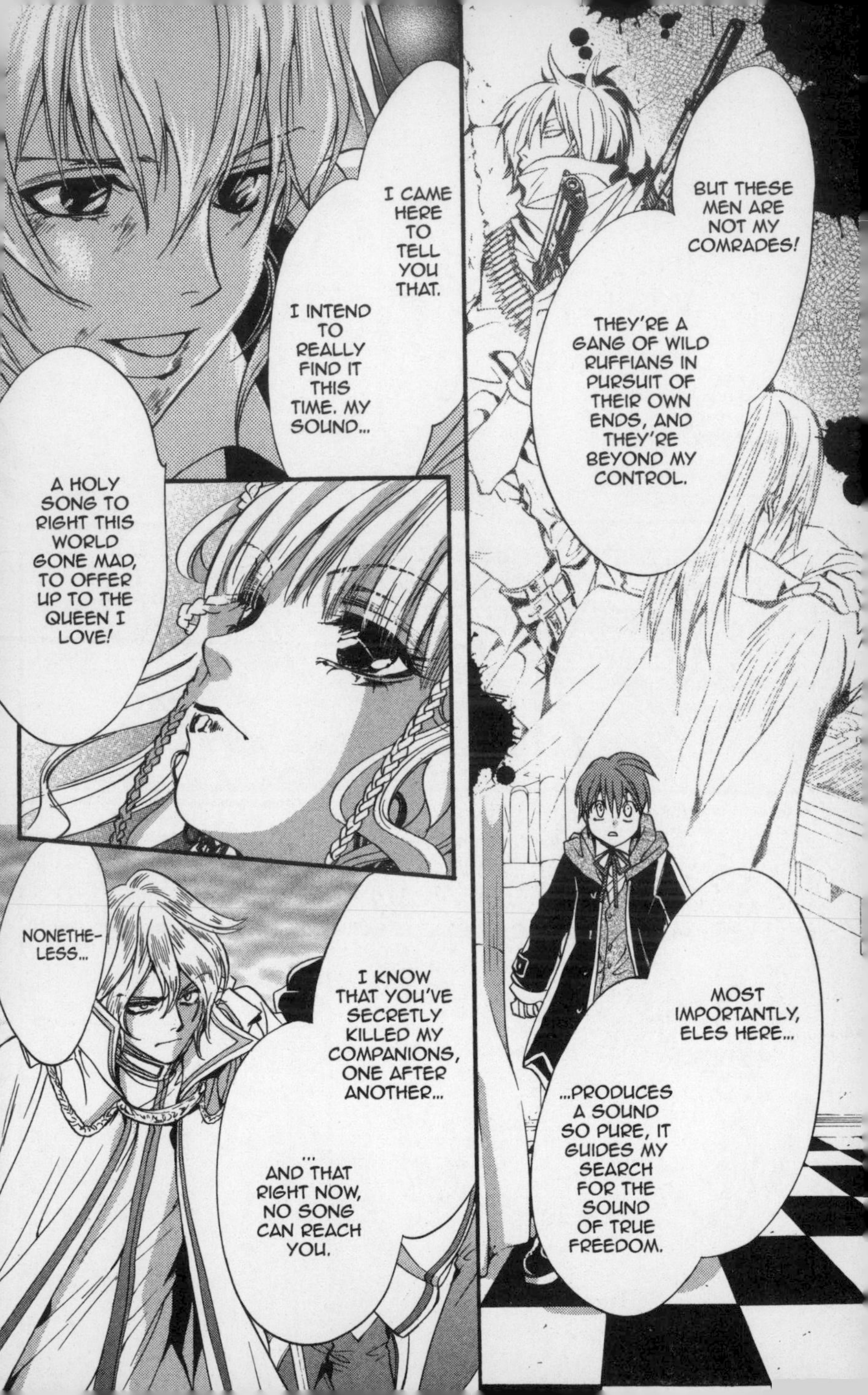
BUT THESE MEN ARE NOT MY COMRADES!
THEY'RE A GANG OF WILD RUFFIANS IN PURSUIT OF THEIR OWN ENDS, AND THEY'RE BEYOND MY CONTROL.
MOST IMPORTANTLY, ELES HERE...
...PRODUCES A SOUND SO PURE, IT GUIDES MY SEARCH FOR THE SOUND OF TRUE FREEDOM.
I CAME HERE TO TELL YOU THAT.
I INTEND TO REALLY FIND IT THIS TIME. MY SOUND...
A HOLY SONG TO RIGHT THIS WORLD GONE MAD, TO OFFER UP TO THE QUEEN I LOVE!
I KNOW THAT YOU'VE SECRETLY KILLED MY COMPANIONS, ONE AFTER ANOTHER...
... AND THAT RIGHT NOW, NO SONG CAN REACH YOU.
NONETHE-LESS...

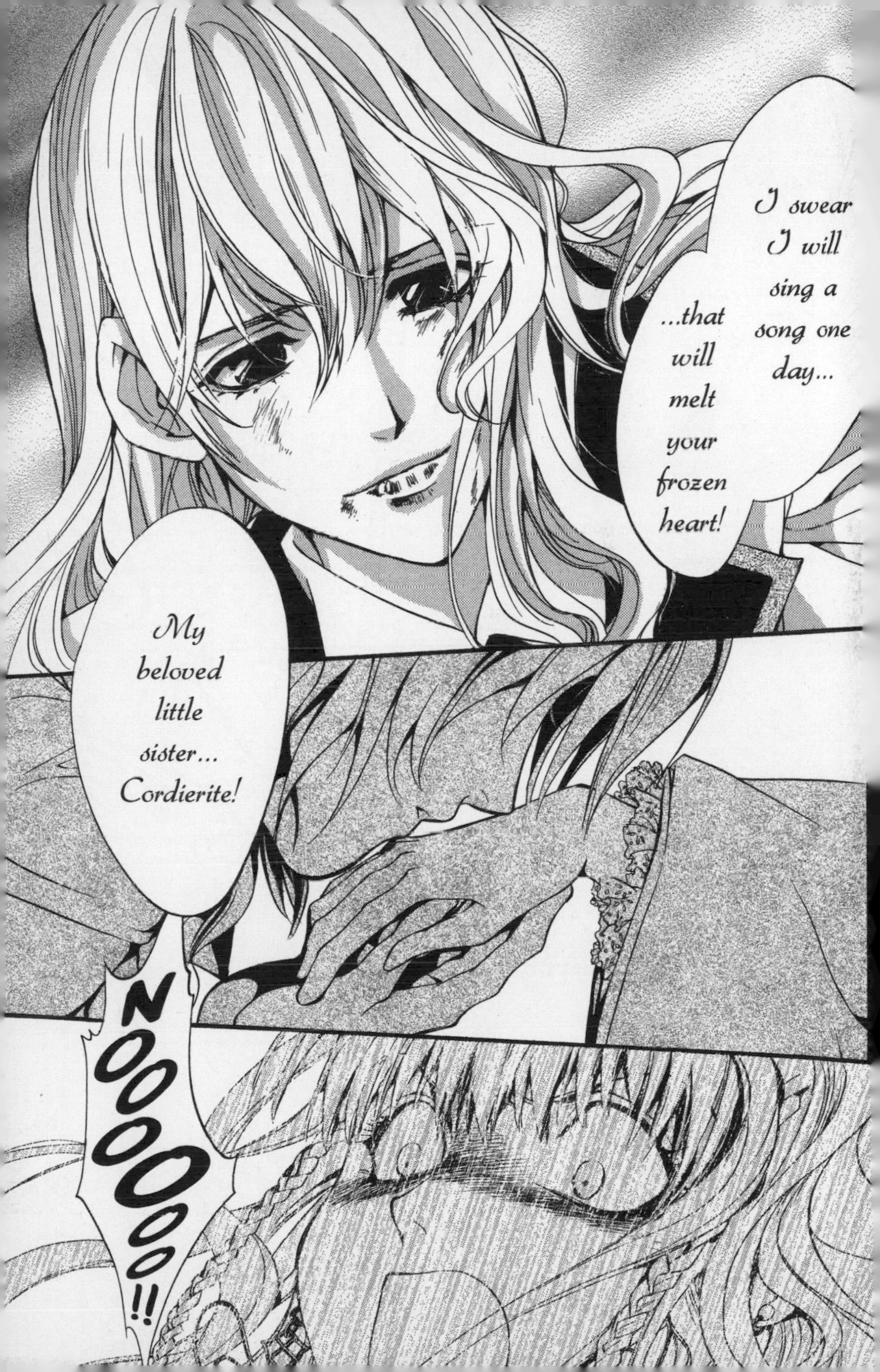
I swear I will sing a song one day...
...that will melt your frozen heart!
My beloved little sister... Cordierite!
NOOOOOOO!!

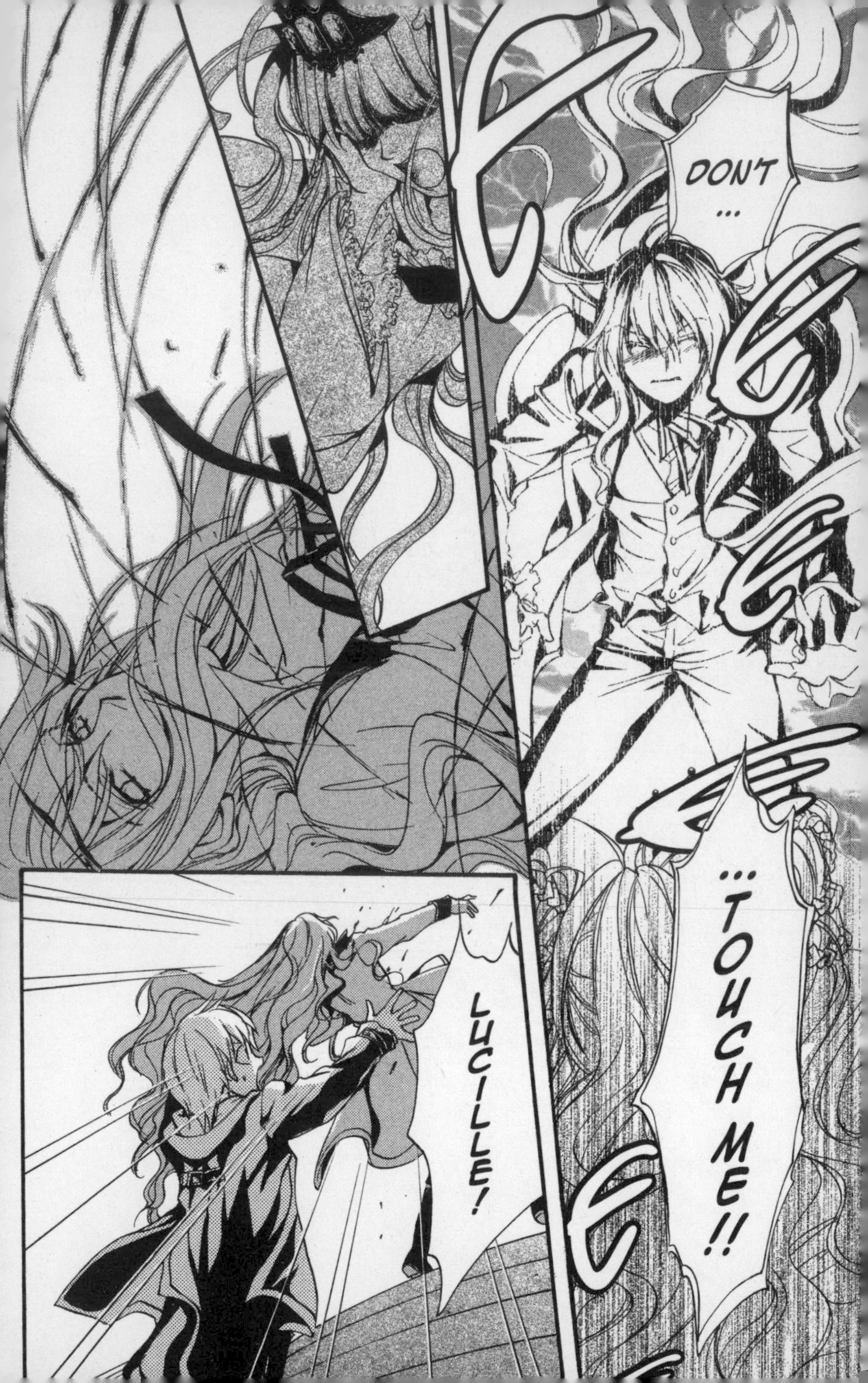
DON'T ...
...TOUCH ME!!
LUCILLE!

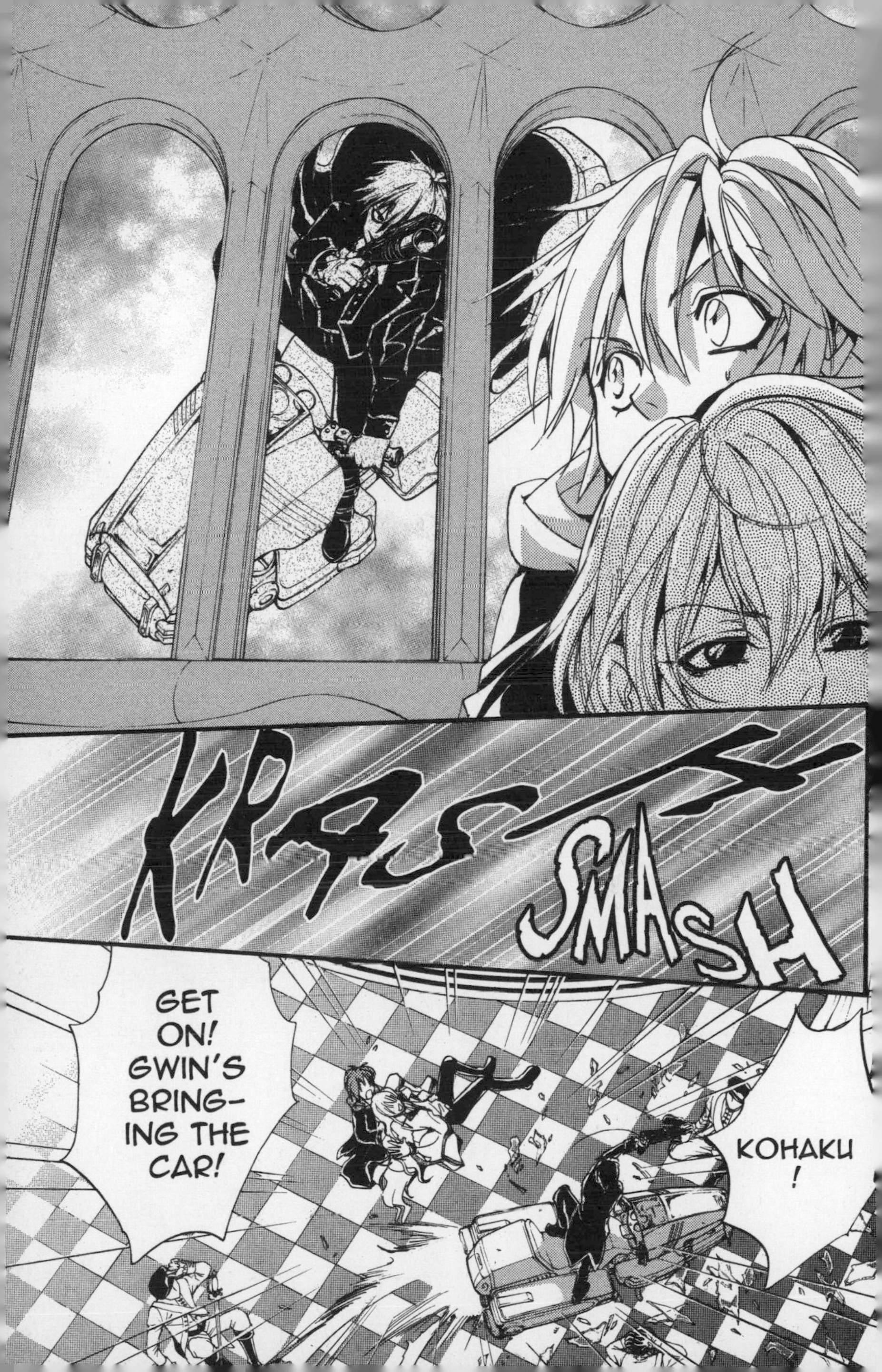
KRASH
SMASH
KOHAKU!
GET ON! GWIN'S BRINGING THE CAR!

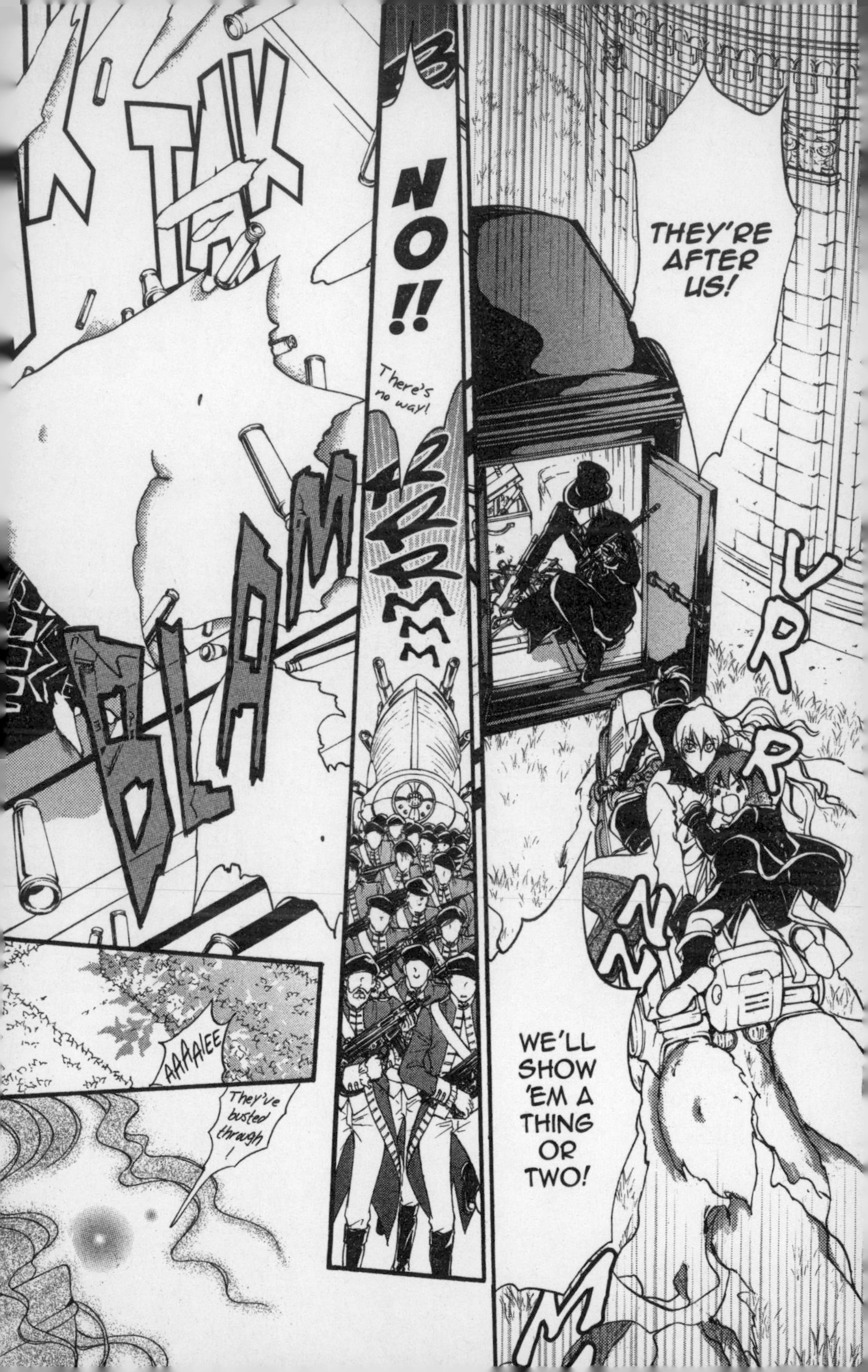
THEY'RE AFTER US!
WE'LL SHOW 'EM A THING OR TWO!
NO!!
There's no way!
TAK
BLAM
AAAAIEE
They've busted through!

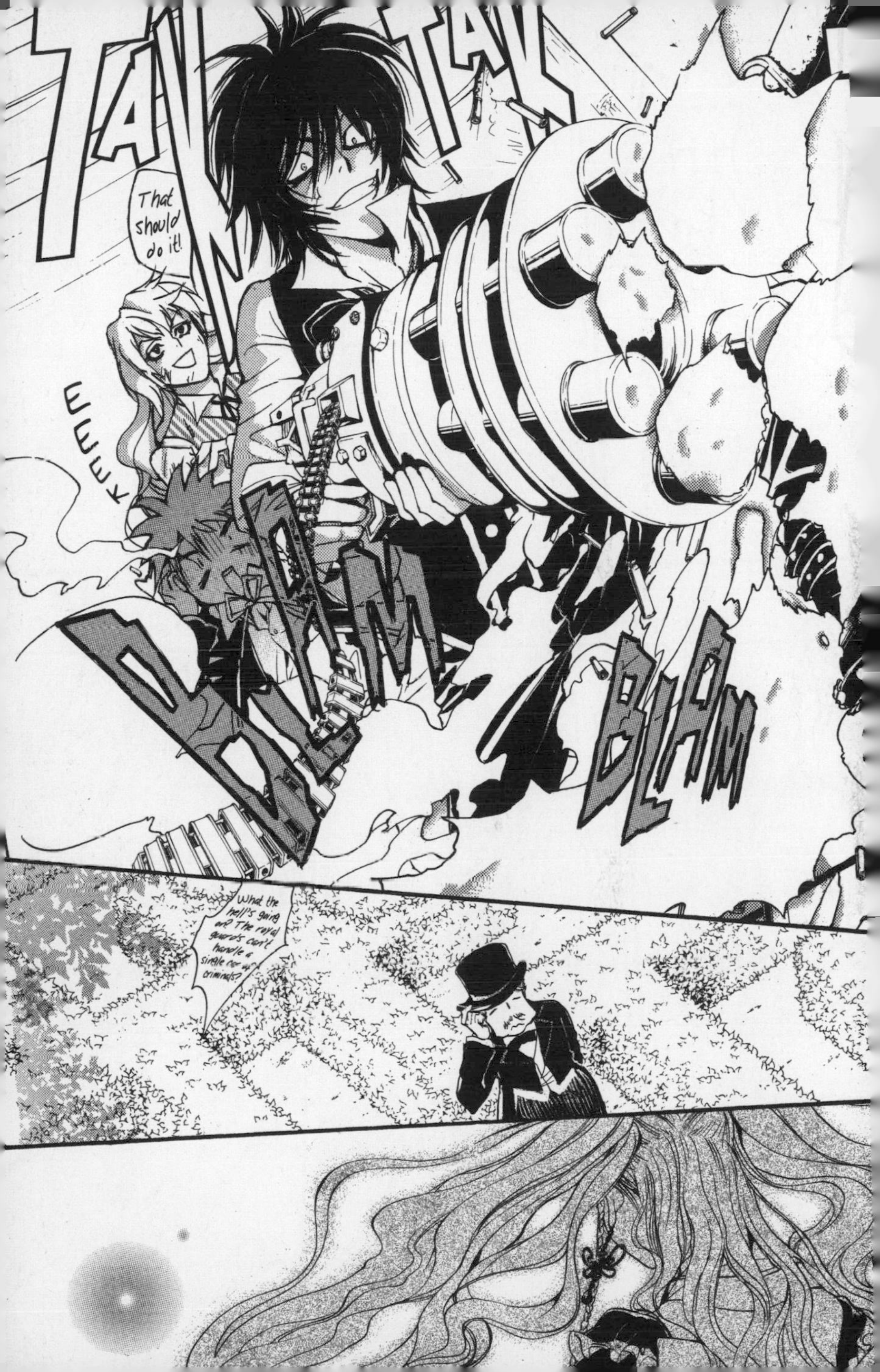
TAK TAK
That should do it!
EEEEK
BLAM
BLAM
What the hell's going on? The royal guards can't handle a single pair of criminals?

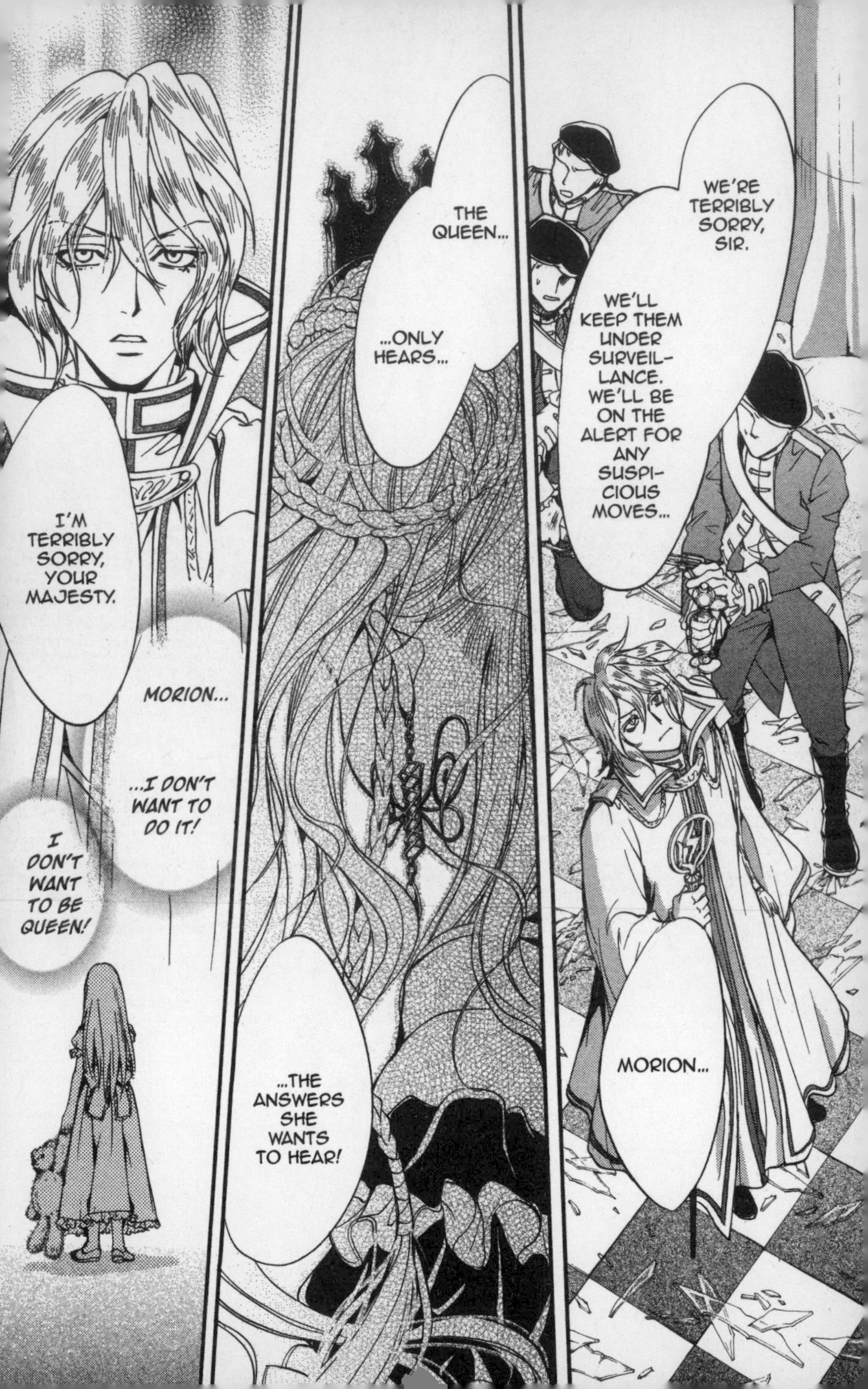
WE'RE TERRIBLY SORRY, SIR.
WE'LL KEEP THEM UNDER SURVEIL-LANCE. WE'LL BE ON THE ALERT FOR ANY SUSPICIOUS MOVES...
MORION...
THE QUEEN...
...ONLY HEARS...
...THE ANSWERS SHE WANTS TO HEAR!
I'M TERRIBLY SORRY, YOUR MAJESTY.
MORION...
...I DON'T WANT TO DO IT!
I DON'T WANT TO BE QUEEN!

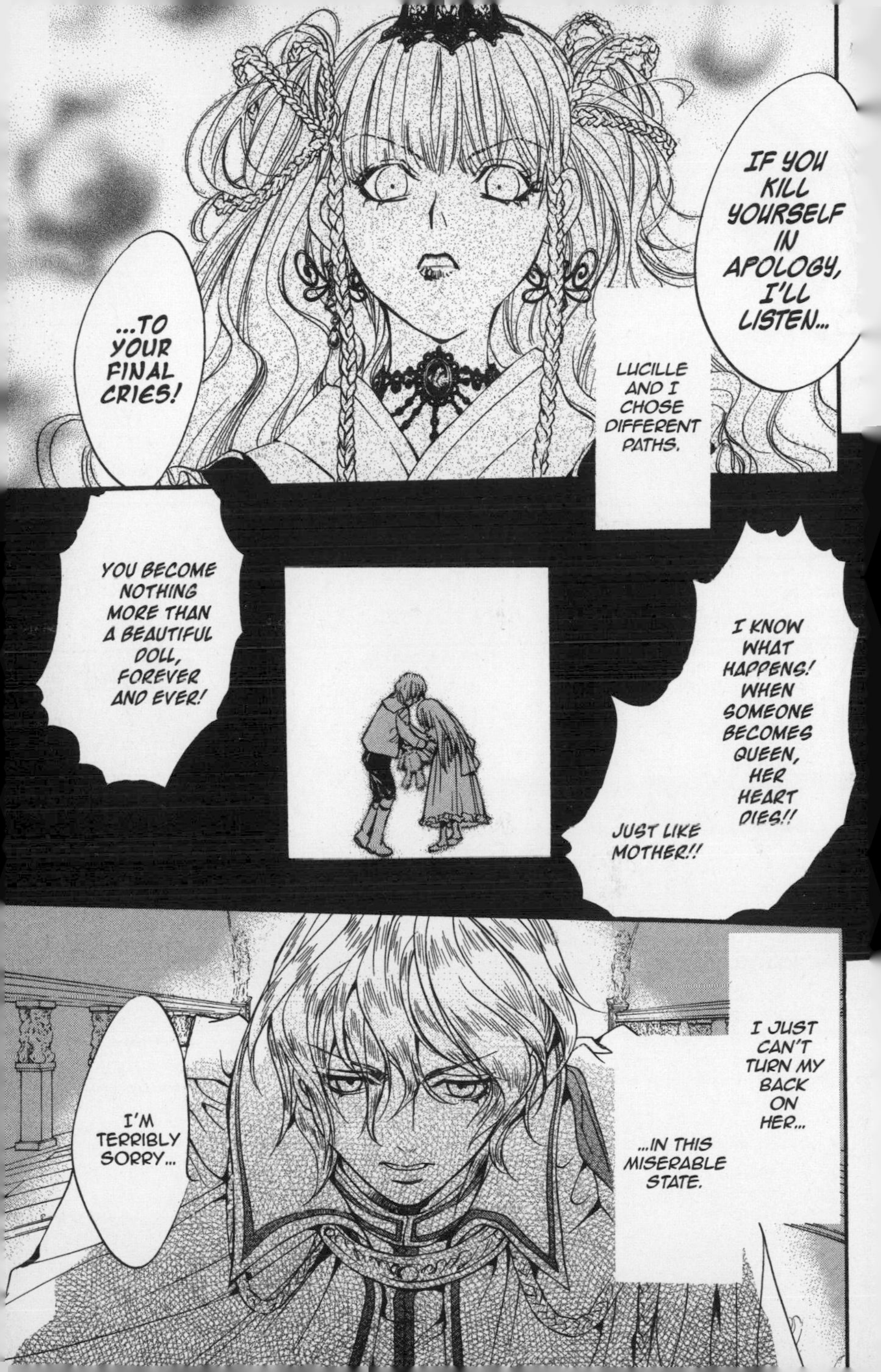
IF YOU KILL YOURSELF IN APOLOGY, I'LL LISTEN...
...TO YOUR FINAL CRIES!
LUCILLE AND I CHOSE DIFFERENT PATHS.
I KNOW WHAT HAPPENS! WHEN SOMEONE BECOMES QUEEN, HER HEART DIES!!
JUST LIKE MOTHER!!
YOU BECOME NOTHING MORE THAN A BEAUTIFUL DOLL, FOREVER AND EVER!
I JUST CAN'T TURN MY BACK ON HER...
...IN THIS MISERABLE STATE.
I'M TERRIBLY SORRY...

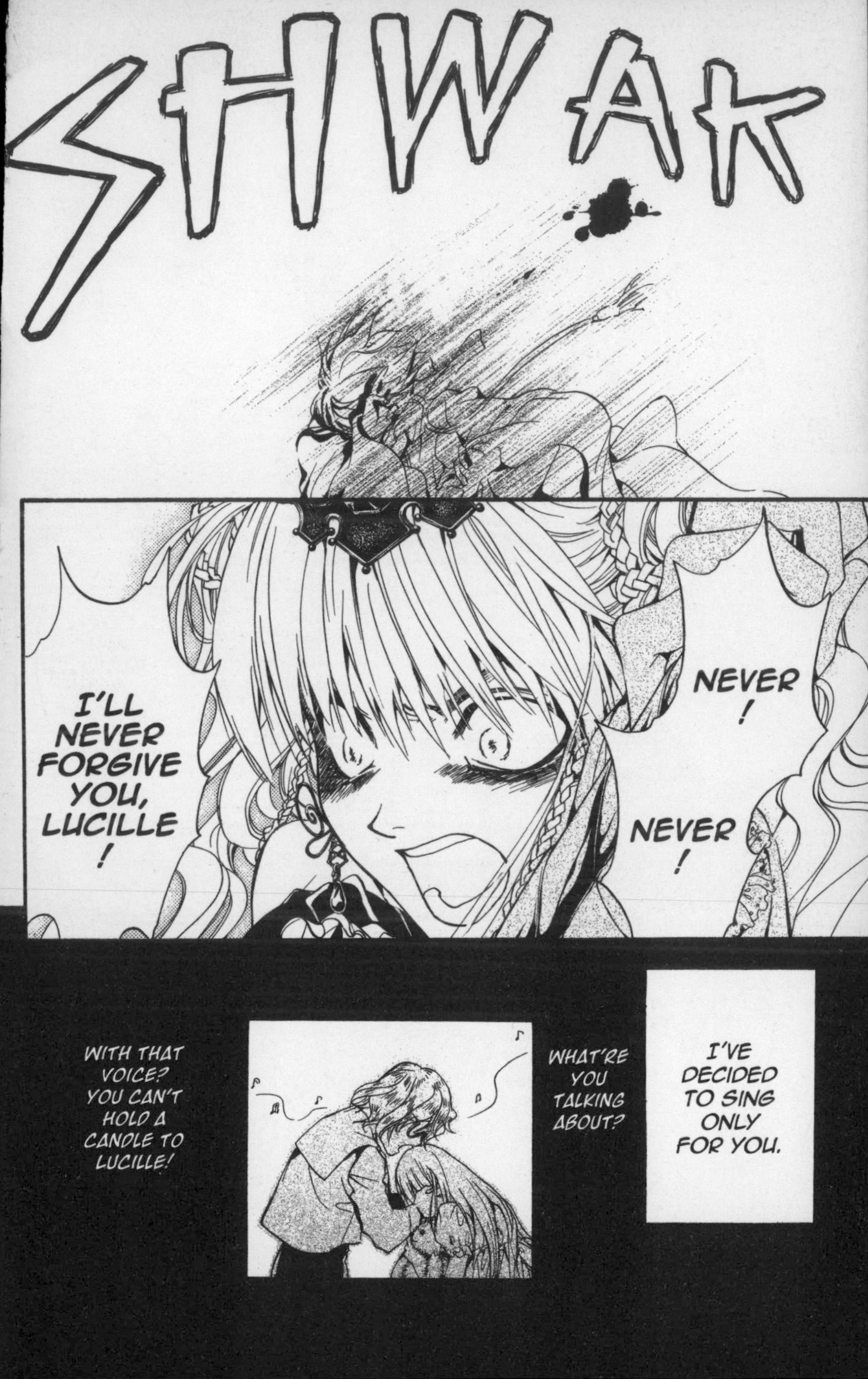
SHWAK
NEVER!
NEVER!
I'LL NEVER FORGIVE YOU, LUCILLE!
I'VE DECIDED TO SING ONLY FOR YOU.
WHAT'RE YOU TALKING ABOUT?
WITH THAT VOICE? YOU CAN'T HOLD A CANDLE TO LUCILLE!

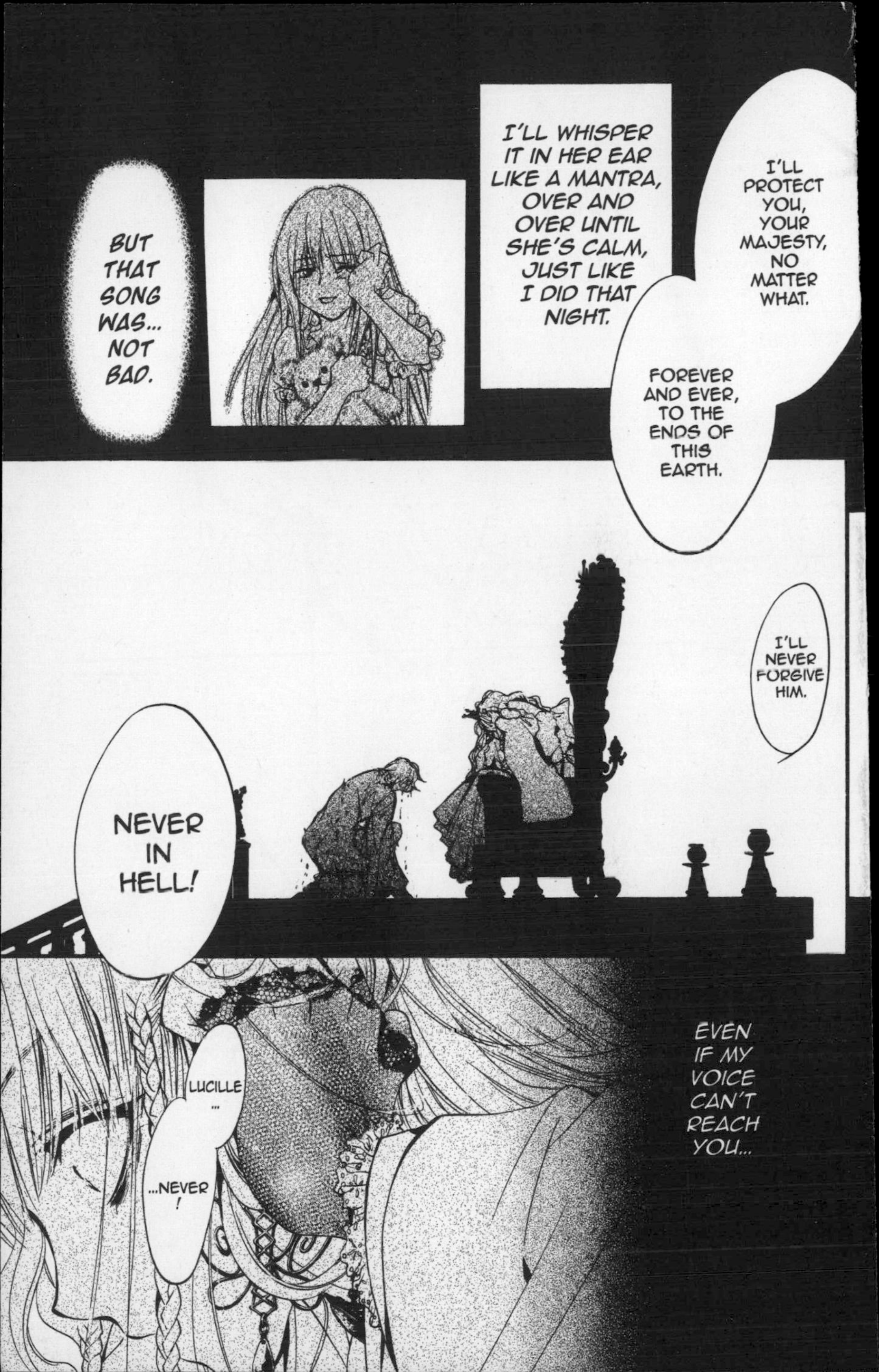
I'LL PROTECT YOU, YOUR MAJESTY, NO MATTER WHAT.
FOREVER AND EVER, TO THE ENDS OF THIS EARTH.
I'LL WHISPER IT IN HER EAR LIKE A MANTRA, OVER AND OVER UNTIL SHE'S CALM, JUST LIKE I DID THAT NIGHT.
BUT THAT SONG WAS... NOT BAD.
I'LL NEVER FORGIVE HIM.
NEVER IN HELL!
EVEN IF MY VOICE CAN'T REACH YOU...
LUCILLE...
...NEVER!

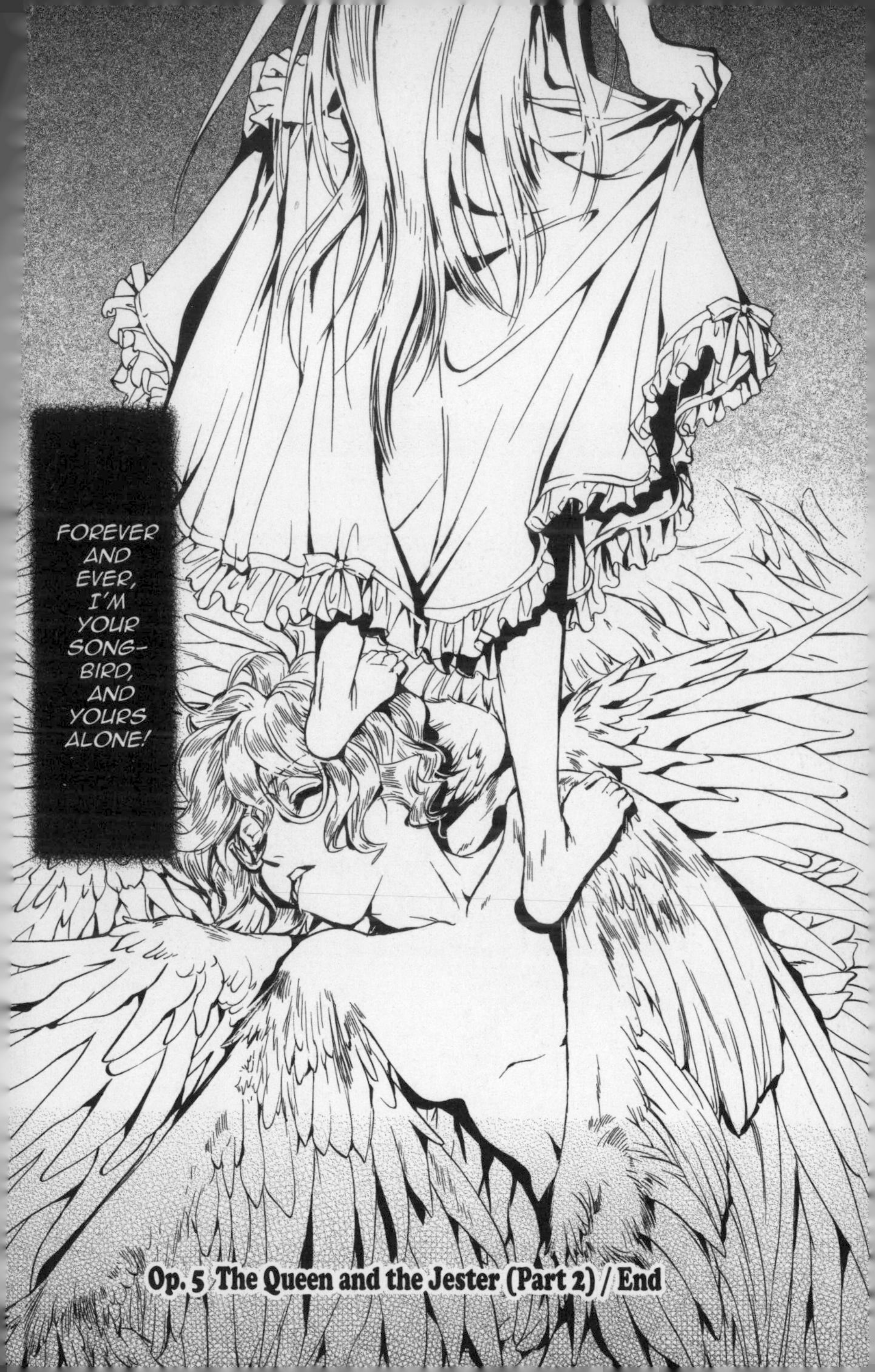
FOREVER AND EVER, I'M YOUR SONG-BIRD, AND YOURS ALONE!

Op. 5 The Queen and the Jester (Part 2) / End

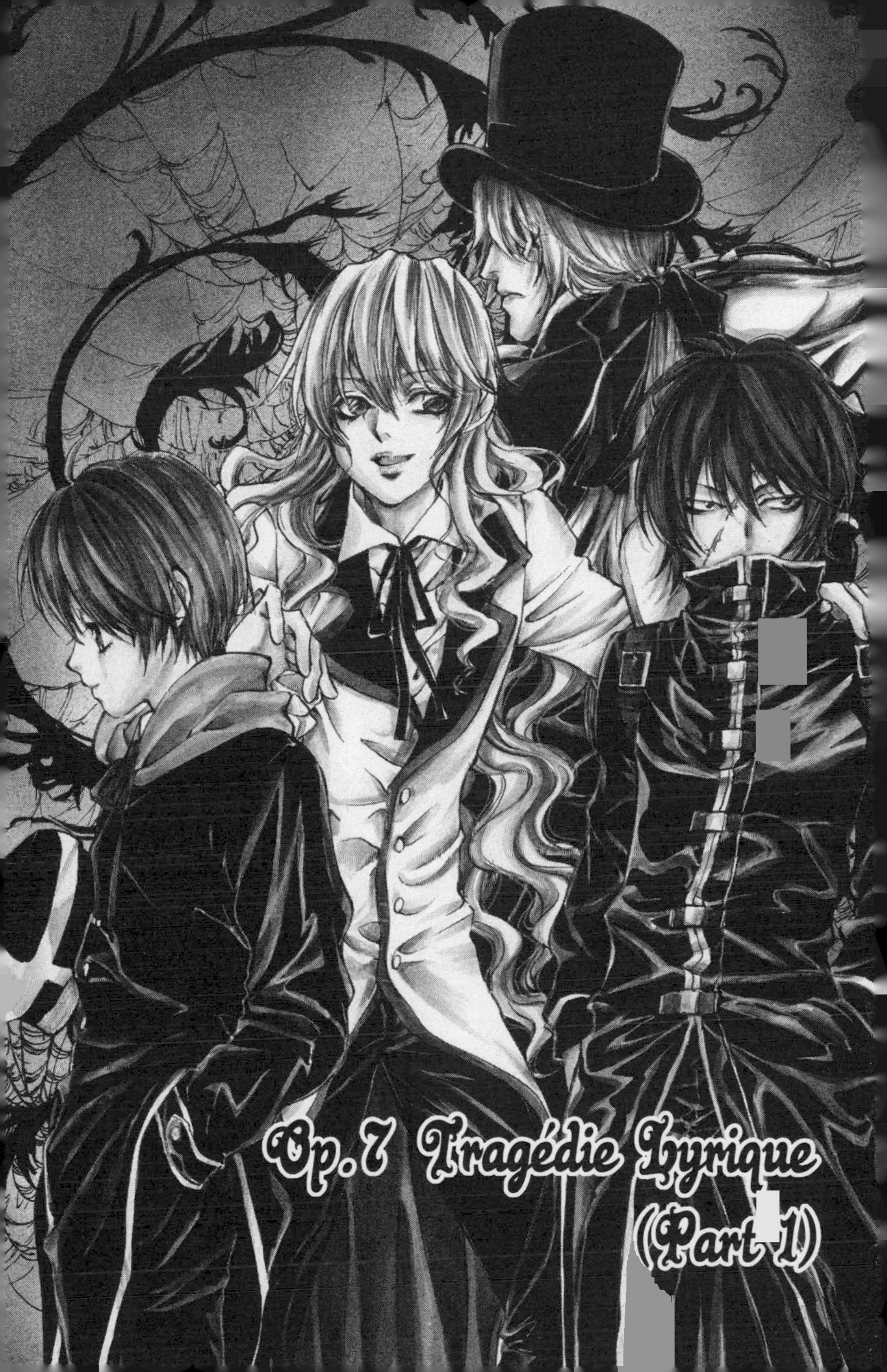
Op.7 Tragédie Lyrique
(Part 1)

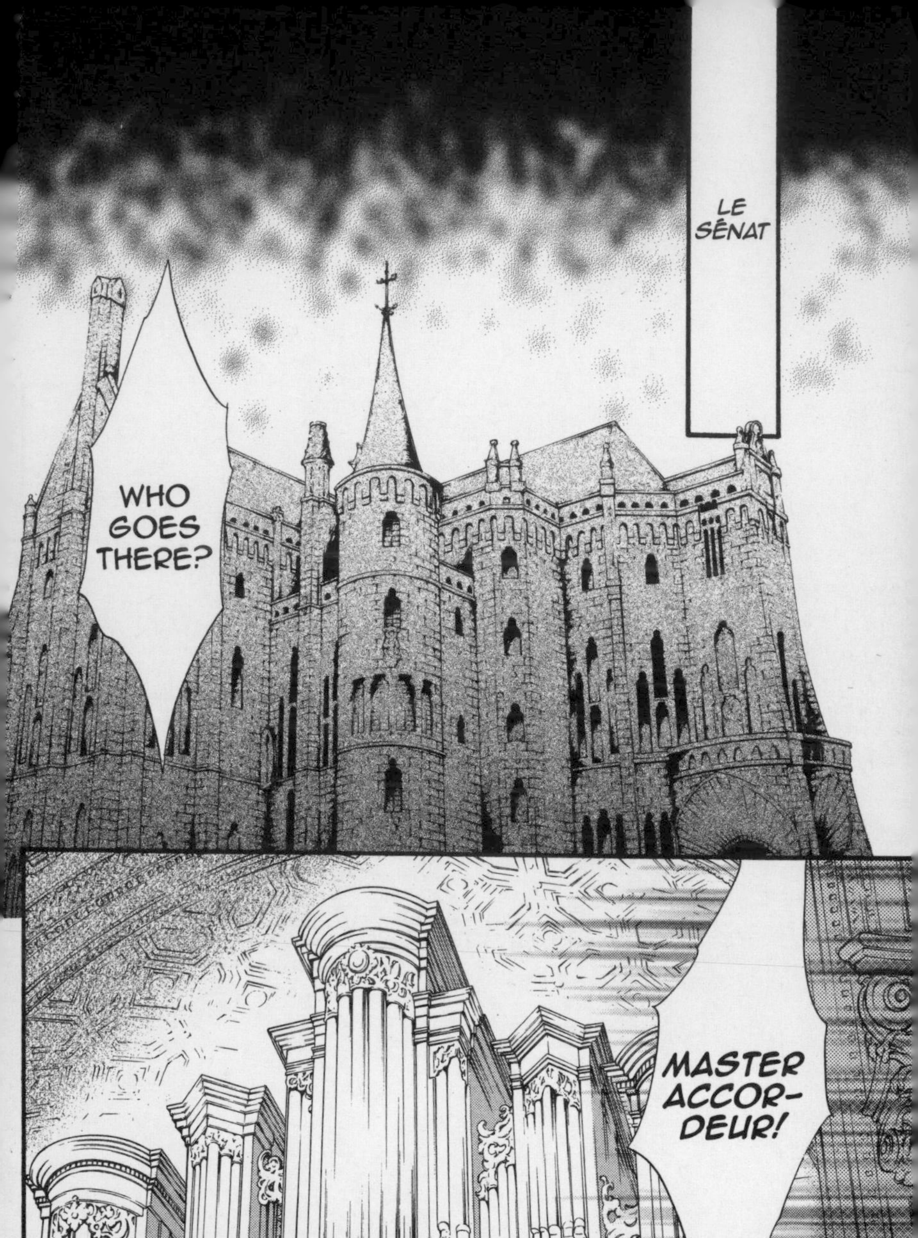
LE SÊNAT
WHO GOES THERE?
MASTER ACCOR-DEUR!

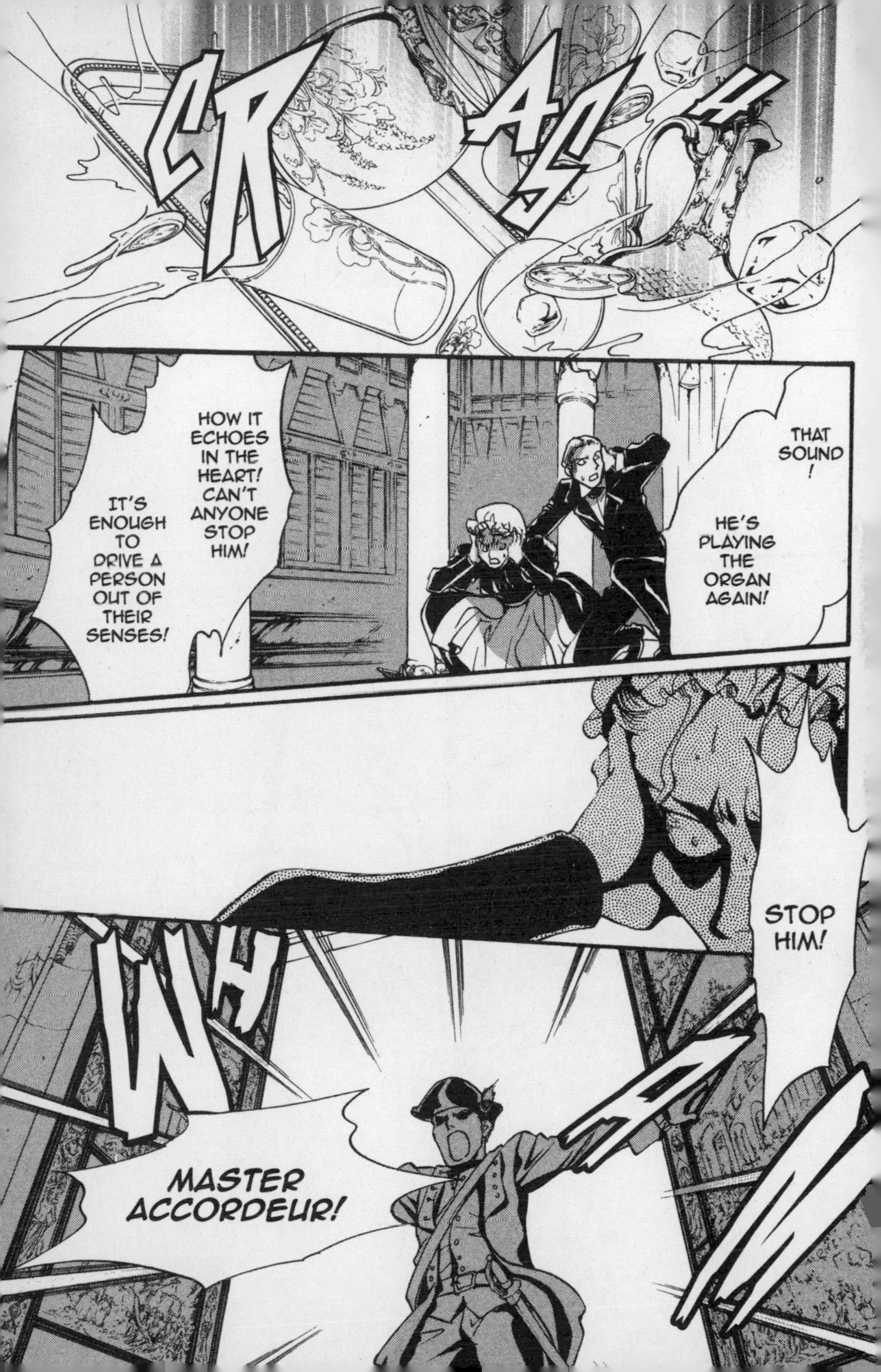
CRASH
THAT SOUND!
HE'S PLAYING THE ORGAN AGAIN!
HOW IT ECHOES IN THE HEART! CAN'T ANYONE STOP HIM!
IT'S ENOUGH TO DRIVE A PERSON OUT OF THEIR SENSES!
STOP HIM!
MASTER ACCORDEUR!

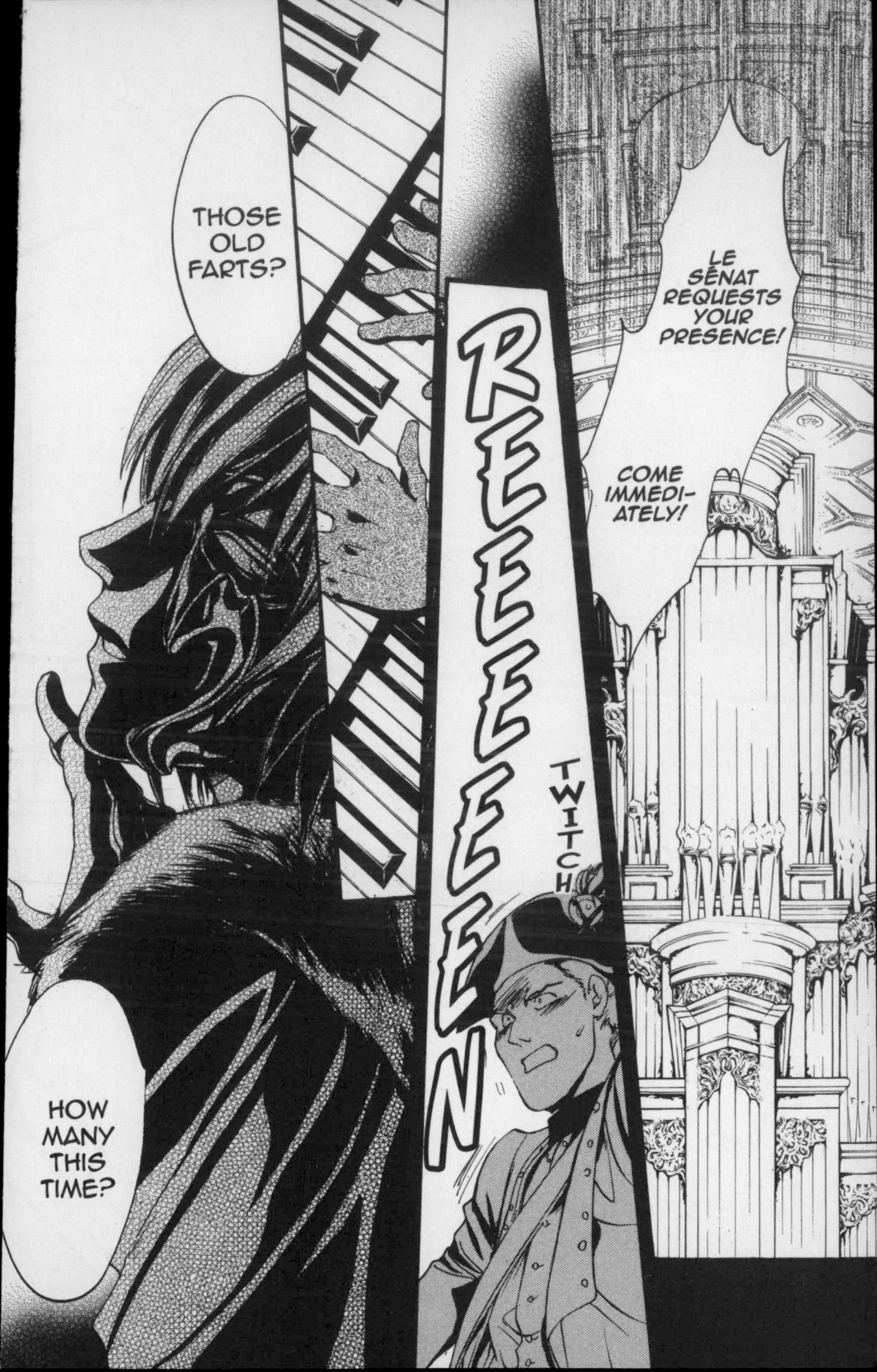
LE SÉNAT REQUESTS YOUR PRESENCE!
COME IMMEDIATELY!
REEEEEEEN
TWITCH
THOSE OLD FARTS?
HOW MANY THIS TIME?

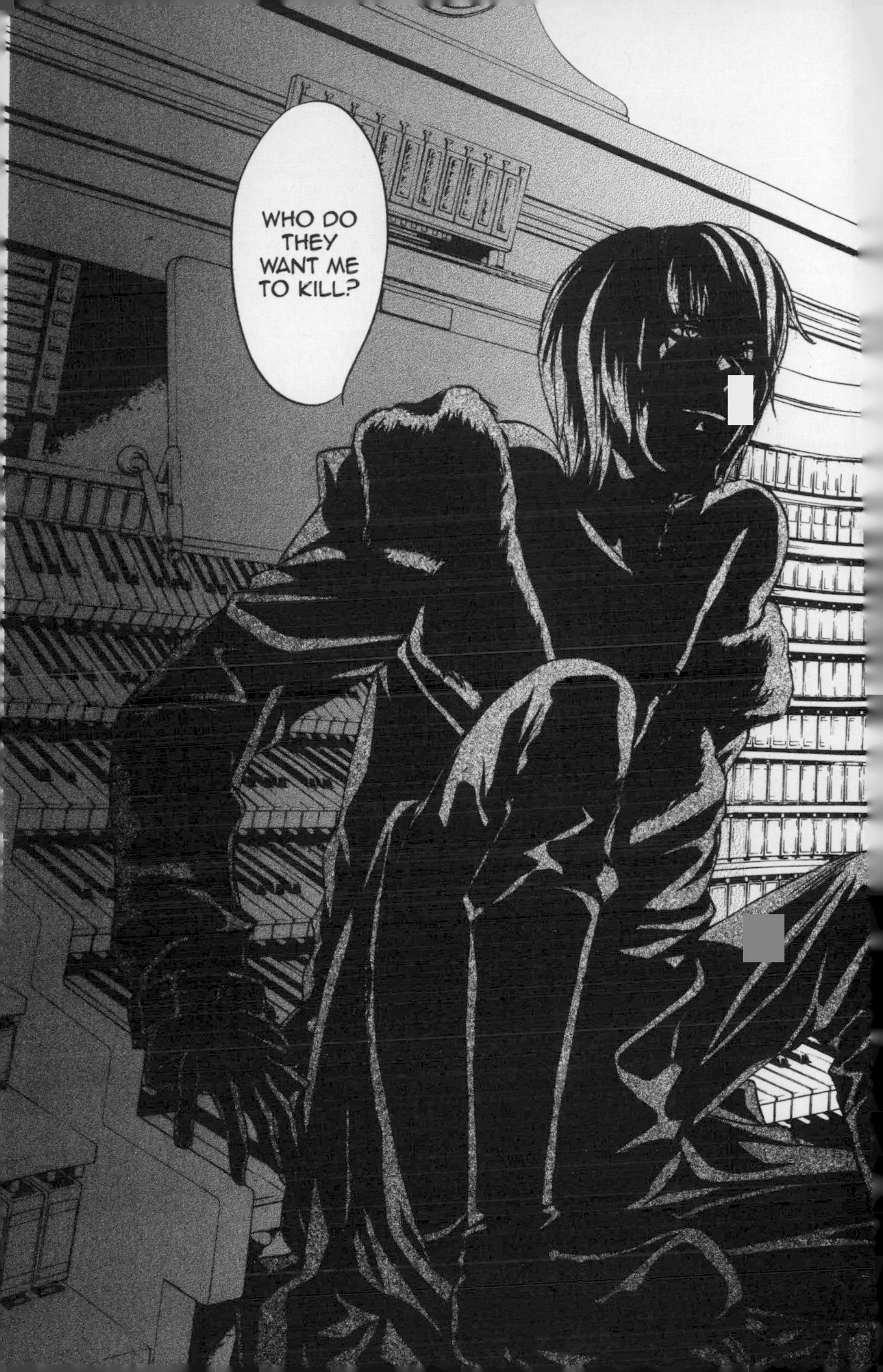
WHO DO THEY WANT ME TO KILL?

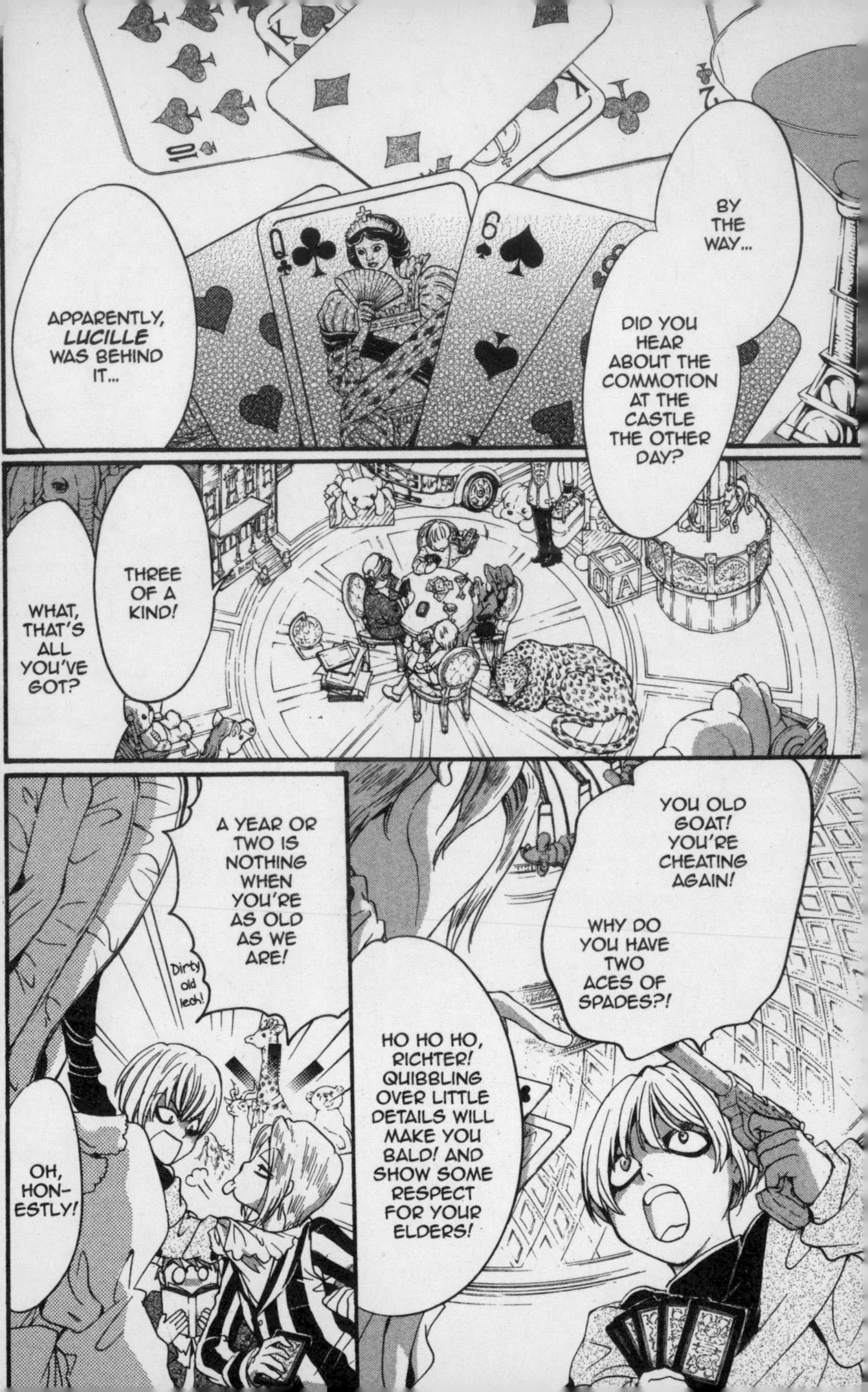
BY THE WAY...
DID YOU HEAR ABOUT THE COMMOTION AT THE CASTLE THE OTHER DAY?
APPARENTLY, *LUCILLE* WAS BEHIND IT...
THREE OF A KIND!
WHAT, THAT'S ALL YOU'VE GOT?
YOU OLD GOAT! YOU'RE CHEATING AGAIN!
WHY DO YOU HAVE TWO ACES OF SPADES?!
HO HO HO, RICHTER! QUIBBLING OVER LITTLE DETAILS WILL MAKE YOU BALD! AND SHOW SOME RESPECT FOR YOUR ELDERS!
A YEAR OR TWO IS NOTHING WHEN YOU'RE AS OLD AS WE ARE!
Dirty old lech!
OH, HON-ESTLY!

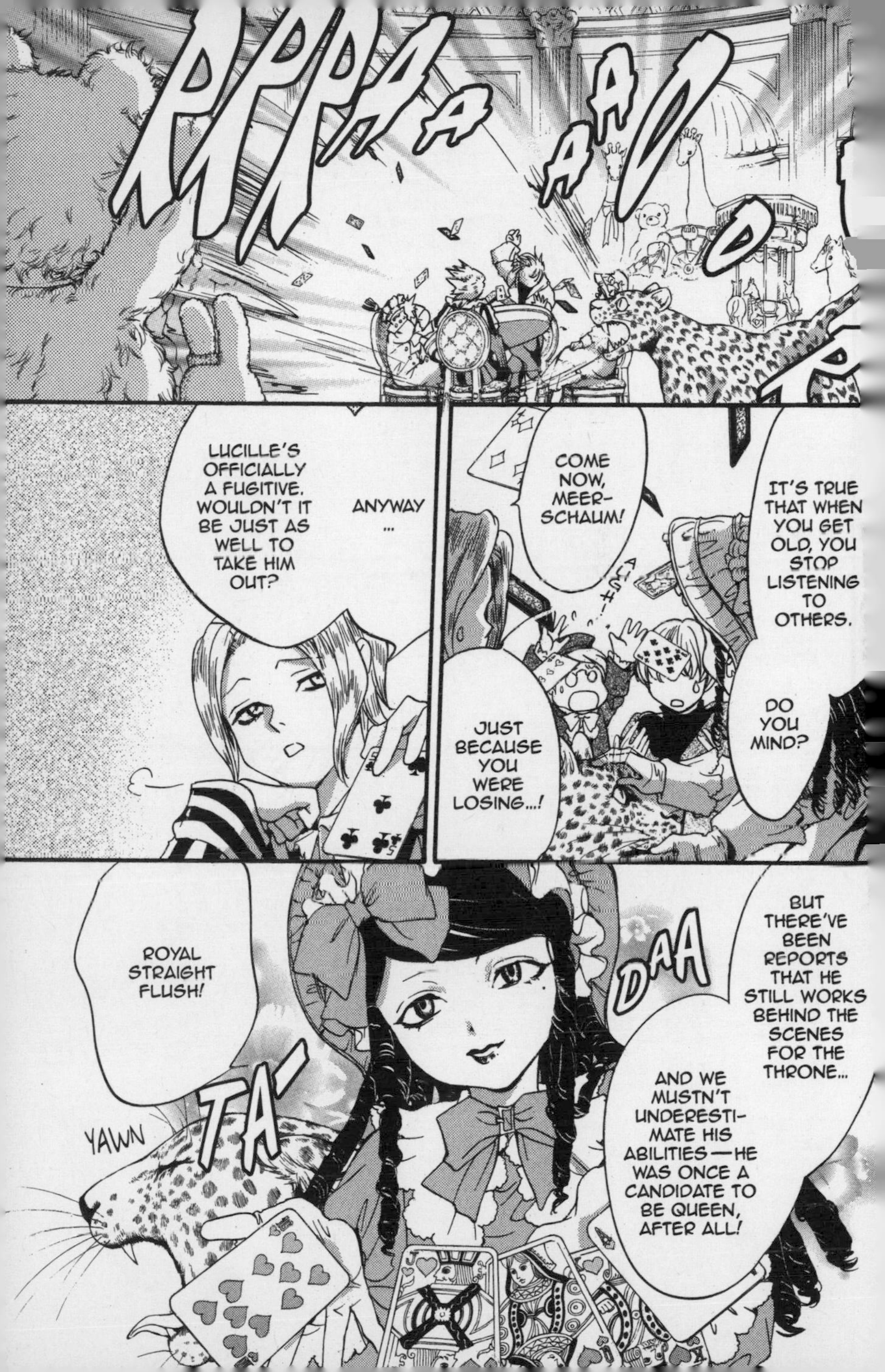
IT'S TRUE THAT WHEN YOU GET OLD, YOU STOP LISTENING TO OTHERS.
COME NOW, MEER-SCHAUM!
DO YOU MIND?
JUST BECAUSE YOU WERE LOSING...!
ANYWAY...
LUCILLE'S OFFICIALLY A FUGITIVE. WOULDN'T IT BE JUST AS WELL TO TAKE HIM OUT?
BUT THERE'VE BEEN REPORTS THAT HE STILL WORKS BEHIND THE SCENES FOR THE THRONE...
AND WE MUSTN'T UNDERESTI-MATE HIS ABILITIES—HE WAS ONCE A CANDIDATE TO BE QUEEN, AFTER ALL!
DAA
ROYAL STRAIGHT FLUSH!
TA'
YAWN

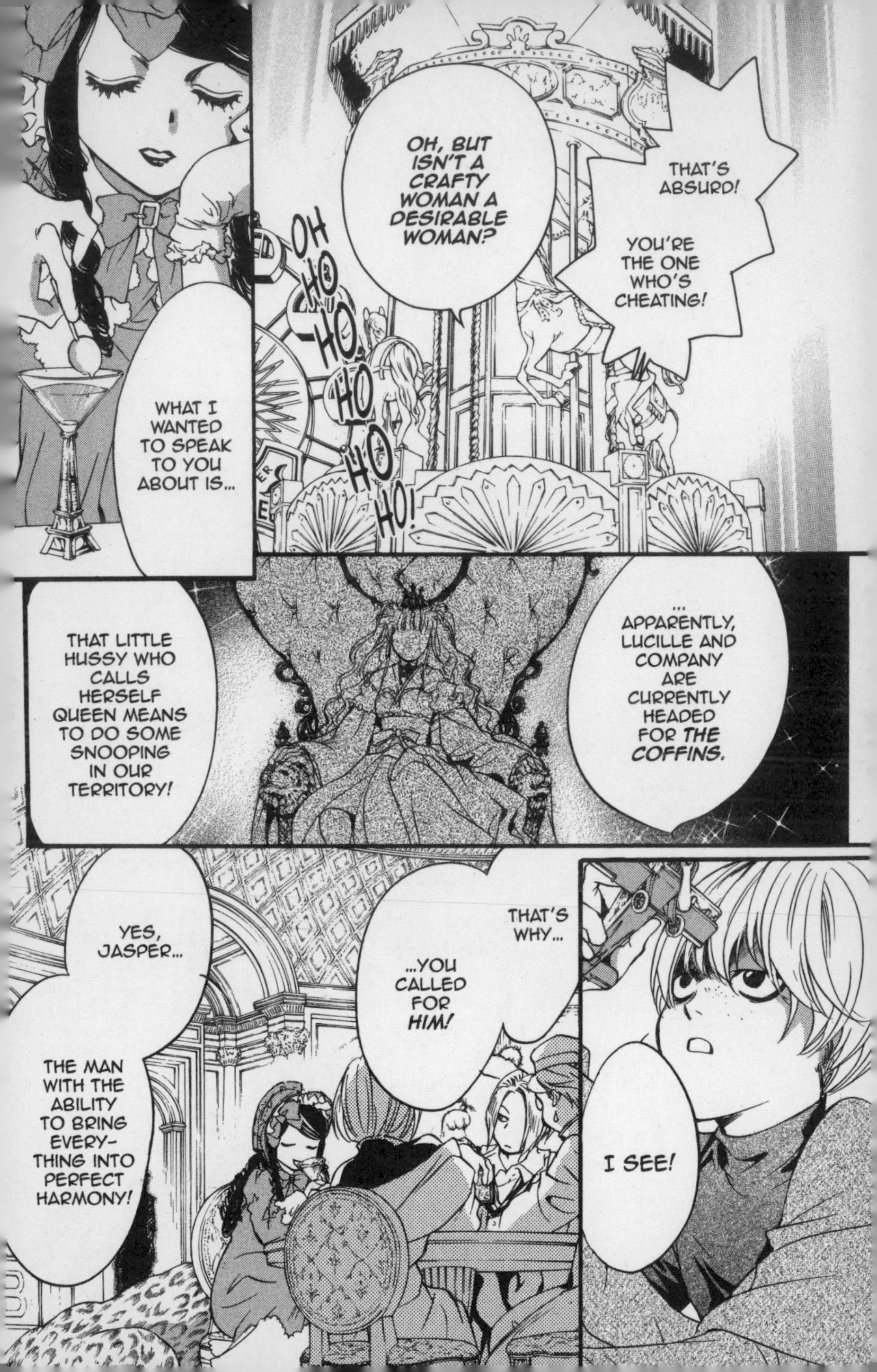
THAT'S ABSURD!
YOU'RE THE ONE WHO'S CHEATING!
OH, BUT ISN'T A CRAFTY WOMAN A DESIRABLE WOMAN?
OH HO HO HO HO HO HO!
WHAT I WANTED TO SPEAK TO YOU ABOUT IS...
... APPARENTLY, LUCILLE AND COMPANY ARE CURRENTLY HEADED FOR *THE COFFINS.*
THAT LITTLE HUSSY WHO CALLS HERSELF QUEEN MEANS TO DO SOME SNOOPING IN OUR TERRITORY!
I SEE!
THAT'S WHY...
...YOU CALLED FOR *HIM!*
YES, JASPER...
THE MAN WITH THE ABILITY TO BRING EVERY-THING INTO PERFECT HARMONY!

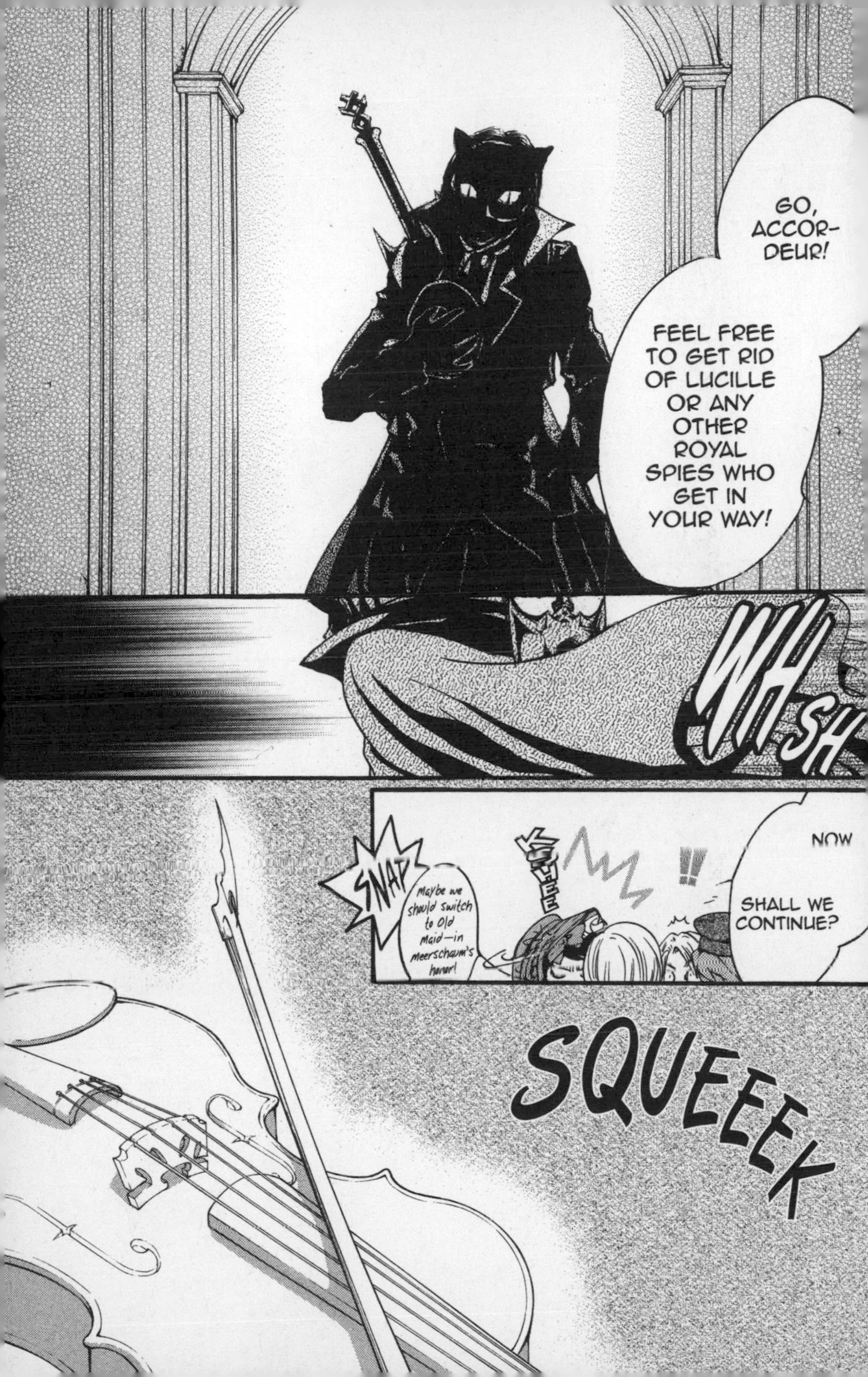
GO, ACCOR-DEUR!
FEEL FREE TO GET RID OF LUCILLE OR ANY OTHER ROYAL SPIES WHO GET IN YOUR WAY!
WHSH
NOW
SHALL WE CONTINUE?
!!
SNAP
Maybe we should switch to Old Maid—in meerschaum's honor!
SQUEEEK

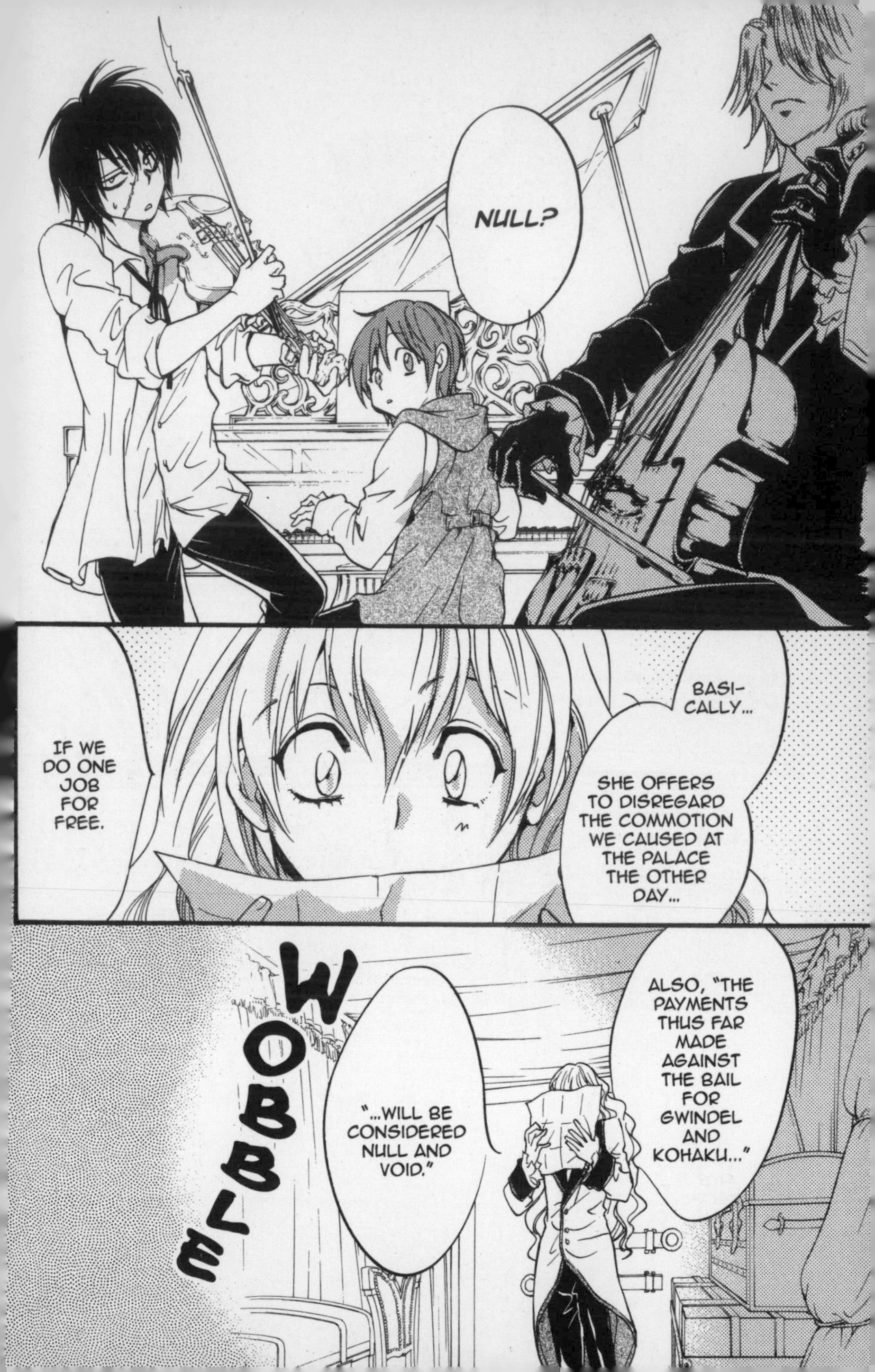
NULL?
BASI-CALLY...
SHE OFFERS TO DISREGARD THE COMMOTION WE CAUSED AT THE PALACE THE OTHER DAY...
IF WE DO ONE JOB FOR FREE.
ALSO, "THE PAYMENTS THUS FAR MADE AGAINST THE BAIL FOR GWINDEL AND KOHAKU..."
"...WILL BE CONSIDERED NULL AND VOID."
WOBBLE

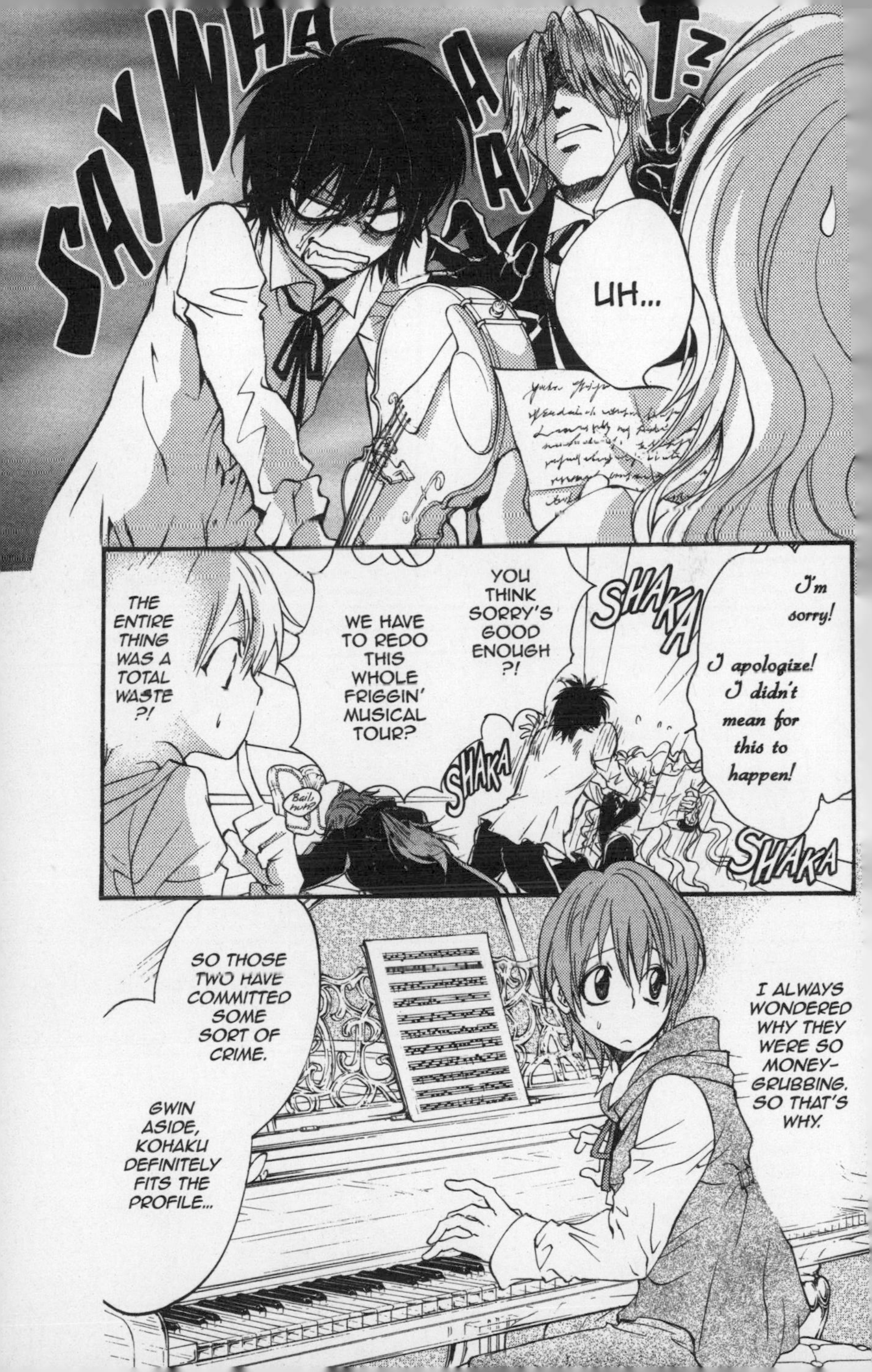

SAY WHAAAT?!
UH...
I'm sorry! I apologize! I didn't mean for this to happen!
SHAKA
YOU THINK SORRY'S GOOD ENOUGH?!
WE HAVE TO REDO THIS WHOLE FRIGGIN' MUSICAL TOUR?
SHAKA
SHAKA
THE ENTIRE THING WAS A TOTAL WASTE?!
I ALWAYS WONDERED WHY THEY WERE SO MONEY-GRUBBING. SO THAT'S WHY.
SO THOSE TWO HAVE COMMITTED SOME SORT OF CRIME.
GWIN ASIDE, KOHAKU DEFINITELY FITS THE PROFILE...

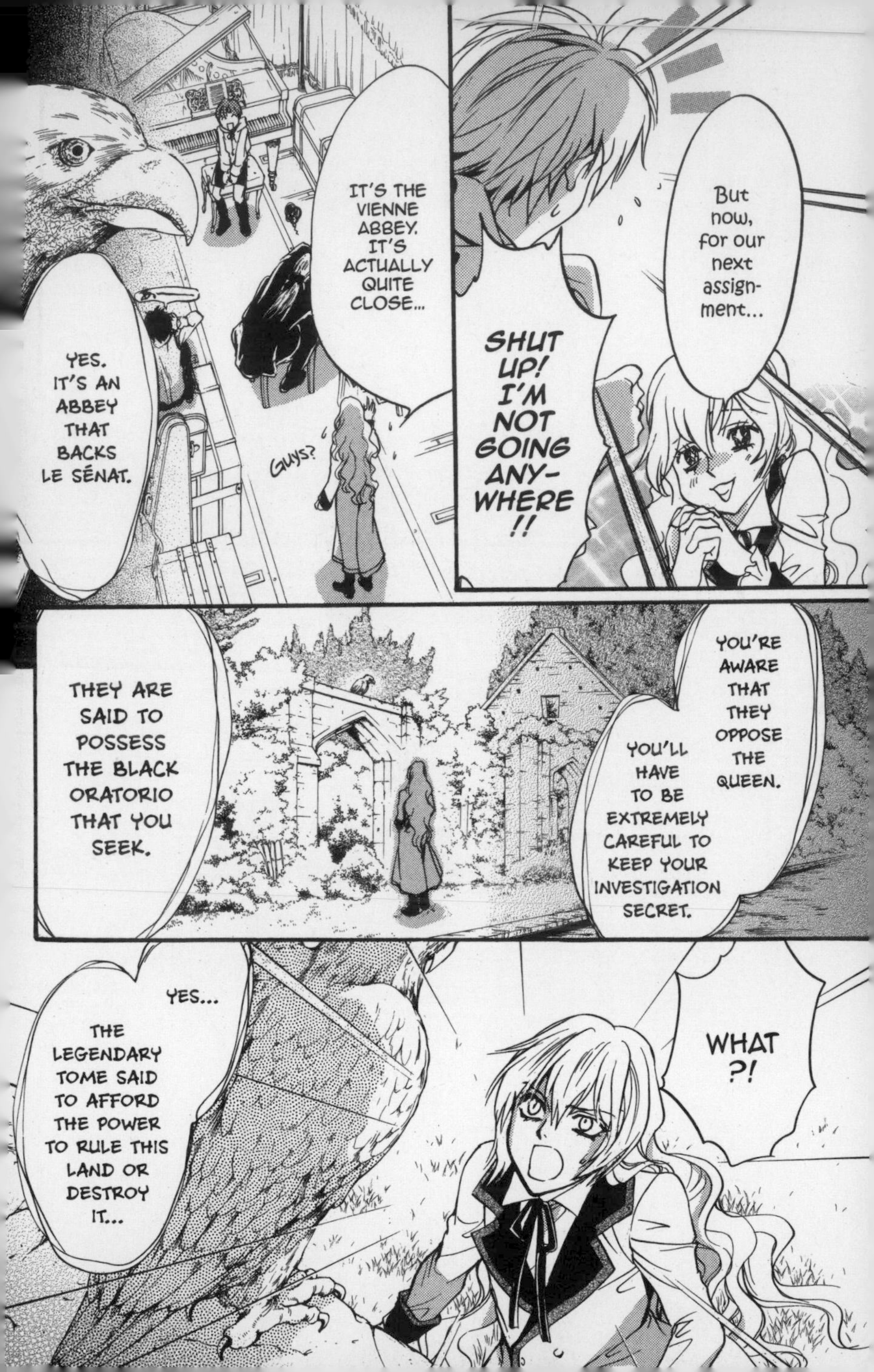
But now, for our next assignment...
SHUT UP! I'M NOT GOING ANYWHERE!!
IT'S THE VIENNE ABBEY. IT'S ACTUALLY QUITE CLOSE...
GUYS?
YES. IT'S AN ABBEY THAT BACKS LE SÉNAT.
YOU'RE AWARE THAT THEY OPPOSE THE QUEEN.
YOU'LL HAVE TO BE EXTREMELY CAREFUL TO KEEP YOUR INVESTIGATION SECRET.
THEY ARE SAID TO POSSESS THE BLACK ORATORIO THAT YOU SEEK.
WHAT?!
YES...
THE LEGENDARY TOME SAID TO AFFORD THE POWER TO RULE THIS LAND OR DESTROY IT...

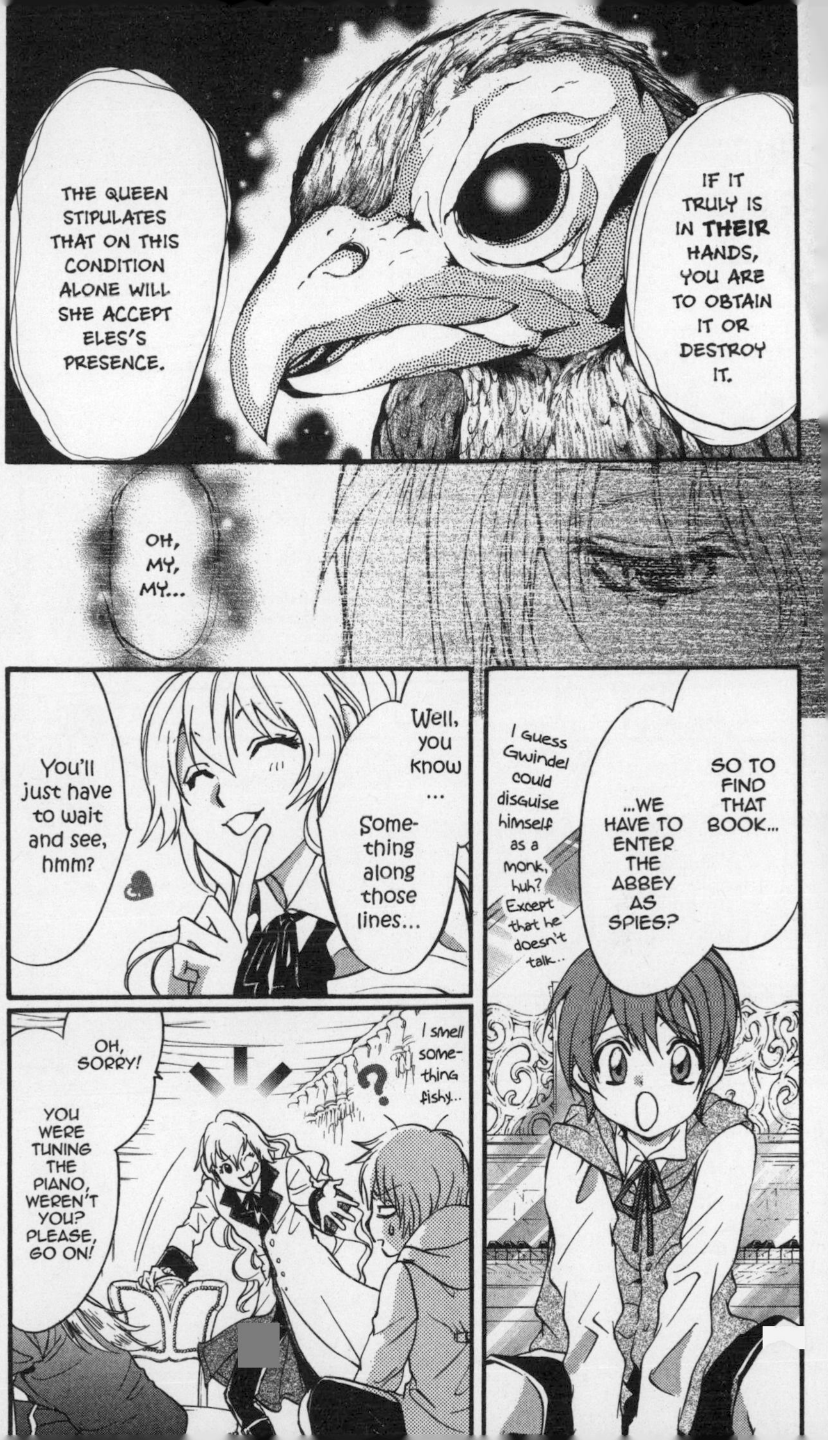
IF IT TRULY IS IN **THEIR** HANDS, YOU ARE TO OBTAIN IT OR DESTROY IT.
THE QUEEN STIPULATES THAT ON THIS CONDITION ALONE WILL SHE ACCEPT ELES'S PRESENCE.
OH, MY, MY...
SO TO FIND THAT BOOK...
...WE HAVE TO ENTER THE ABBEY AS SPIES?
I guess Gwindel could disguise himself as a monk, huh? Except that he doesn't talk...
Well, you know... Something along those lines...
You'll just have to wait and see, hmm?
I smell something fishy...
OH, SORRY!
YOU WERE TUNING THE PIANO, WEREN'T YOU? PLEASE, GO ON!

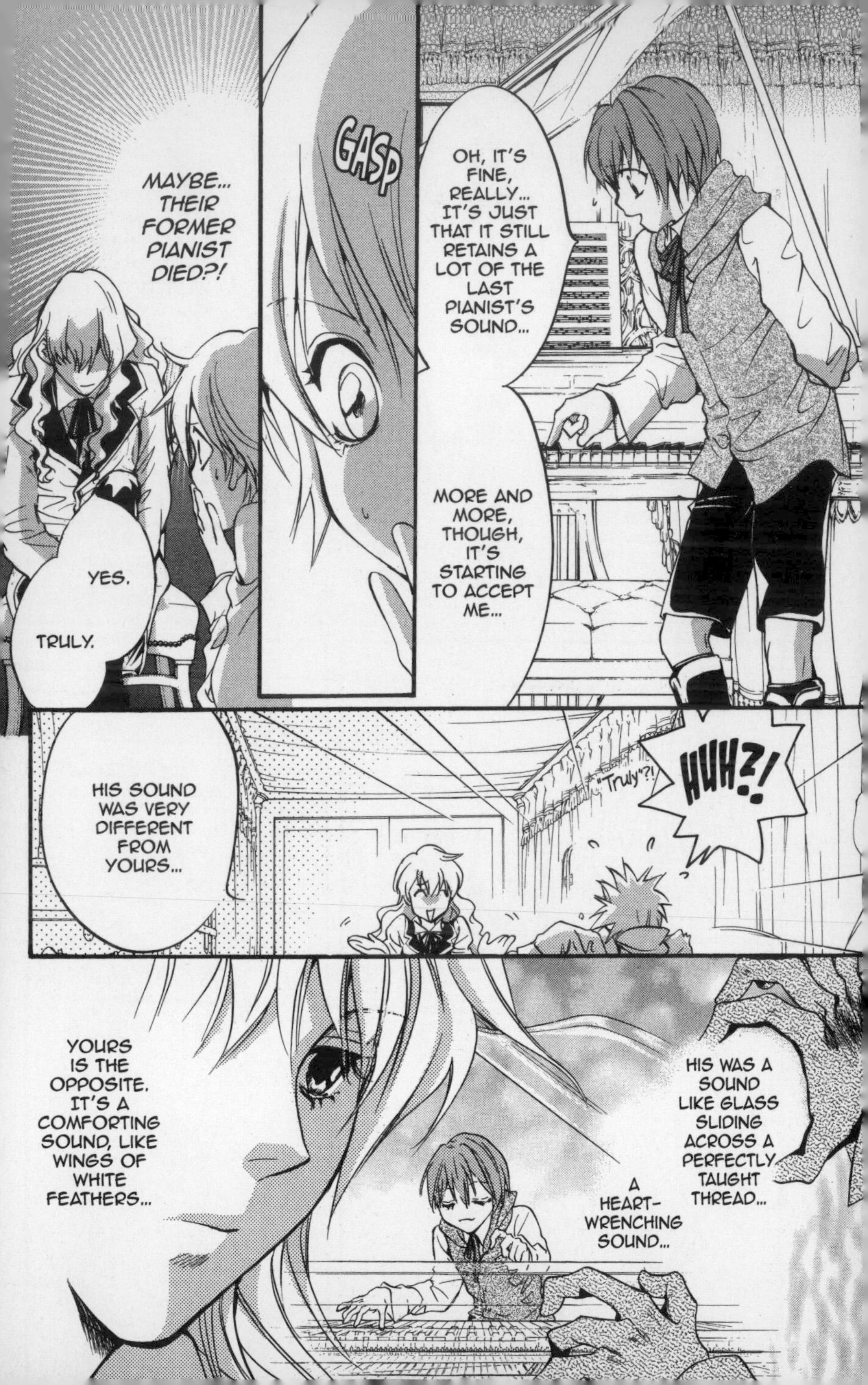
OH, IT'S FINE, REALLY... IT'S JUST THAT IT STILL RETAINS A LOT OF THE LAST PIANIST'S SOUND...
MORE AND MORE, THOUGH, IT'S STARTING TO ACCEPT ME...
GASP
MAYBE... THEIR FORMER PIANIST DIED?!
YES.
TRULY.
HUH?!
"Truly"?!
HIS SOUND WAS VERY DIFFERENT FROM YOURS...
HIS WAS A SOUND LIKE GLASS SLIDING ACROSS A PERFECTLY TAUGHT THREAD...
A HEART-WRENCHING SOUND...
YOURS IS THE OPPOSITE. IT'S A COMFORTING SOUND, LIKE WINGS OF WHITE FEATHERS...

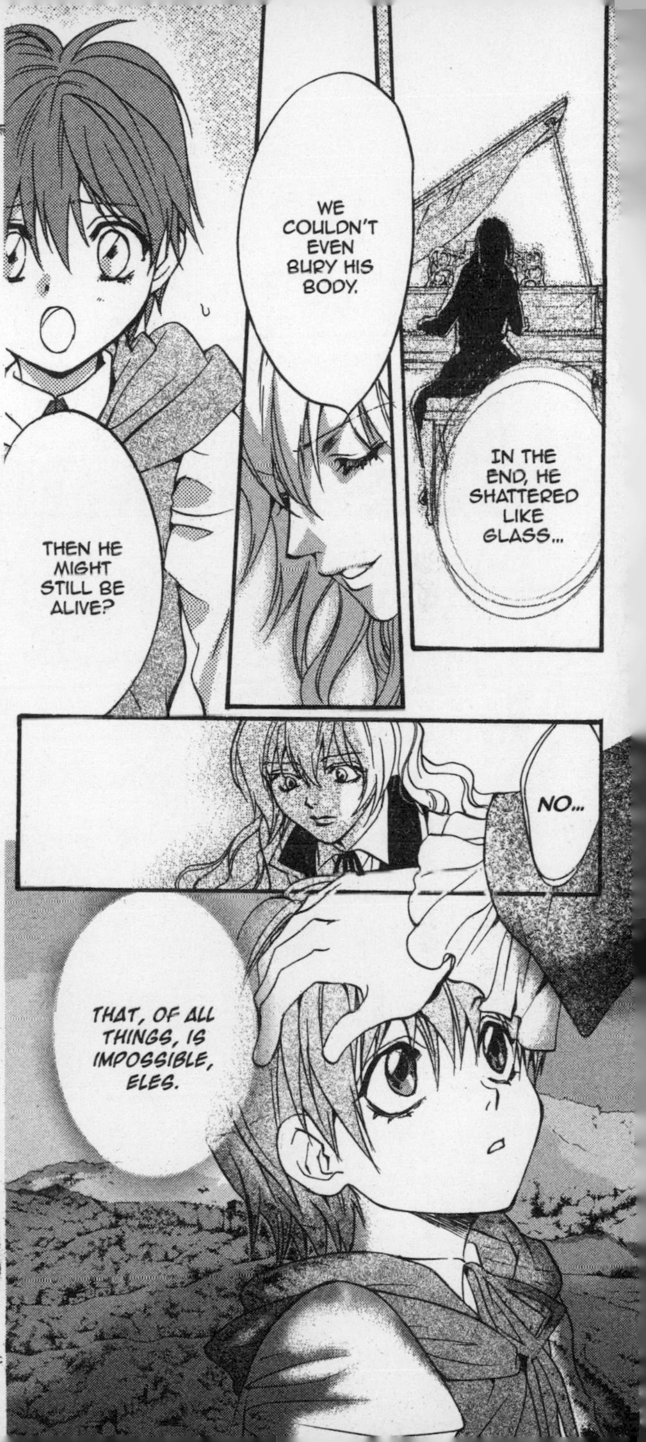
IN THE END, HE SHATTERED LIKE GLASS...
WE COULDN'T EVEN BURY HIS BODY.
THEN HE MIGHT STILL BE ALIVE?
NO...
THAT, OF ALL THINGS, IS IMPOSSIBLE, ELES.

One reason I came up with this story was to give Eles a chance to dress like a girl...but uniforms are really a pain to draw. After I draw them, I keep finding parts I left out or drew wrong. And the novitiates have a different design. But still, I'm just happy I get to draw a lot of girls for once!

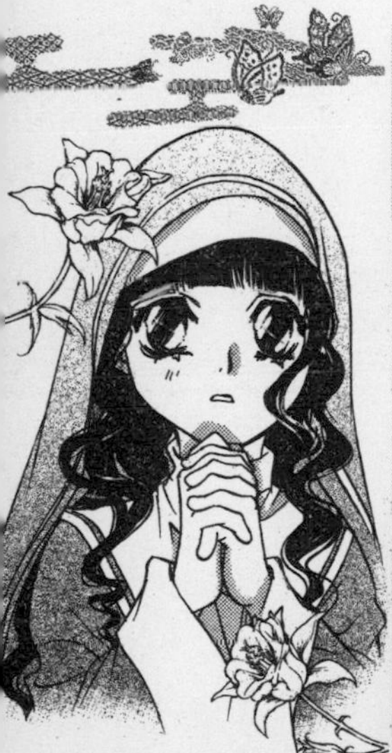

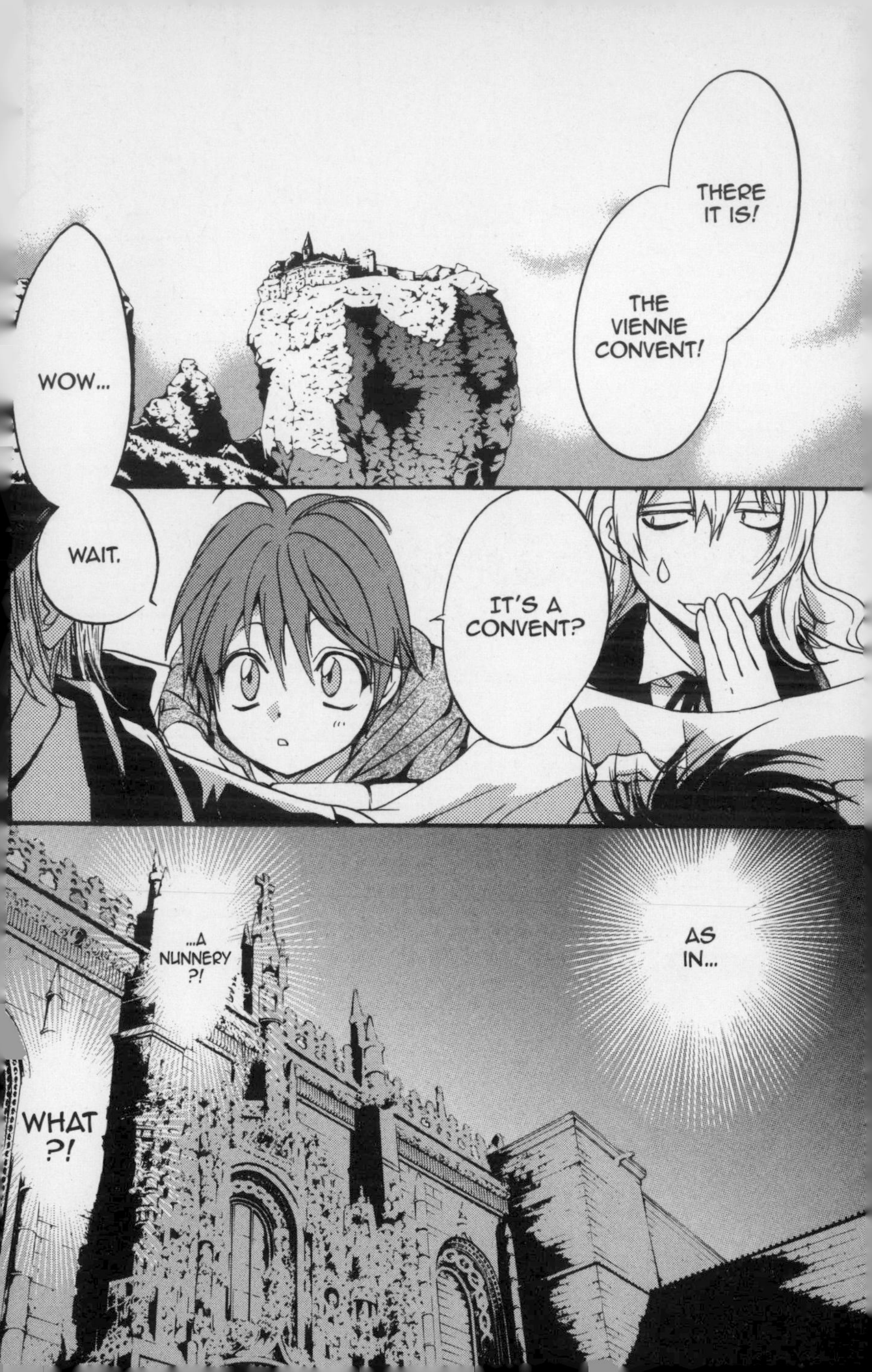
THERE IT IS!
THE VIENNE CONVENT!
WOW...
WAIT.
IT'S A CONVENT?
AS IN...
...A NUNNERY?!
WHAT?!

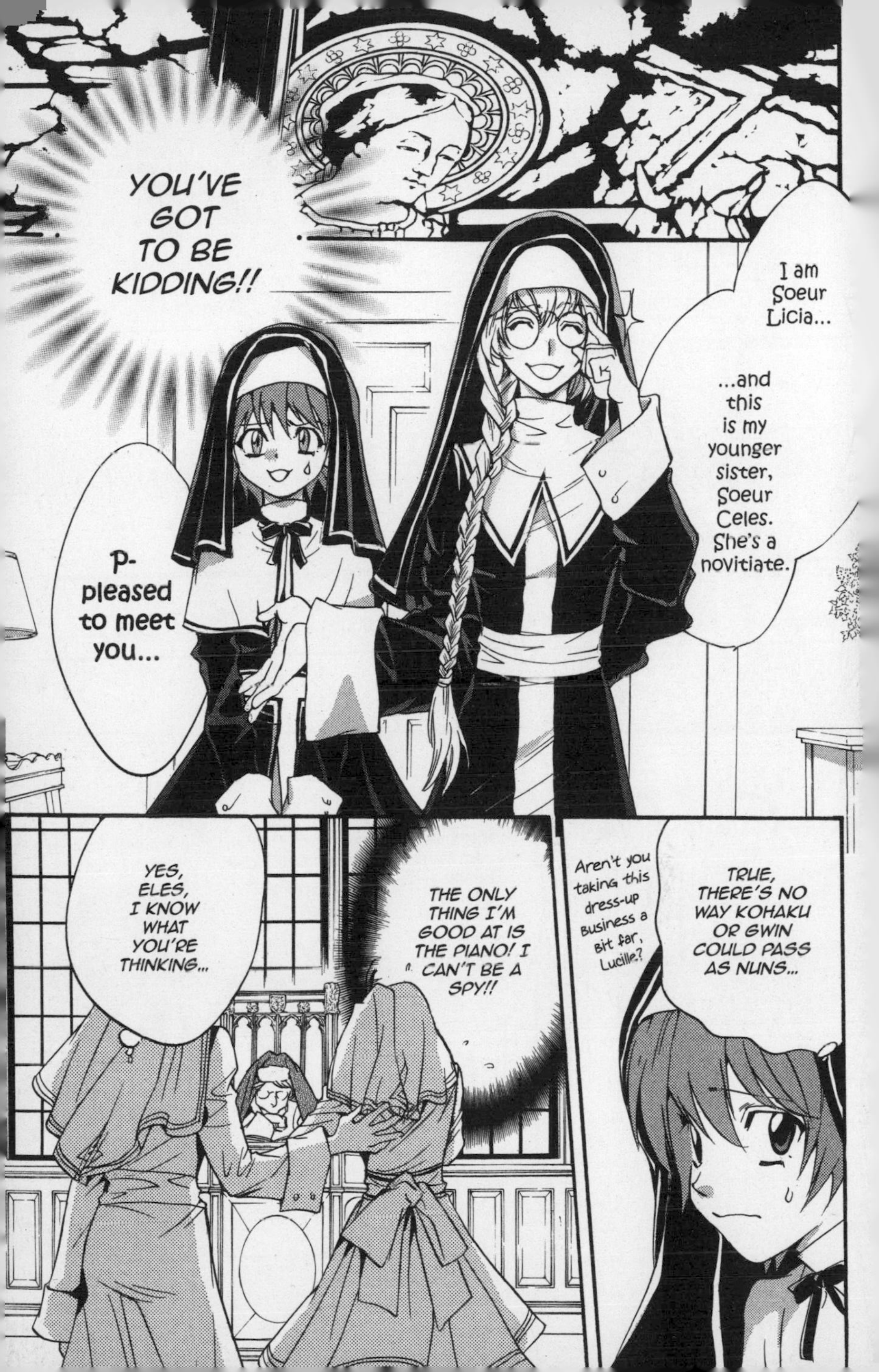
I am Soeur Licia...
...and this is my younger sister, Soeur Celes. She's a novitiate.
YOU'VE GOT TO BE KIDDING!!
P-pleased to meet you...
Aren't you taking this dress-up business a bit far, Lucille?
TRUE, THERE'S NO WAY KOHAKU OR GWIN COULD PASS AS NUNS...
THE ONLY THING I'M GOOD AT IS THE PIANO! I CAN'T BE A SPY!!
YES, ELES, I KNOW WHAT YOU'RE THINKING...

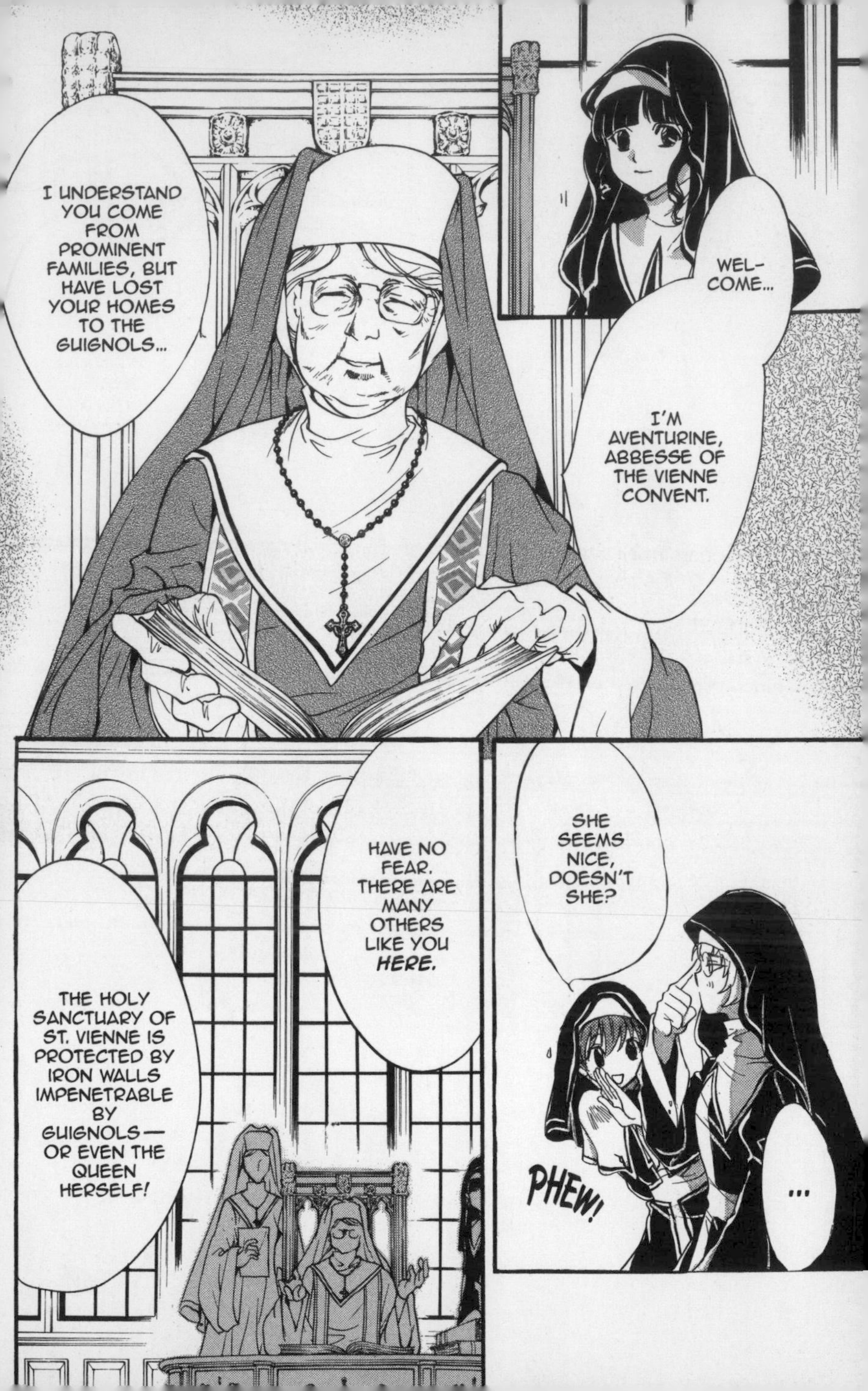
WEL-COME...
I'M AVENTURINE, ABBESSE OF THE VIENNE CONVENT.
I UNDERSTAND YOU COME FROM PROMINENT FAMILIES, BUT HAVE LOST YOUR HOMES TO THE GUIGNOLS...
SHE SEEMS NICE, DOESN'T SHE?
...
PHEW!
HAVE NO FEAR. THERE ARE MANY OTHERS LIKE YOU *HERE.*
THE HOLY SANCTUARY OF ST. VIENNE IS PROTECTED BY IRON WALLS IMPENETRABLE BY GUIGNOLS—OR EVEN THE QUEEN HERSELF!

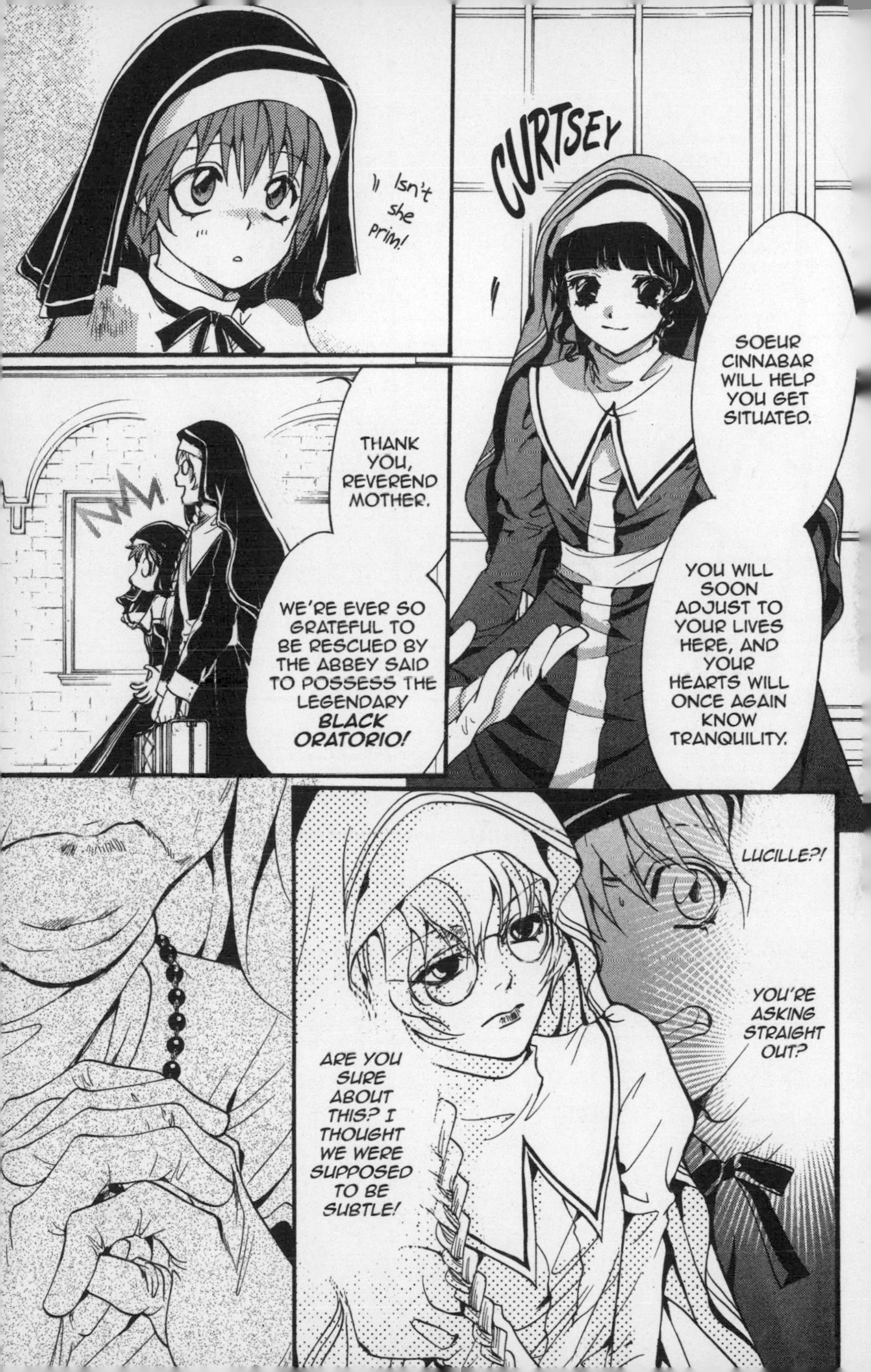
CURTSEY
SOEUR CINNABAR WILL HELP YOU GET SITUATED.
YOU WILL SOON ADJUST TO YOUR LIVES HERE, AND YOUR HEARTS WILL ONCE AGAIN KNOW TRANQUILITY.
Isn't she prim!
THANK YOU, REVEREND MOTHER.
WE'RE EVER SO GRATEFUL TO BE RESCUED BY THE ABBEY SAID TO POSSESS THE LEGENDARY BLACK ORATORIO!
LUCILLE?!
YOU'RE ASKING STRAIGHT OUT?
ARE YOU SURE ABOUT THIS? I THOUGHT WE WERE SUPPOSED TO BE SUBTLE!

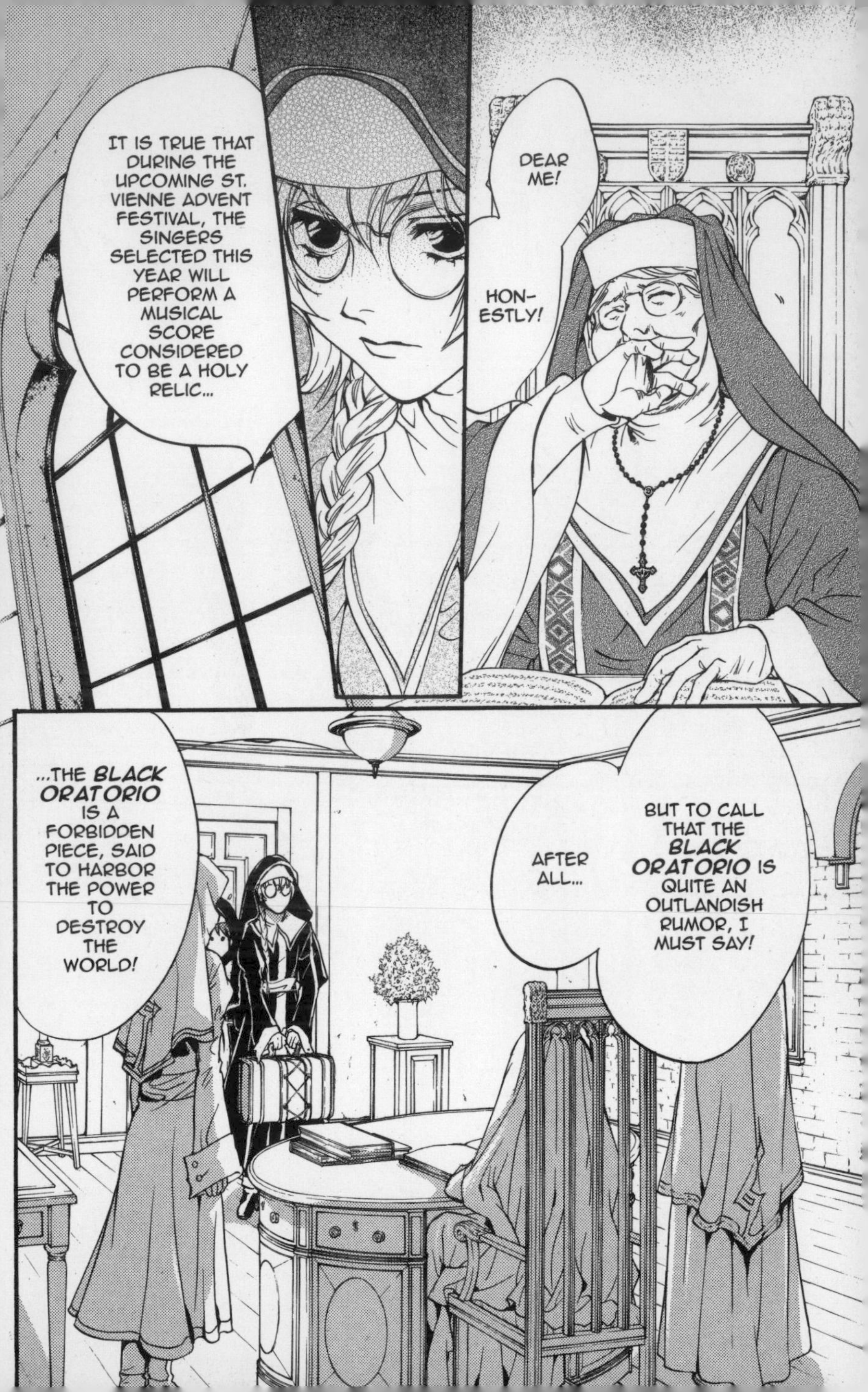
DEAR ME!
HON-ESTLY!
IT IS TRUE THAT DURING THE UPCOMING ST. VIENNE ADVENT FESTIVAL, THE SINGERS SELECTED THIS YEAR WILL PERFORM A MUSICAL SCORE CONSIDERED TO BE A HOLY RELIC...
AFTER ALL...
BUT TO CALL THAT THE *BLACK ORATORIO* IS QUITE AN OUTLANDISH RUMOR, I MUST SAY!
...THE *BLACK ORATORIO* IS A FORBIDDEN PIECE, SAID TO HARBOR THE POWER TO DESTROY THE WORLD!

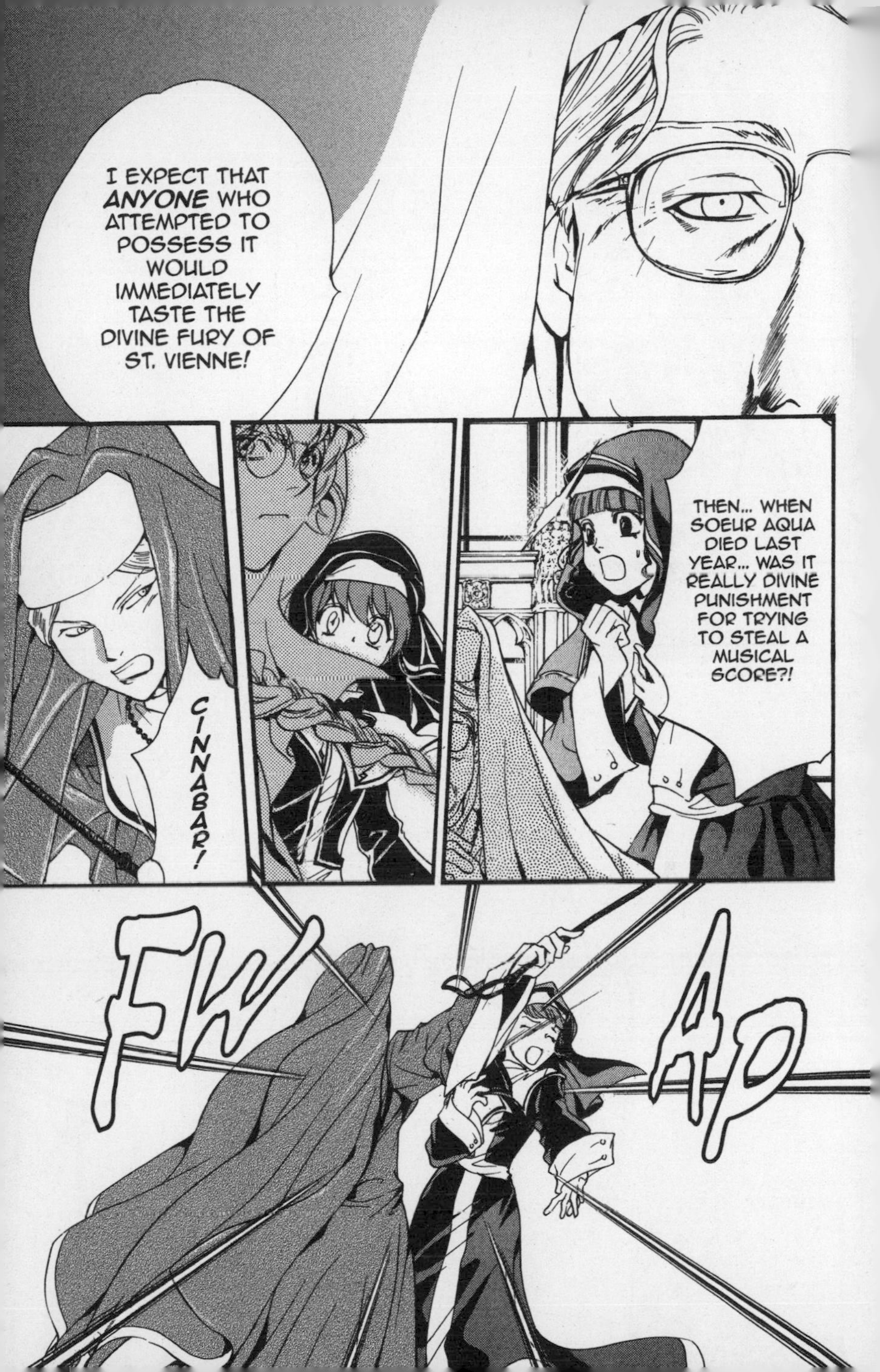
I EXPECT THAT ANYONE WHO ATTEMPTED TO POSSESS IT WOULD IMMEDIATELY TASTE THE DIVINE FURY OF ST. VIENNE!
THEN... WHEN SOEUR AQUA DIED LAST YEAR... WAS IT REALLY DIVINE PUNISHMENT FOR TRYING TO STEAL A MUSICAL SCORE?!
CINNABAR!
FWAP

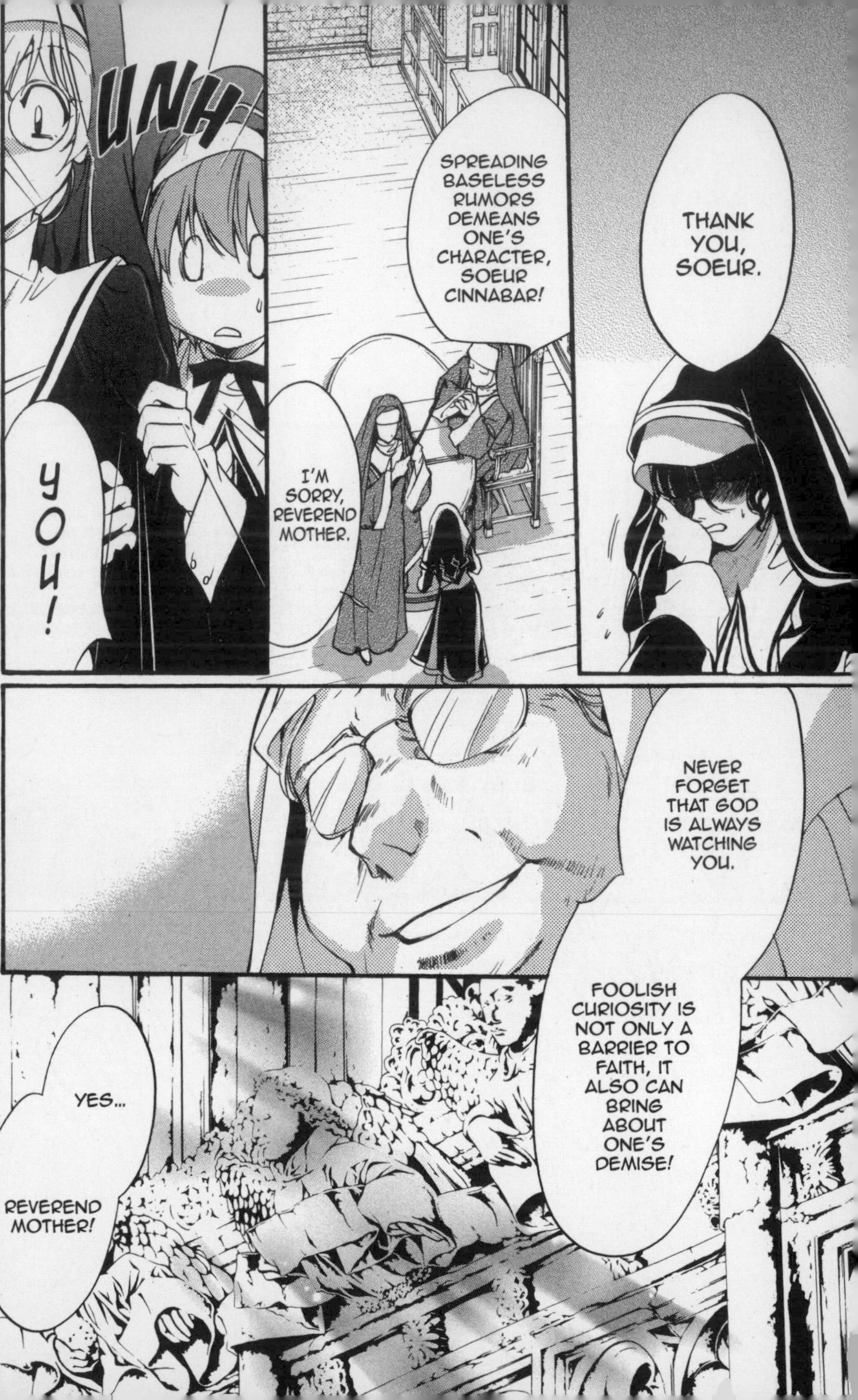
THANK YOU, SOEUR.
SPREADING BASELESS RUMORS DEMEANS ONE'S CHARACTER, SOEUR CINNABAR!
I'M SORRY, REVEREND MOTHER.
UNH
YOU!
NEVER FORGET THAT GOD IS ALWAYS WATCHING YOU.
FOOLISH CURIOSITY IS NOT ONLY A BARRIER TO FAITH, IT ALSO CAN BRING ABOUT ONE'S DEMISE!
YES...
REVEREND MOTHER!

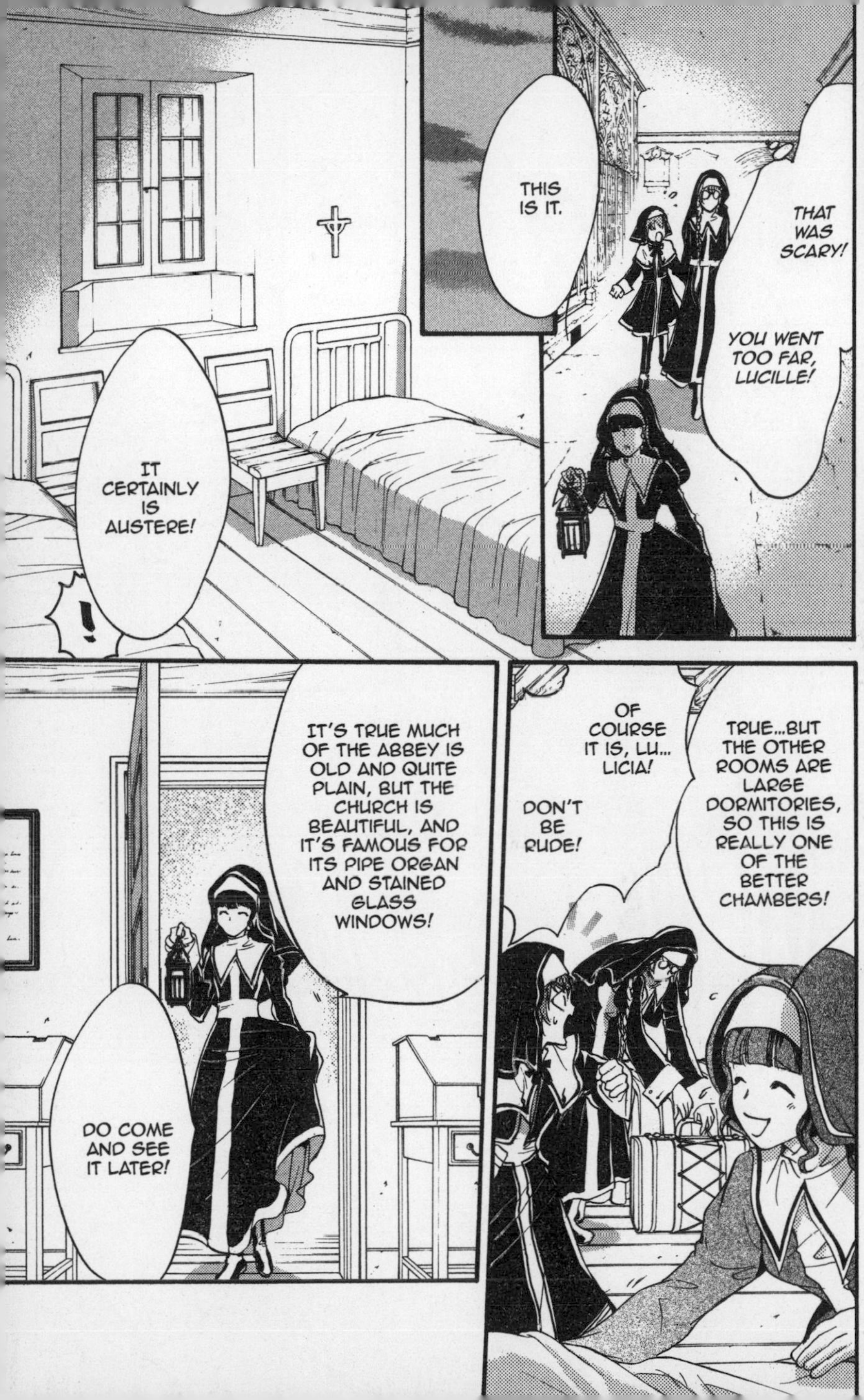
THAT WAS SCARY!
YOU WENT TOO FAR, LUCILLE!
THIS IS IT.
IT CERTAINLY IS AUSTERE!
!
TRUE...BUT THE OTHER ROOMS ARE LARGE DORMITORIES, SO THIS IS REALLY ONE OF THE BETTER CHAMBERS!
OF COURSE IT IS, LU... LICIA!
DON'T BE RUDE!
IT'S TRUE MUCH OF THE ABBEY IS OLD AND QUITE PLAIN, BUT THE CHURCH IS BEAUTIFUL, AND IT'S FAMOUS FOR ITS PIPE ORGAN AND STAINED GLASS WINDOWS!
DO COME AND SEE IT LATER!

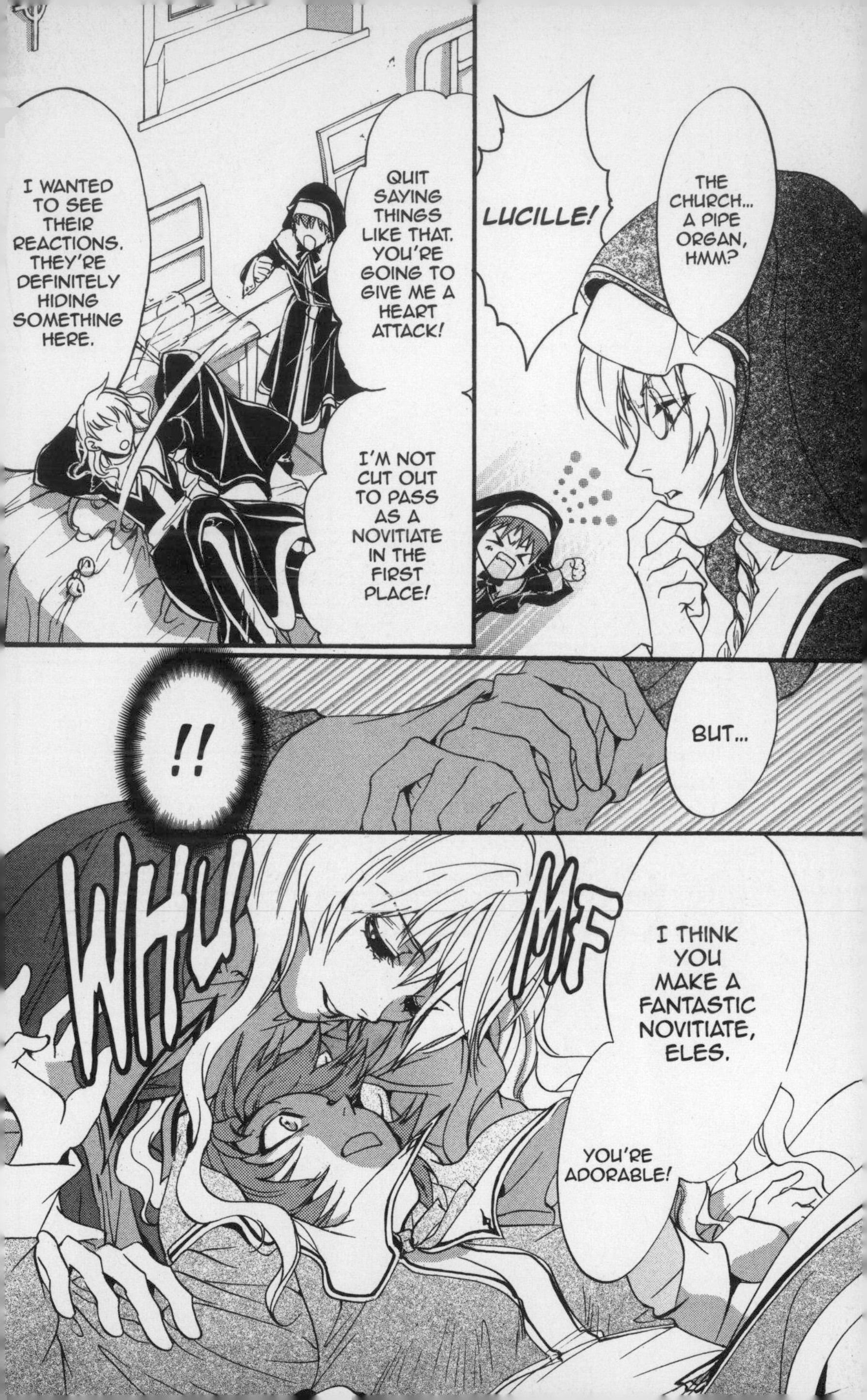
THE CHURCH... A PIPE ORGAN, HMM?
LUCILLE!
QUIT SAYING THINGS LIKE THAT. YOU'RE GOING TO GIVE ME A HEART ATTACK!
I'M NOT CUT OUT TO PASS AS A NOVITIATE IN THE FIRST PLACE!
I WANTED TO SEE THEIR REACTIONS. THEY'RE DEFINITELY HIDING SOMETHING HERE.
BUT...
!!
I THINK YOU MAKE A FANTASTIC NOVITIATE, ELES.
YOU'RE ADORABLE!
WHU MF

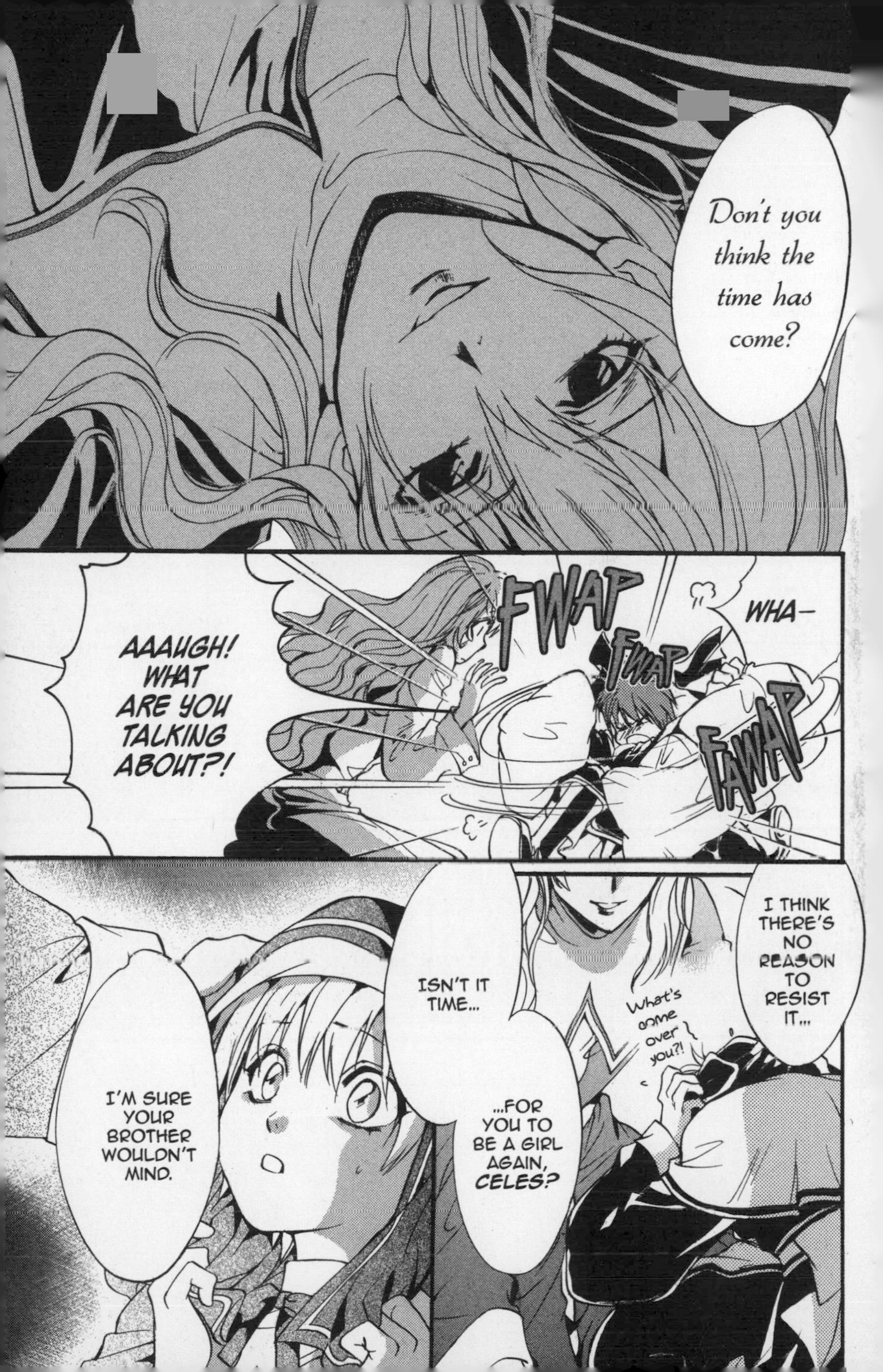

Don't you think the time has come?
WHA–
FWAP
FWAP
FWAP
AAAUGH! WHAT ARE YOU TALKING ABOUT?!
I THINK THERE'S NO REASON TO RESIST IT...
What's come over you?!
ISN'T IT TIME...
...FOR YOU TO BE A GIRL AGAIN, CELES?
I'M SURE YOUR BROTHER WOULDN'T MIND.

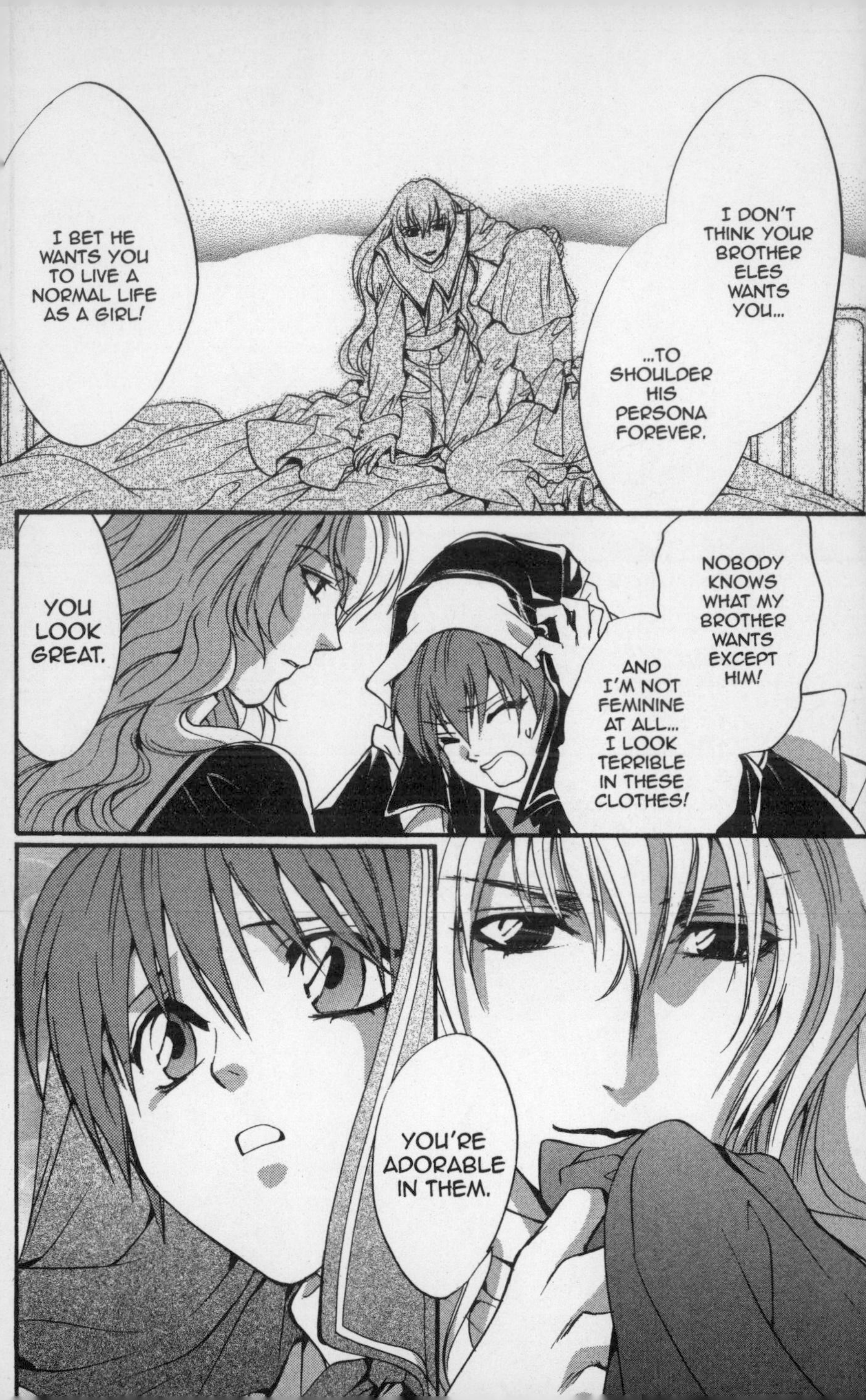
I DON'T THINK YOUR BROTHER ELES WANTS YOU...
...TO SHOULDER HIS PERSONA FOREVER.
I BET HE WANTS YOU TO LIVE A NORMAL LIFE AS A GIRL!
NOBODY KNOWS WHAT MY BROTHER WANTS EXCEPT HIM!
AND I'M NOT FEMININE AT ALL... I LOOK TERRIBLE IN THESE CLOTHES!
YOU LOOK GREAT.
YOU'RE ADORABLE IN THEM.

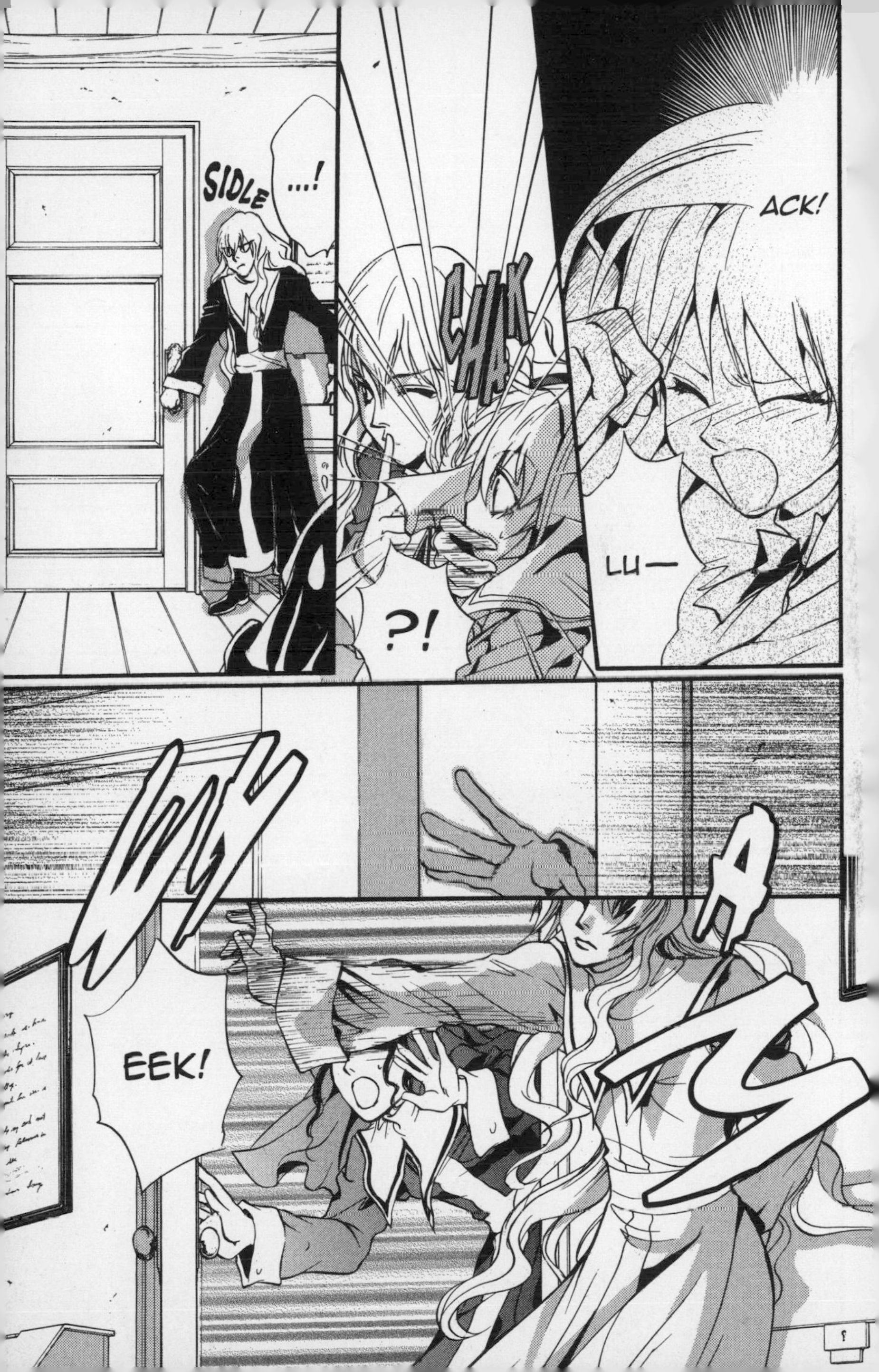
ACK!
LU—
CHAK
?!
SIDLE
...!
EEK!

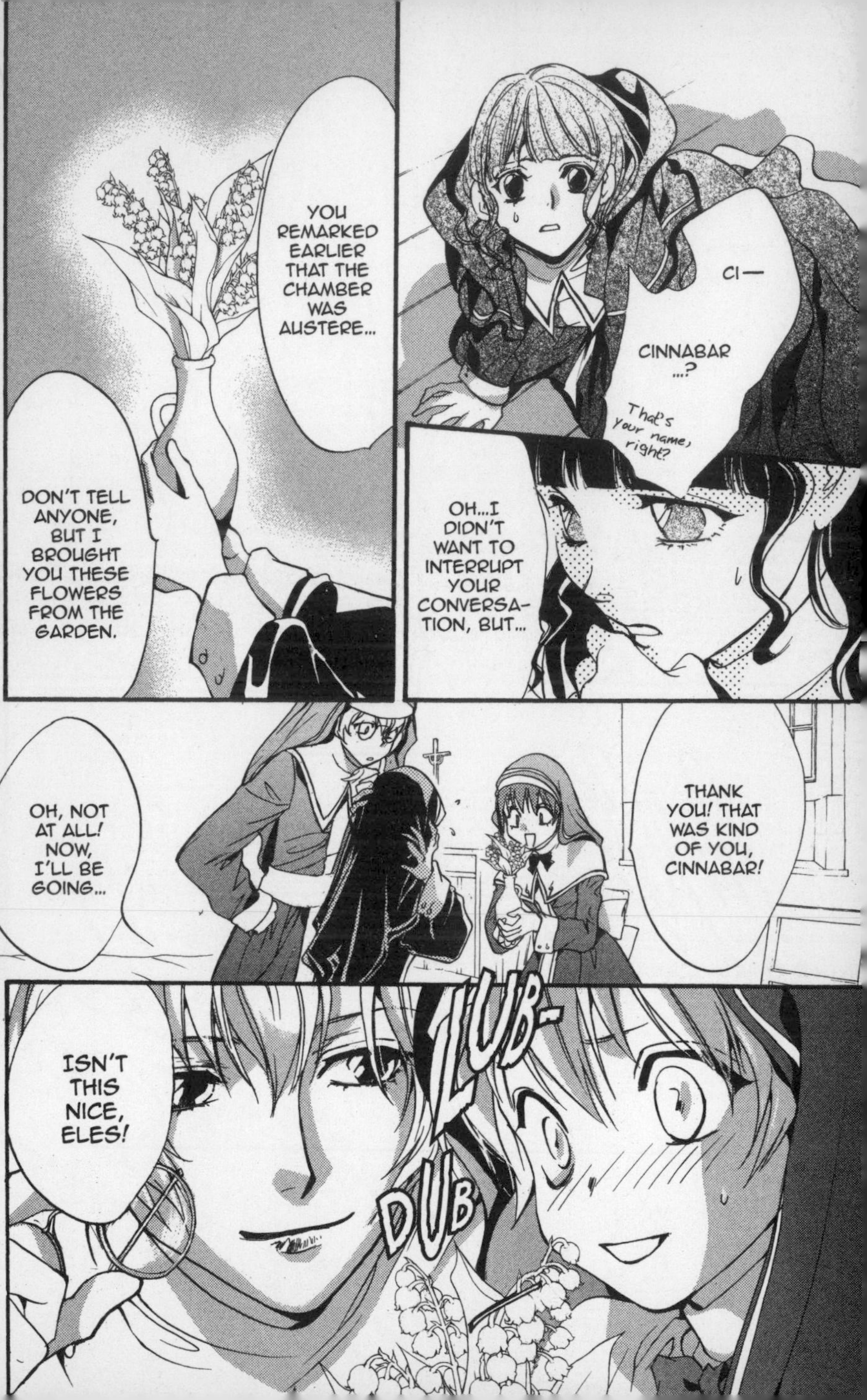
CI—
CINNABAR ...?
That's your name, right?
OH...I DIDN'T WANT TO INTERRUPT YOUR CONVERSATION, BUT...
YOU REMARKED EARLIER THAT THE CHAMBER WAS AUSTERE...
DON'T TELL ANYONE, BUT I BROUGHT YOU THESE FLOWERS FROM THE GARDEN.
THANK YOU! THAT WAS KIND OF YOU, CINNABAR!
OH, NOT AT ALL! NOW, I'LL BE GOING...
ZUB-
DUB
ISN'T THIS NICE, ELES!

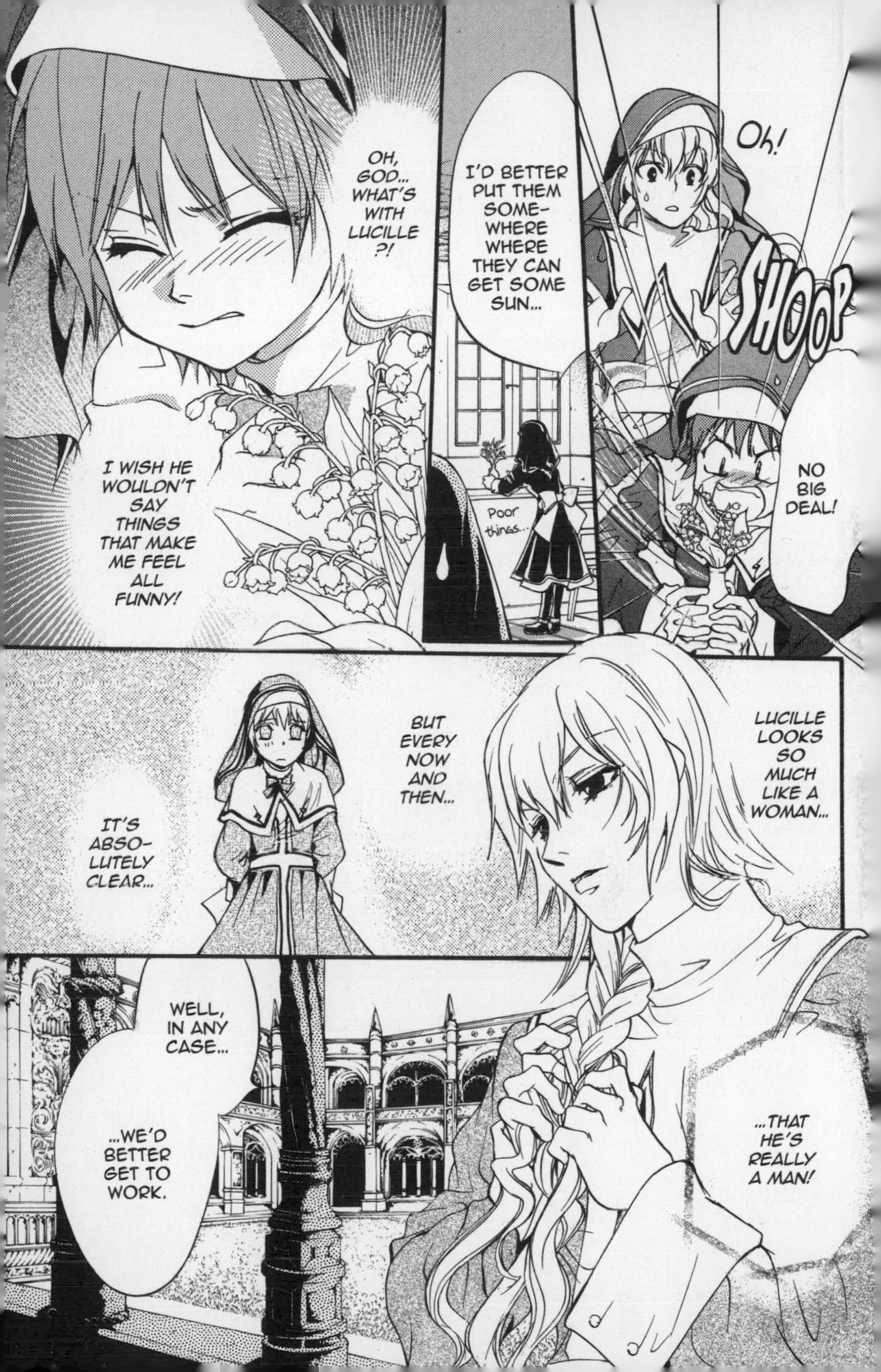

Oh!
SHOOP
NO BIG DEAL!
I'D BETTER PUT THEM SOME-WHERE WHERE THEY CAN GET SOME SUN...
Poor things...
OH, GOD... WHAT'S WITH LUCILLE ?!
I WISH HE WOULDN'T SAY THINGS THAT MAKE ME FEEL ALL FUNNY!
LUCILLE LOOKS SO MUCH LIKE A WOMAN...
BUT EVERY NOW AND THEN...
IT'S ABSO-LUTELY CLEAR...
...THAT HE'S REALLY A MAN!
WELL, IN ANY CASE...
...WE'D BETTER GET TO WORK.

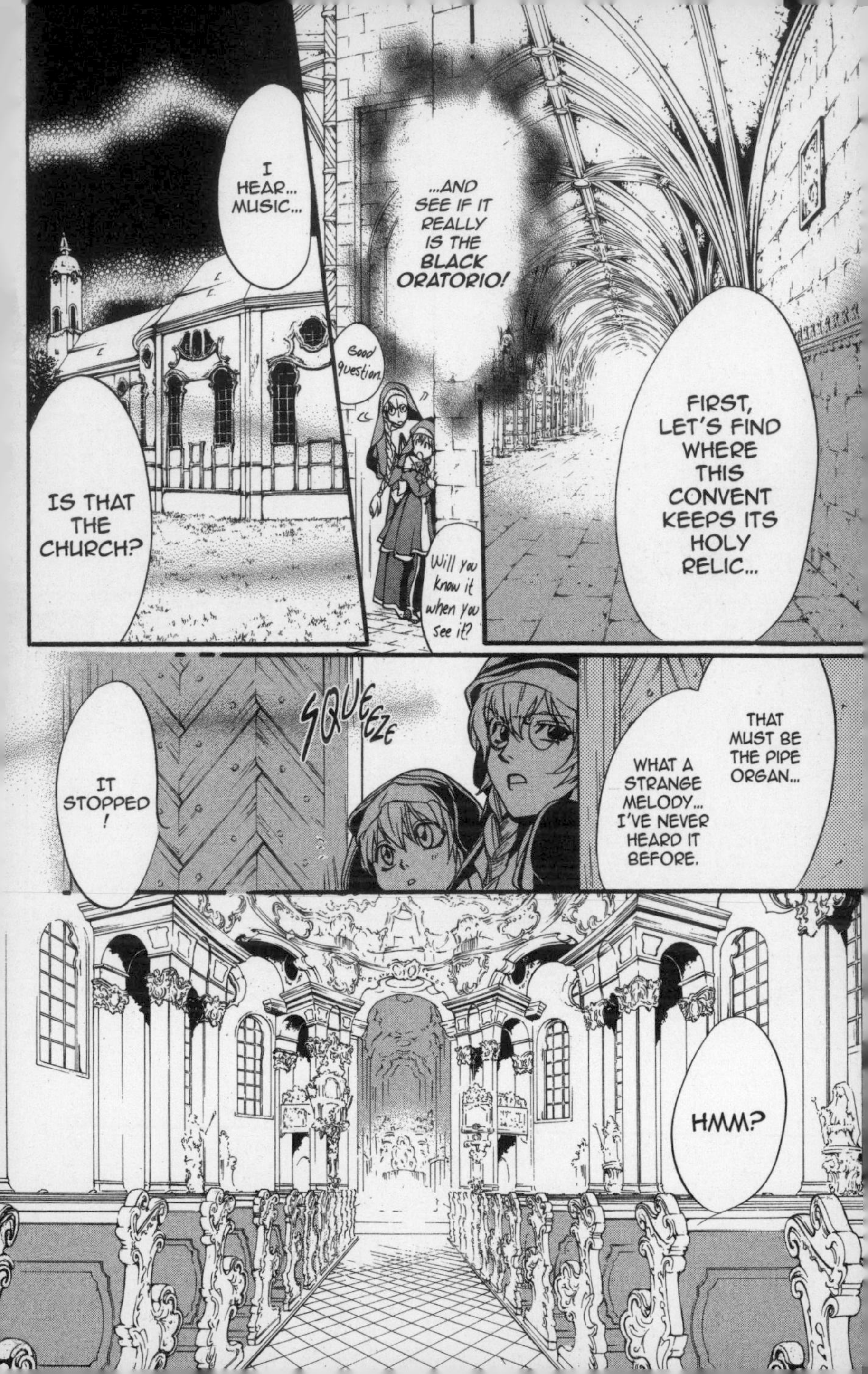
FIRST, LET'S FIND WHERE THIS CONVENT KEEPS ITS HOLY RELIC...
...AND SEE IF IT REALLY IS THE BLACK ORATORIO!
Will you know it when you see it?
Good question.
I HEAR... MUSIC...
IS THAT THE CHURCH?
THAT MUST BE THE PIPE ORGAN...
WHAT A STRANGE MELODY... I'VE NEVER HEARD IT BEFORE.
SQUEEZE
IT STOPPED!
HMM?

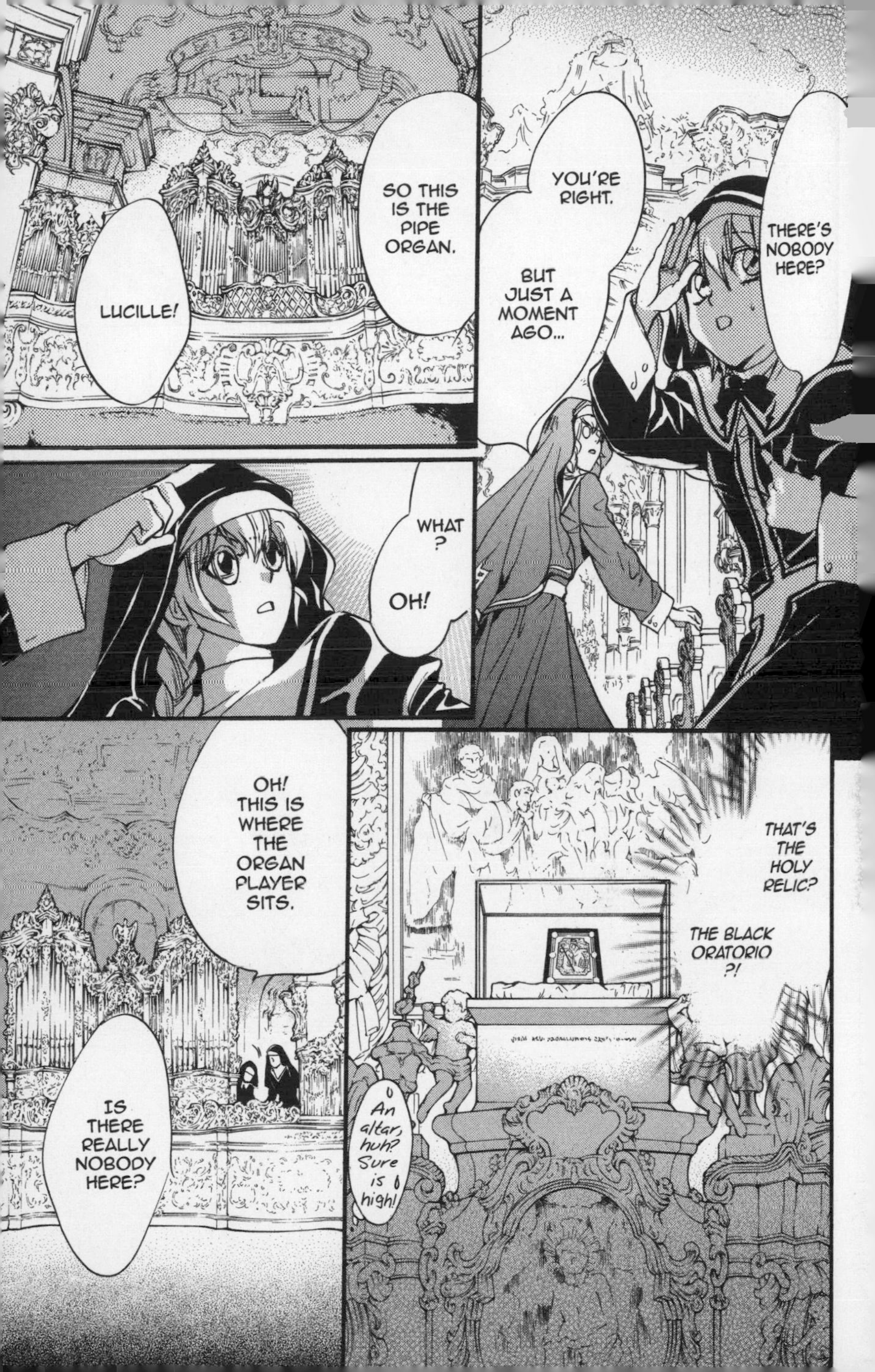
THERE'S NOBODY HERE?
YOU'RE RIGHT.
BUT JUST A MOMENT AGO...
SO THIS IS THE PIPE ORGAN.
LUCILLE!
WHAT?
OH!
THAT'S THE HOLY RELIC?
THE BLACK ORATORIO?!
An altar, huh? Sure is high!
OH! THIS IS WHERE THE ORGAN PLAYER SITS.
IS THERE REALLY NOBODY HERE?

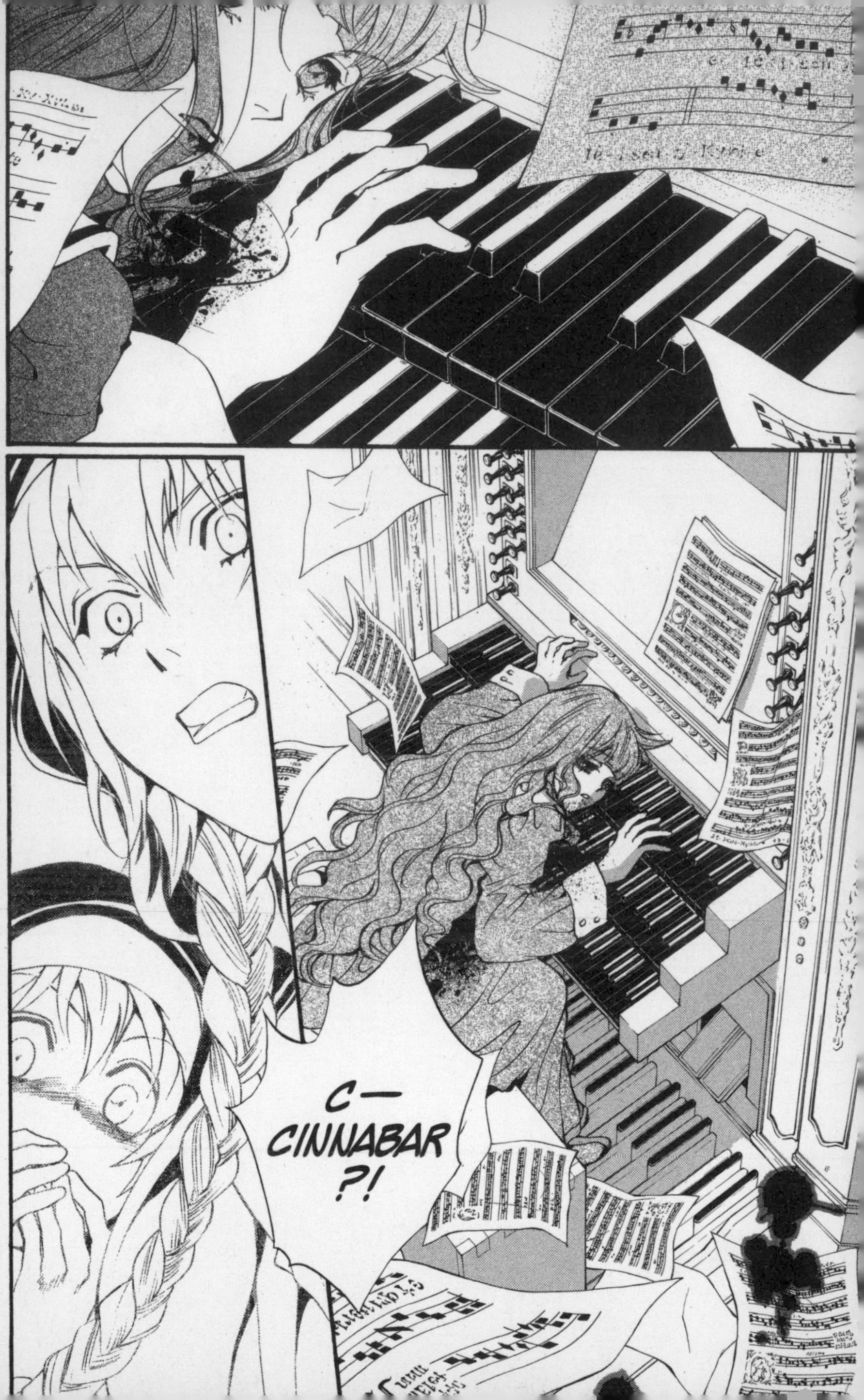
C— CINNABAR ?!

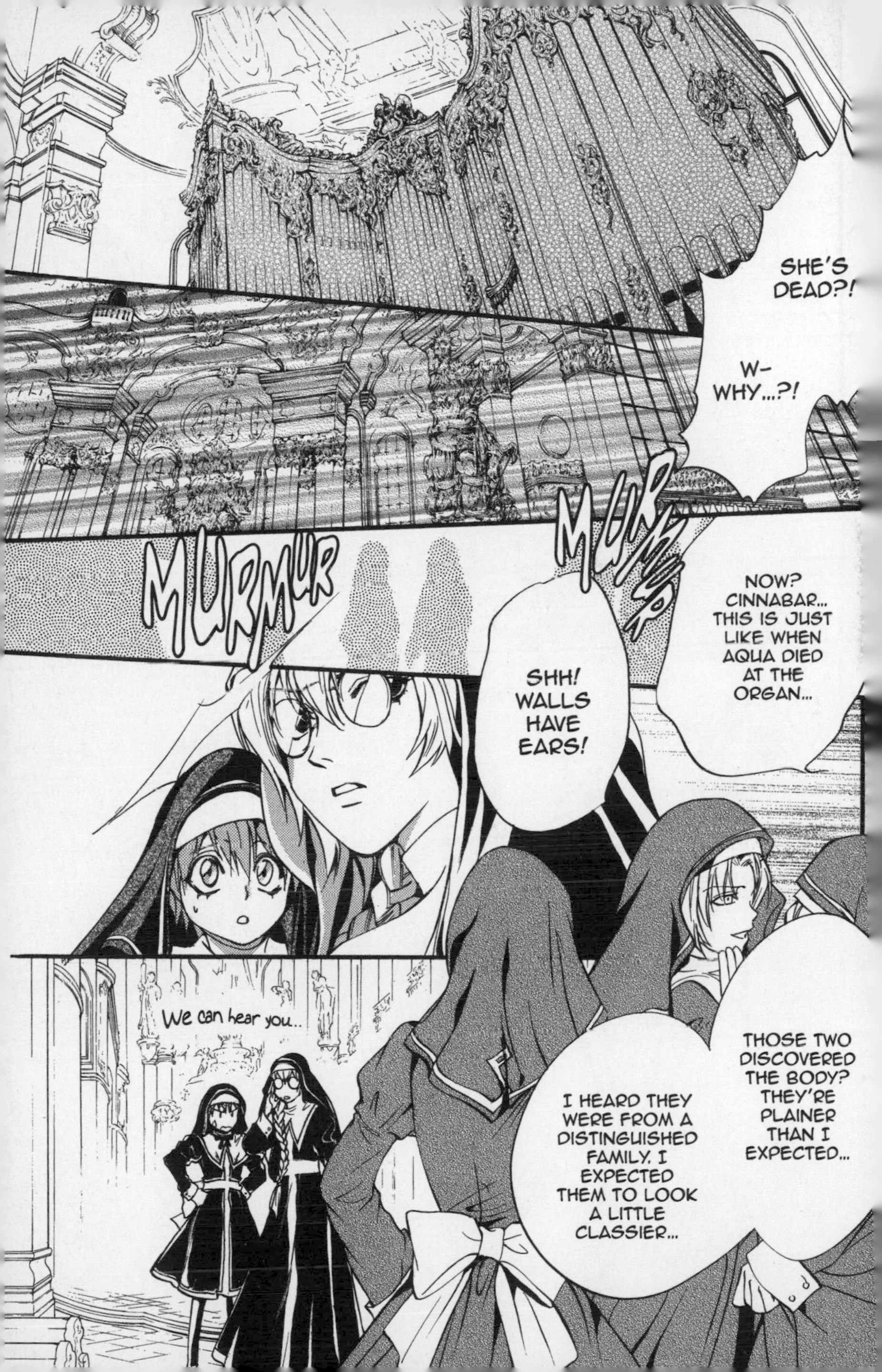
SHE'S DEAD?!
W-WHY...?!
MURMUR
MURMUR
NOW? CINNABAR... THIS IS JUST LIKE WHEN AQUA DIED AT THE ORGAN...
SHH! WALLS HAVE EARS!
THOSE TWO DISCOVERED THE BODY? THEY'RE PLAINER THAN I EXPECTED...
I HEARD THEY WERE FROM A DISTINGUISHED FAMILY. I EXPECTED THEM TO LOOK A LITTLE CLASSIER...
We can hear you..

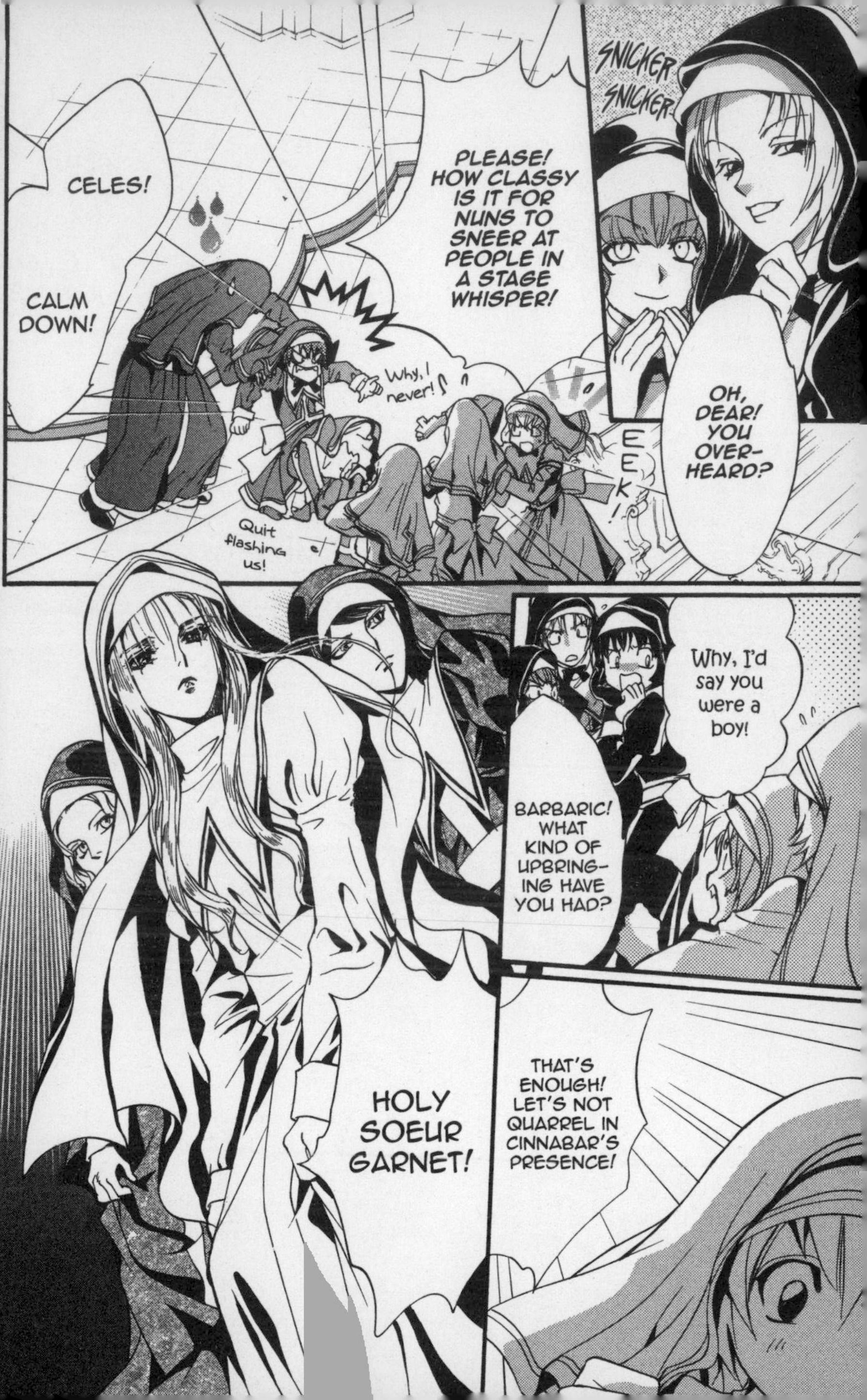
SNICKER SNICKER
OH, DEAR! YOU OVER-HEARD?
PLEASE! HOW CLASSY IS IT FOR NUNS TO SNEER AT PEOPLE IN A STAGE WHISPER!
CELES!
EEK!
Why, I never!
CALM DOWN!
Quit flashing us!
Why, I'd say you were a boy!
BARBARIC! WHAT KIND OF UPBRING-ING HAVE YOU HAD?
THAT'S ENOUGH! LET'S NOT QUARREL IN CINNABAR'S PRESENCE!
HOLY SOEUR GARNET!

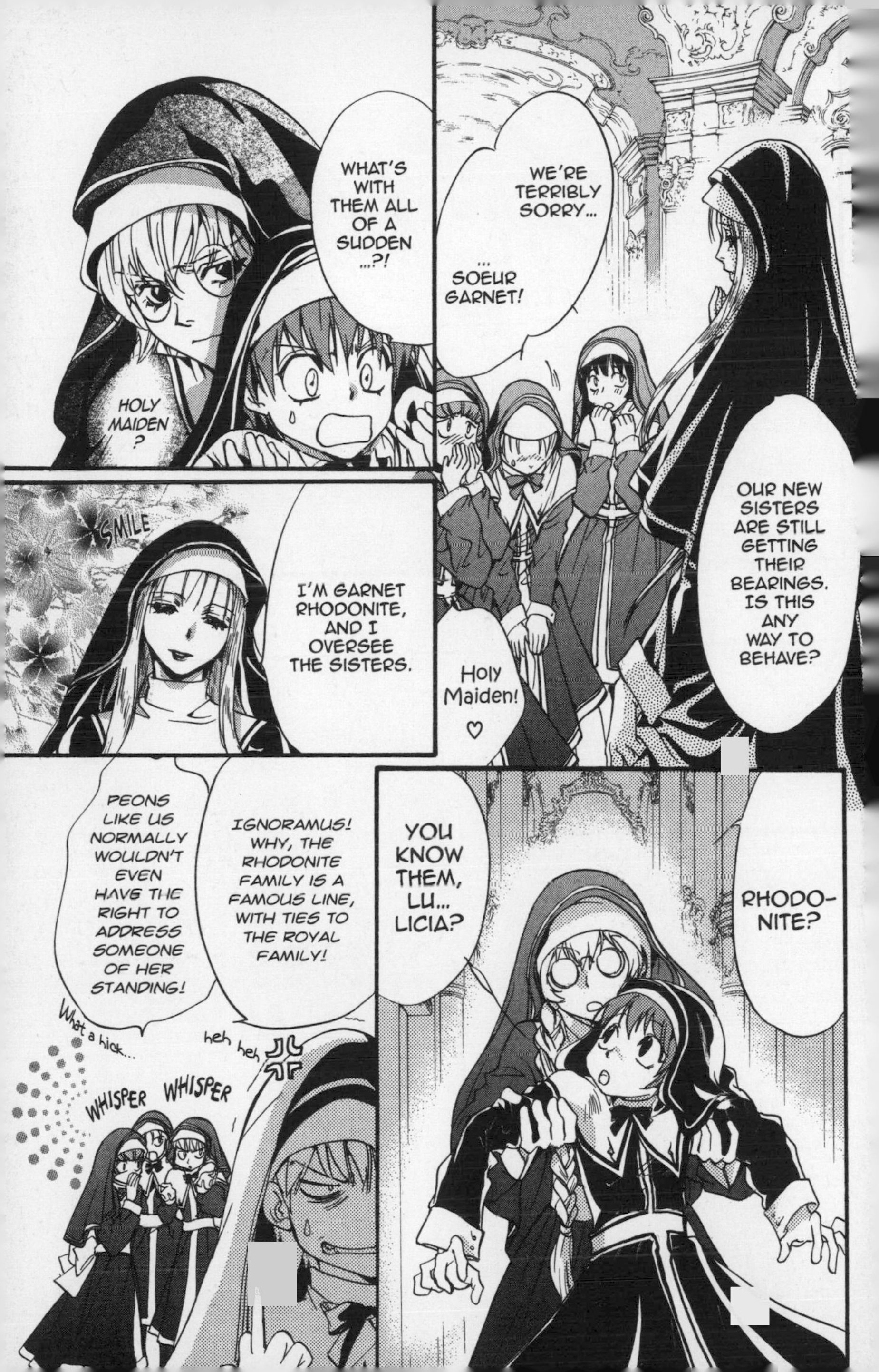
WE'RE TERRIBLY SORRY... ...SOEUR GARNET!
OUR NEW SISTERS ARE STILL GETTING THEIR BEARINGS. IS THIS ANY WAY TO BEHAVE?
Holy Maiden! ♡
WHAT'S WITH THEM ALL OF A SUDDEN ...?!
HOLY MAIDEN?
SMILE
I'M GARNET RHODONITE, AND I OVERSEE THE SISTERS.
RHODO-NITE?
YOU KNOW THEM, LU... LICIA?
IGNORAMUS! WHY, THE RHODONITE FAMILY IS A FAMOUS LINE, WITH TIES TO THE ROYAL FAMILY!
PEONS LIKE US NORMALLY WOULDN'T EVEN HAVE THE RIGHT TO ADDRESS SOMEONE OF HER STANDING!
What a hick...
heh heh
WHISPER WHISPER

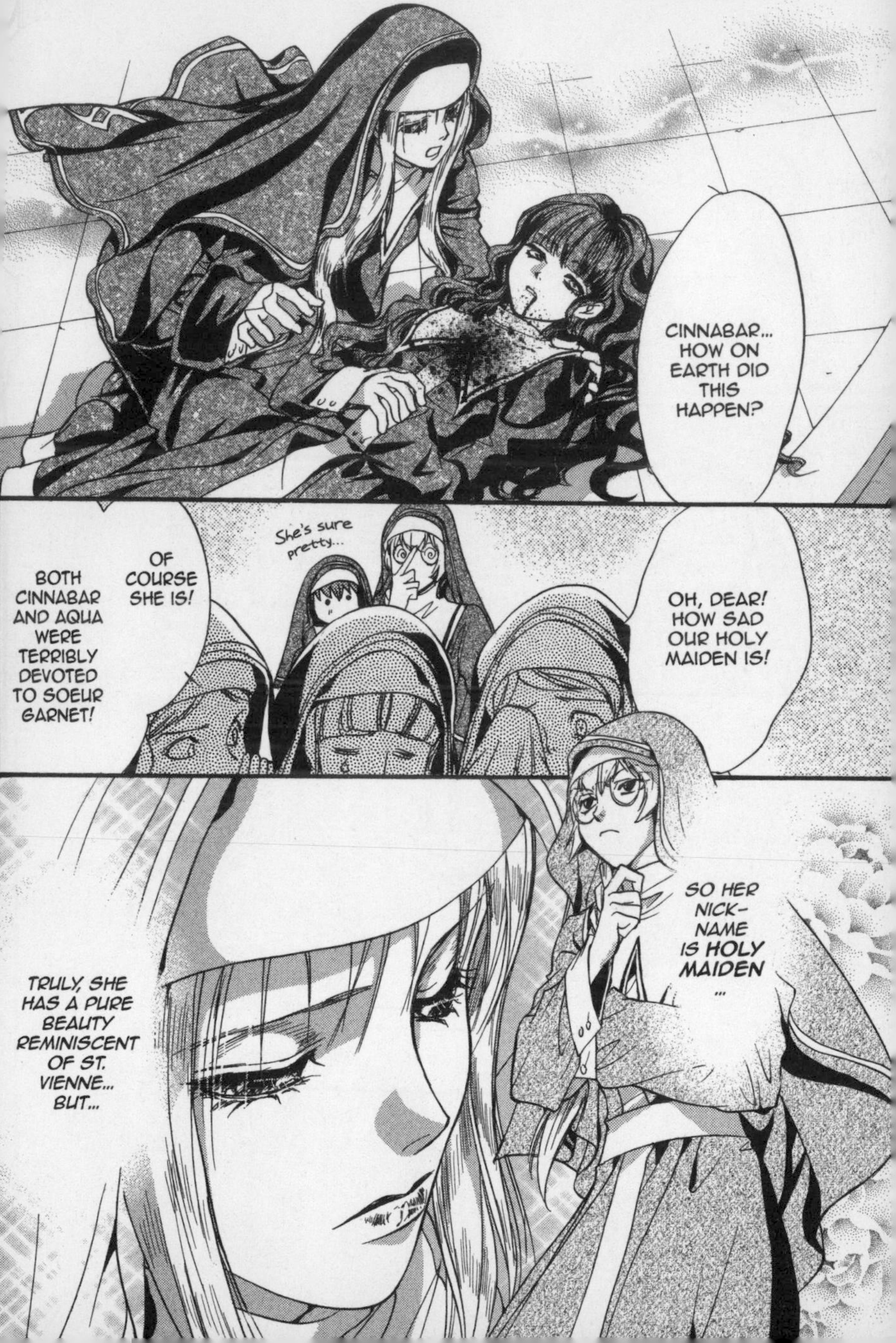
CINNABAR... HOW ON EARTH DID THIS HAPPEN?
OH, DEAR! HOW SAD OUR HOLY MAIDEN IS!
She's sure pretty...
OF COURSE SHE IS!
BOTH CINNABAR AND AQUA WERE TERRIBLY DEVOTED TO SOEUR GARNET!
SO HER NICK-NAME IS HOLY MAIDEN ...
TRULY, SHE HAS A PURE BEAUTY REMINISCENT OF ST. VIENNE... BUT...

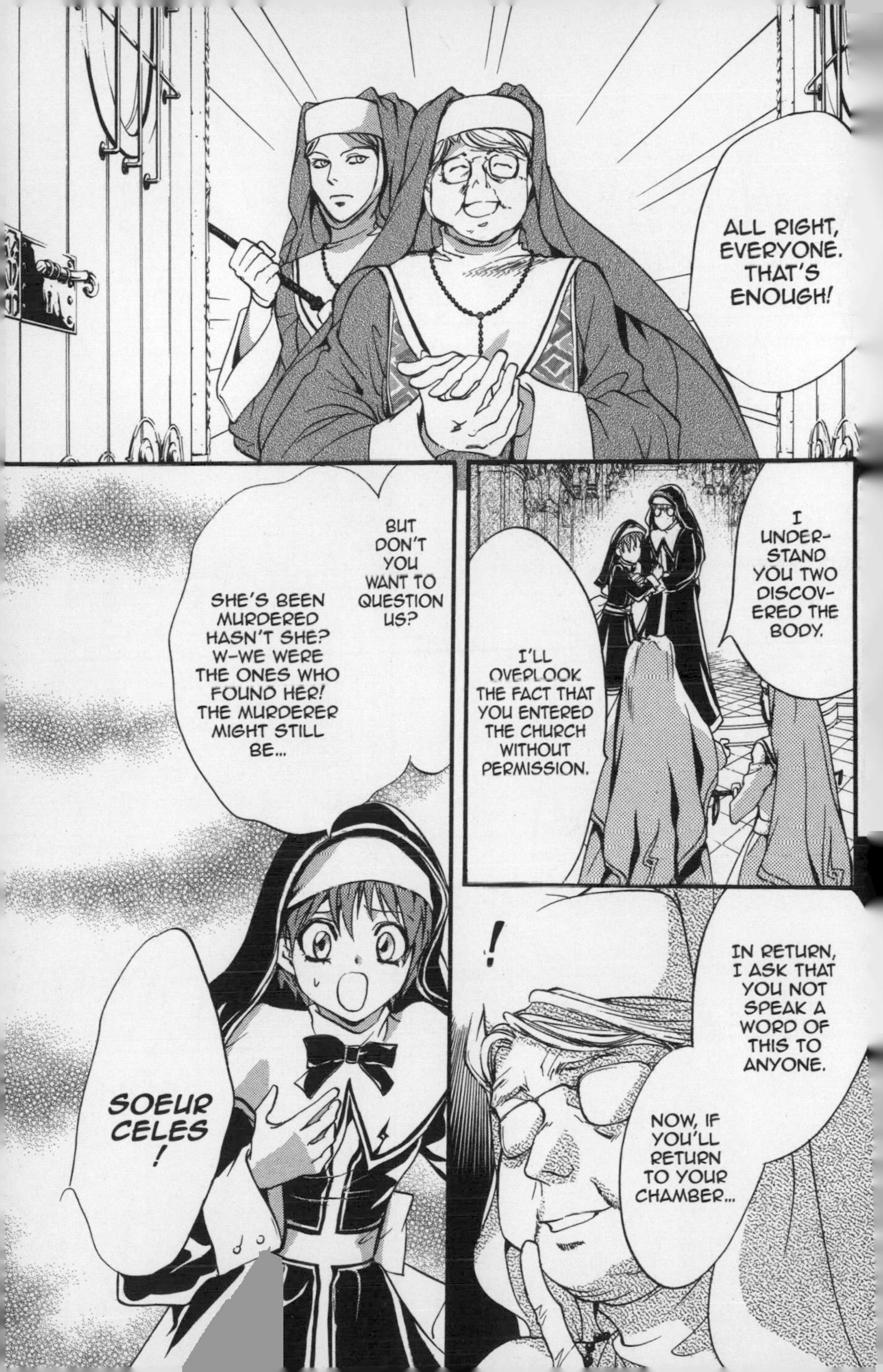
ALL RIGHT, EVERYONE. THAT'S ENOUGH!
I UNDER-STAND YOU TWO DISCOV-ERED THE BODY.
I'LL OVERLOOK THE FACT THAT YOU ENTERED THE CHURCH WITHOUT PERMISSION.
!
IN RETURN, I ASK THAT YOU NOT SPEAK A WORD OF THIS TO ANYONE.
NOW, IF YOU'LL RETURN TO YOUR CHAMBER...
BUT DON'T YOU WANT TO QUESTION US?
SHE'S BEEN MURDERED HASN'T SHE? W-WE WERE THE ONES WHO FOUND HER! THE MURDERER MIGHT STILL BE...
SOEUR CELES!

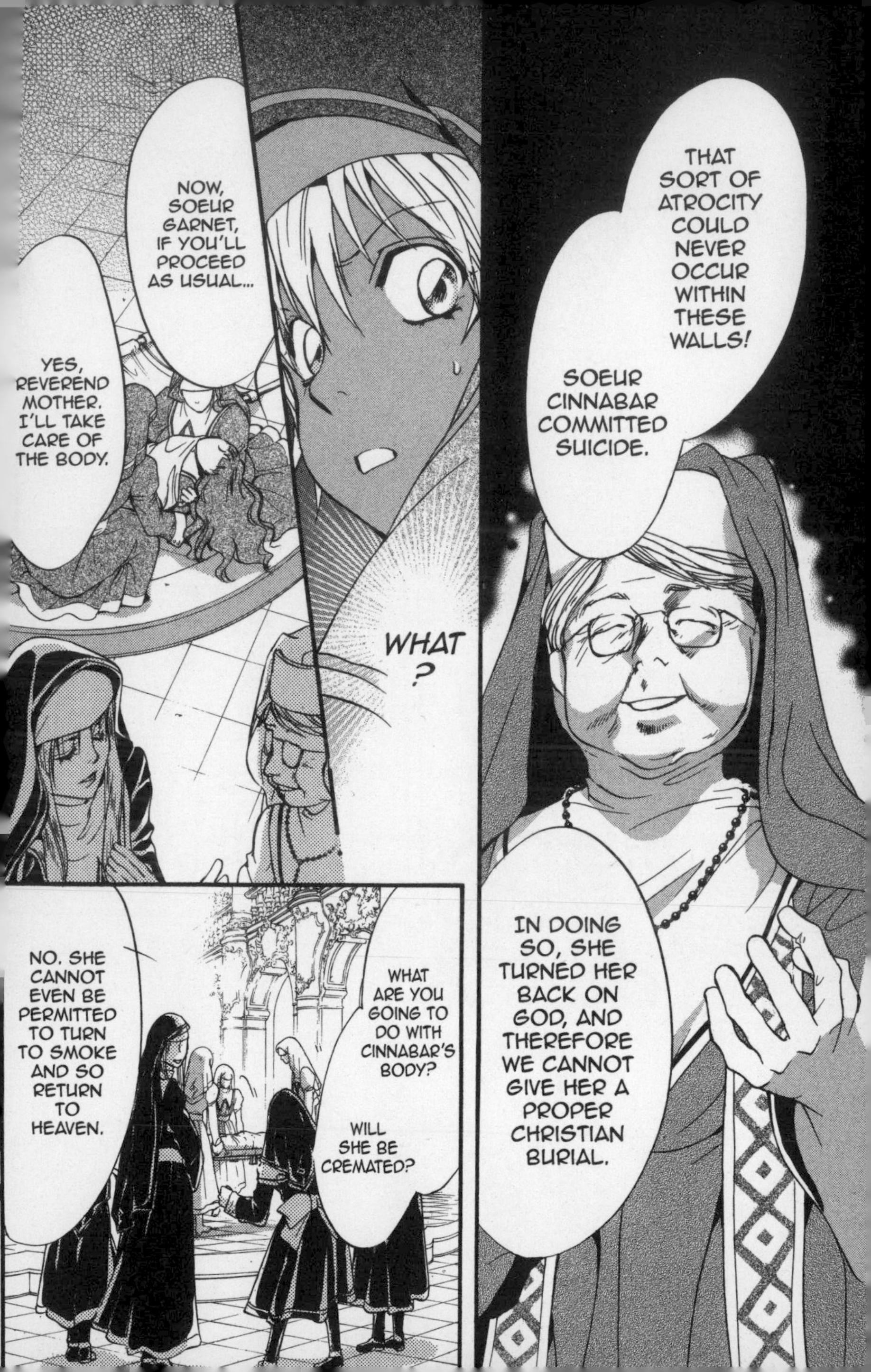
THAT SORT OF ATROCITY COULD NEVER OCCUR WITHIN THESE WALLS!
SOEUR CINNABAR COMMITTED SUICIDE.
IN DOING SO, SHE TURNED HER BACK ON GOD, AND THEREFORE WE CANNOT GIVE HER A PROPER CHRISTIAN BURIAL.
WHAT?
NOW, SOEUR GARNET, IF YOU'LL PROCEED AS USUAL...
YES, REVEREND MOTHER. I'LL TAKE CARE OF THE BODY.
WHAT ARE YOU GOING TO DO WITH CINNABAR'S BODY?
WILL SHE BE CREMATED?
NO. SHE CANNOT EVEN BE PERMITTED TO TURN TO SMOKE AND SO RETURN TO HEAVEN.

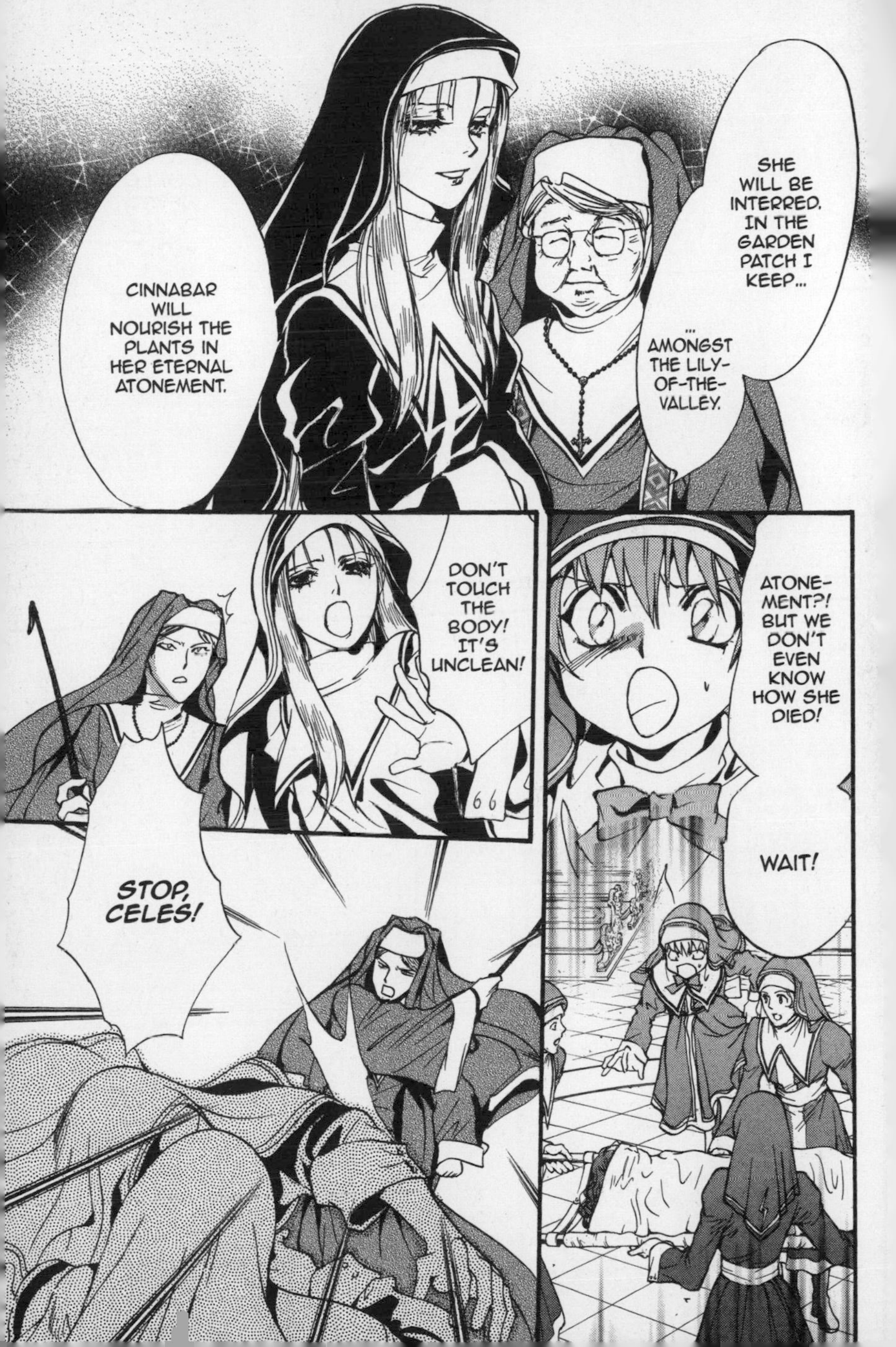
SHE WILL BE INTERRED. IN THE GARDEN PATCH I KEEP...
...AMONGST THE LILY-OF-THE-VALLEY.
CINNABAR WILL NOURISH THE PLANTS IN HER ETERNAL ATONEMENT.
ATONEMENT?! BUT WE DON'T EVEN KNOW HOW SHE DIED!
WAIT!
DON'T TOUCH THE BODY! IT'S UNCLEAN!
STOP, CELES!

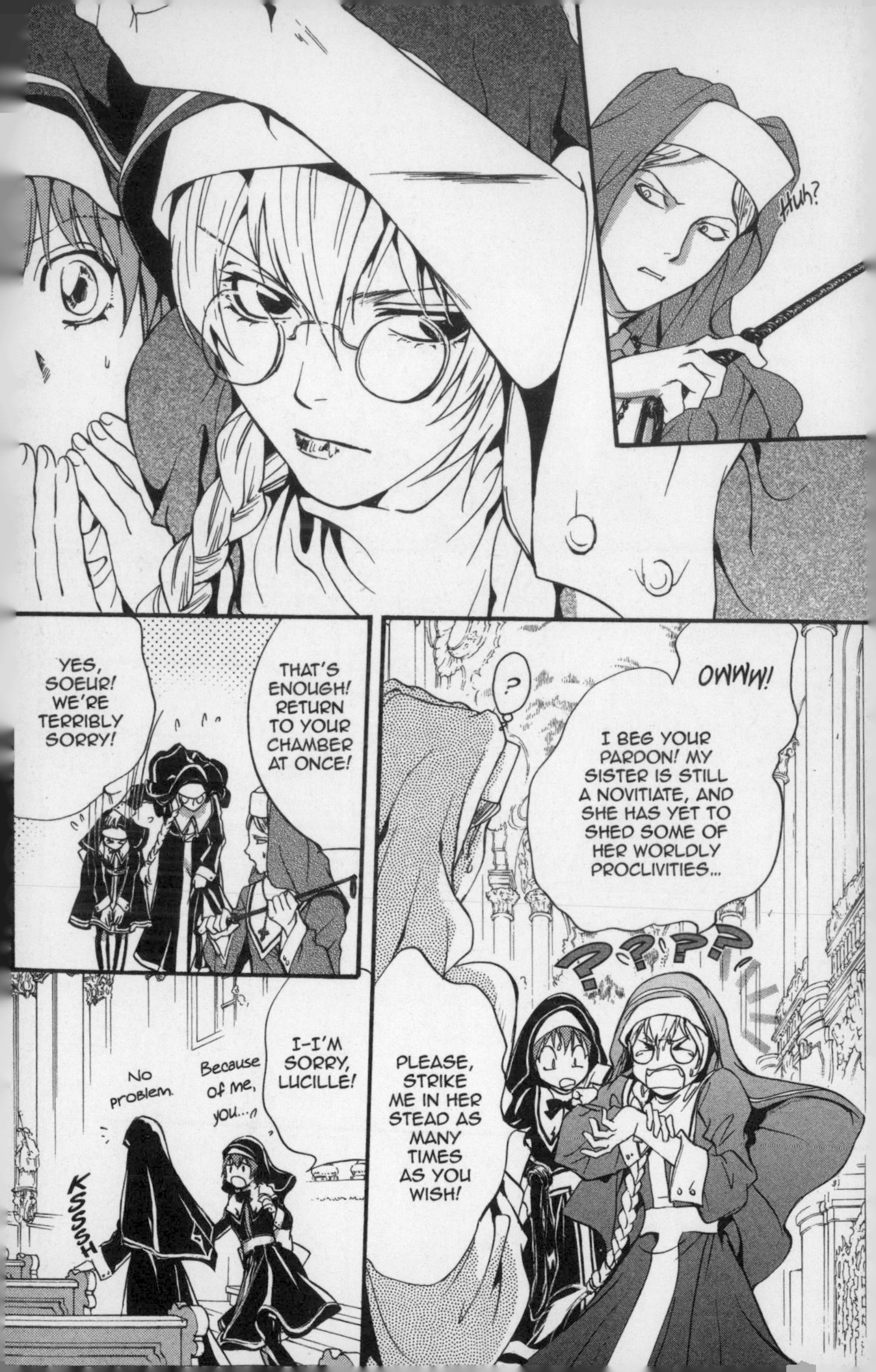
Huh?
OWWW!
?
I BEG YOUR PARDON! MY SISTER IS STILL A NOVITIATE, AND SHE HAS YET TO SHED SOME OF HER WORLDLY PROCLIVITIES...
?????
PLEASE, STRIKE ME IN HER STEAD AS MANY TIMES AS YOU WISH!
THAT'S ENOUGH! RETURN TO YOUR CHAMBER AT ONCE!
YES, SOEUR! WE'RE TERRIBLY SORRY!
I-I'M SORRY, LUCILLE!
Because of me, you...
No problem.
KSSSH

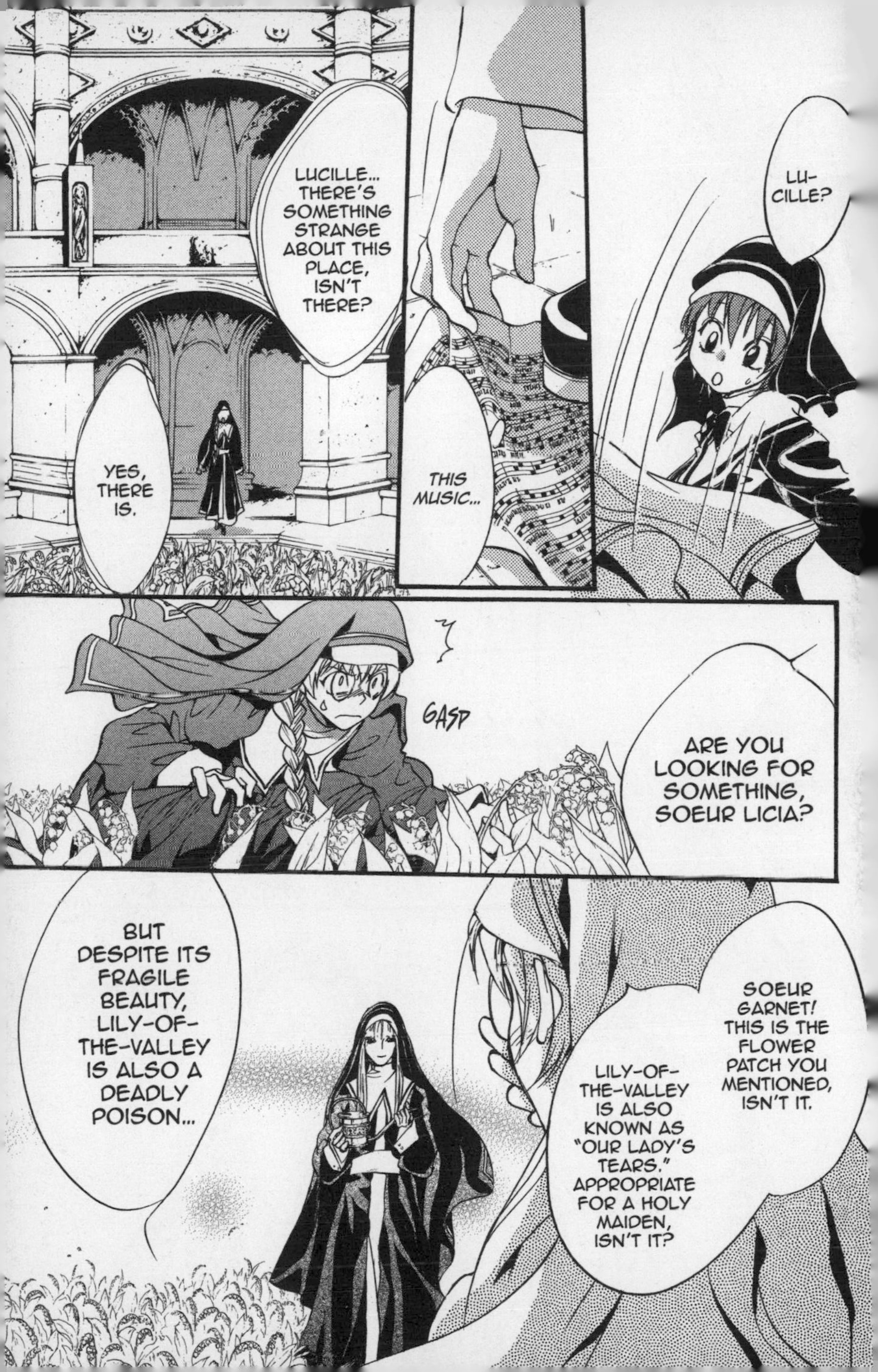
LU-CILLE?
THIS MUSIC...
LUCILLE... THERE'S SOMETHING STRANGE ABOUT THIS PLACE, ISN'T THERE?
YES, THERE IS.
ARE YOU LOOKING FOR SOMETHING, SOEUR LICIA?
GASP
SOEUR GARNET! THIS IS THE FLOWER PATCH YOU MENTIONED, ISN'T IT.
LILY-OF-THE-VALLEY IS ALSO KNOWN AS "OUR LADY'S TEARS." APPROPRIATE FOR A HOLY MAIDEN, ISN'T IT?
BUT DESPITE ITS FRAGILE BEAUTY, LILY-OF-THE-VALLEY IS ALSO A DEADLY POISON...

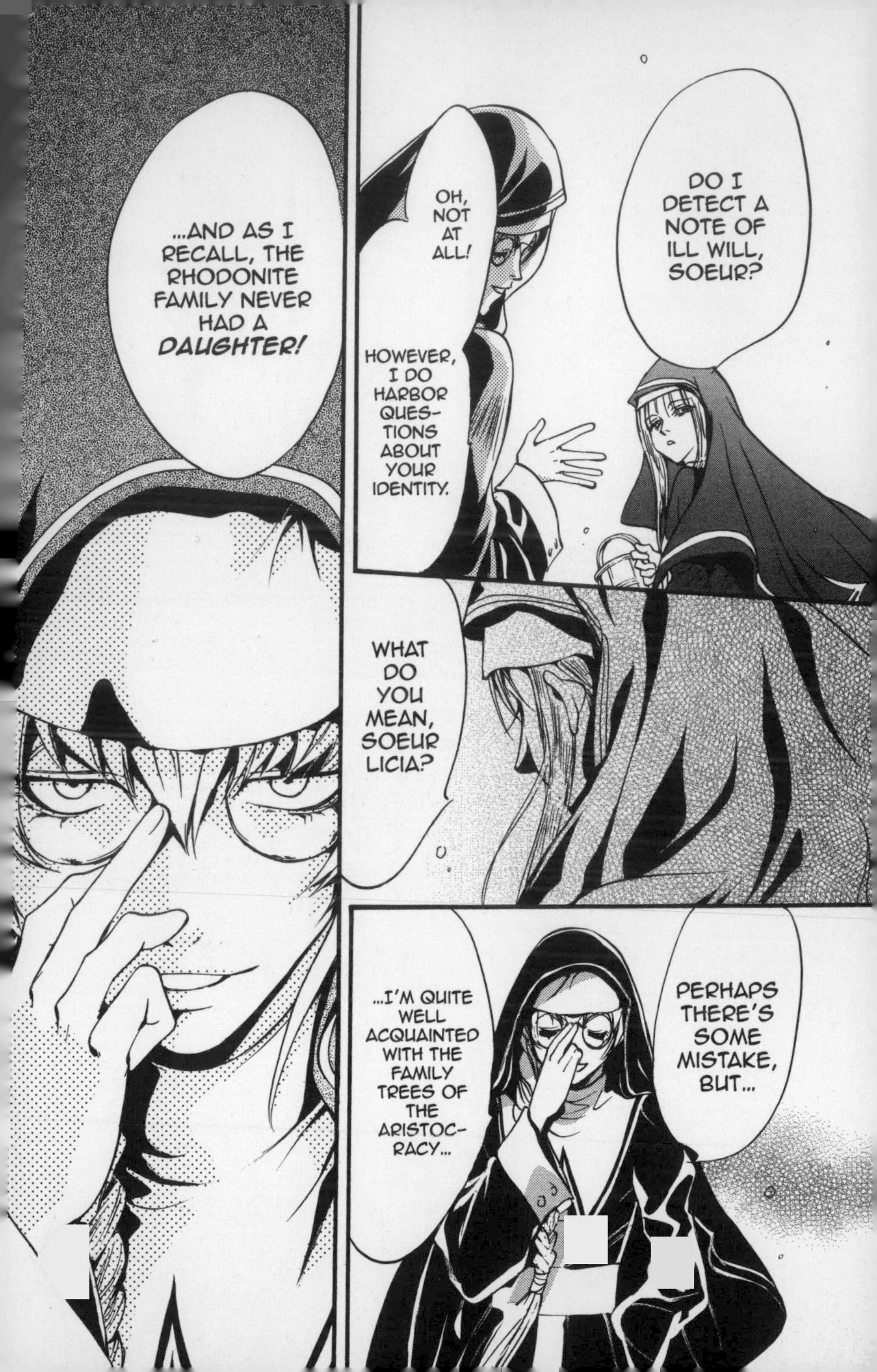
DO I DETECT A NOTE OF ILL WILL, SOEUR?
OH, NOT AT ALL!
HOWEVER, I DO HARBOR QUES-TIONS ABOUT YOUR IDENTITY.
WHAT DO YOU MEAN, SOEUR LICIA?
PERHAPS THERE'S SOME MISTAKE, BUT...
...I'M QUITE WELL ACQUAINTED WITH THE FAMILY TREES OF THE ARISTOC-RACY...
...AND AS I RECALL, THE RHODONITE FAMILY NEVER HAD A *DAUGHTER!*

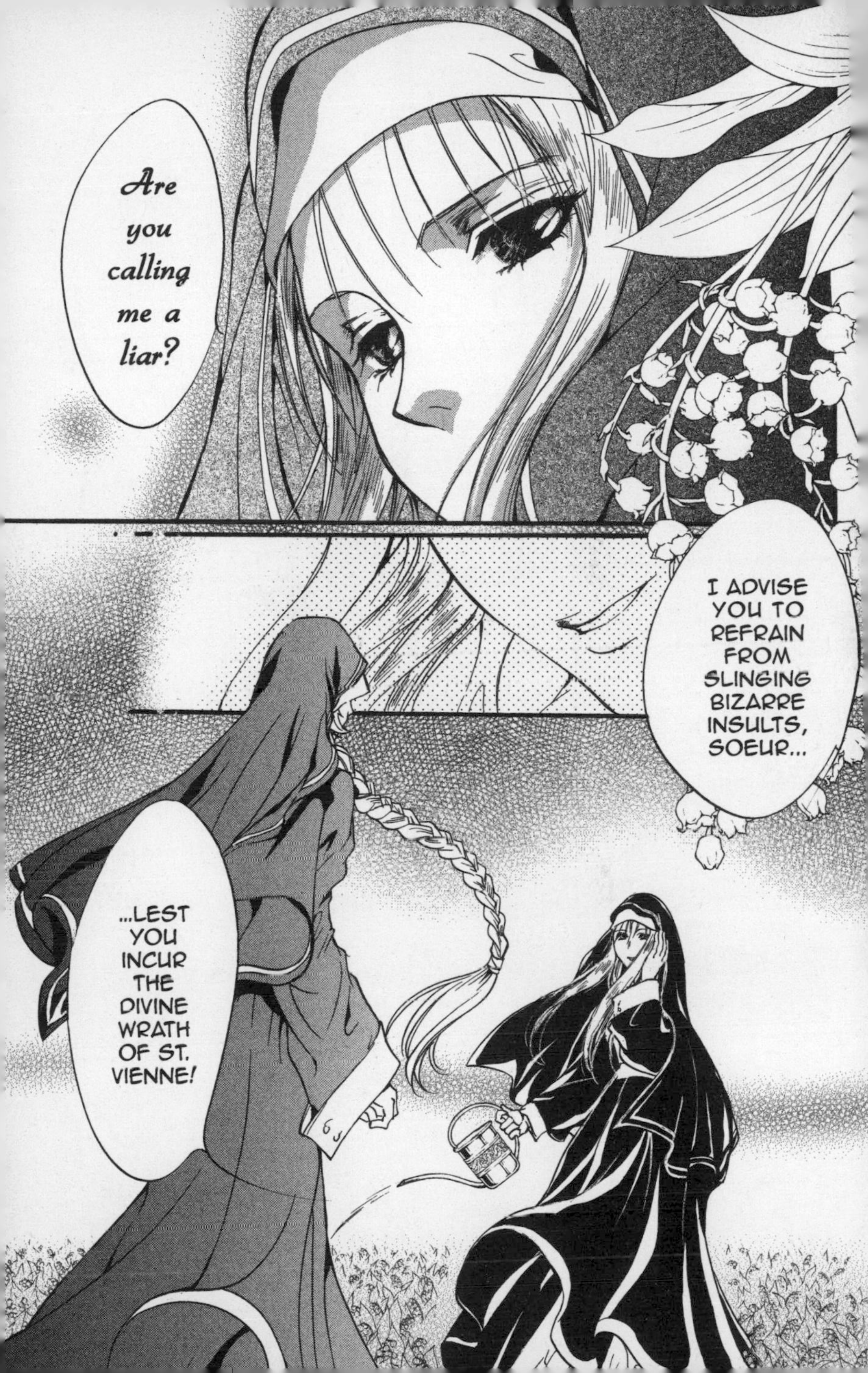
Are you calling me a liar?
I ADVISE YOU TO REFRAIN FROM SLINGING BIZARRE INSULTS, SOEUR...
...LEST YOU INCUR THE DIVINE WRATH OF ST. VIENNE!

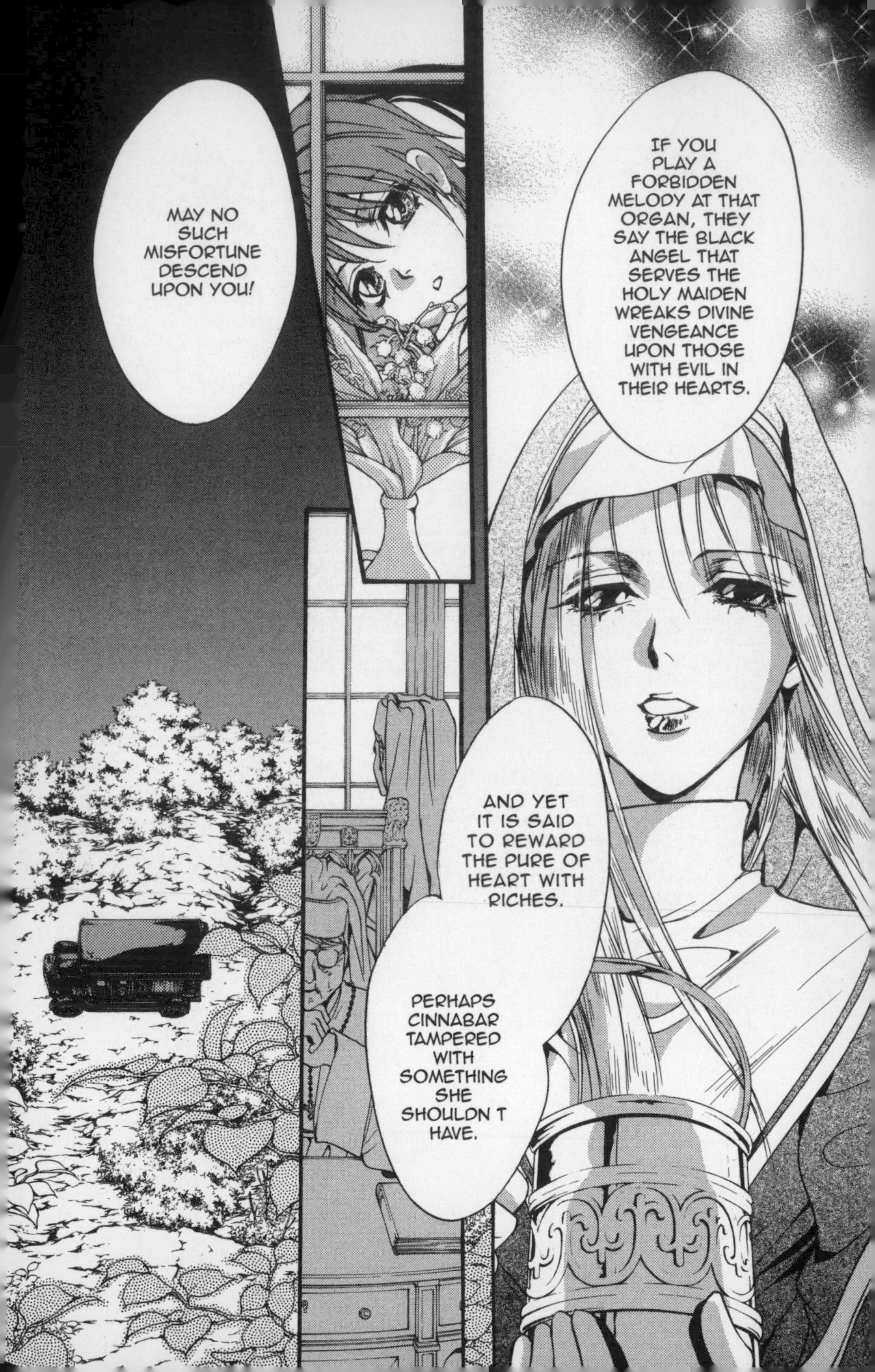
IF YOU PLAY A FORBIDDEN MELODY AT THAT ORGAN, THEY SAY THE BLACK ANGEL THAT SERVES THE HOLY MAIDEN WREAKS DIVINE VENGEANCE UPON THOSE WITH EVIL IN THEIR HEARTS.
AND YET IT IS SAID TO REWARD THE PURE OF HEART WITH RICHES.
PERHAPS CINNABAR TAMPERED WITH SOMETHING SHE SHOULDN T HAVE.
MAY NO SUCH MISFORTUNE DESCEND UPON YOU!

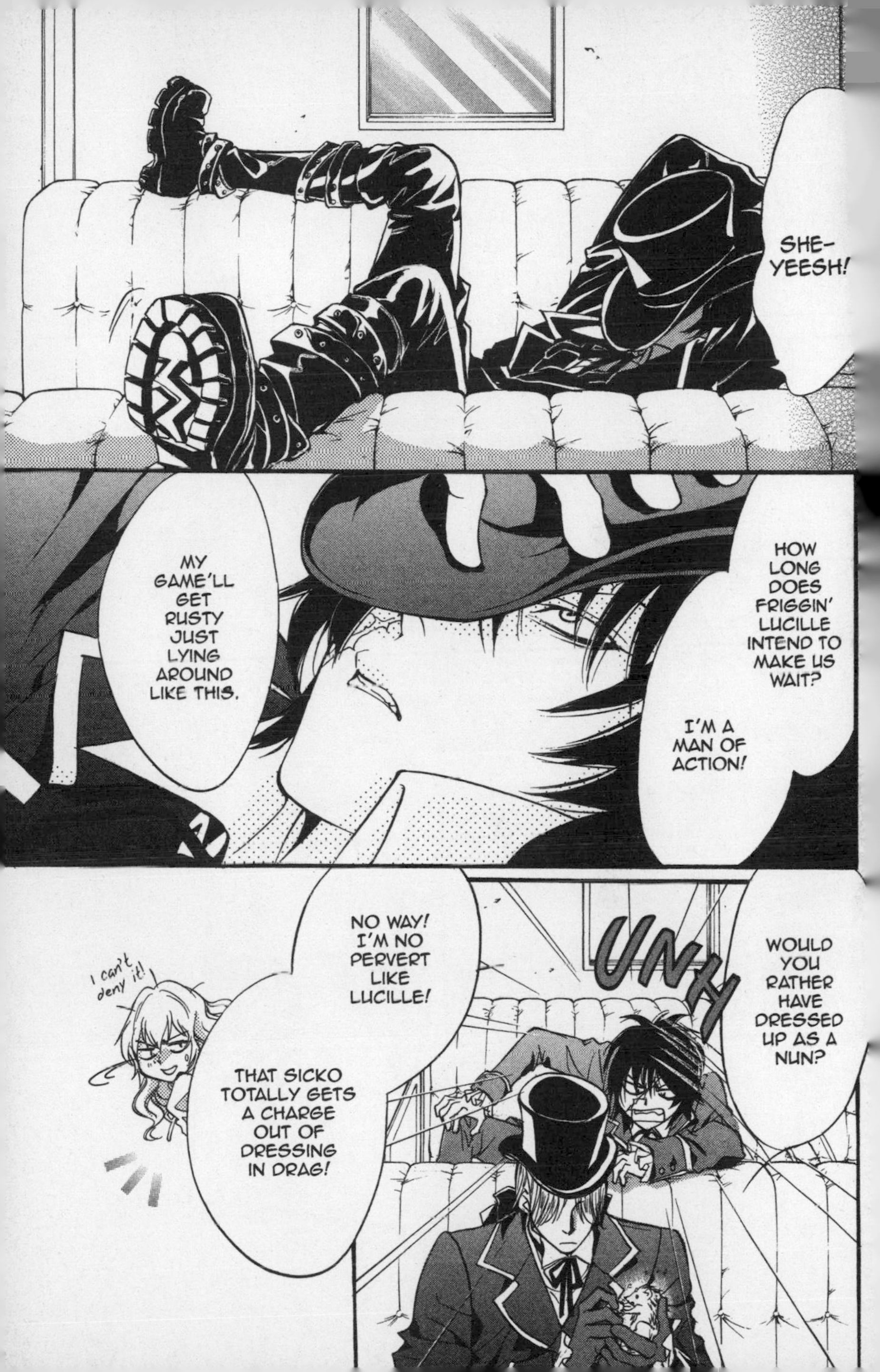
SHE-YEESH!
HOW LONG DOES FRIGGIN' LUCILLE INTEND TO MAKE US WAIT?
I'M A MAN OF ACTION!
MY GAME'LL GET RUSTY JUST LYING AROUND LIKE THIS.
WOULD YOU RATHER HAVE DRESSED UP AS A NUN?
UNH
NO WAY! I'M NO PERVERT LIKE LUCILLE!
THAT SICKO TOTALLY GETS A CHARGE OUT OF DRESSING IN DRAG!
I can't deny it!

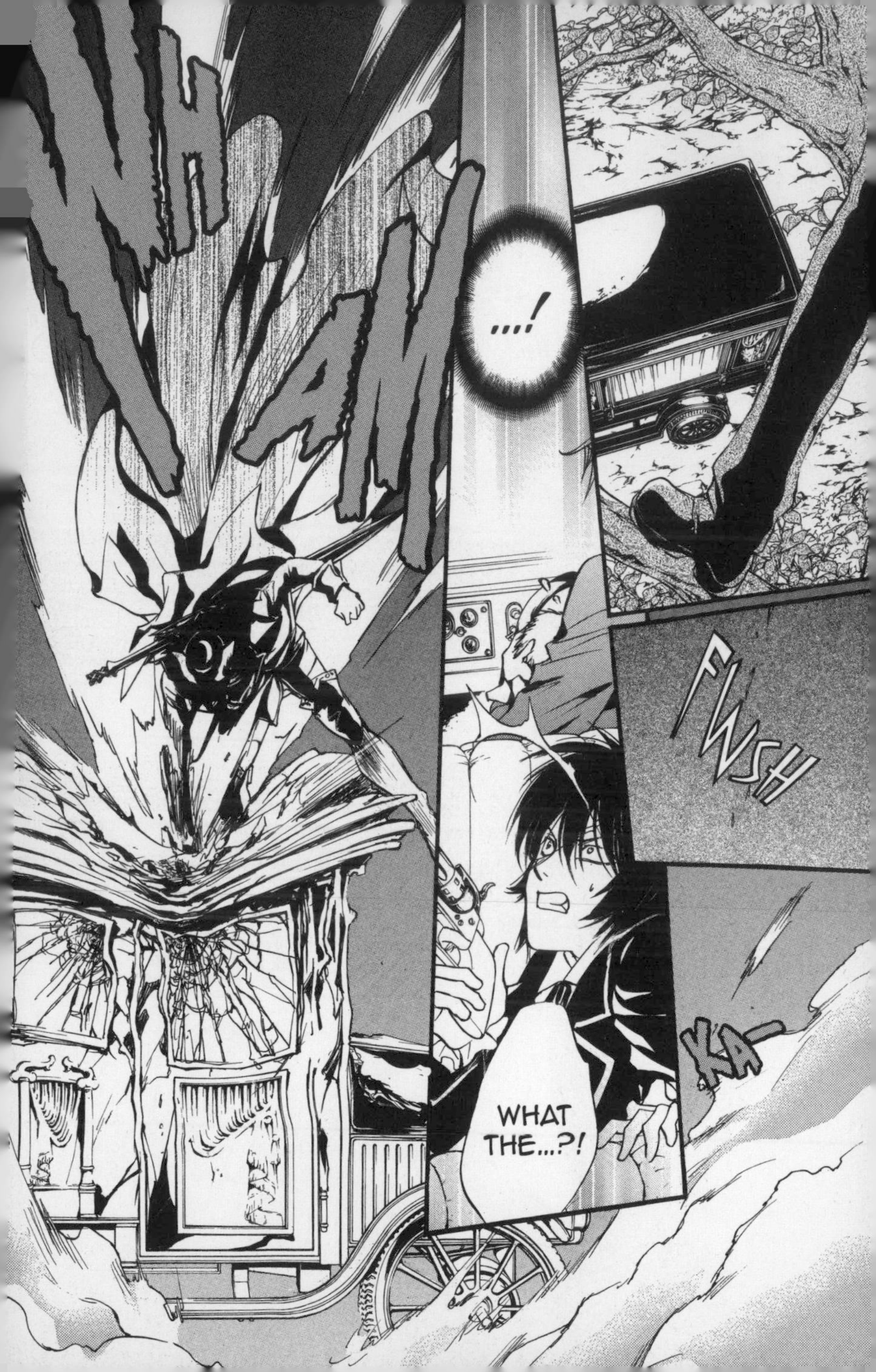
FWSH
KA-
...!
WHAT THE...?!
WHAM

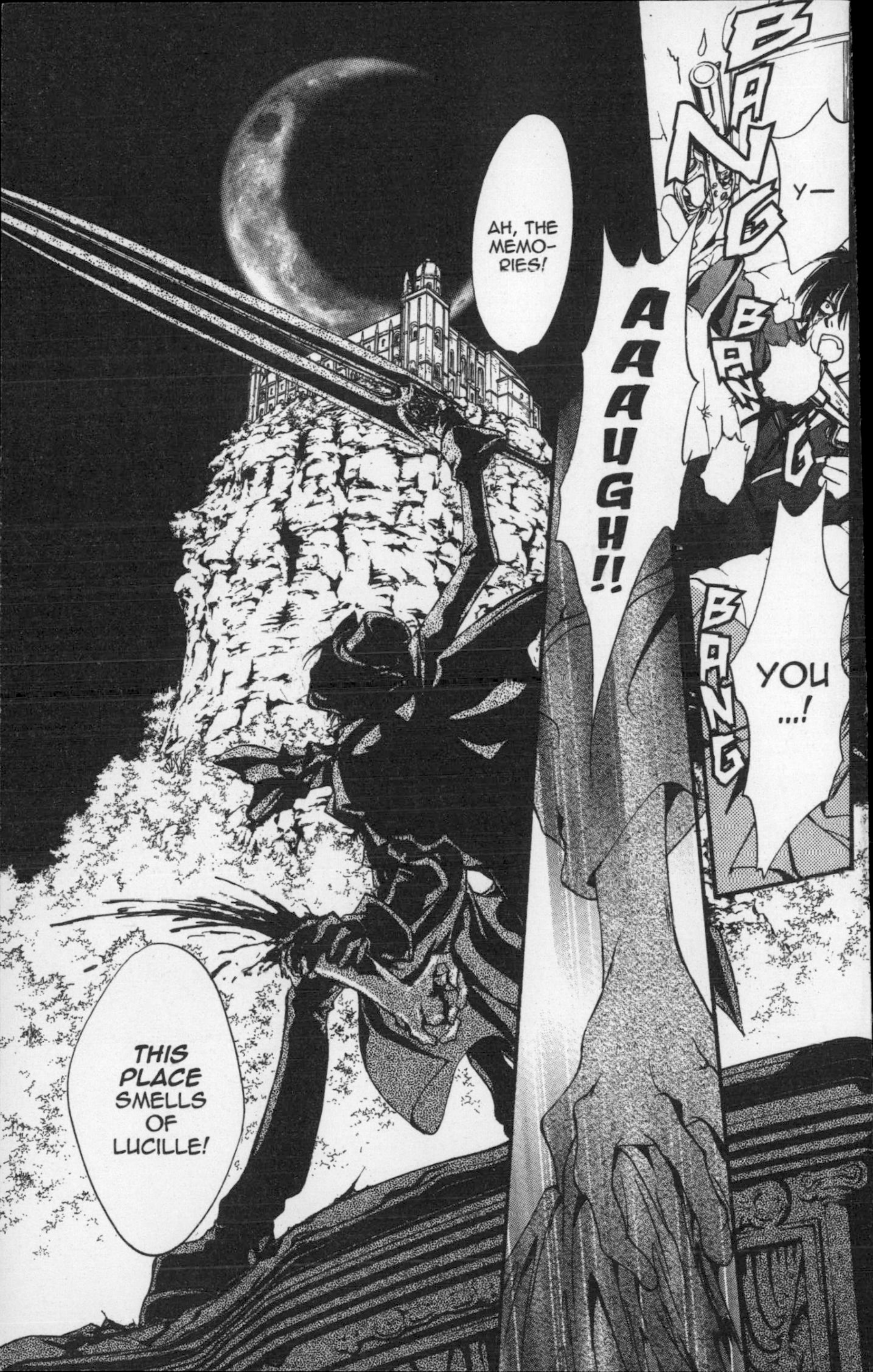
BANG
Y—
BANG
BANG
YOU ...!
AAAAUGH!!
AH, THE MEMO-RIES!
THIS PLACE SMELLS OF LUCILLE!

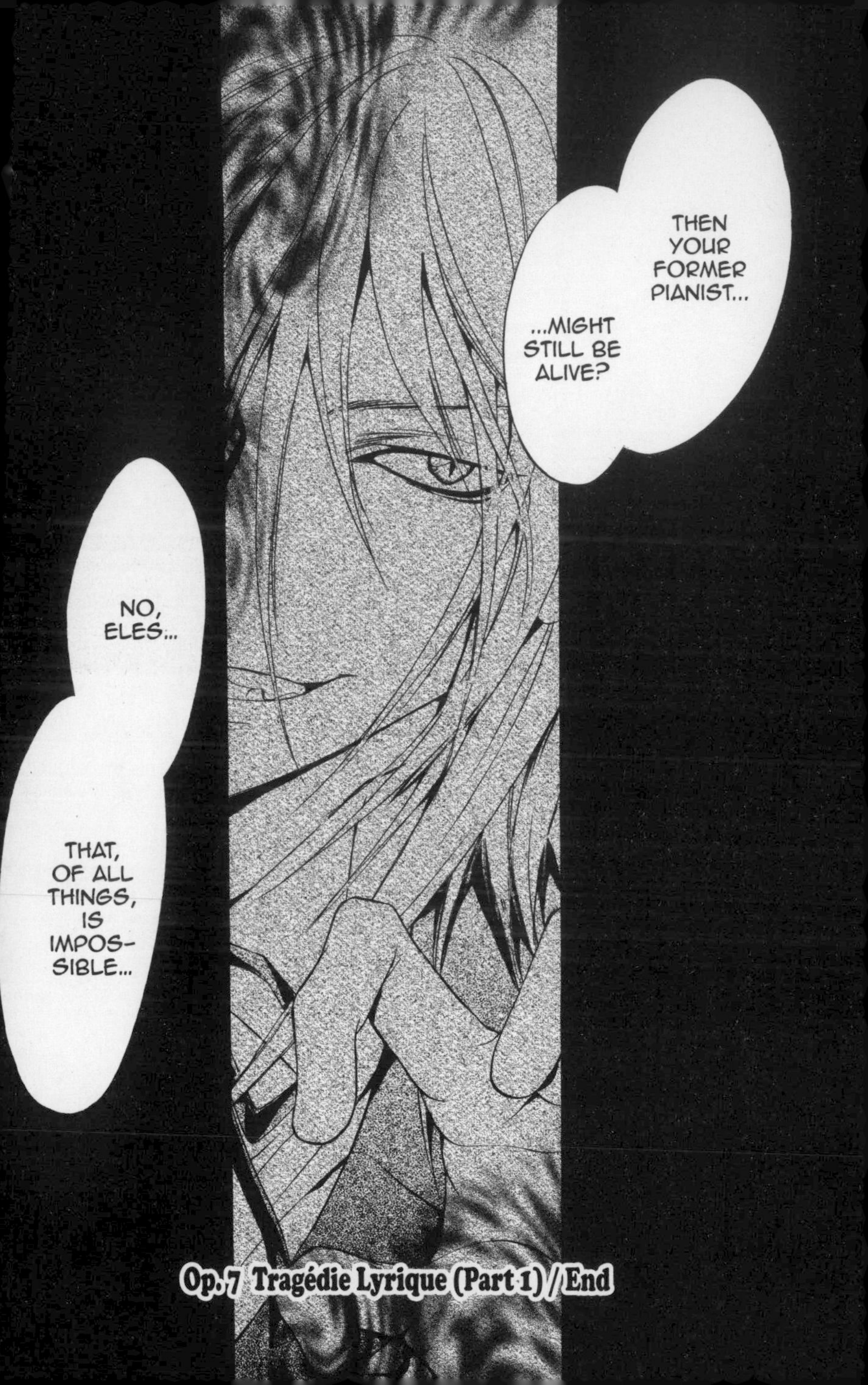
THEN YOUR FORMER PIANIST...
...MIGHT STILL BE ALIVE?
NO, ELES...
THAT, OF ALL THINGS, IS IMPOSSIBLE...
Op. 7 Tragédie Lyrique (Part 1) / End

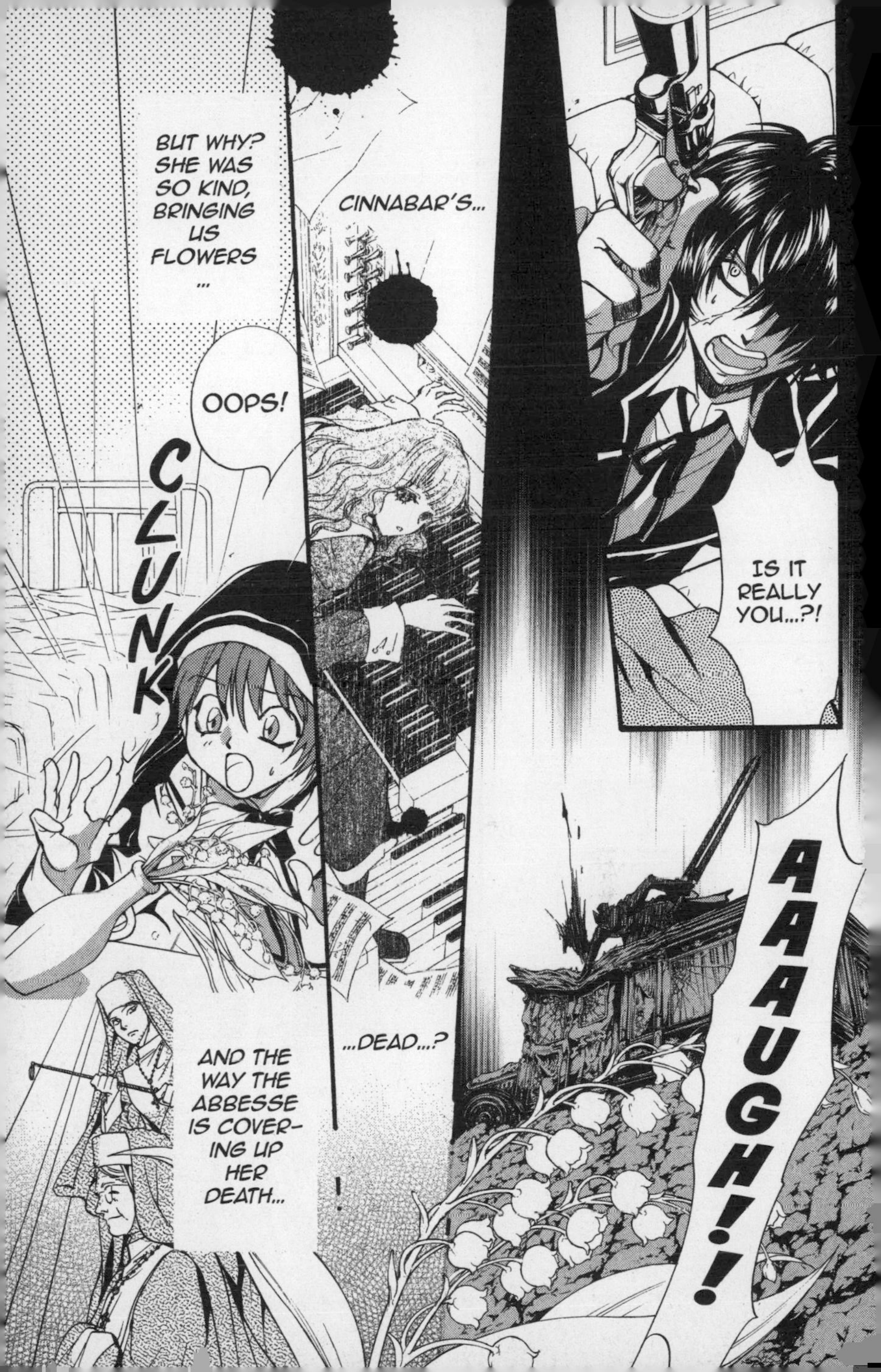
IS IT REALLY YOU...?!
AAAUGH!!!
CINNABAR'S...
...DEAD...?
!
BUT WHY? SHE WAS SO KIND, BRINGING US FLOWERS ...
OOPS!
CLUNK
AND THE WAY THE ABBESSE IS COVERING UP HER DEATH...

Op. 8 Tragédie Lyrique (Part 2)

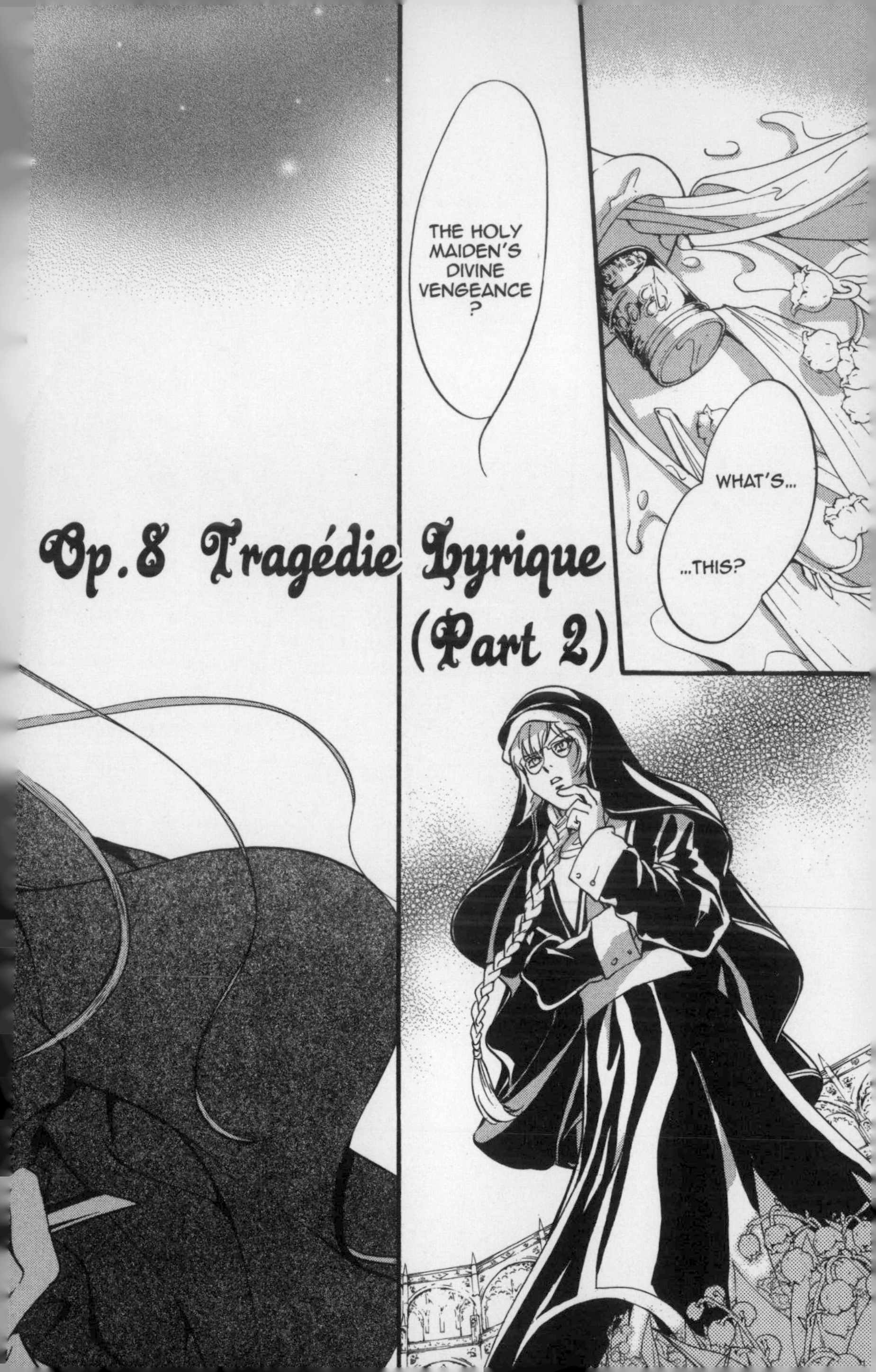
WHAT'S...
...THIS?
THE HOLY MAIDEN'S DIVINE VENGEANCE?

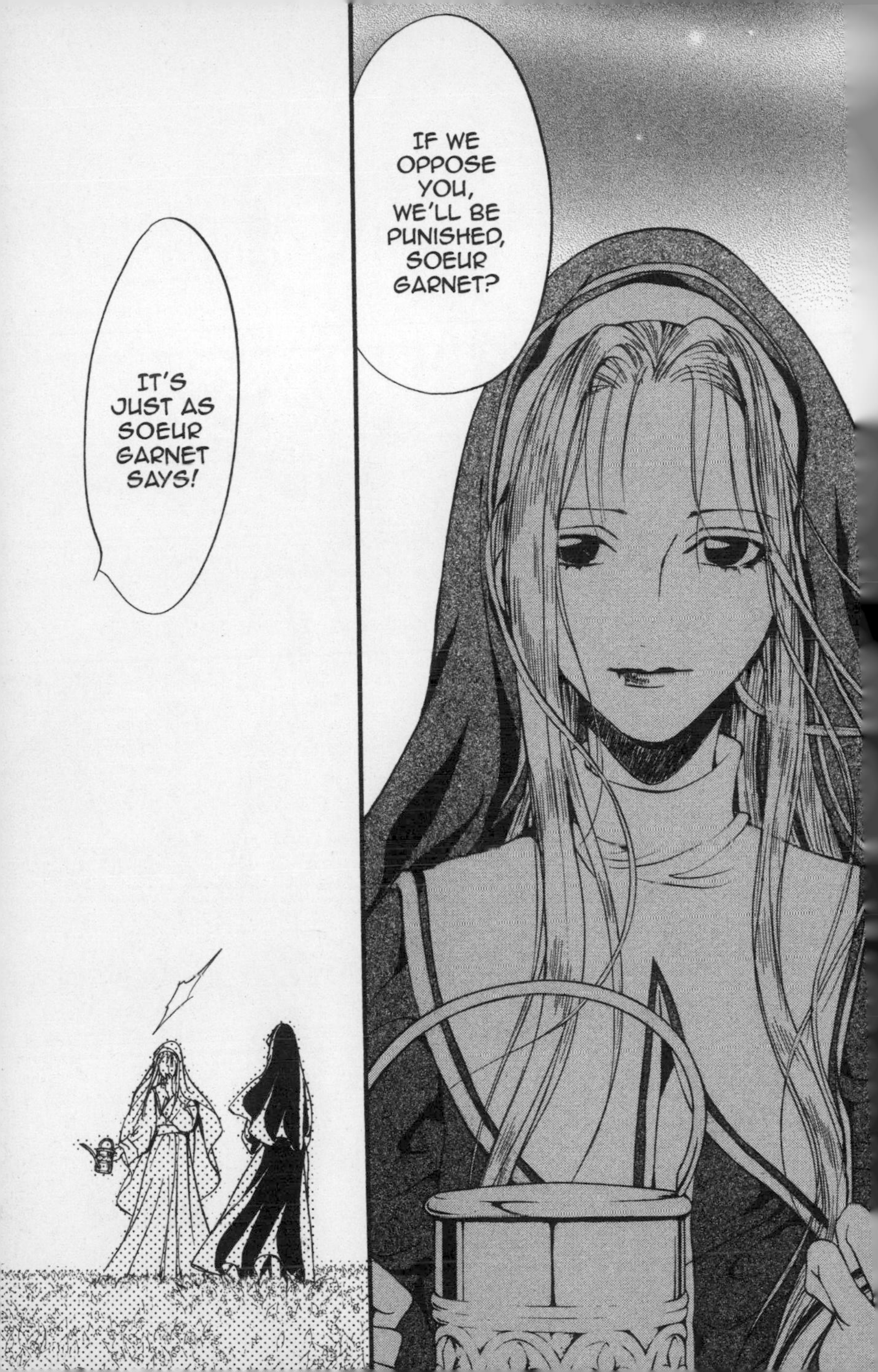
IF WE OPPOSE YOU, WE'LL BE PUNISHED, SOEUR GARNET?
IT'S JUST AS SOEUR GARNET SAYS!

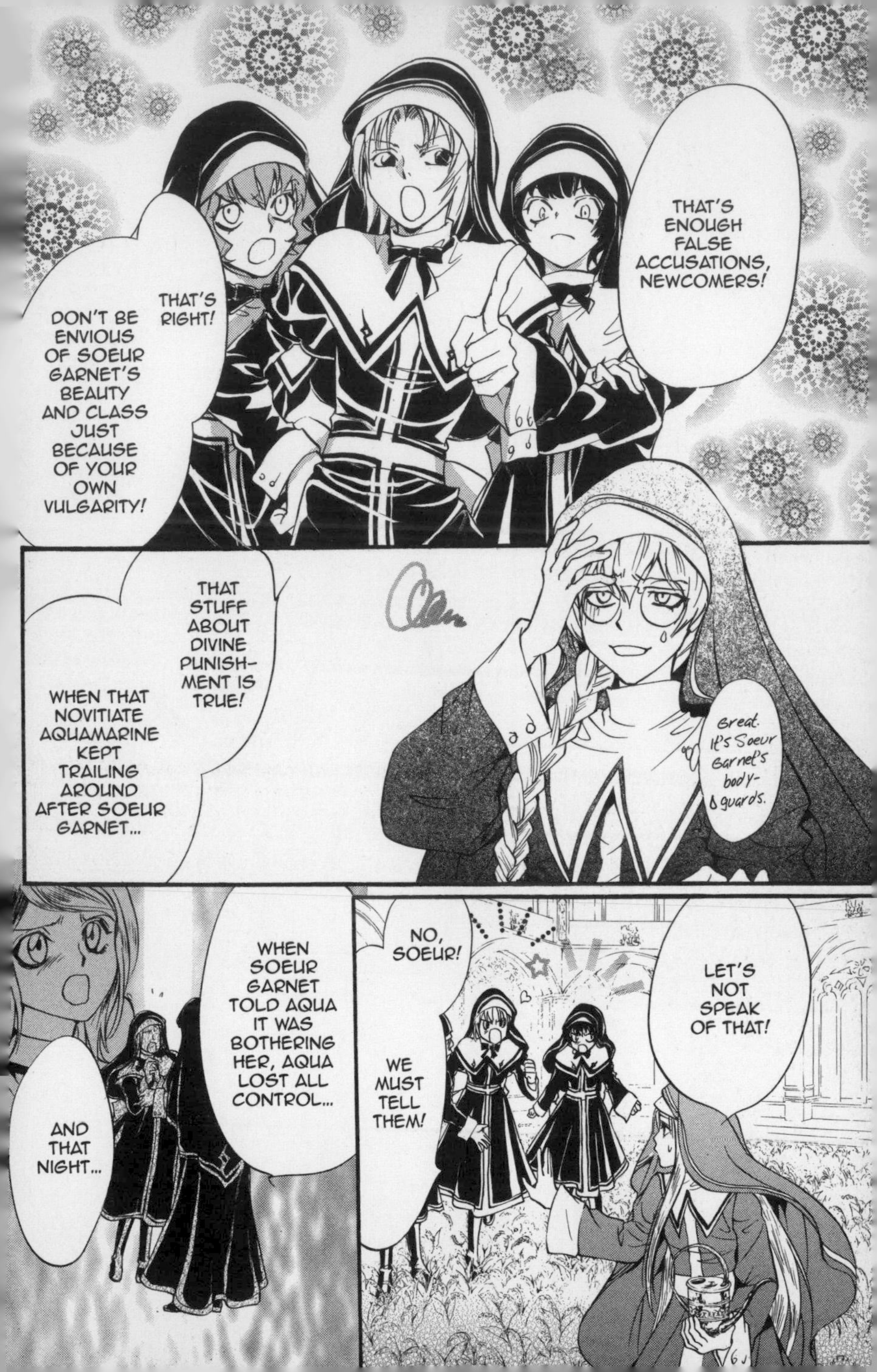
THAT'S ENOUGH FALSE ACCUSATIONS, NEWCOMERS!
THAT'S RIGHT!
DON'T BE ENVIOUS OF SOEUR GARNET'S BEAUTY AND CLASS JUST BECAUSE OF YOUR OWN VULGARITY!
Great. It's Soeur Garnet's body-guards.
THAT STUFF ABOUT DIVINE PUNISH-MENT IS TRUE!
WHEN THAT NOVITIATE AQUAMARINE KEPT TRAILING AROUND AFTER SOEUR GARNET...
LET'S NOT SPEAK OF THAT!
NO, SOEUR!
WE MUST TELL THEM!
WHEN SOEUR GARNET TOLD AQUA IT WAS BOTHERING HER, AQUA LOST ALL CONTROL...
AND THAT NIGHT...

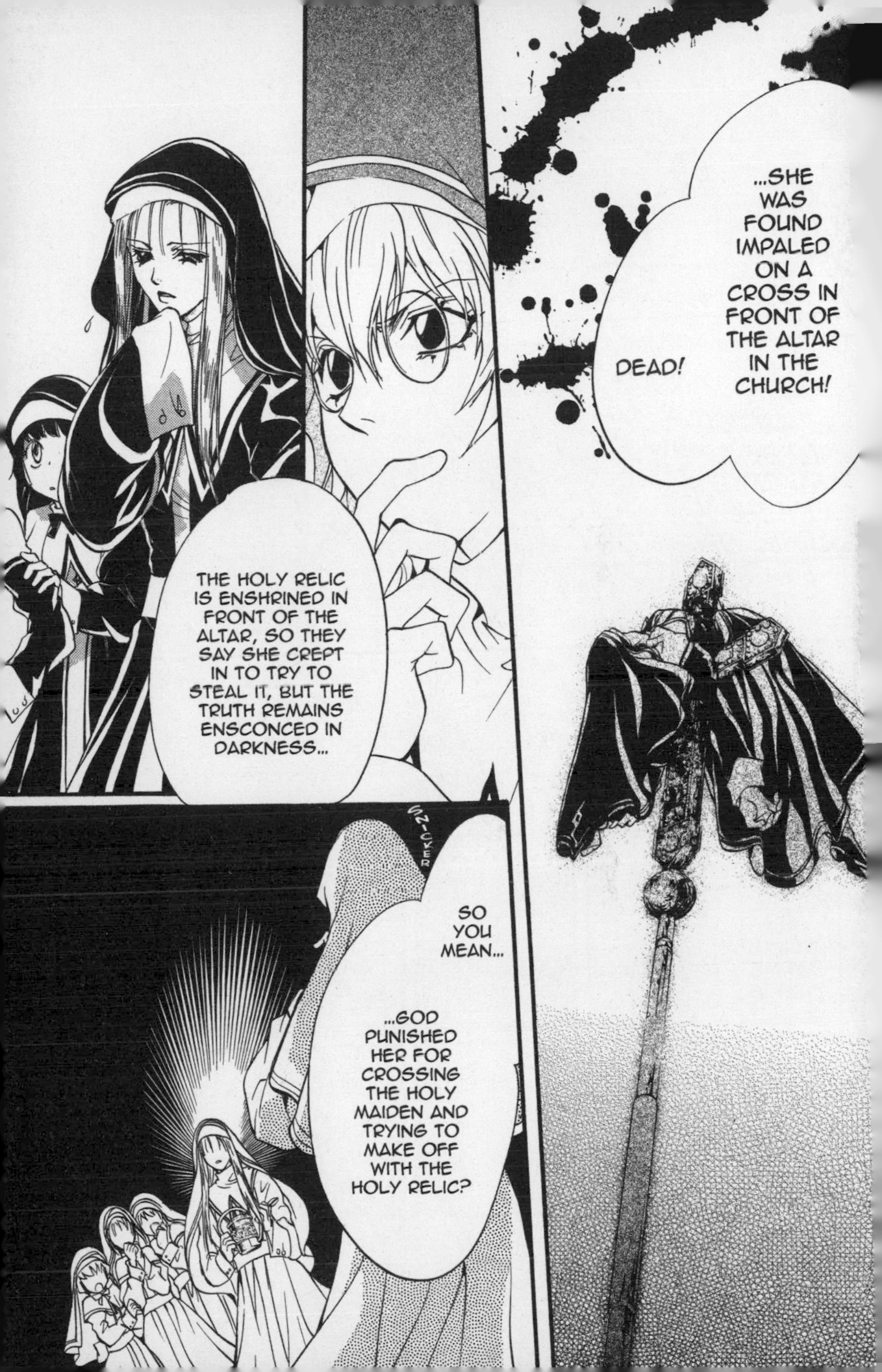
...SHE WAS FOUND IMPALED ON A CROSS IN FRONT OF THE ALTAR IN THE CHURCH!
DEAD!
THE HOLY RELIC IS ENSHRINED IN FRONT OF THE ALTAR, SO THEY SAY SHE CREPT IN TO TRY TO STEAL IT, BUT THE TRUTH REMAINS ENSCONCED IN DARKNESS...
SNICKER
SO YOU MEAN...
...GOD PUNISHED HER FOR CROSSING THE HOLY MAIDEN AND TRYING TO MAKE OFF WITH THE HOLY RELIC?

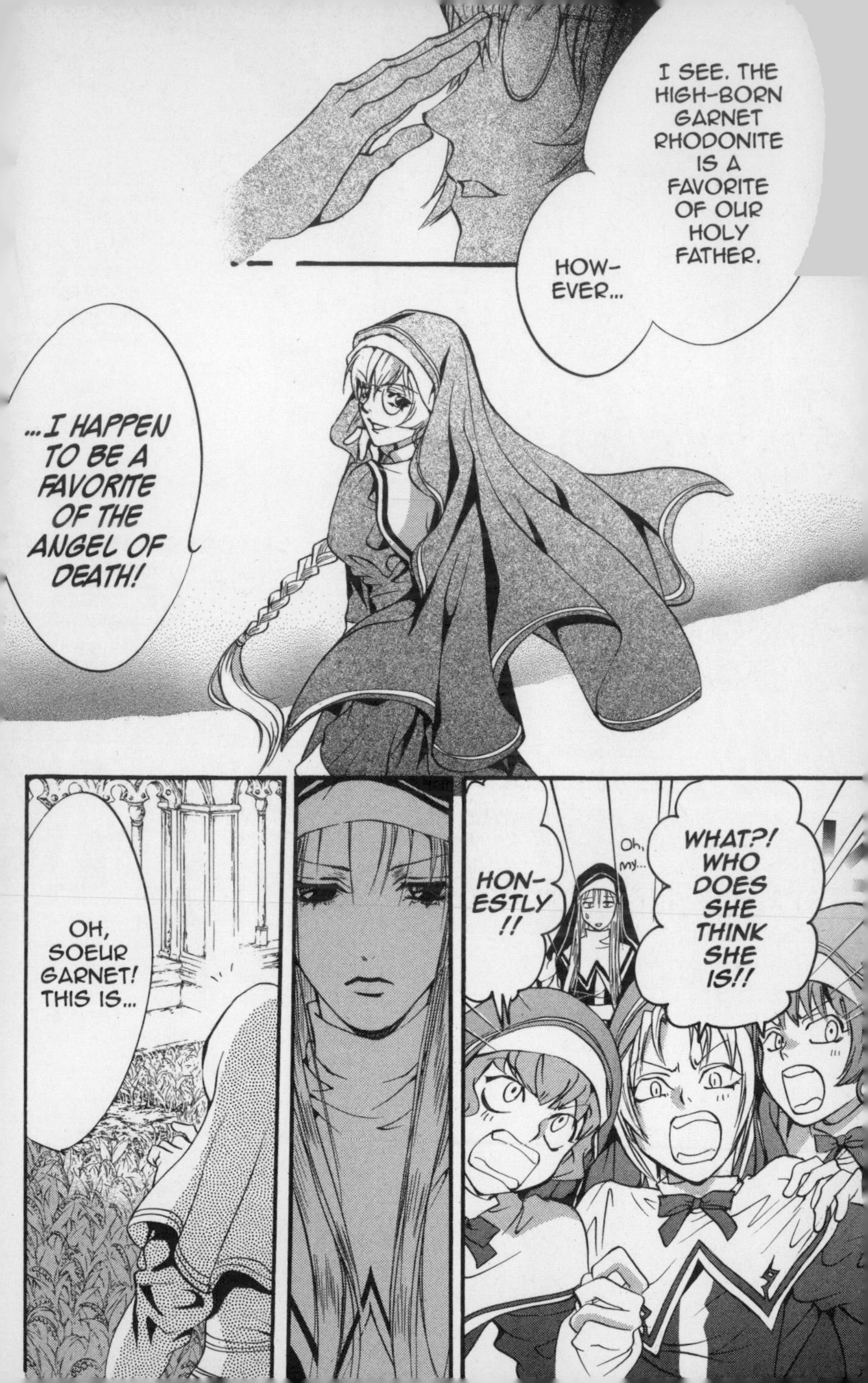
I SEE. THE HIGH-BORN GARNET RHODONITE IS A FAVORITE OF OUR HOLY FATHER.
HOW-EVER...
...I HAPPEN TO BE A FAVORITE OF THE ANGEL OF DEATH!
WHAT?! WHO DOES SHE THINK SHE IS!!
Oh, my...
HON-ESTLY!!
OH, SOEUR GARNET! THIS IS...

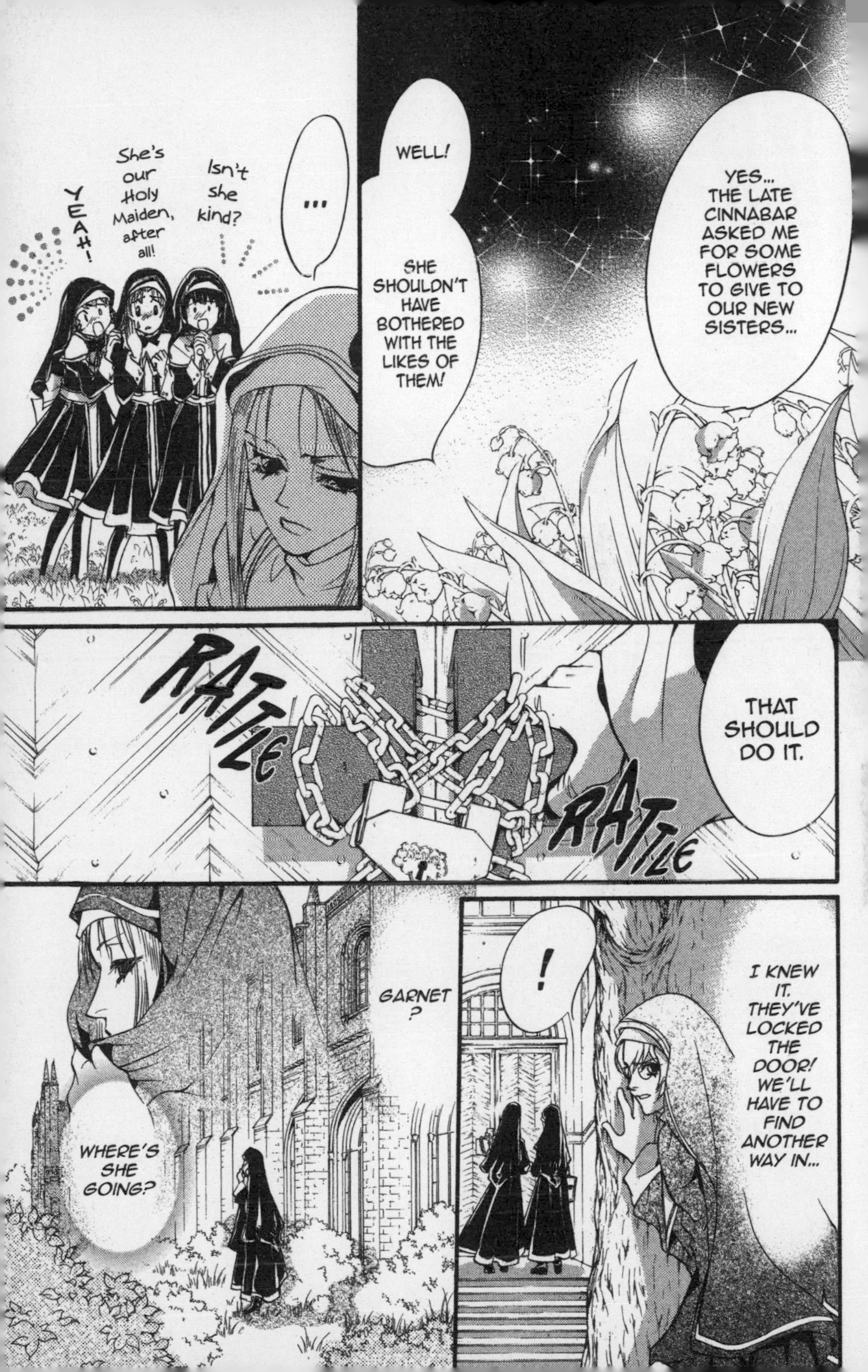
YES... THE LATE CINNABAR ASKED ME FOR SOME FLOWERS TO GIVE TO OUR NEW SISTERS...
WELL! SHE SHOULDN'T HAVE BOTHERED WITH THE LIKES OF THEM!
...
Isn't she kind?
She's our Holy Maiden, after all!
YEAH!
THAT SHOULD DO IT.
RATTLE
RATTLE
I KNEW IT. THEY'VE LOCKED THE DOOR! WE'LL HAVE TO FIND ANOTHER WAY IN...
!
GARNET?
WHERE'S SHE GOING?

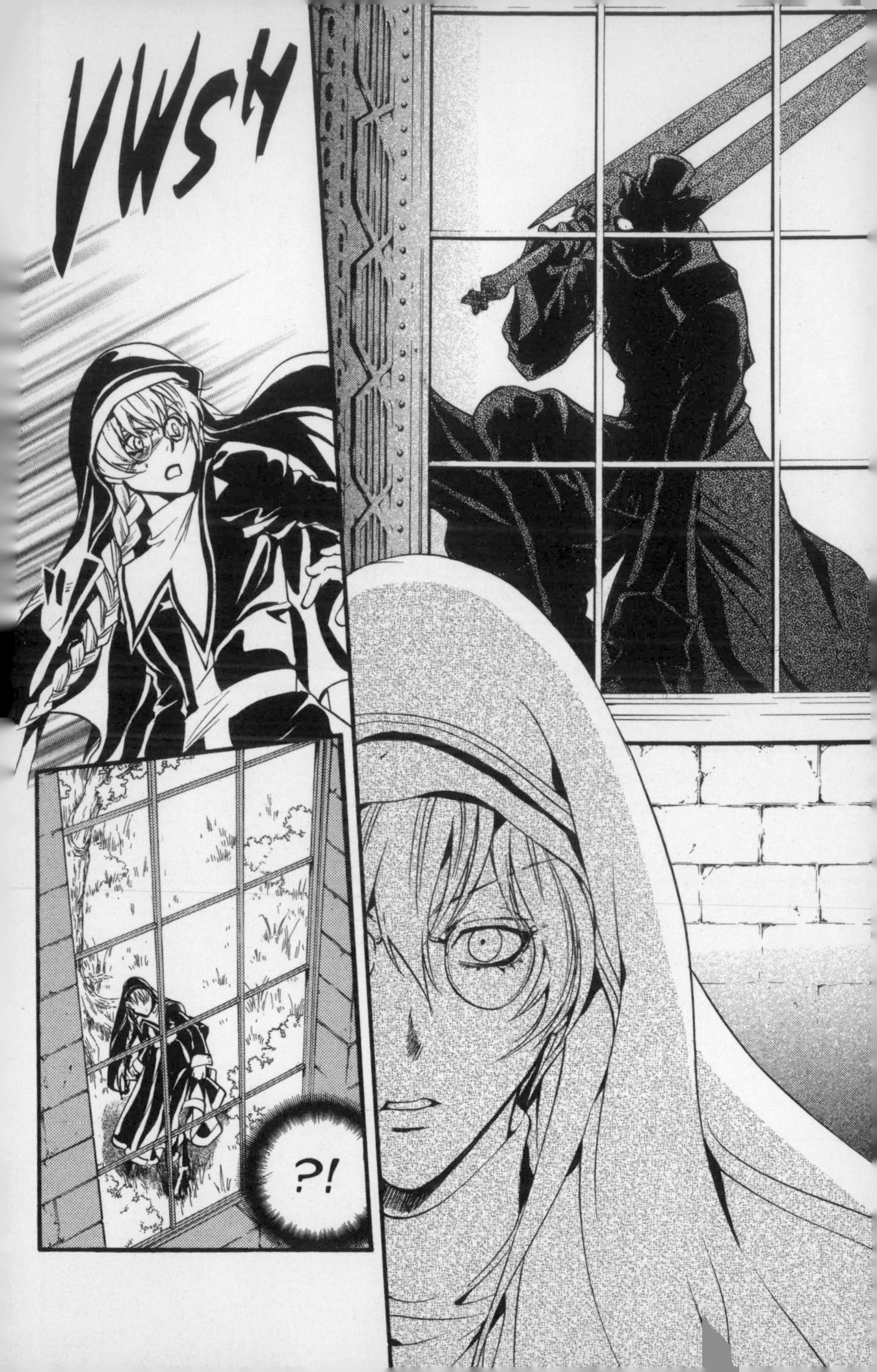
VWSH
?!

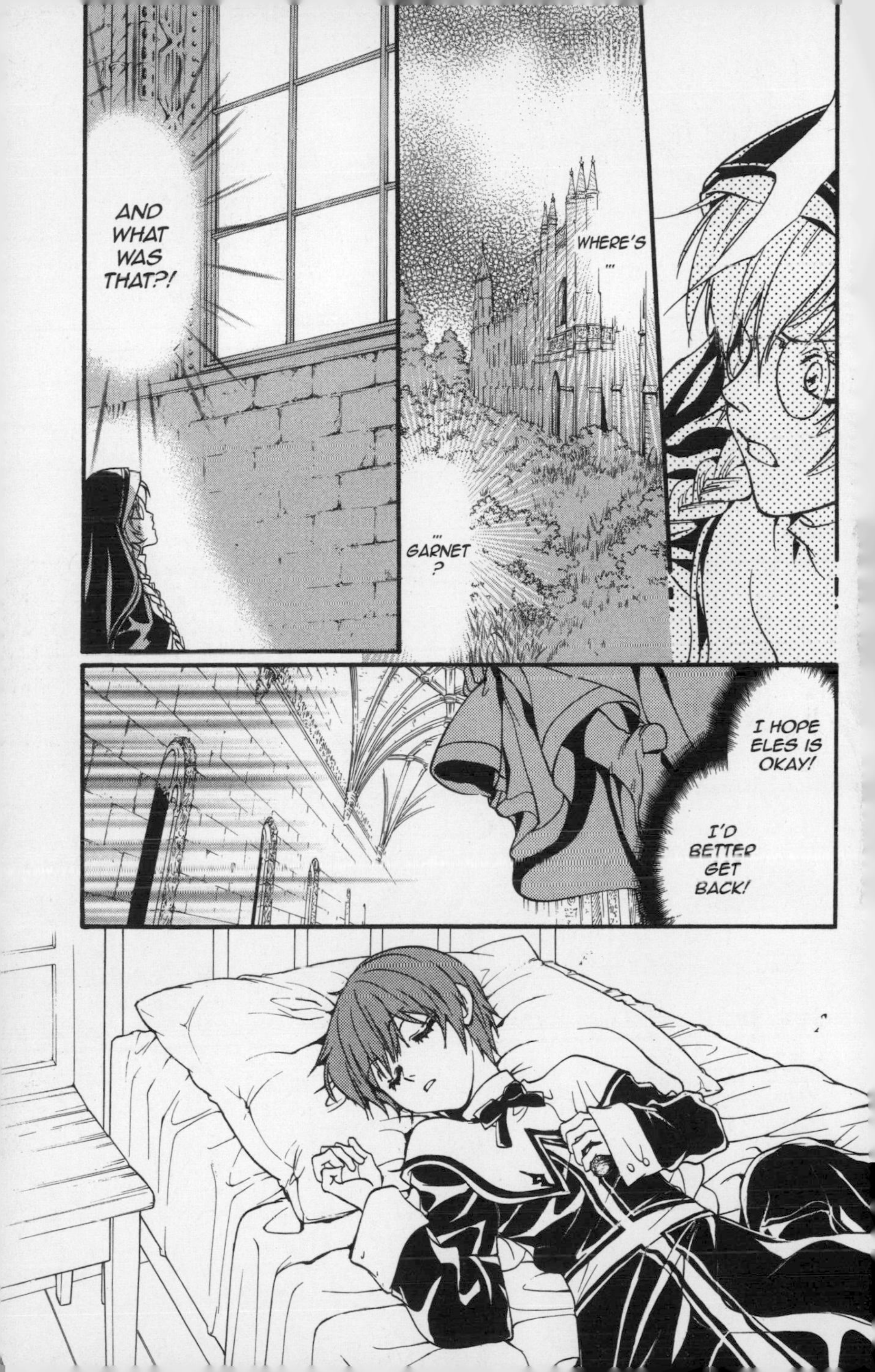
WHERE'S ...
... GARNET ?
AND WHAT WAS THAT?!
I HOPE ELES IS OKAY!
I'D BETTER GET BACK!

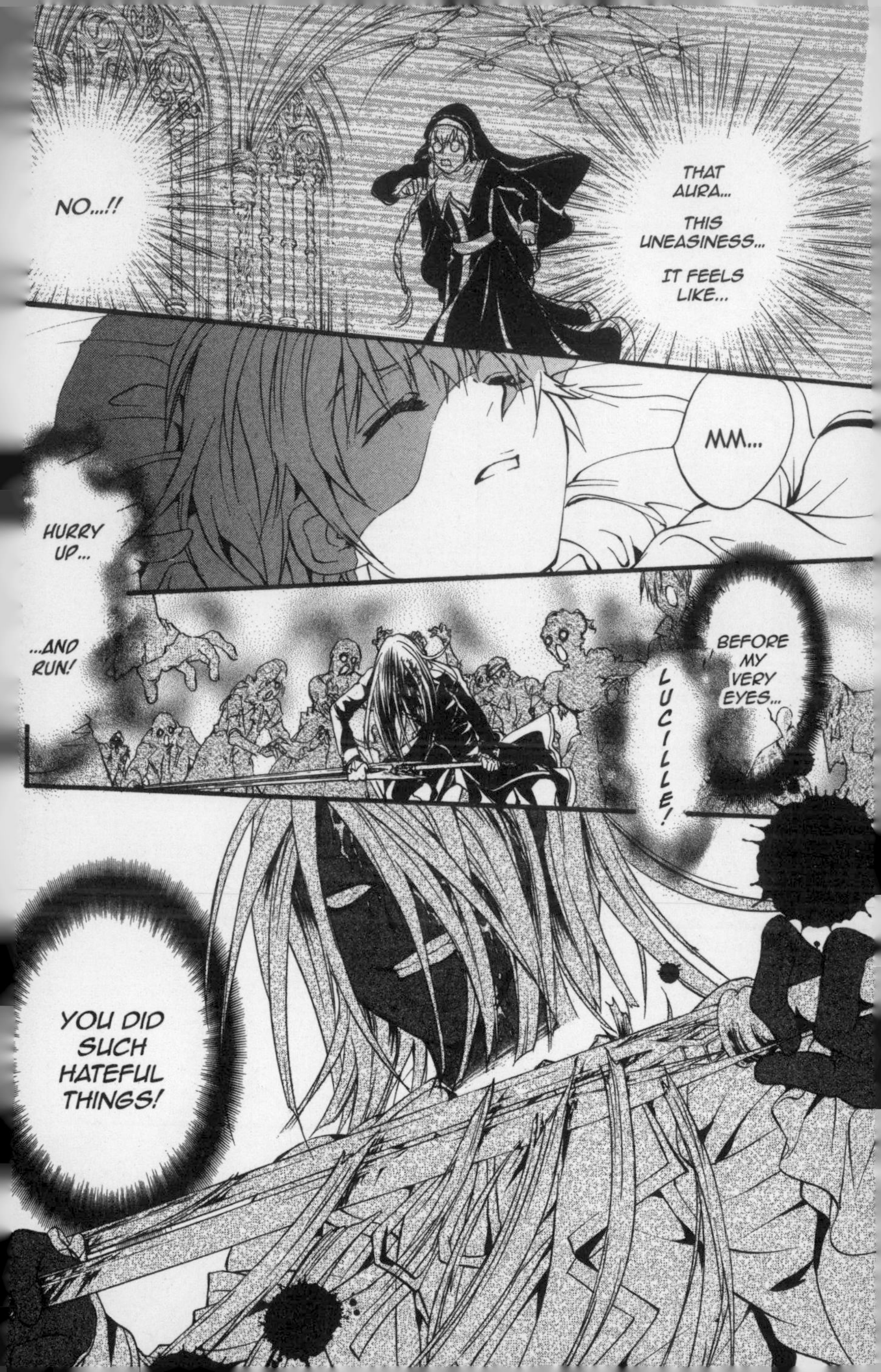
THAT AURA... THIS UNEASINESS... IT FEELS LIKE...
NO...!!
MM...
HURRY UP...
BEFORE MY VERY EYES...
LUCILLE!
...AND RUN!
YOU DID SUCH HATEFUL THINGS!

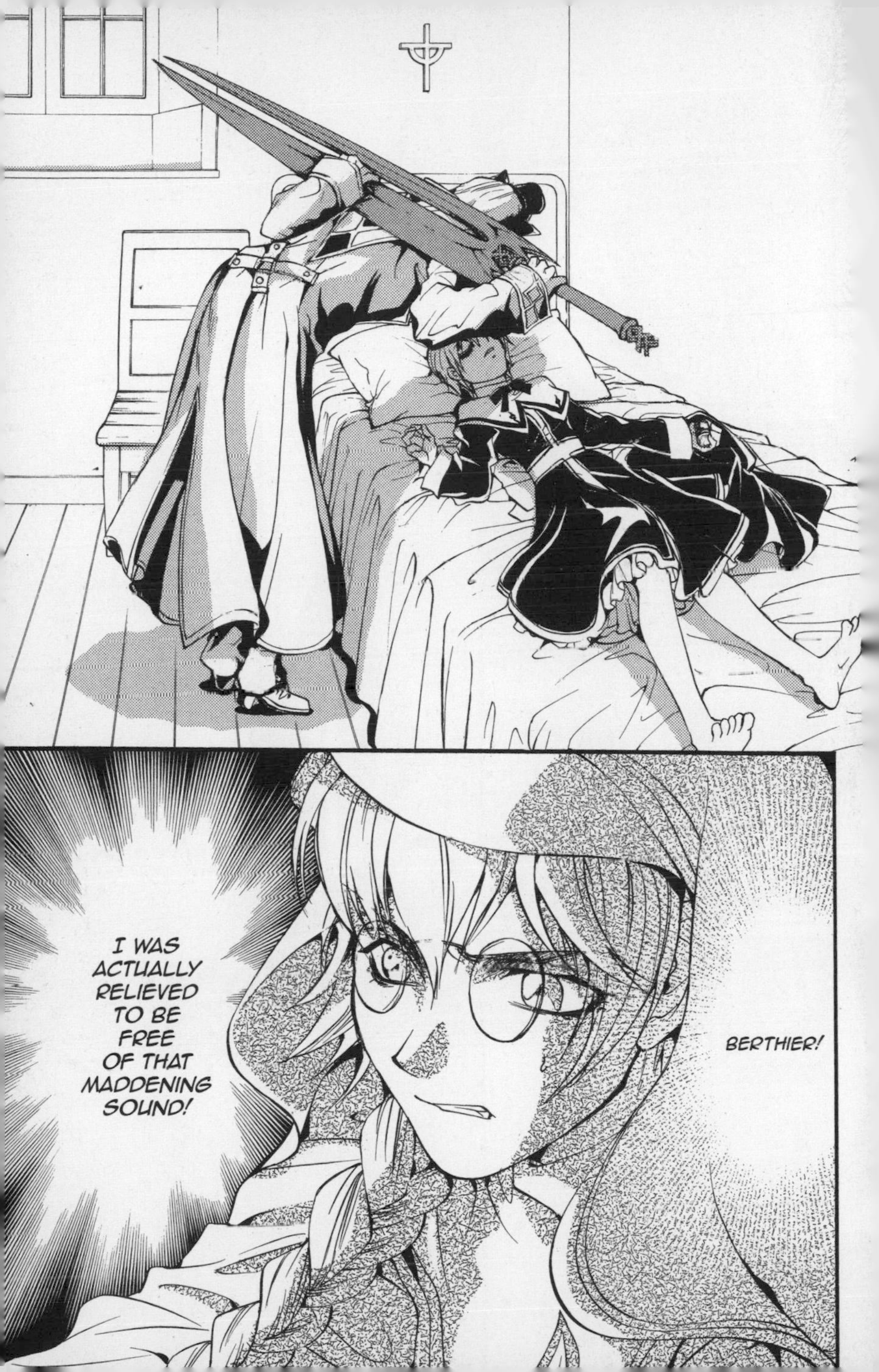
BERTHIER!
I WAS ACTUALLY RELIEVED TO BE FREE OF THAT MADDENING SOUND!

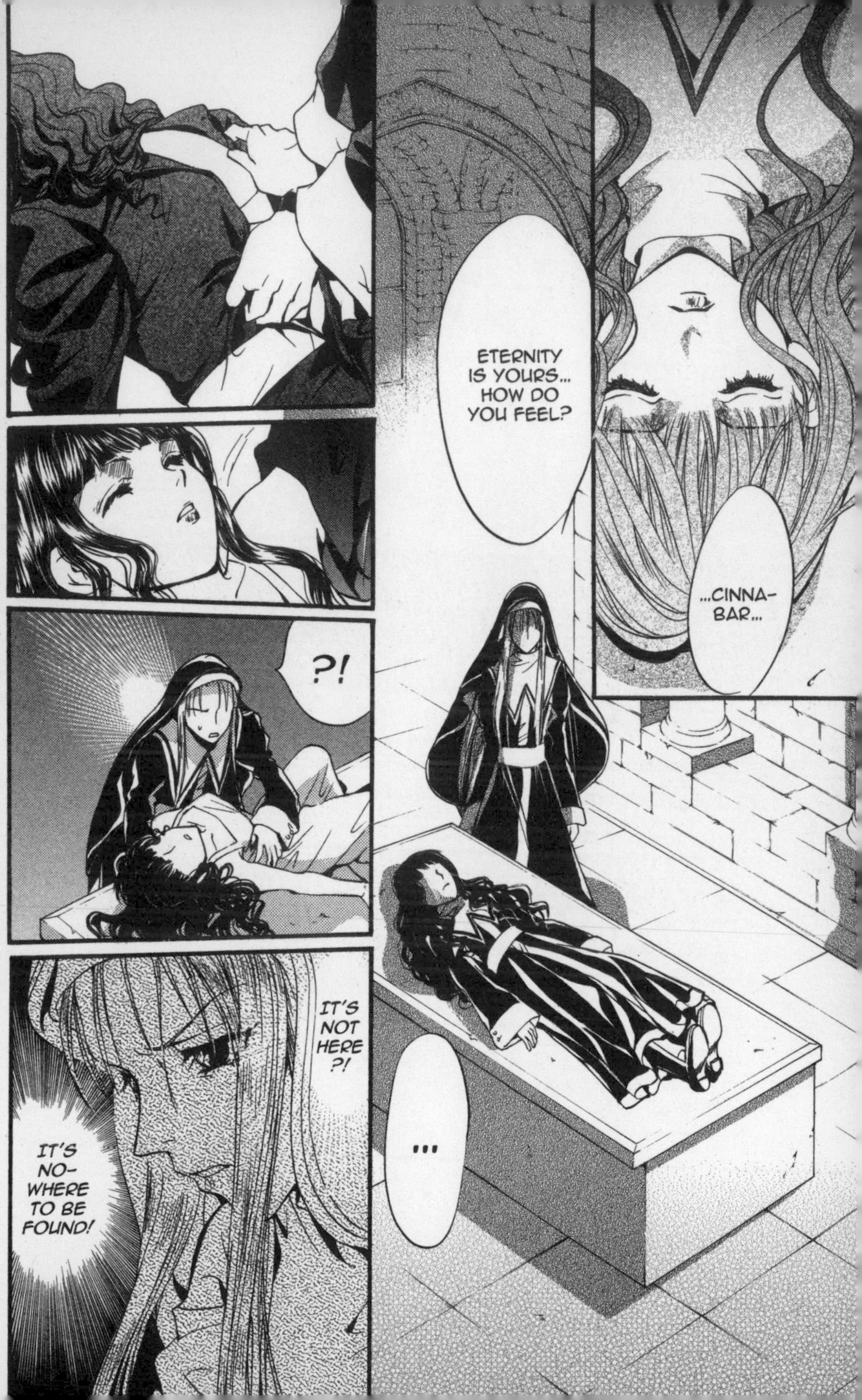
...CINNA-BAR...
ETERNITY IS YOURS... HOW DO YOU FEEL?
...
?!
IT'S NOT HERE?!
IT'S NO-WHERE TO BE FOUND!

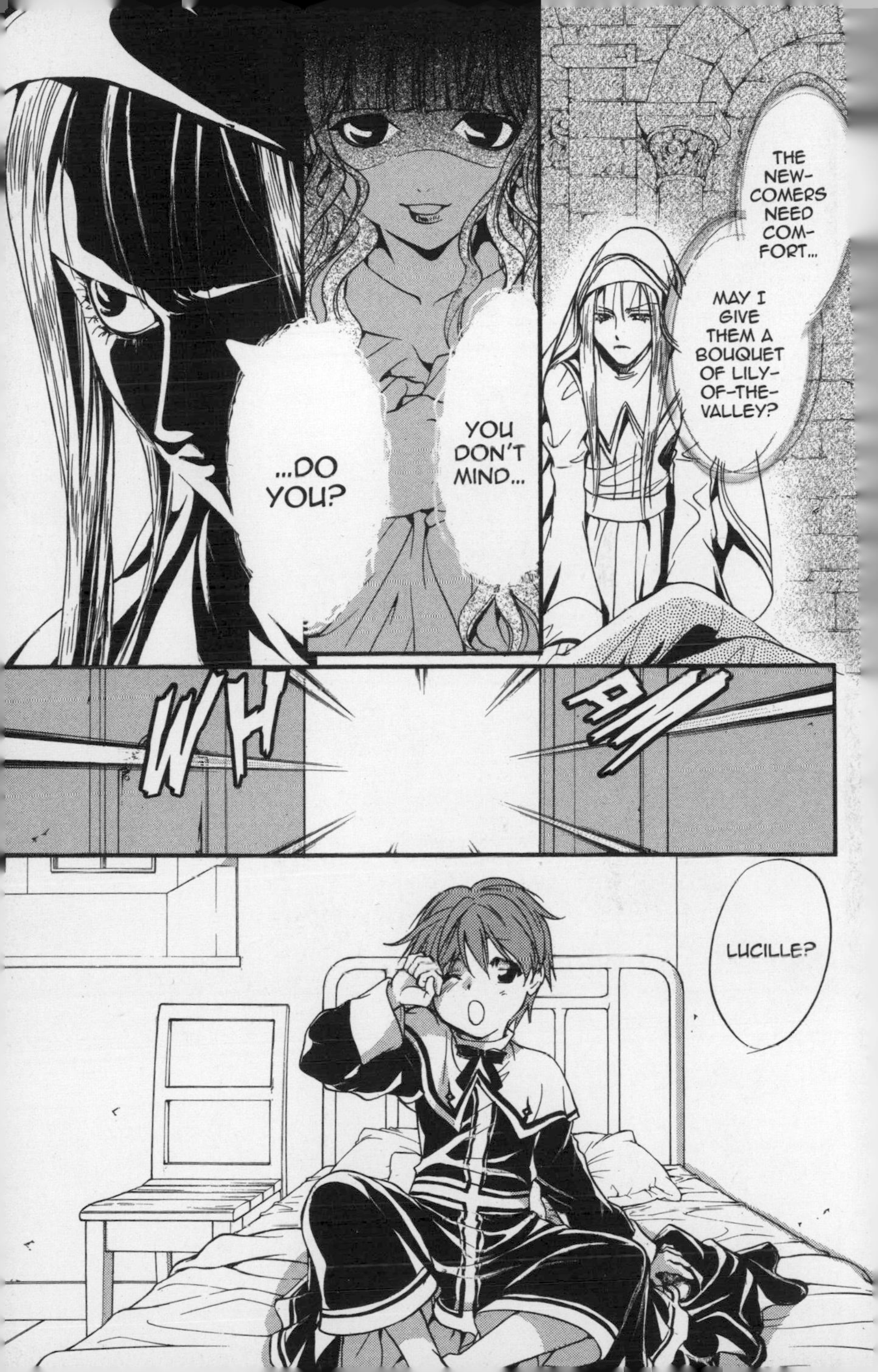
THE NEW-COMERS NEED COM-FORT...
MAY I GIVE THEM A BOUQUET OF LILY-OF-THE-VALLEY?
YOU DON'T MIND...
...DO YOU?
WHA
LUCILLE?

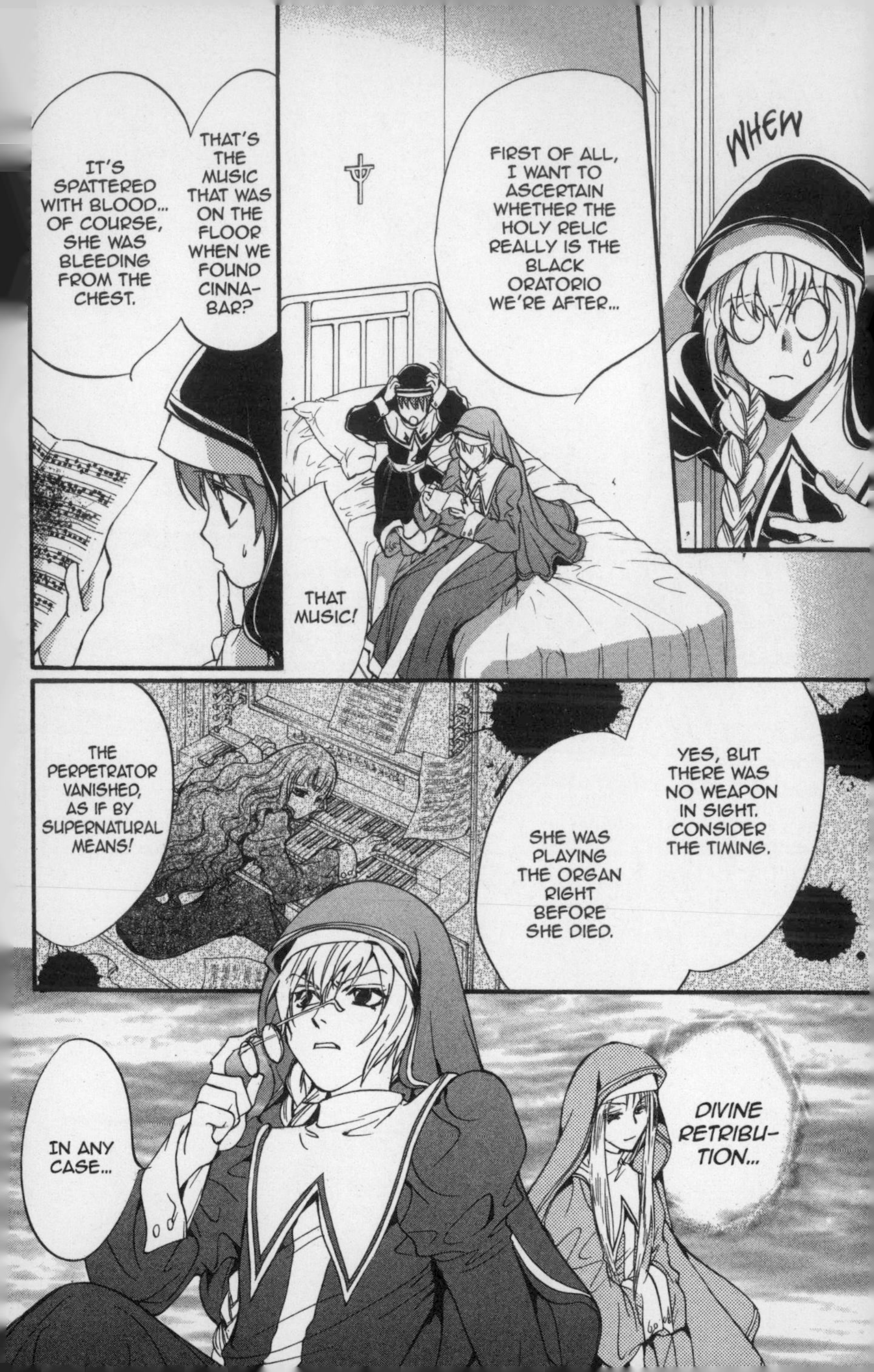
WHEW
FIRST OF ALL, I WANT TO ASCERTAIN WHETHER THE HOLY RELIC REALLY IS THE BLACK ORATORIO WE'RE AFTER...
THAT'S THE MUSIC THAT WAS ON THE FLOOR WHEN WE FOUND CINNA-BAR?
IT'S SPATTERED WITH BLOOD... OF COURSE, SHE WAS BLEEDING FROM THE CHEST.
THAT MUSIC!
YES, BUT THERE WAS NO WEAPON IN SIGHT. CONSIDER THE TIMING.
SHE WAS PLAYING THE ORGAN RIGHT BEFORE SHE DIED.
THE PERPETRATOR VANISHED, AS IF BY SUPERNATURAL MEANS!
DIVINE RETRIBU-TION...
IN ANY CASE...

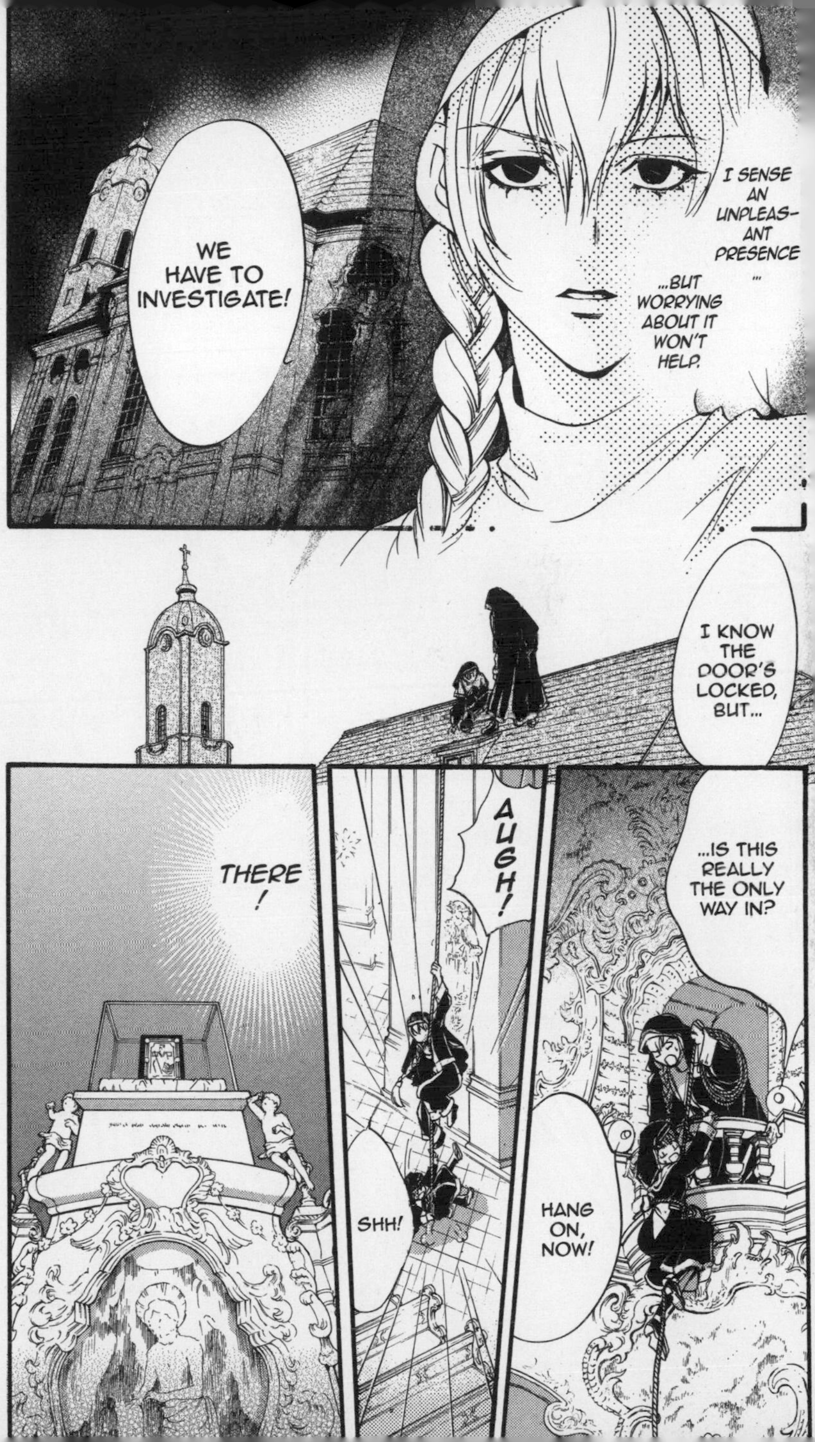
I SENSE AN UNPLEAS-ANT PRESENCE ...
...BUT WORRYING ABOUT IT WON'T HELP.
WE HAVE TO INVESTIGATE!
I KNOW THE DOOR'S LOCKED, BUT...
...IS THIS REALLY THE ONLY WAY IN?
HANG ON, NOW!
AUGH!
SHH!
THERE!

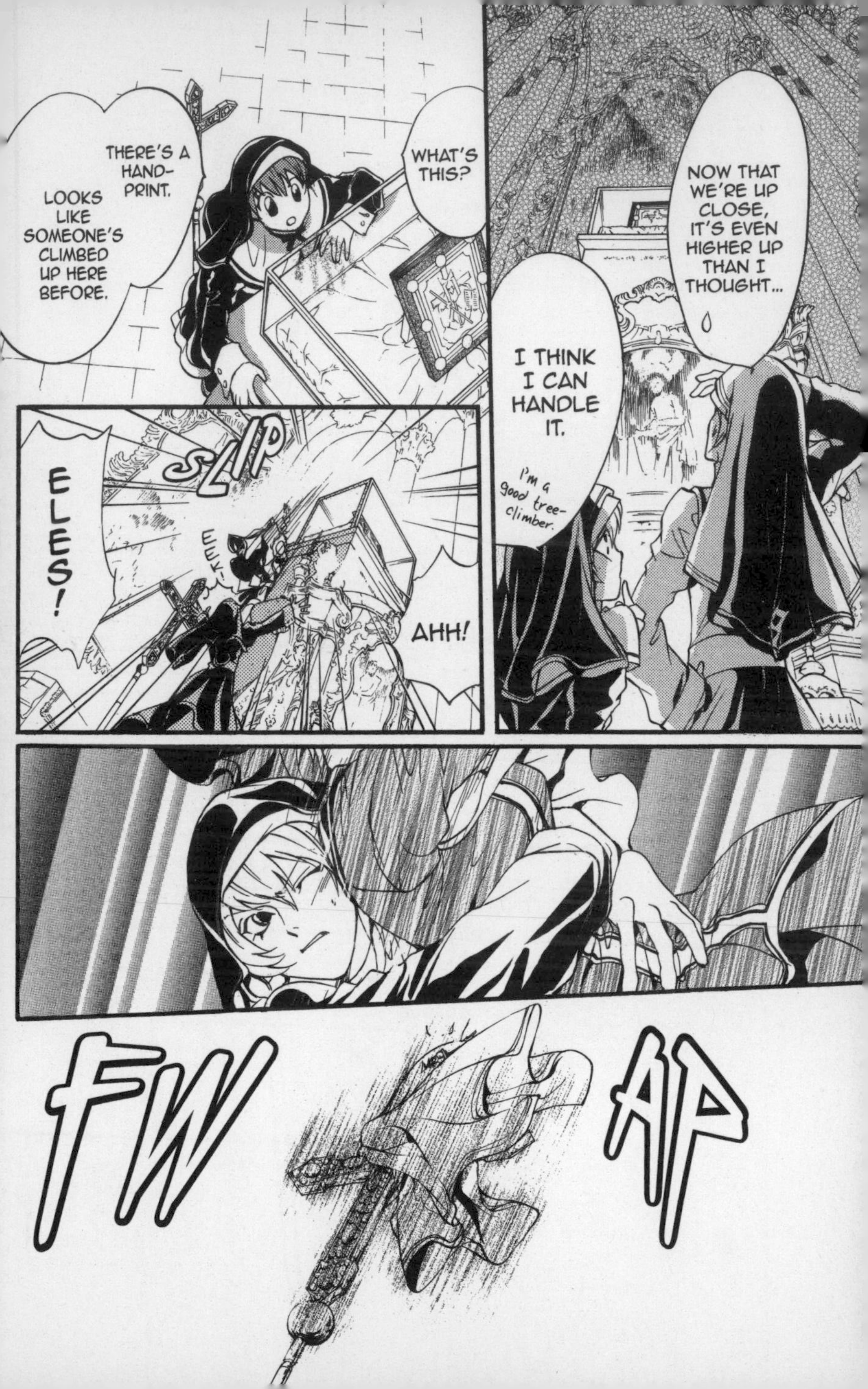
NOW THAT WE'RE UP CLOSE, IT'S EVEN HIGHER UP THAN I THOUGHT...
I THINK I CAN HANDLE IT.
I'm a good tree-climber.
WHAT'S THIS?
THERE'S A HAND-PRINT.
LOOKS LIKE SOMEONE'S CLIMBED UP HERE BEFORE.
SLIP
EEK!
ELES!
AHH!
FWAP

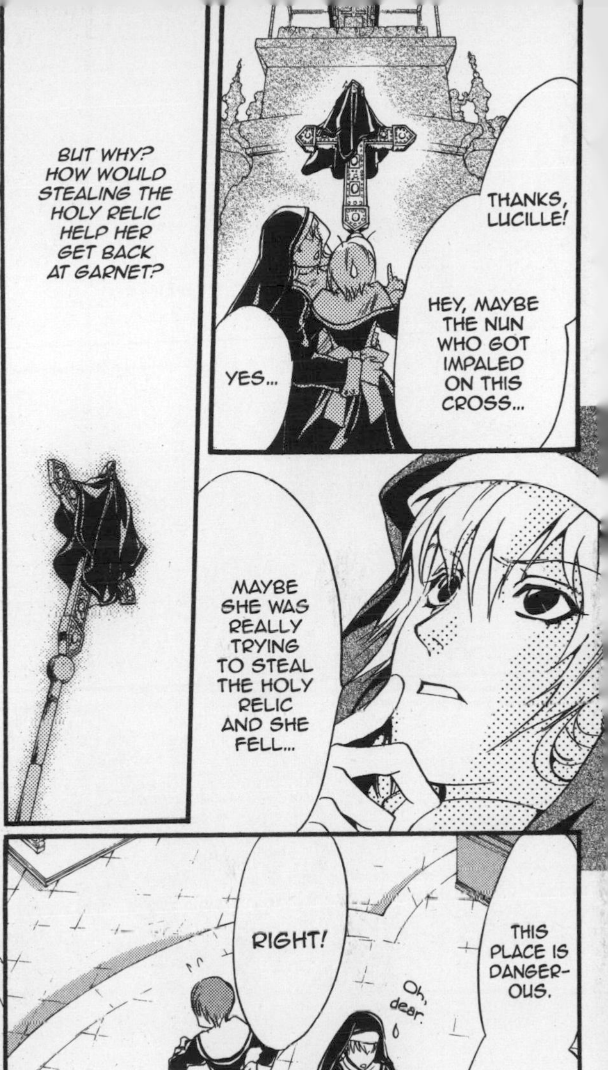
THANKS, LUCILLE!
HEY, MAYBE THE NUN WHO GOT IMPALED ON THIS CROSS...
YES...
MAYBE SHE WAS REALLY TRYING TO STEAL THE HOLY RELIC AND SHE FELL...
BUT WHY? HOW WOULD STEALING THE HOLY RELIC HELP HER GET BACK AT GARNET?
THIS PLACE IS DANGER-OUS.
LET'S CHECK OUT THE ORGAN FIRST.
RIGHT!
Oh, dear.

At first, I was going to have the cat man wearing a full-body animal suit, but then I thought that would be too comical. That's how he turned out the way he did. I had so much trouble settling on a character design, he came out pretty wild in his first appearance. Oh, dear. This manga is really getting full of strange men. I don't do it on purpose...

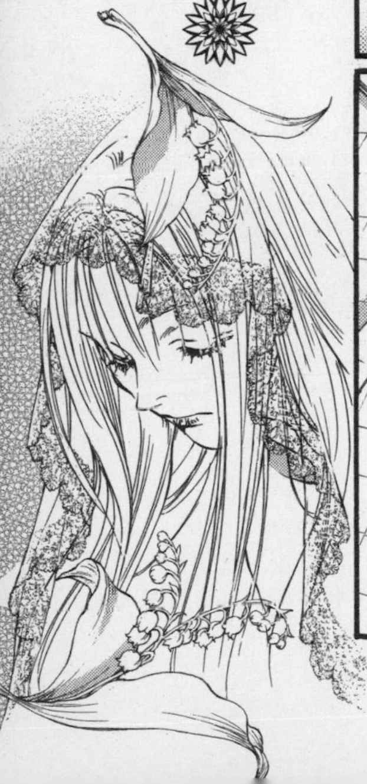

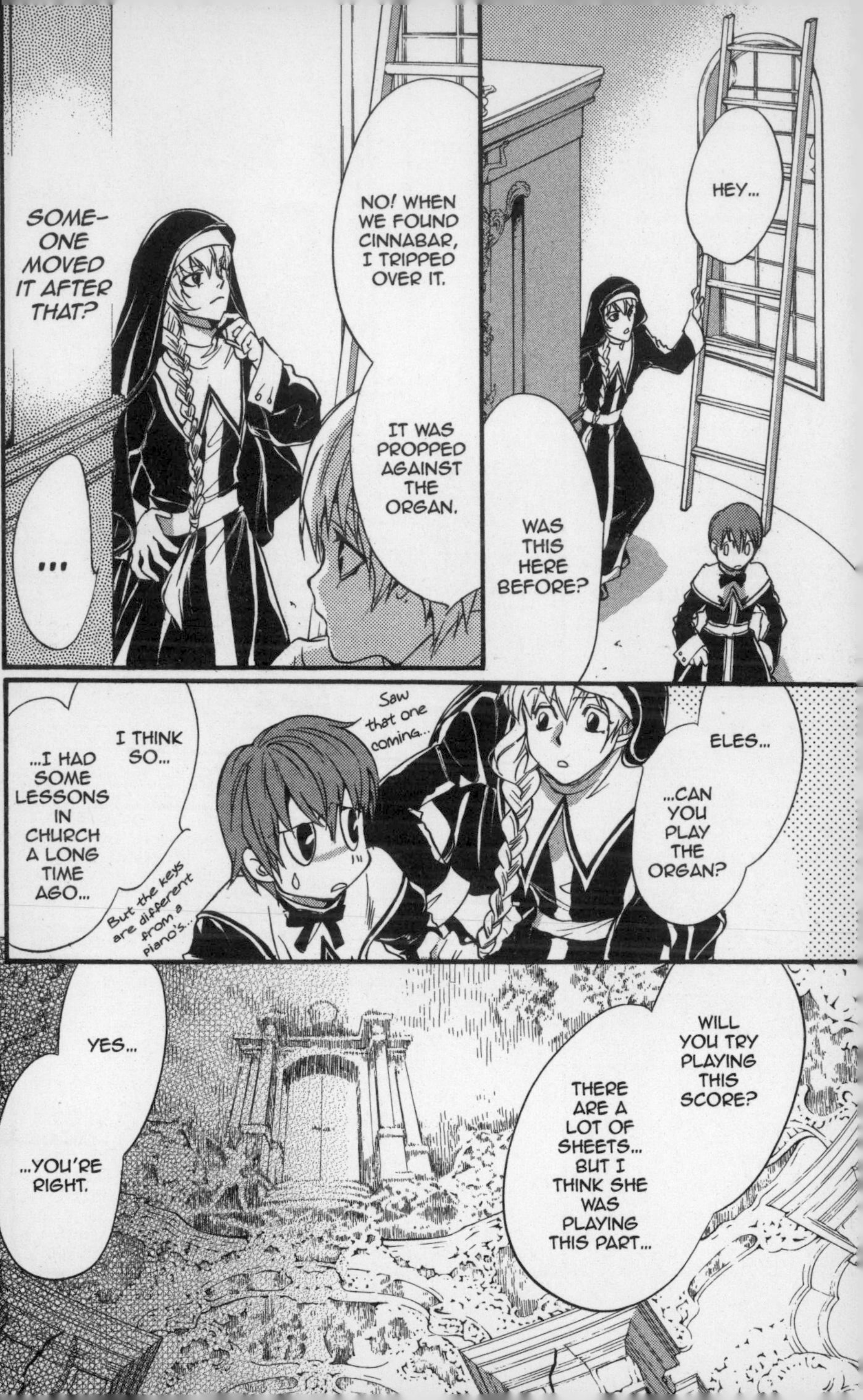
HEY...
WAS THIS HERE BEFORE?
NO! WHEN WE FOUND CINNABAR, I TRIPPED OVER IT.
IT WAS PROPPED AGAINST THE ORGAN.
SOME-ONE MOVED IT AFTER THAT?
...
ELES...
...CAN YOU PLAY THE ORGAN?
Saw that one coming...
I THINK SO...
...I HAD SOME LESSONS IN CHURCH A LONG TIME AGO...
But the keys are different from a piano's...
WILL YOU TRY PLAYING THIS SCORE?
THERE ARE A LOT OF SHEETS... BUT I THINK SHE WAS PLAYING THIS PART...
YES...
...YOU'RE RIGHT.

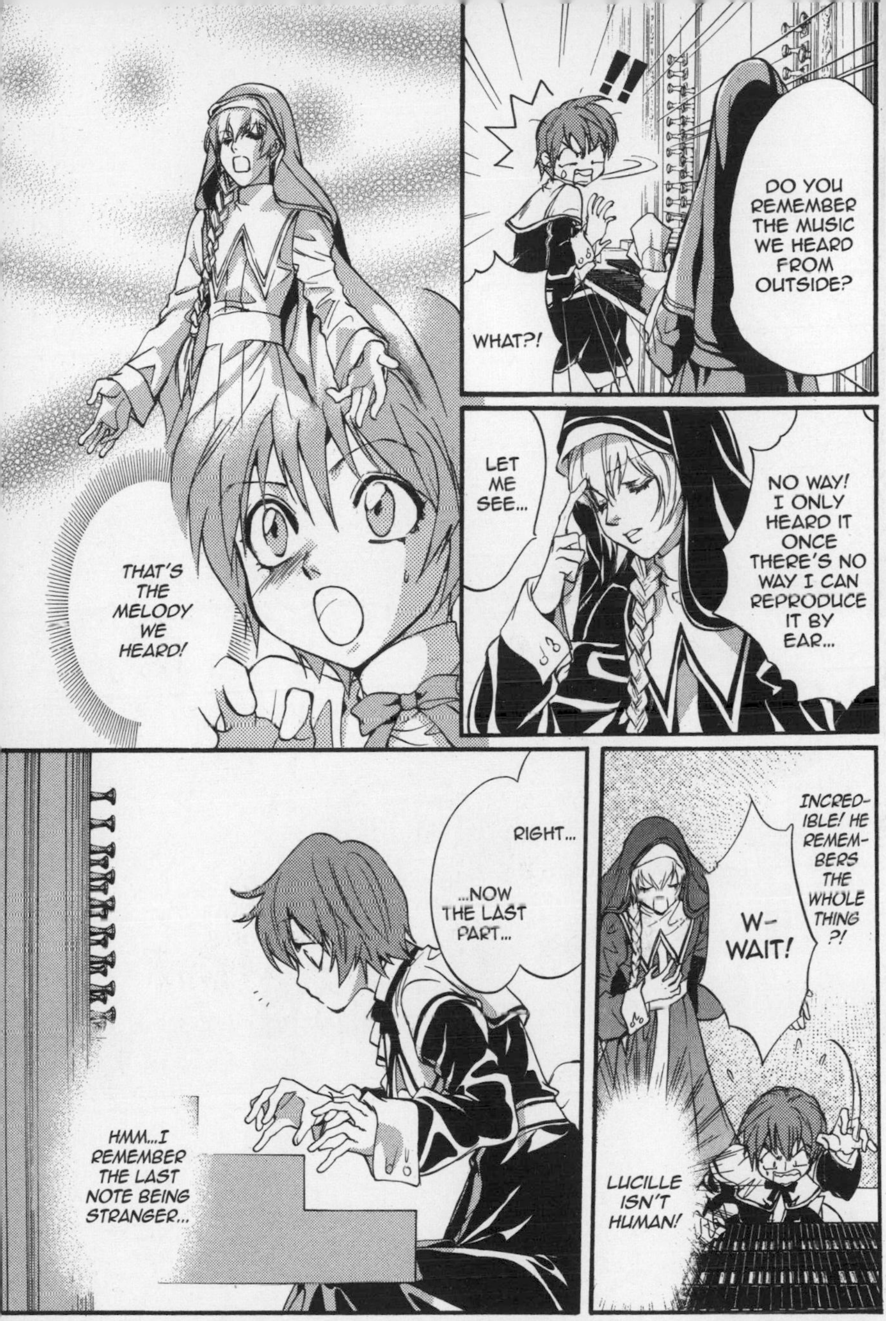
DO YOU REMEMBER THE MUSIC WE HEARD FROM OUTSIDE?
!!
WHAT?!
NO WAY! I ONLY HEARD IT ONCE THERE'S NO WAY I CAN REPRODUCE IT BY EAR...
LET ME SEE...
THAT'S THE MELODY WE HEARD!
INCREDIBLE! HE REMEMBERS THE WHOLE THING?!
W-WAIT!
LUCILLE ISN'T HUMAN!
RIGHT...
...NOW THE LAST PART...
HMM...I REMEMBER THE LAST NOTE BEING STRANGER...

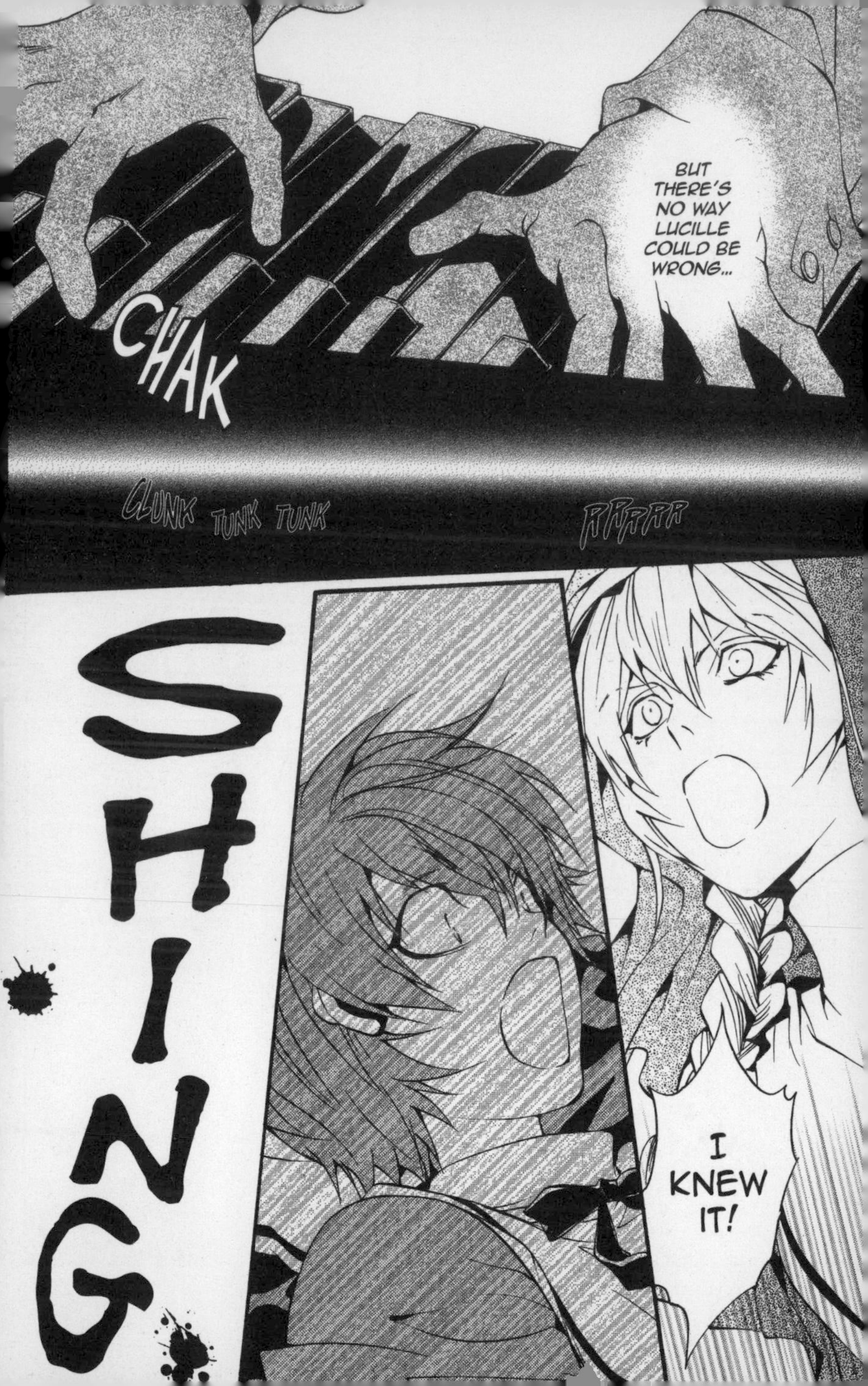
BUT THERE'S NO WAY LUCILLE COULD BE WRONG...
CHAK
RRRRRR
CLUNK TUNK TUNK
I KNEW IT!
SHING

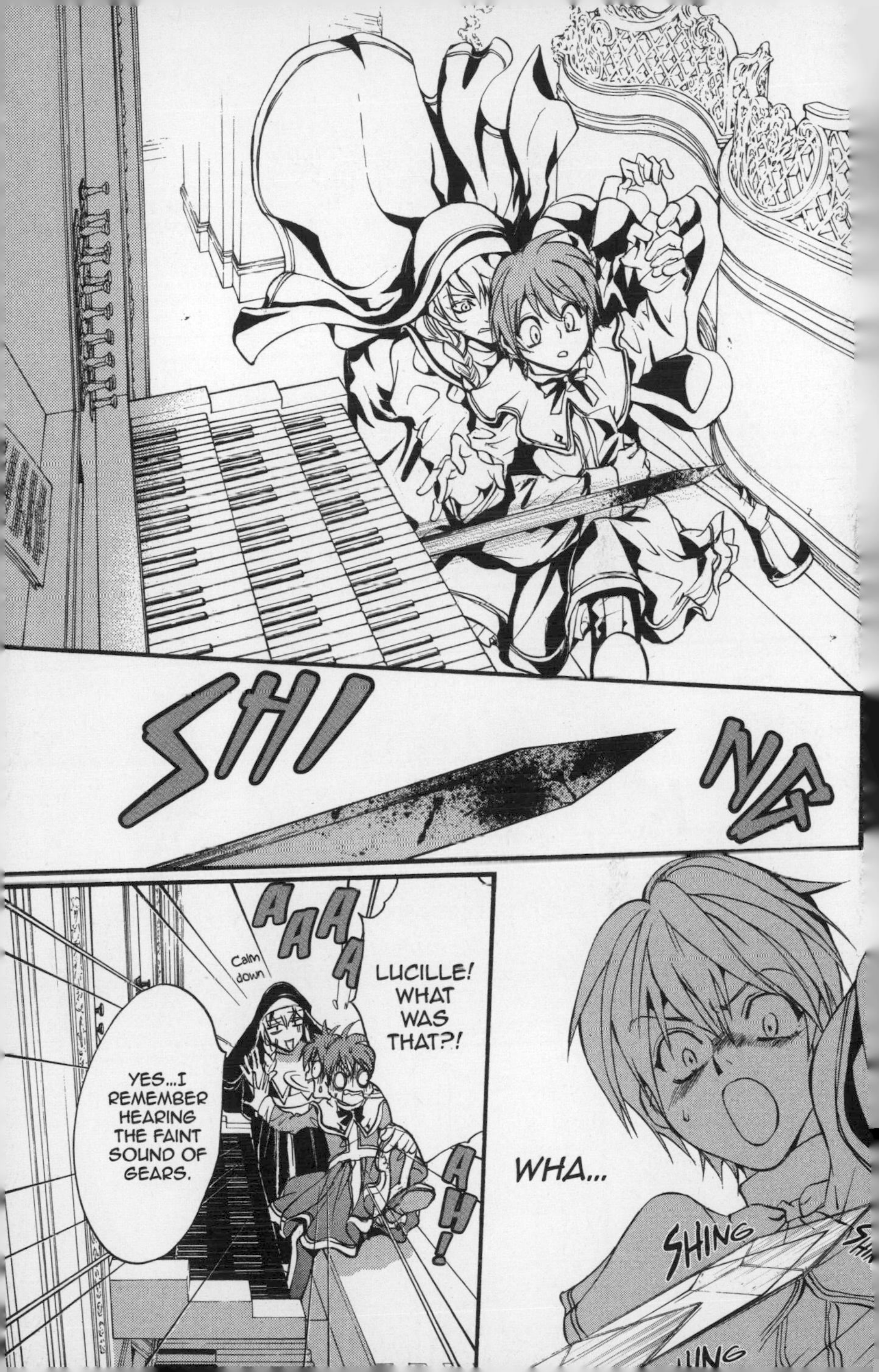
SHI NG
WHA...
SHING
AAAAA
LUCILLE! WHAT WAS THAT?!
Calm down
AH!
YES...I REMEMBER HEARING THE FAINT SOUND OF GEARS.

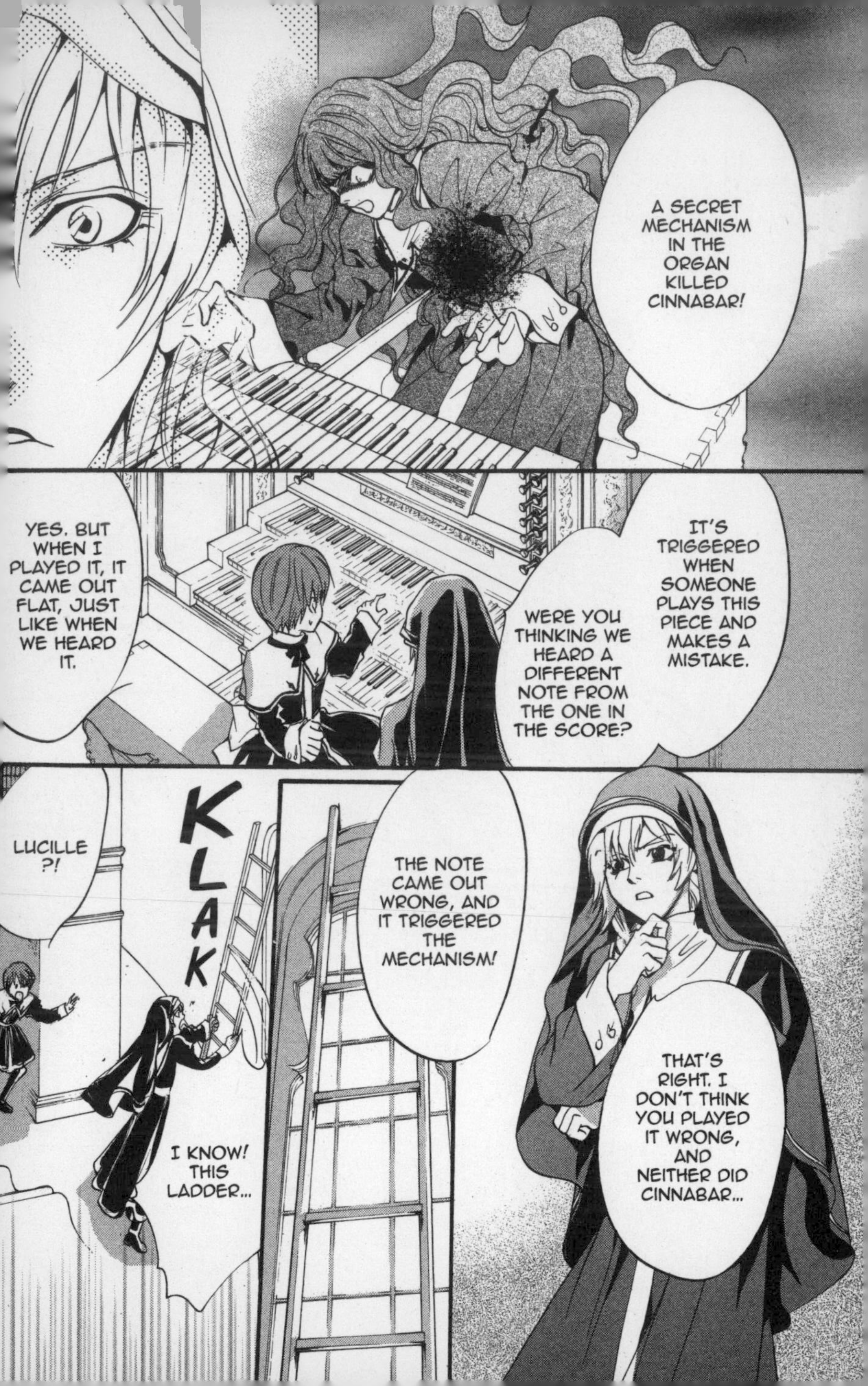
A SECRET MECHANISM IN THE ORGAN KILLED CINNABAR!
IT'S TRIGGERED WHEN SOMEONE PLAYS THIS PIECE AND MAKES A MISTAKE.
WERE YOU THINKING WE HEARD A DIFFERENT NOTE FROM THE ONE IN THE SCORE?
YES. BUT WHEN I PLAYED IT, IT CAME OUT FLAT, JUST LIKE WHEN WE HEARD IT.
THE NOTE CAME OUT WRONG, AND IT TRIGGERED THE MECHANISM!
THAT'S RIGHT. I DON'T THINK YOU PLAYED IT WRONG, AND NEITHER DID CINNABAR...
KLAK
LUCILLE ?!
I KNOW! THIS LADDER...

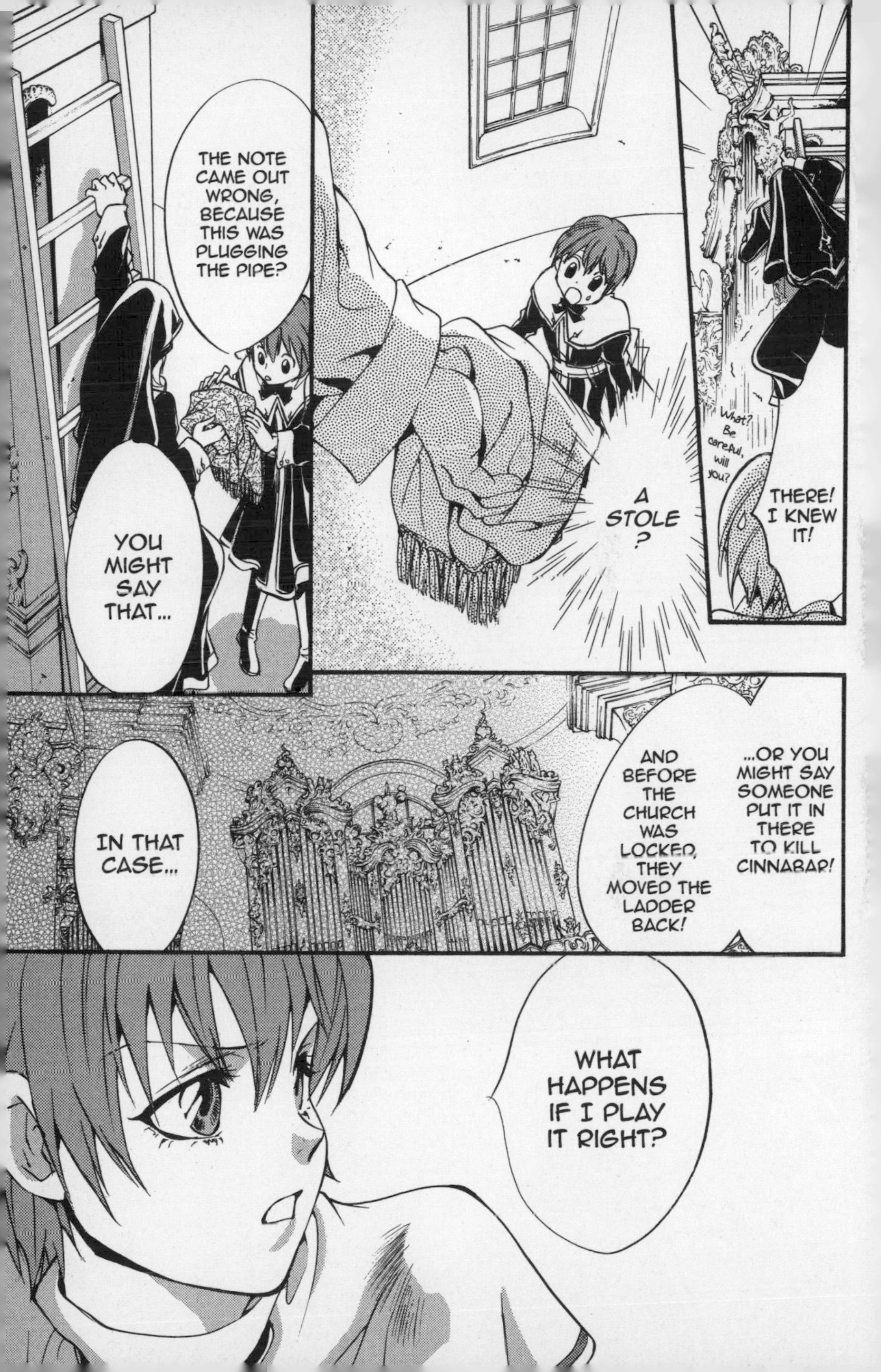
THERE! I KNEW IT!
What? Be careful, will you?
A STOLE?
THE NOTE CAME OUT WRONG, BECAUSE THIS WAS PLUGGING THE PIPE?
YOU MIGHT SAY THAT...
...OR YOU MIGHT SAY SOMEONE PUT IT IN THERE TO KILL CINNABAR!
AND BEFORE THE CHURCH WAS LOCKED, THEY MOVED THE LADDER BACK!
IN THAT CASE...
WHAT HAPPENS IF I PLAY IT RIGHT?

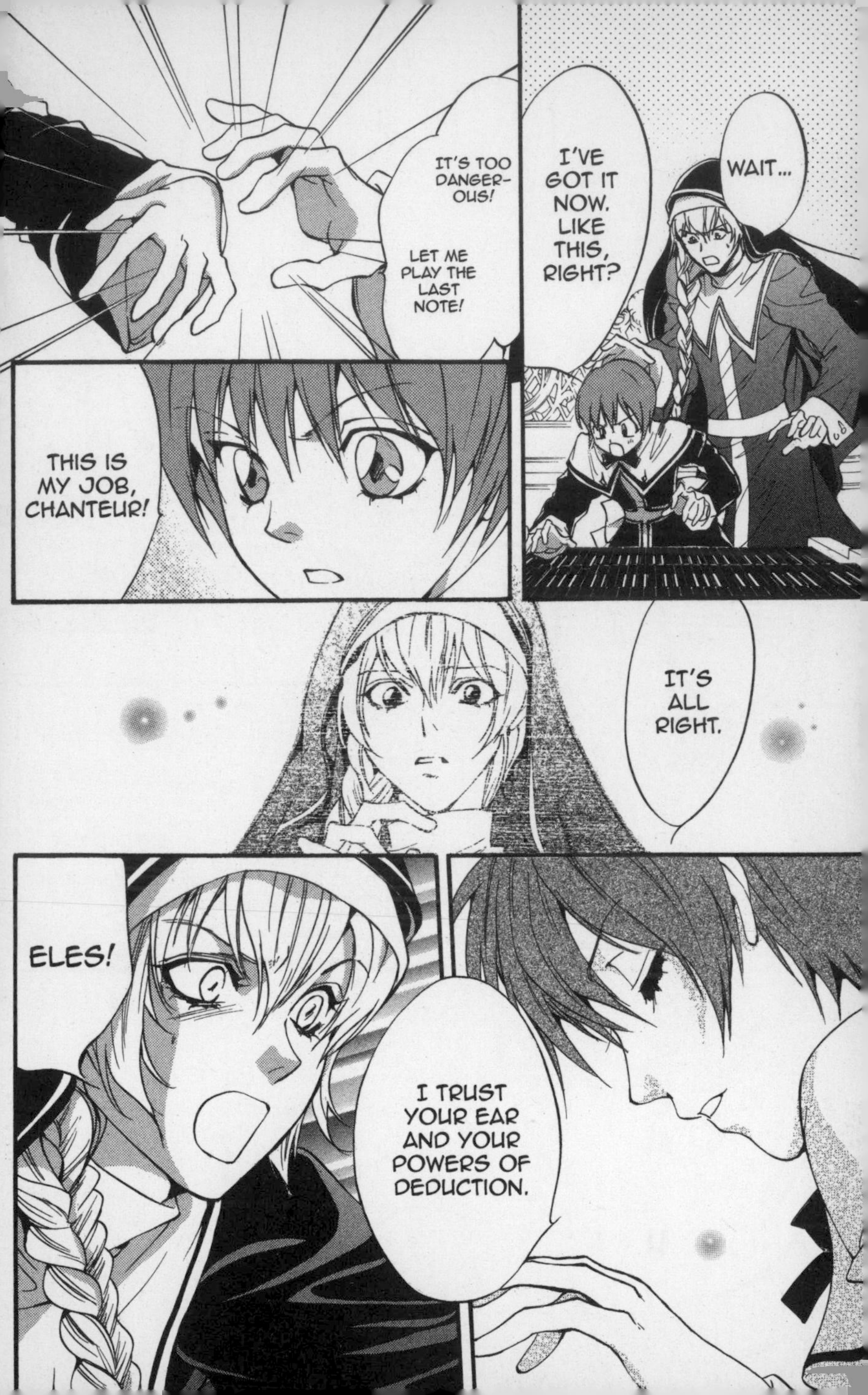
WAIT...
I'VE GOT IT NOW. LIKE THIS, RIGHT?
IT'S TOO DANGER-OUS!
LET ME PLAY THE LAST NOTE!
THIS IS MY JOB, CHANTEUR!
IT'S ALL RIGHT.
I TRUST YOUR EAR AND YOUR POWERS OF DEDUCTION.
ELES!

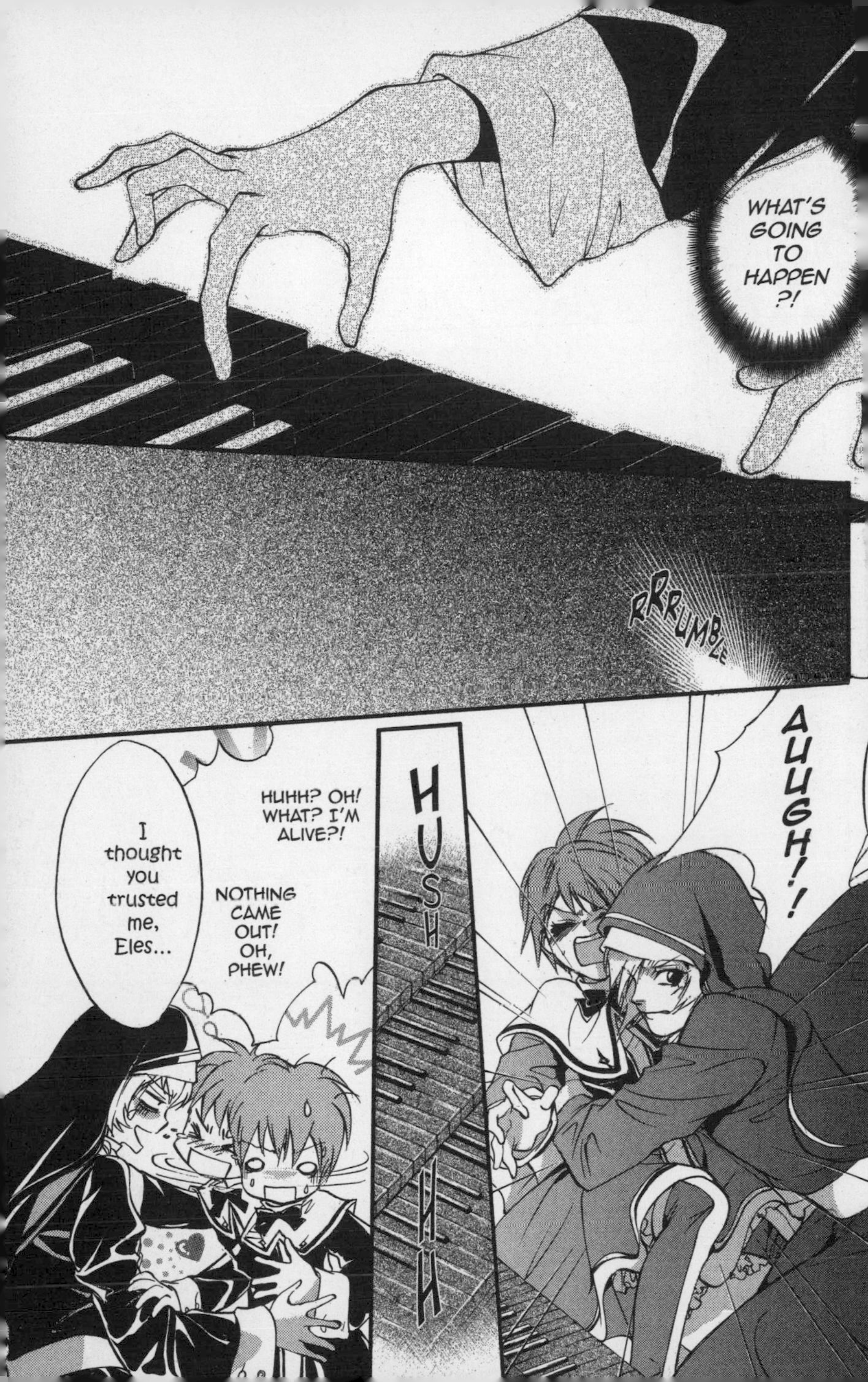
WHAT'S GOING TO HAPPEN?!
RRRUMBLE
AUUGH!!!
HUSH
HUHH? OH! WHAT? I'M ALIVE?!
I thought you trusted me, Eles...
NOTHING CAME OUT! OH, PHEW!

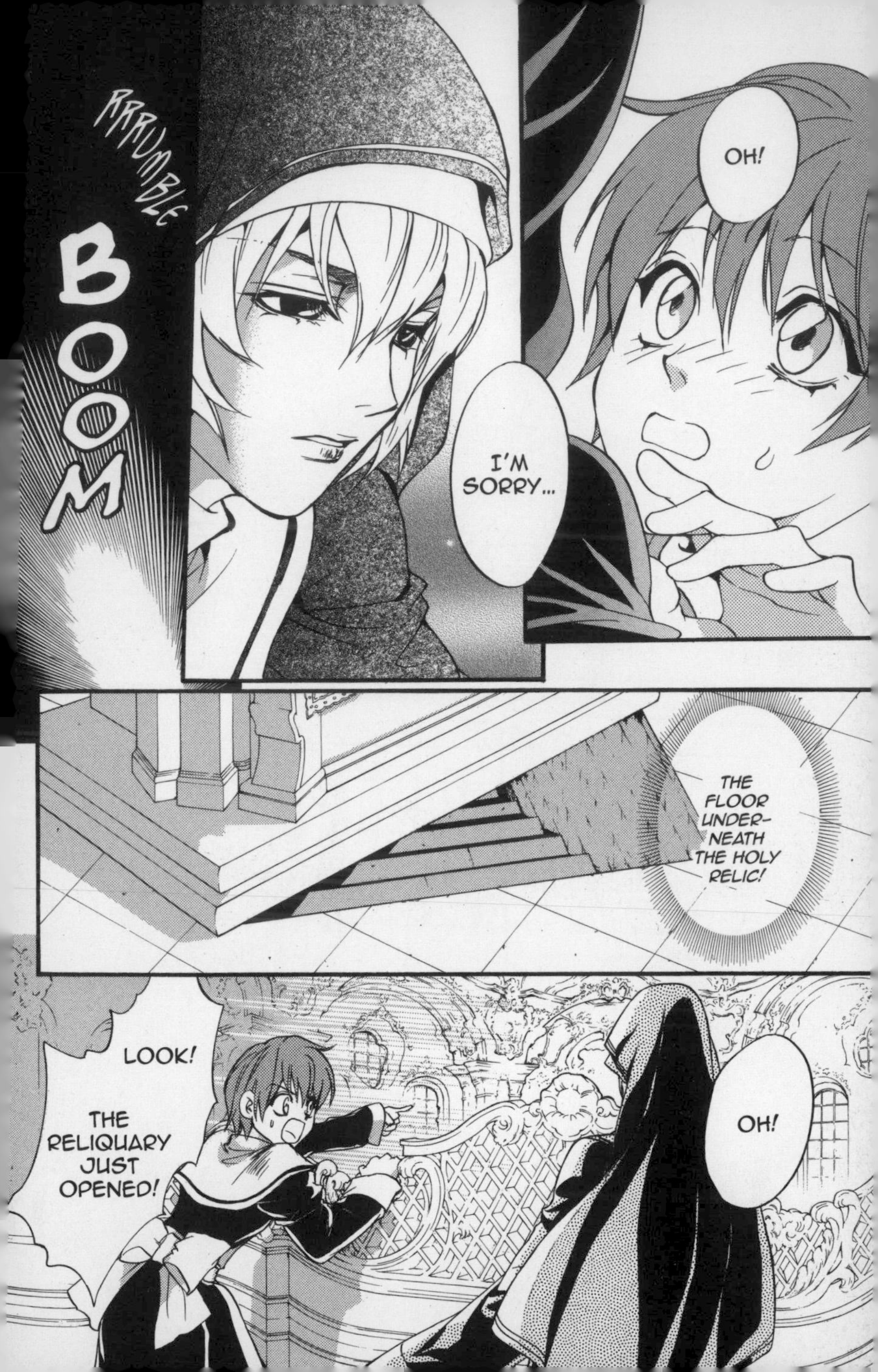
OH!
I'M SORRY...
RRRUMBLE
BOOM
THE FLOOR UNDER-NEATH THE HOLY RELIC!
LOOK!
THE RELIQUARY JUST OPENED!
OH!

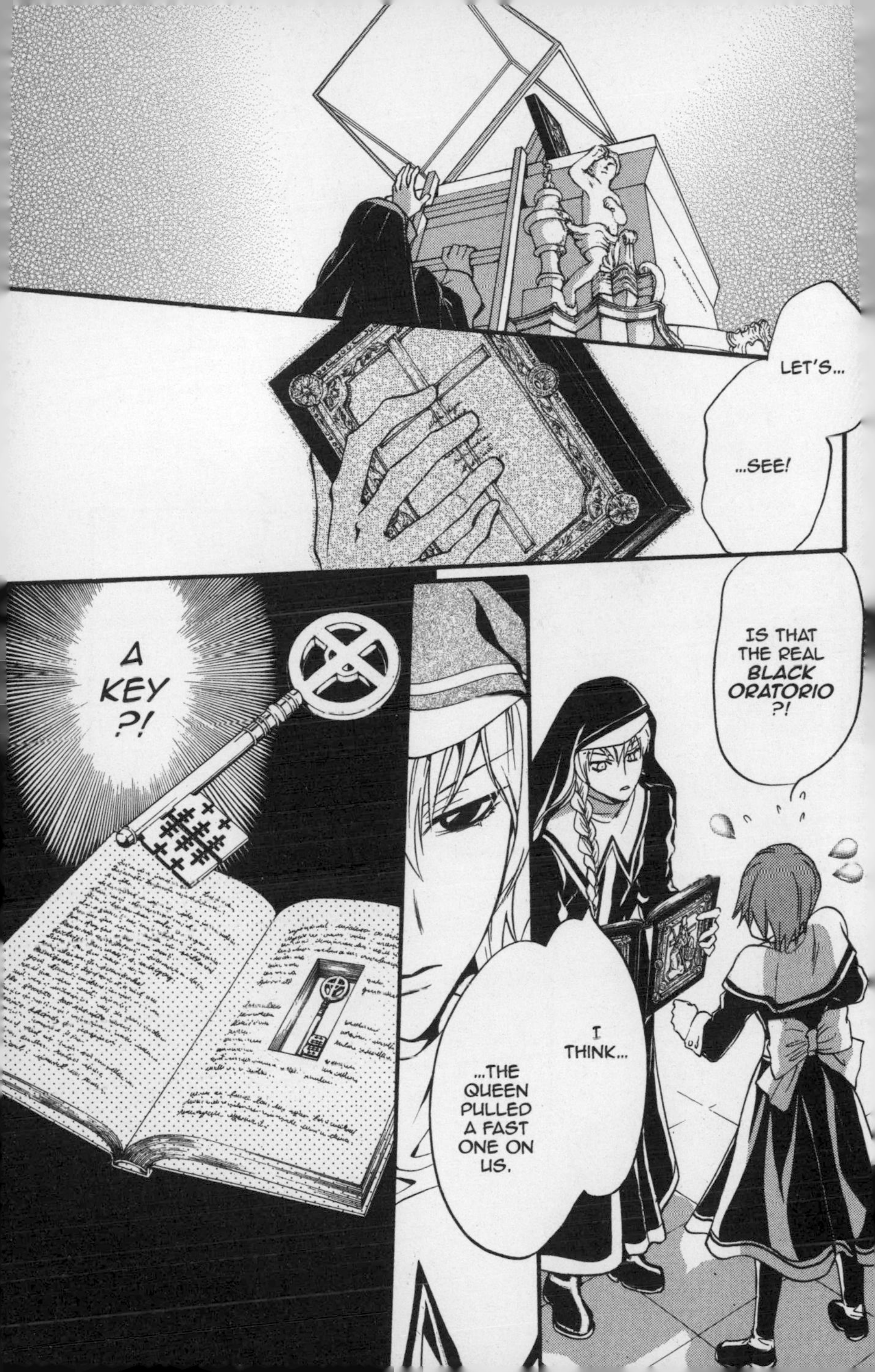

LET'S...
...SEE!
IS THAT THE REAL BLACK ORATORIO ?!
I THINK...
...THE QUEEN PULLED A FAST ONE ON US.
A KEY ?!

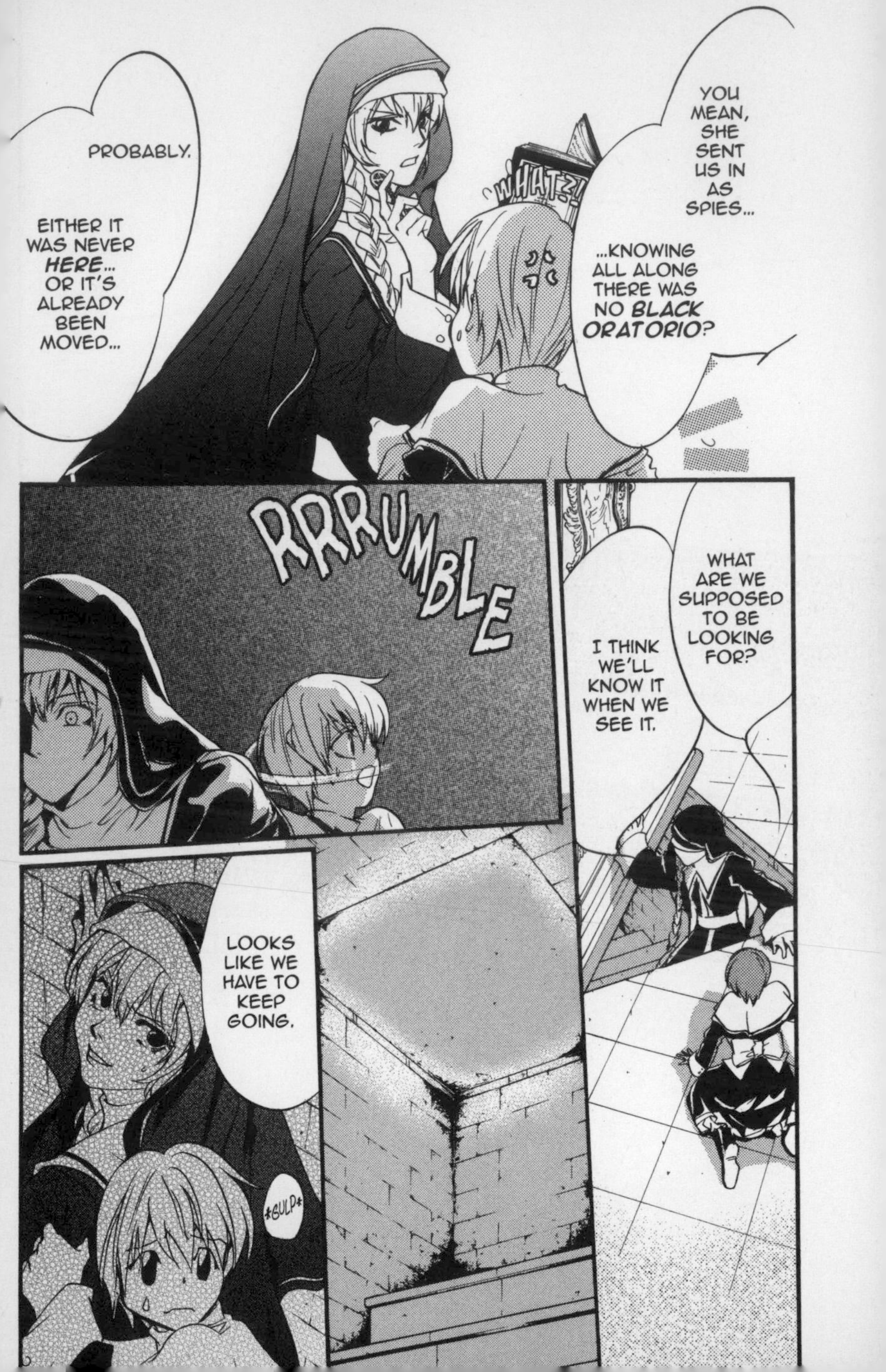
WHAT?!
YOU MEAN, SHE SENT US IN AS SPIES...
...KNOWING ALL ALONG THERE WAS NO BLACK ORATORIO?
PROBABLY.
EITHER IT WAS NEVER HERE... OR IT'S ALREADY BEEN MOVED...
WHAT ARE WE SUPPOSED TO BE LOOKING FOR?
I THINK WE'LL KNOW IT WHEN WE SEE IT.
RRRUMBLE
LOOKS LIKE WE HAVE TO KEEP GOING.
GULP

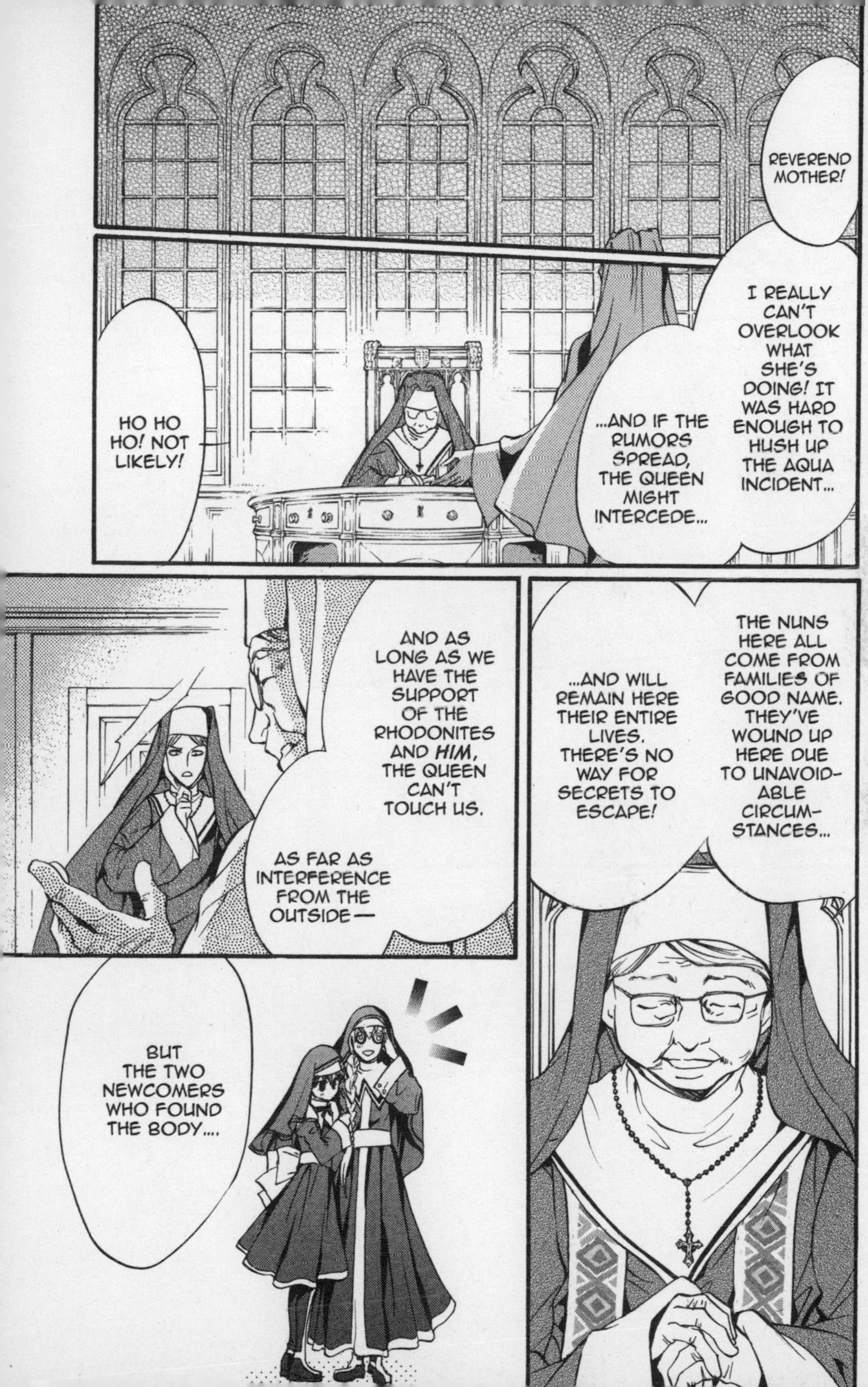
REVEREND MOTHER!
I REALLY CAN'T OVERLOOK WHAT SHE'S DOING! IT WAS HARD ENOUGH TO HUSH UP THE AQUA INCIDENT...
...AND IF THE RUMORS SPREAD, THE QUEEN MIGHT INTERCEDE...
HO HO HO! NOT LIKELY!
THE NUNS HERE ALL COME FROM FAMILIES OF GOOD NAME. THEY'VE WOUND UP HERE DUE TO UNAVOID-ABLE CIRCUM-STANCES...
...AND WILL REMAIN HERE THEIR ENTIRE LIVES. THERE'S NO WAY FOR SECRETS TO ESCAPE!
AND AS LONG AS WE HAVE THE SUPPORT OF THE RHODONITES AND *HIM*, THE QUEEN CAN'T TOUCH US.
AS FAR AS INTERFERENCE FROM THE OUTSIDE—
BUT THE TWO NEWCOMERS WHO FOUND THE BODY....

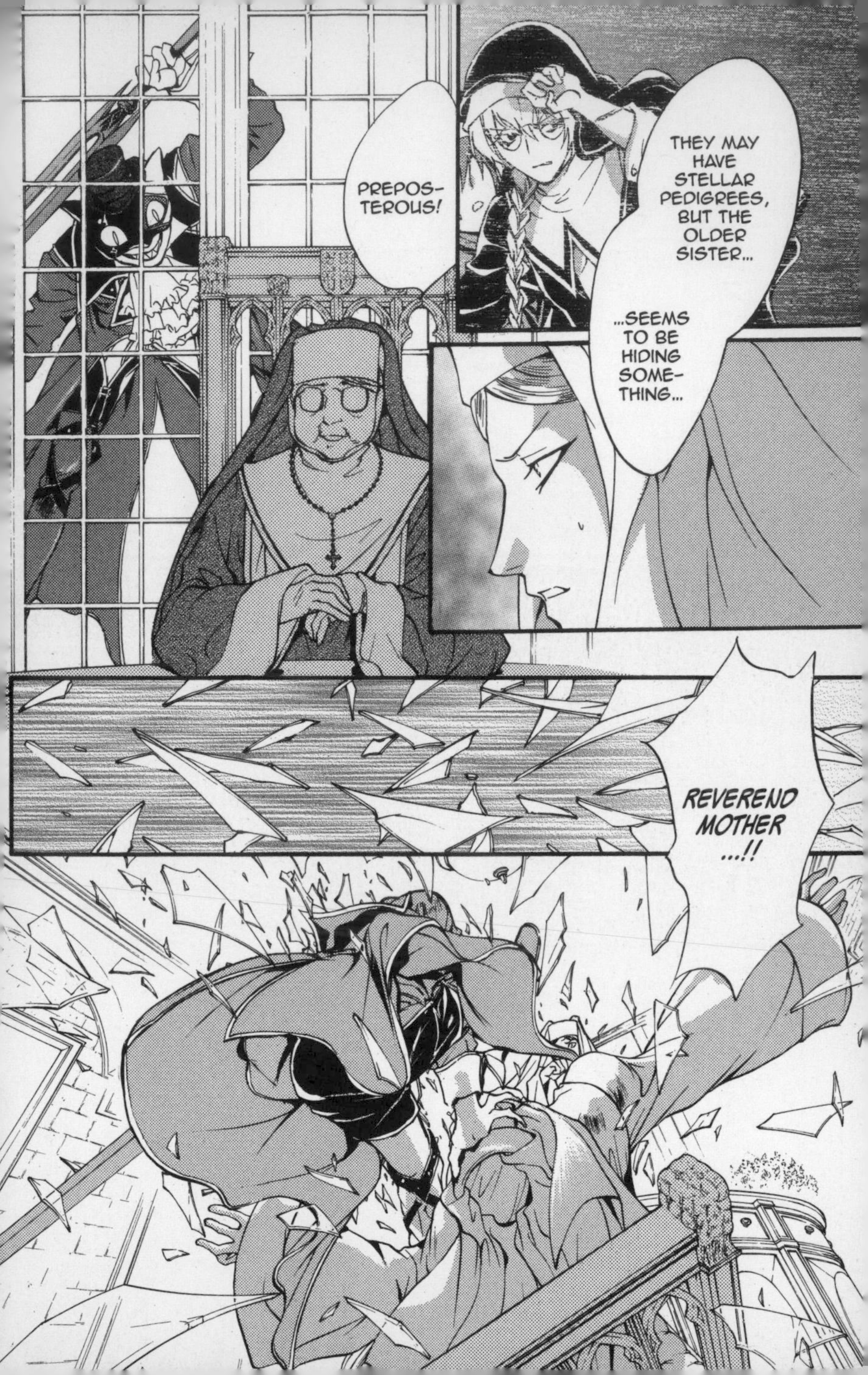
THEY MAY HAVE STELLAR PEDIGREES, BUT THE OLDER SISTER...
...SEEMS TO BE HIDING SOME-THING...
PREPOS-TEROUS!
REVEREND MOTHER ...!!

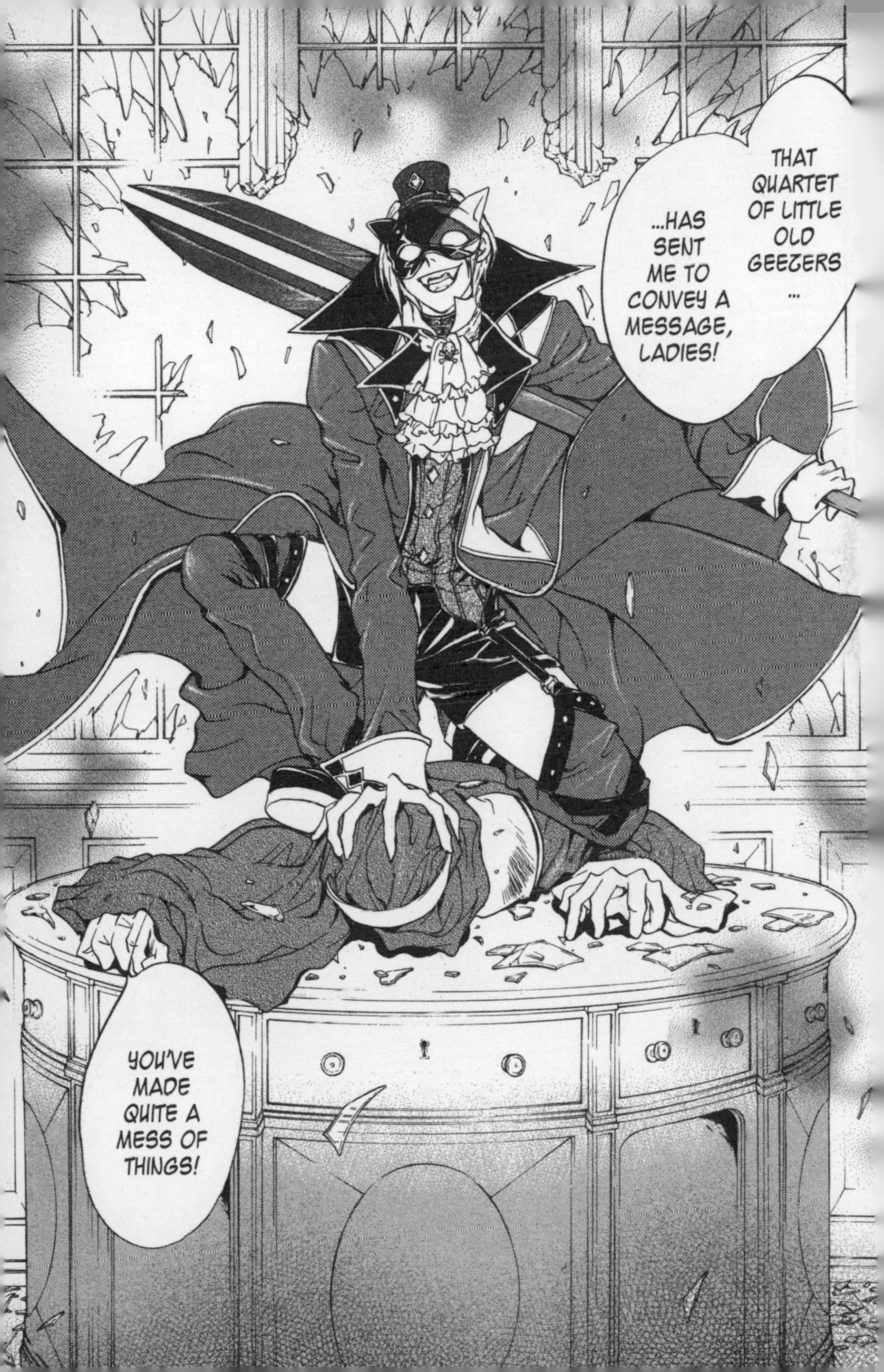
THAT QUARTET OF LITTLE OLD GEEZERS ...
...HAS SENT ME TO CONVEY A MESSAGE, LADIES!
YOU'VE MADE QUITE A MESS OF THINGS!

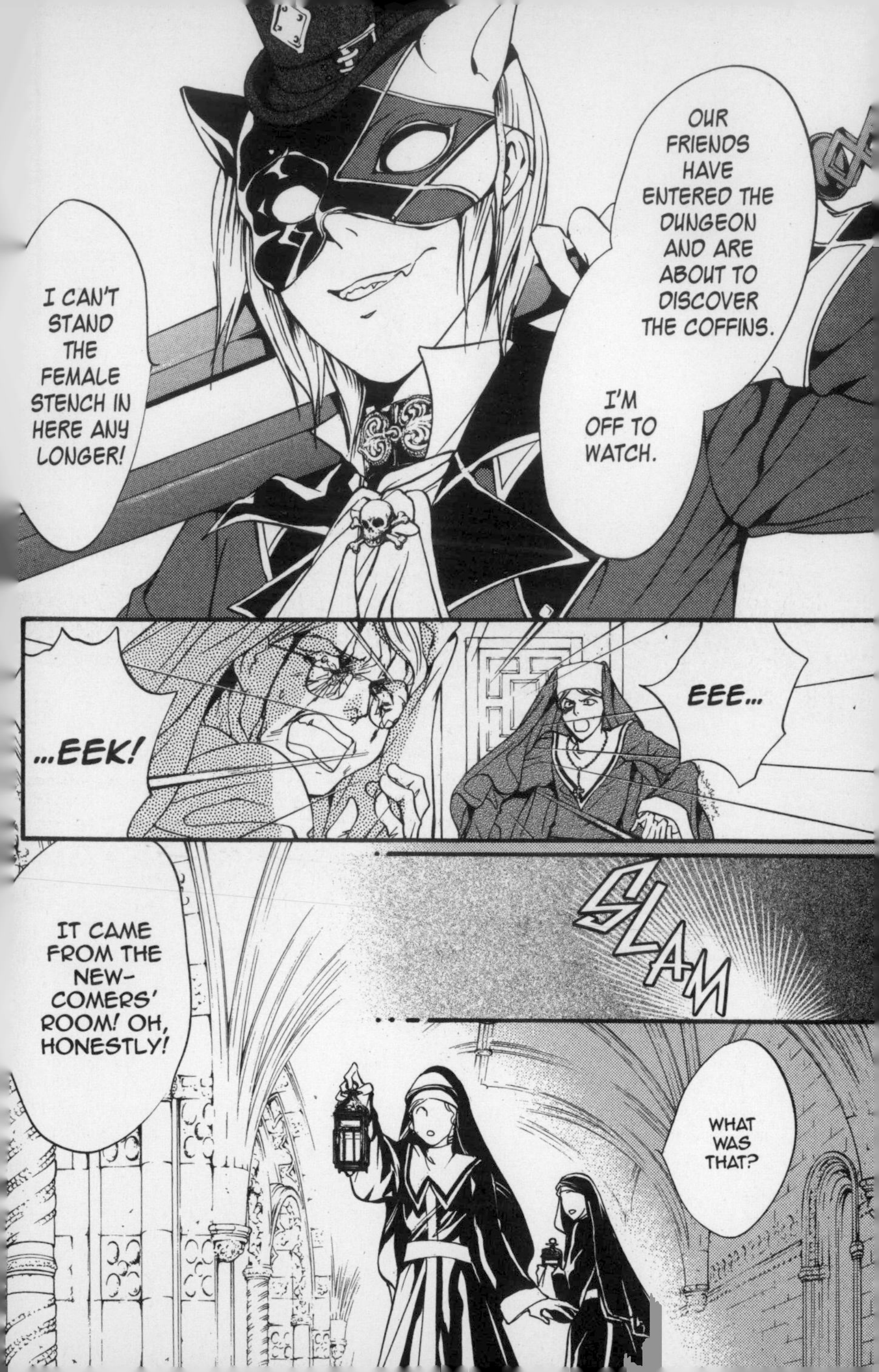
OUR FRIENDS HAVE ENTERED THE DUNGEON AND ARE ABOUT TO DISCOVER THE COFFINS.
I'M OFF TO WATCH.
I CAN'T STAND THE FEMALE STENCH IN HERE ANY LONGER!
EEE...
...EEK!
SLAM
WHAT WAS THAT?
IT CAME FROM THE NEW-COMERS' ROOM! OH, HONESTLY!

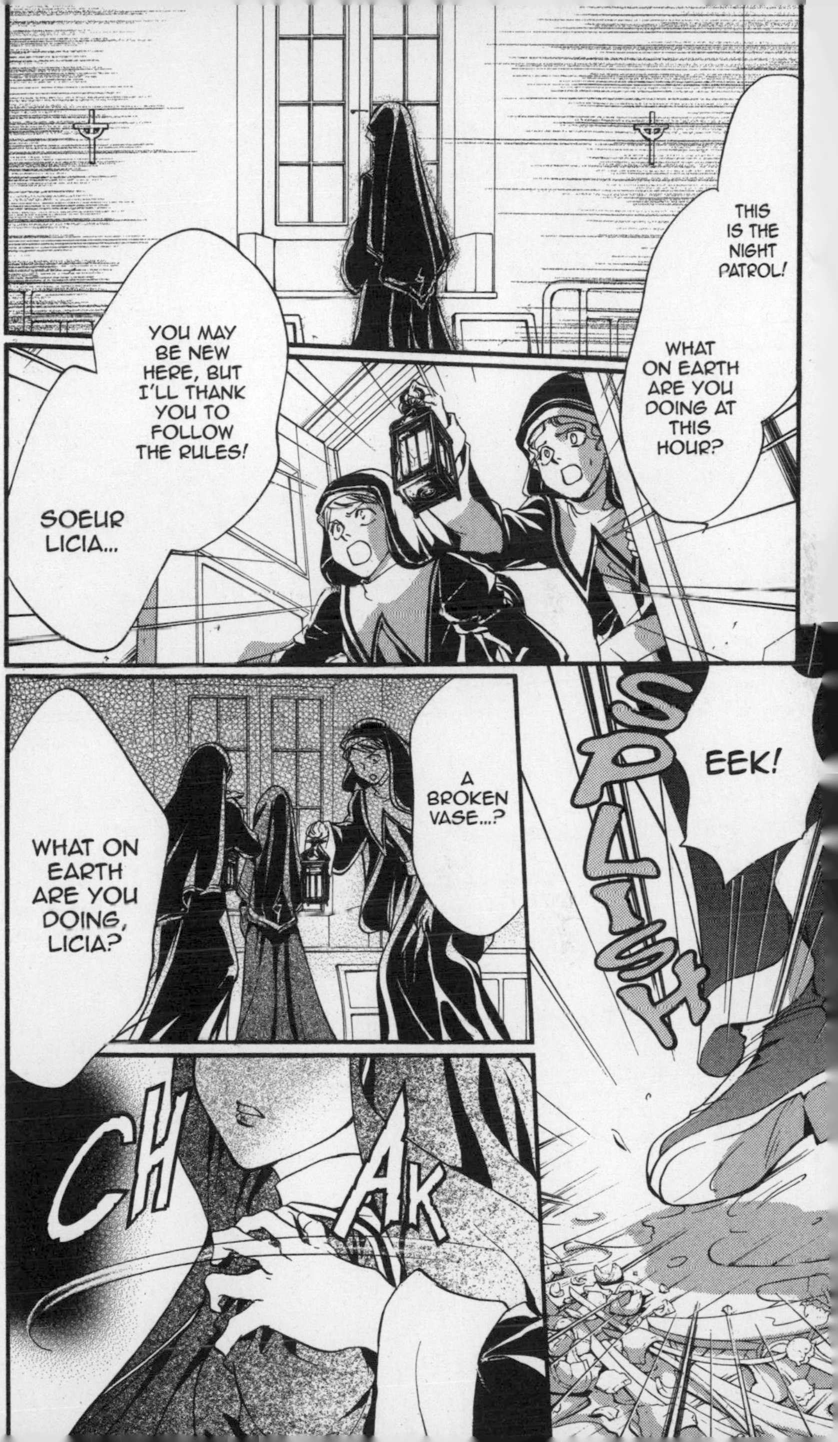
THIS IS THE NIGHT PATROL!
WHAT ON EARTH ARE YOU DOING AT THIS HOUR?
YOU MAY BE NEW HERE, BUT I'LL THANK YOU TO FOLLOW THE RULES!
SOEUR LICIA...
EEK!
SPLISH
A BROKEN VASE...?
WHAT ON EARTH ARE YOU DOING, LICIA?
CHAK

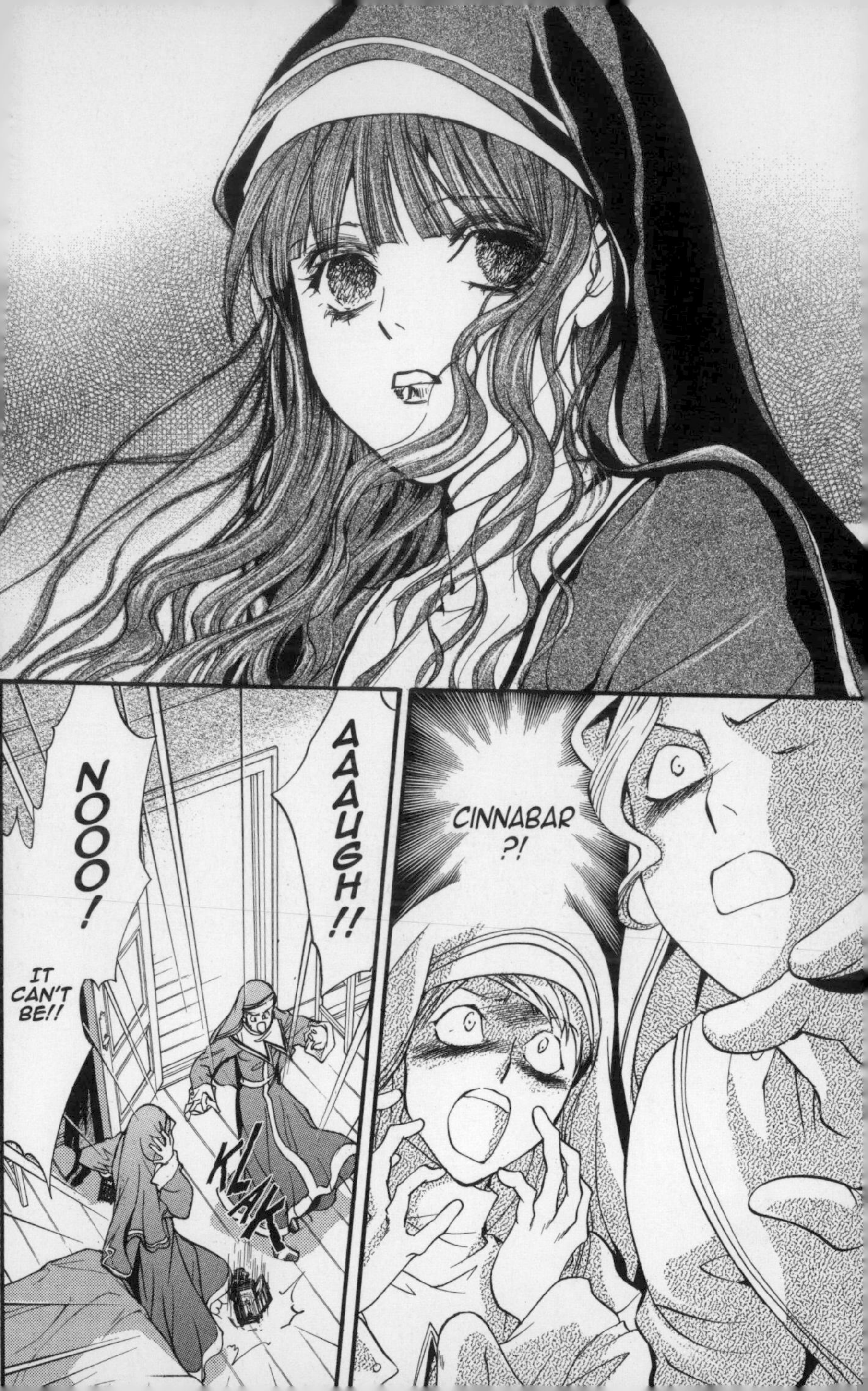
CINNABAR ?!
AAAUGH!!
NOOOO!
IT CAN'T BE!!
KLAK

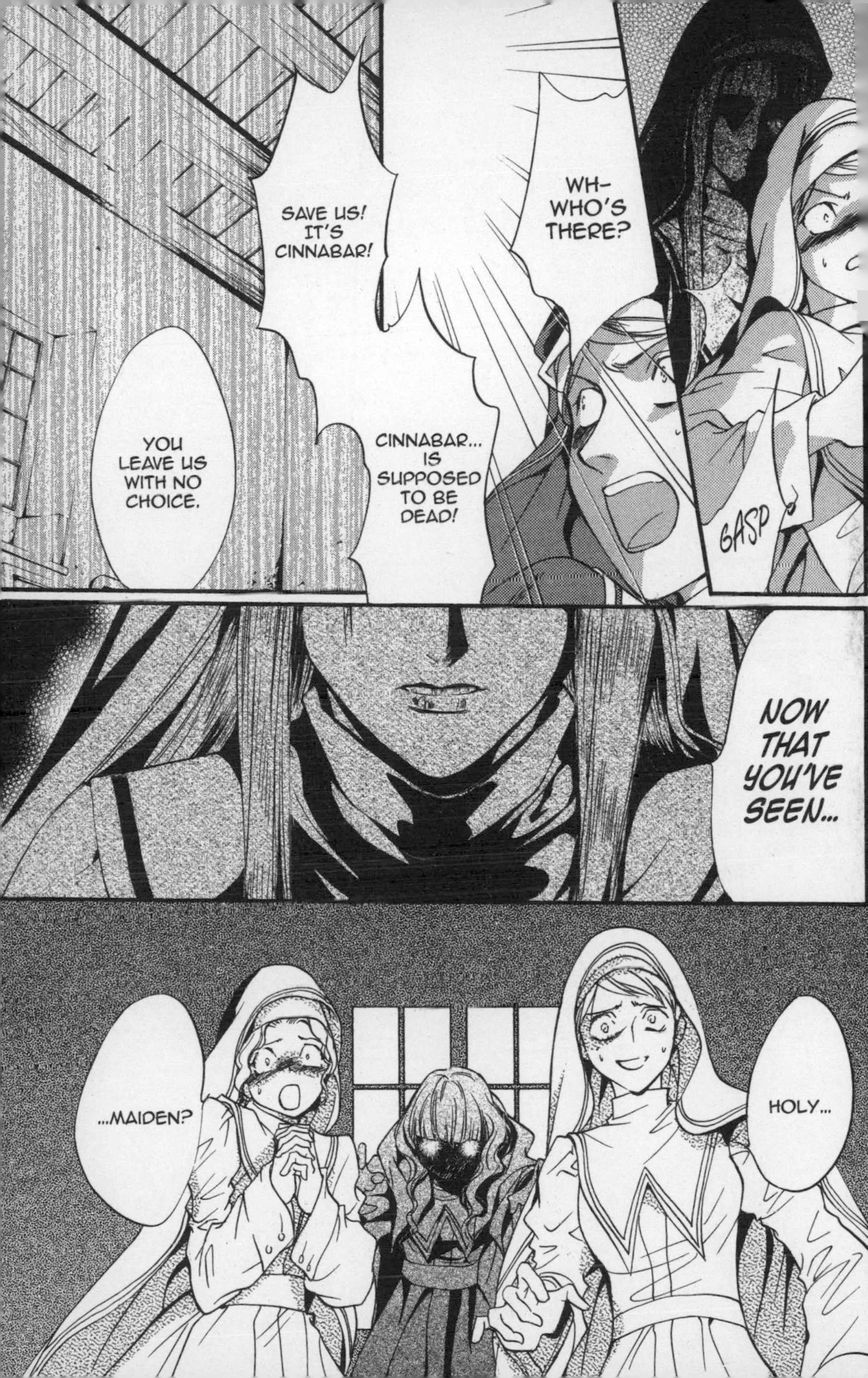
WH- WHO'S THERE?
GASP
SAVE US! IT'S CINNABAR!
CINNABAR... IS SUPPOSED TO BE DEAD!
YOU LEAVE US WITH NO CHOICE.
NOW THAT YOU'VE SEEN...
HOLY...
...MAIDEN?

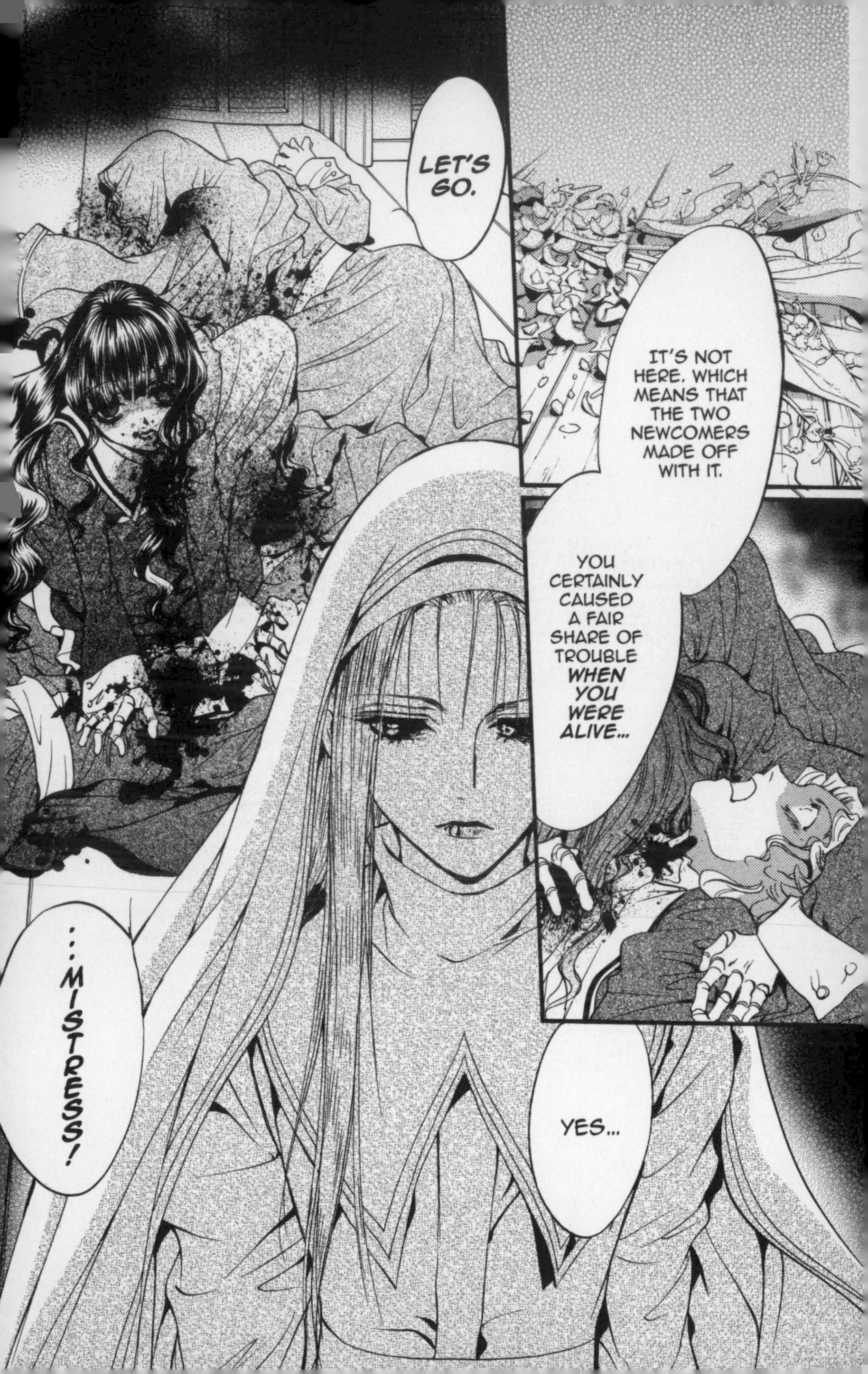
IT'S NOT HERE. WHICH MEANS THAT THE TWO NEWCOMERS MADE OFF WITH IT.
YOU CERTAINLY CAUSED A FAIR SHARE OF TROUBLE WHEN YOU WERE ALIVE...
LET'S GO.
YES...
...MISTRESS!

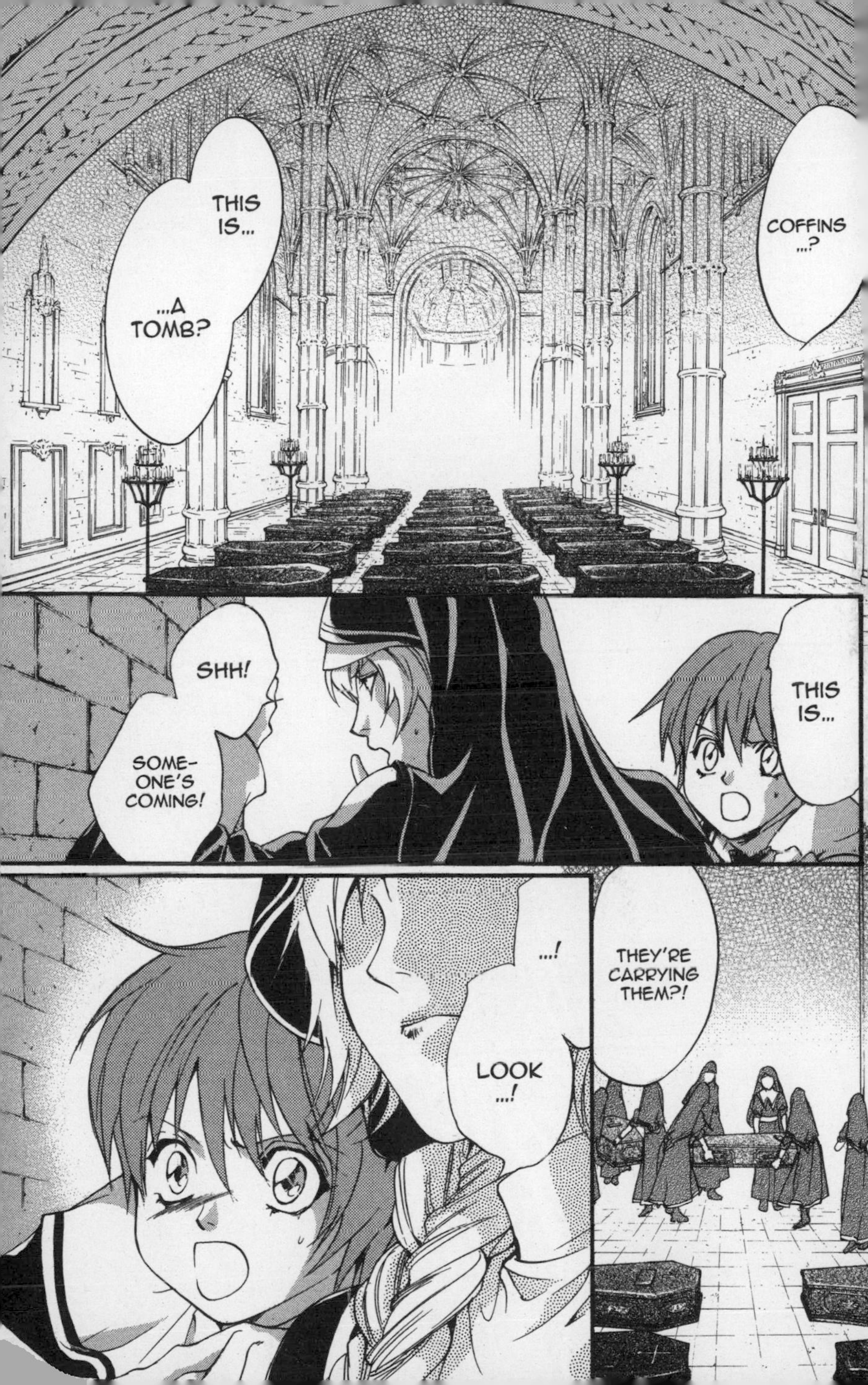
COFFINS ...?
THIS IS... ...A TOMB?
THIS IS...
SHH! SOME-ONE'S COMING!
THEY'RE CARRYING THEM?!
...!
LOOK ...!

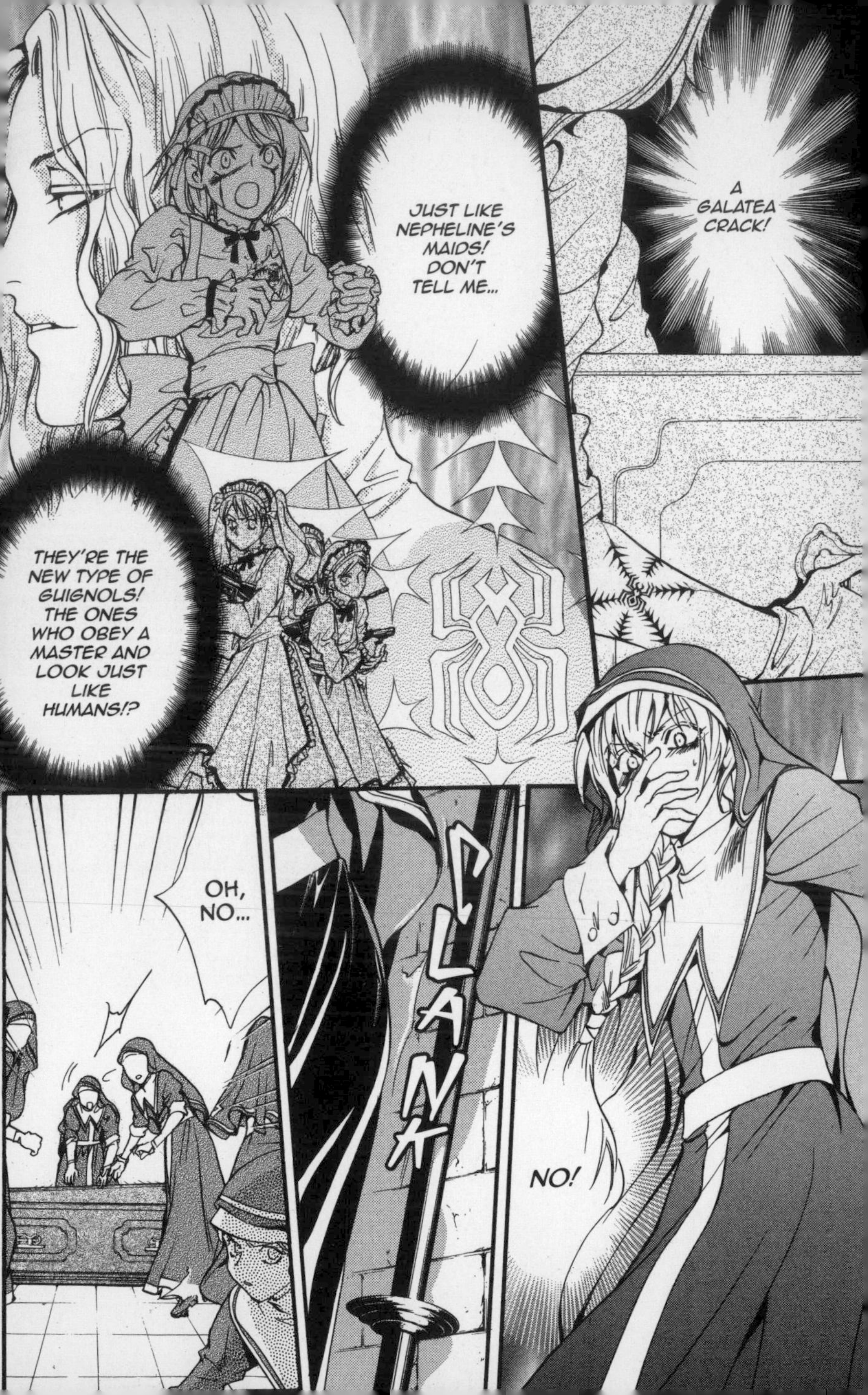
A GALATEA CRACK!
JUST LIKE NEPHELINE'S MAIDS! DON'T TELL ME...
THEY'RE THE NEW TYPE OF GUIGNOLS! THE ONES WHO OBEY A MASTER AND LOOK JUST LIKE HUMANS!?
NO!
CLANK
OH, NO...

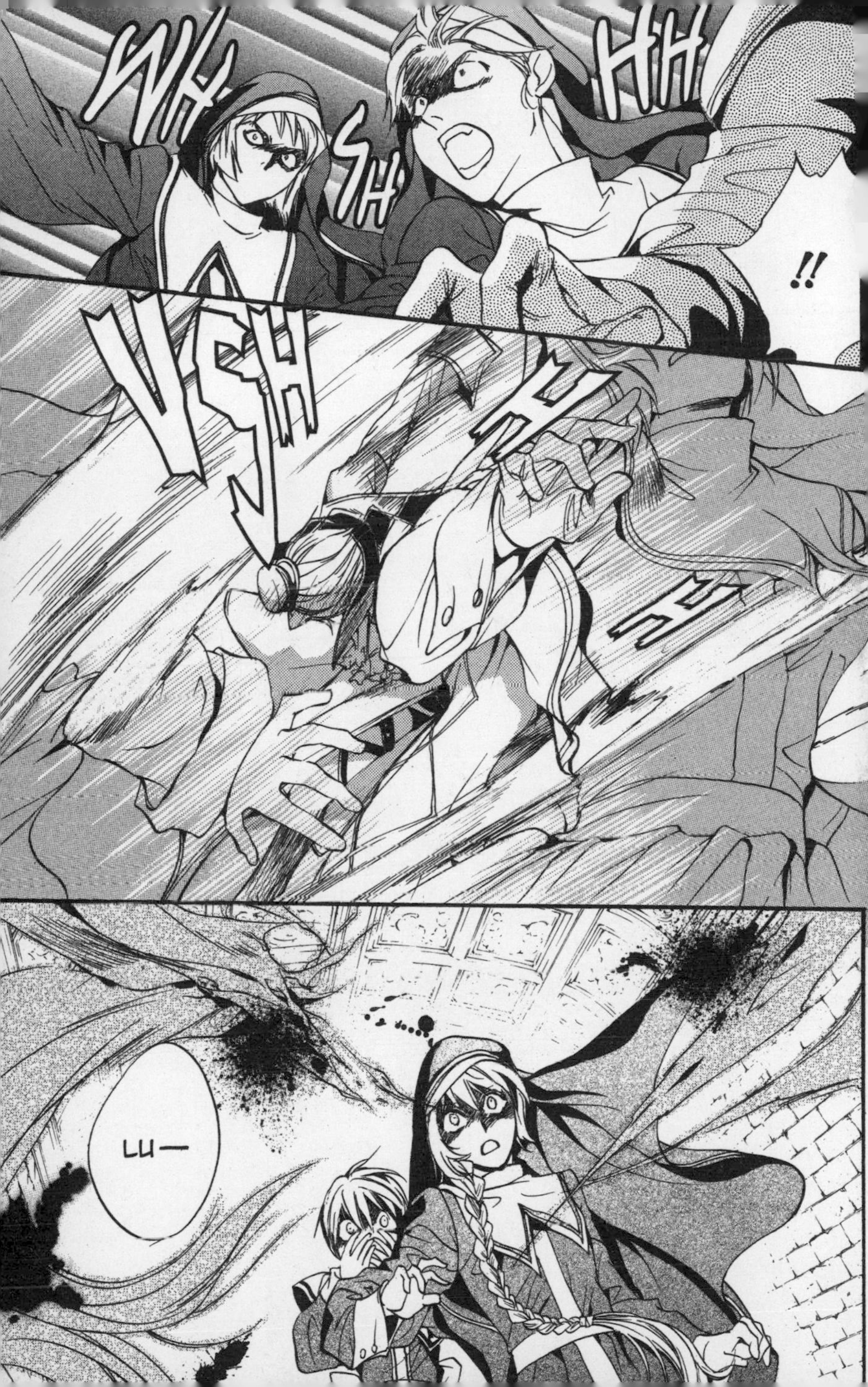
!!
HH
SH
WH
VSH
LU—

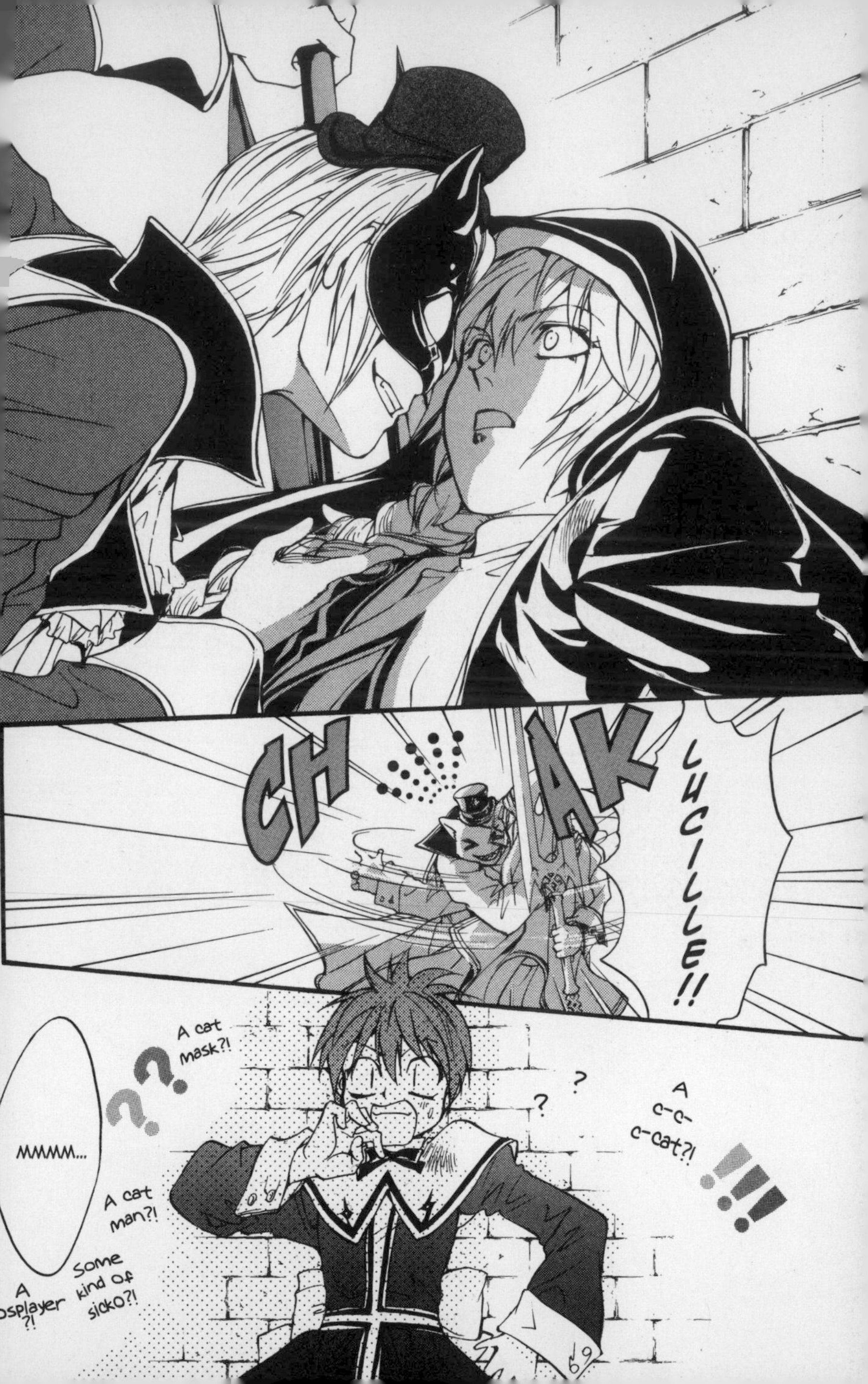
CHAK
LUCILLE!!
A c-c-c-cat?!
?
?
A cat mask?!
A cat man?!
Some kind of sicko?!
A cosplayer?!
MMMM...

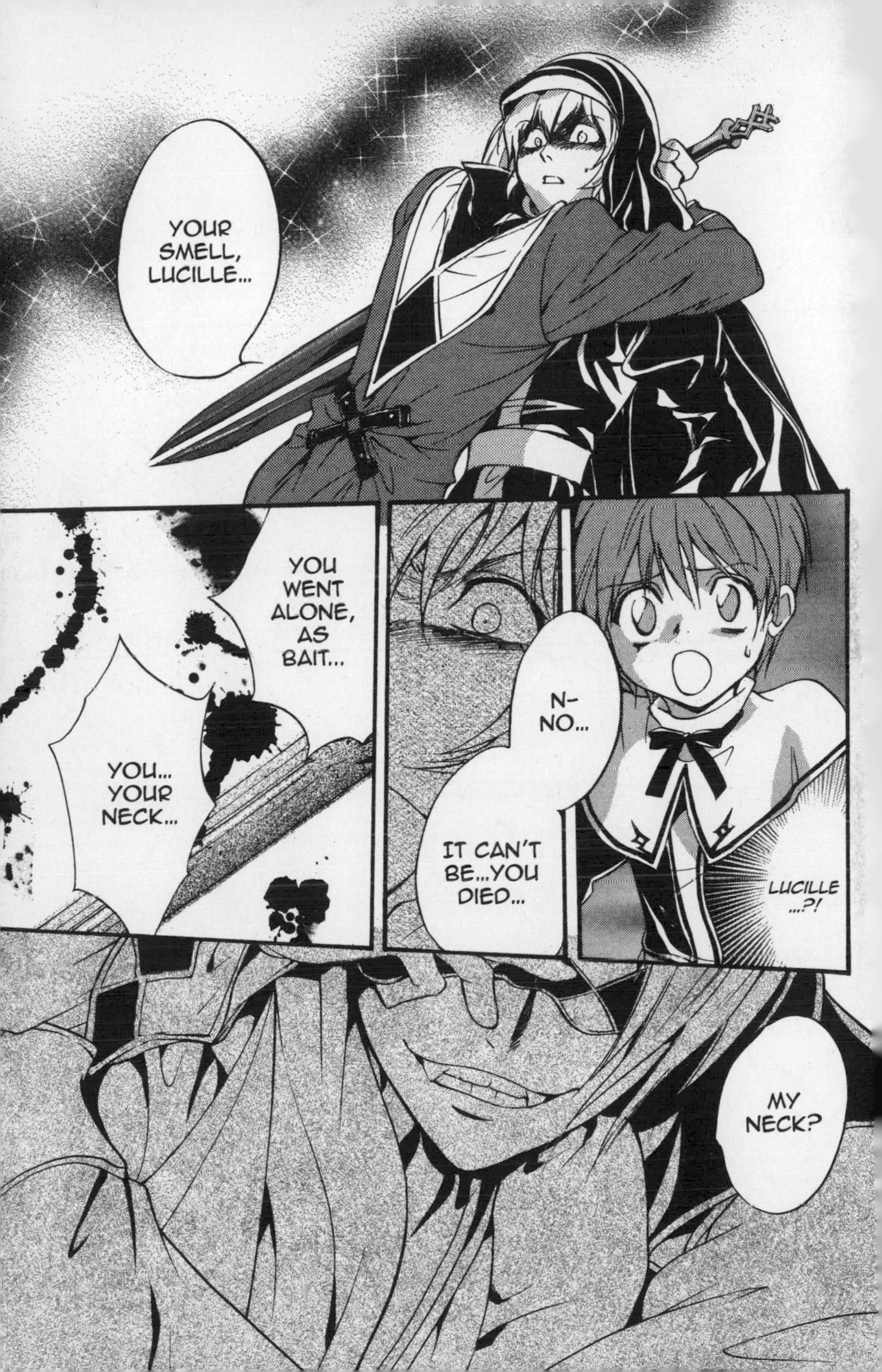
YOUR SMELL, LUCILLE...
LUCILLE ...?!
N-NO...
IT CAN'T BE...YOU DIED...
YOU WENT ALONE, AS BAIT...
YOU... YOUR NECK...
MY NECK?

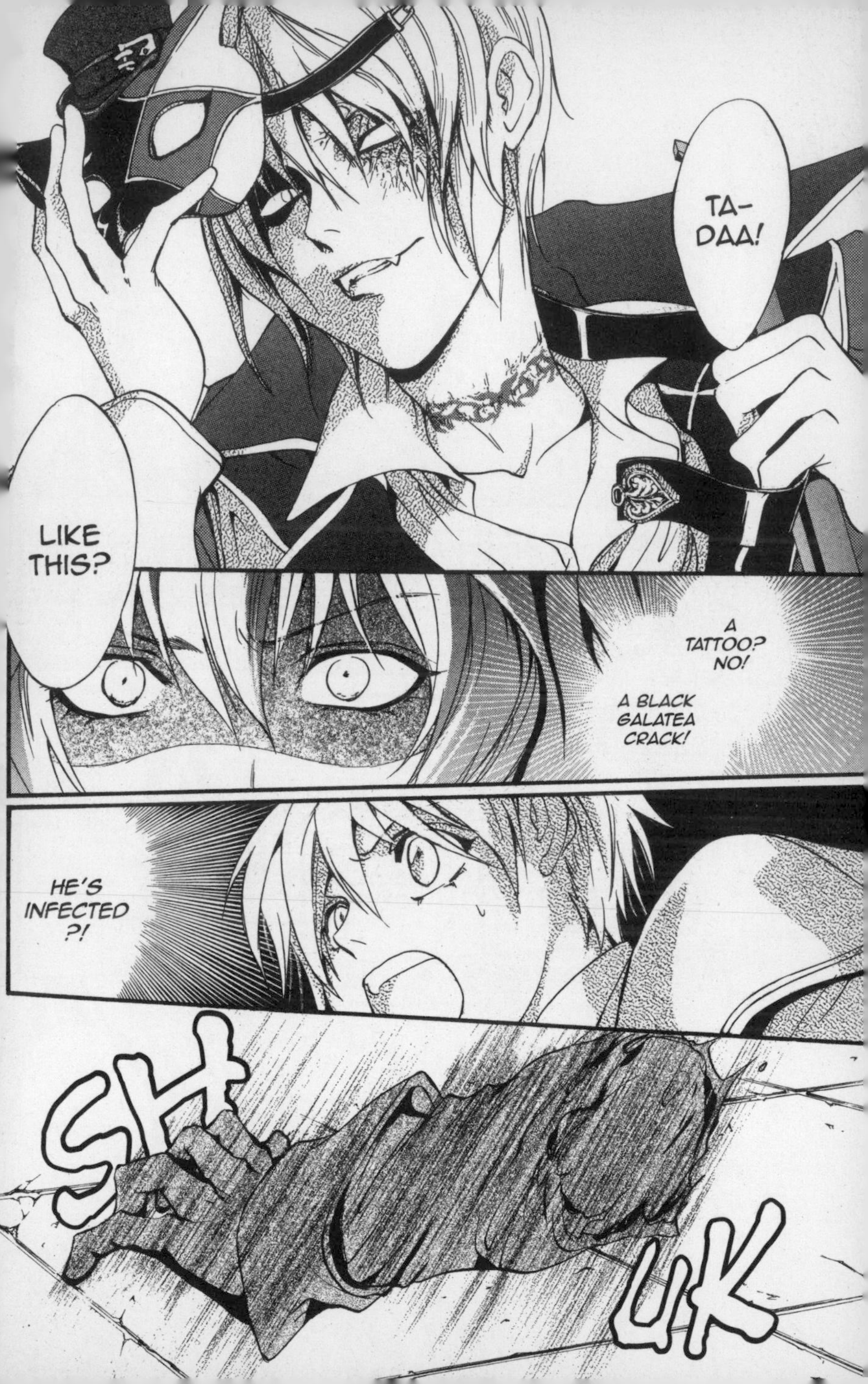
TA-DAA!
LIKE THIS?
A TATTOO? NO!
A BLACK GALATEA CRACK!
HE'S INFECTED ?!
SHUK

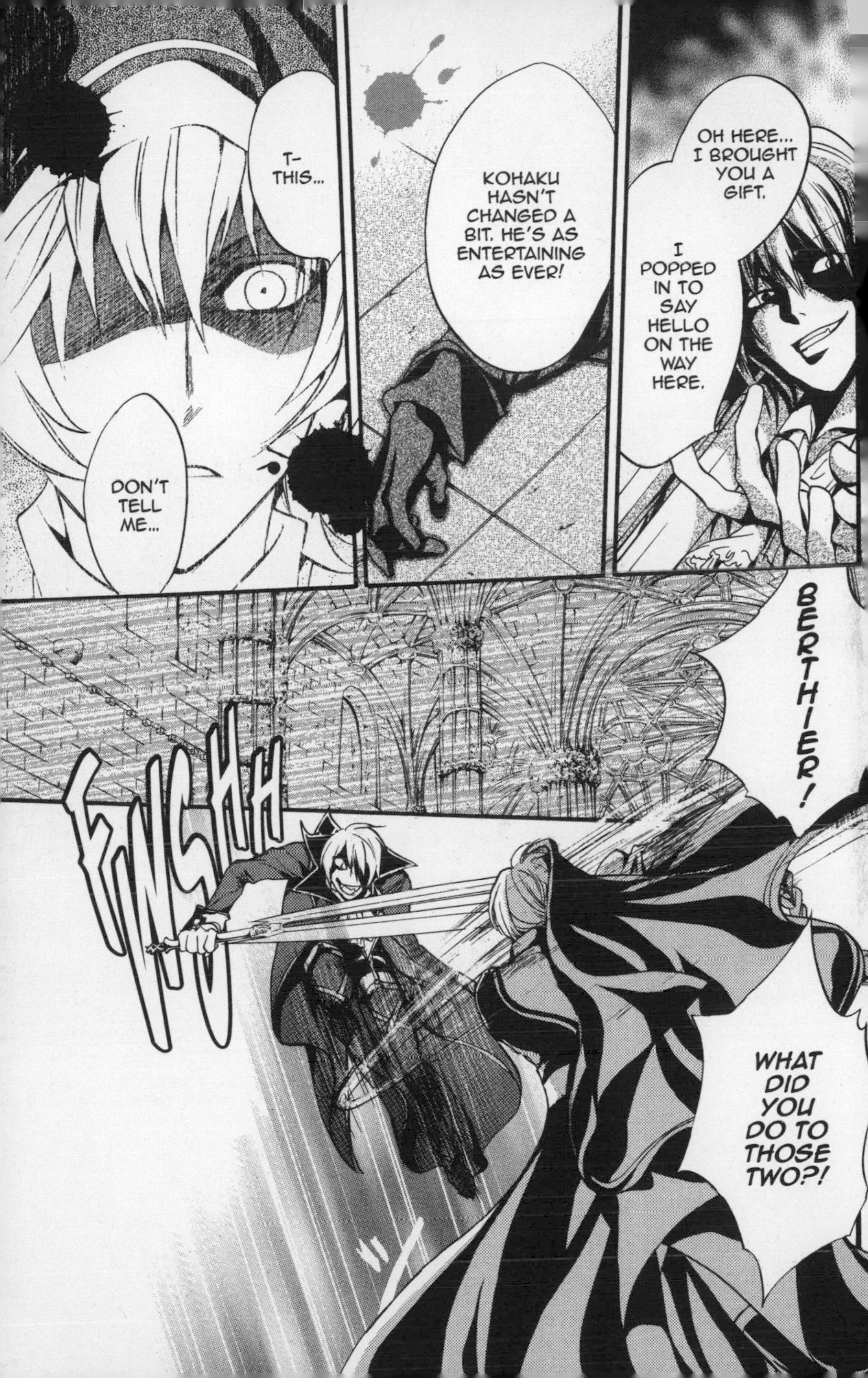
OH HERE... I BROUGHT YOU A GIFT.
I POPPED IN TO SAY HELLO ON THE WAY HERE.
KOHAKU HASN'T CHANGED A BIT. HE'S AS ENTERTAINING AS EVER!
T-THIS...
DON'T TELL ME...
BERTHIER!
FINSHH
WHAT DID YOU DO TO THOSE TWO?!

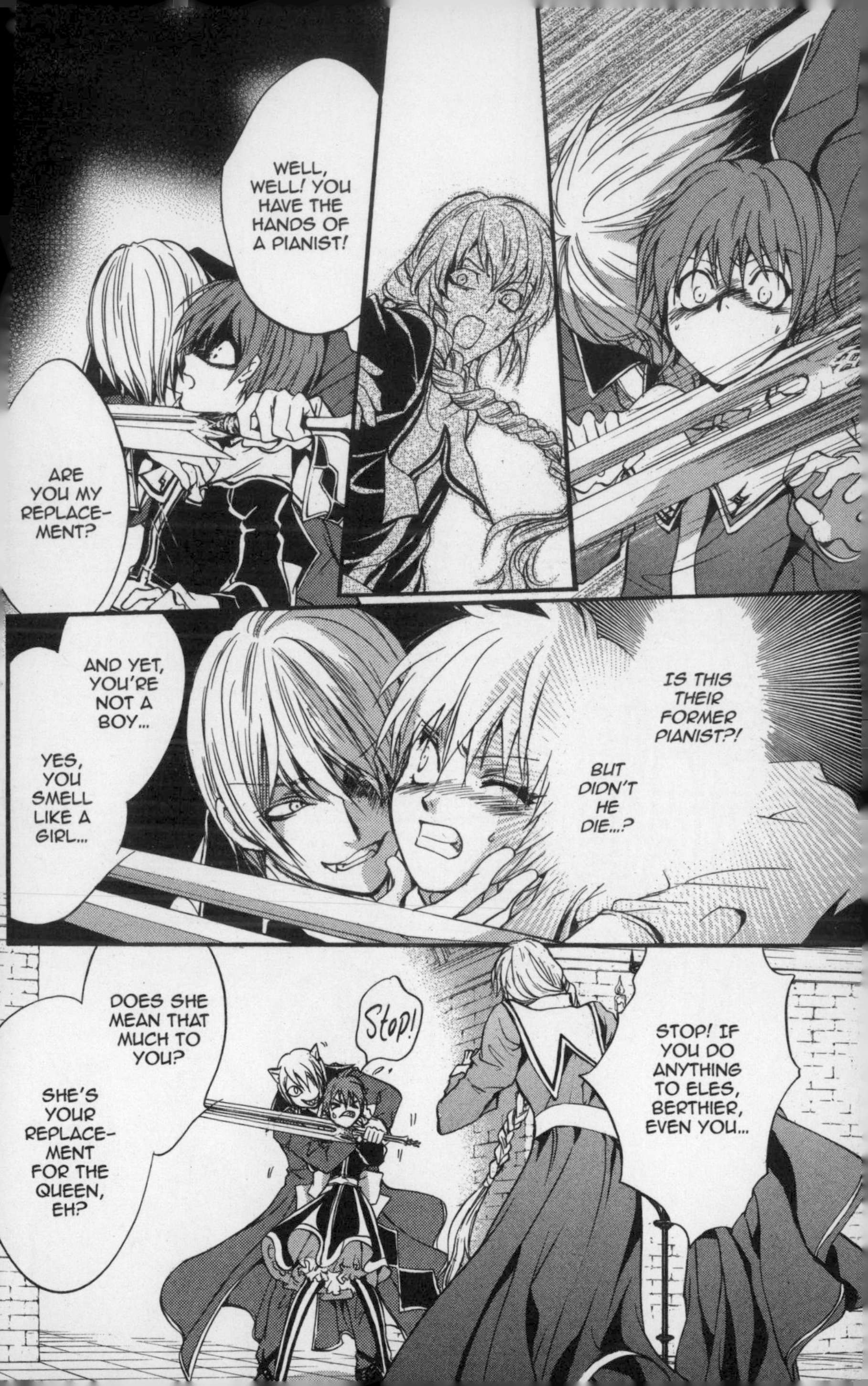
WELL, WELL! YOU HAVE THE HANDS OF A PIANIST!
ARE YOU MY REPLACEMENT?
IS THIS THEIR FORMER PIANIST?!
BUT DIDN'T HE DIE...?
AND YET, YOU'RE NOT A BOY...
YES, YOU SMELL LIKE A GIRL...
STOP! IF YOU DO ANYTHING TO ELES, BERTHIER, EVEN YOU...
Stop!
DOES SHE MEAN THAT MUCH TO YOU?
SHE'S YOUR REPLACEMENT FOR THE QUEEN, EH?

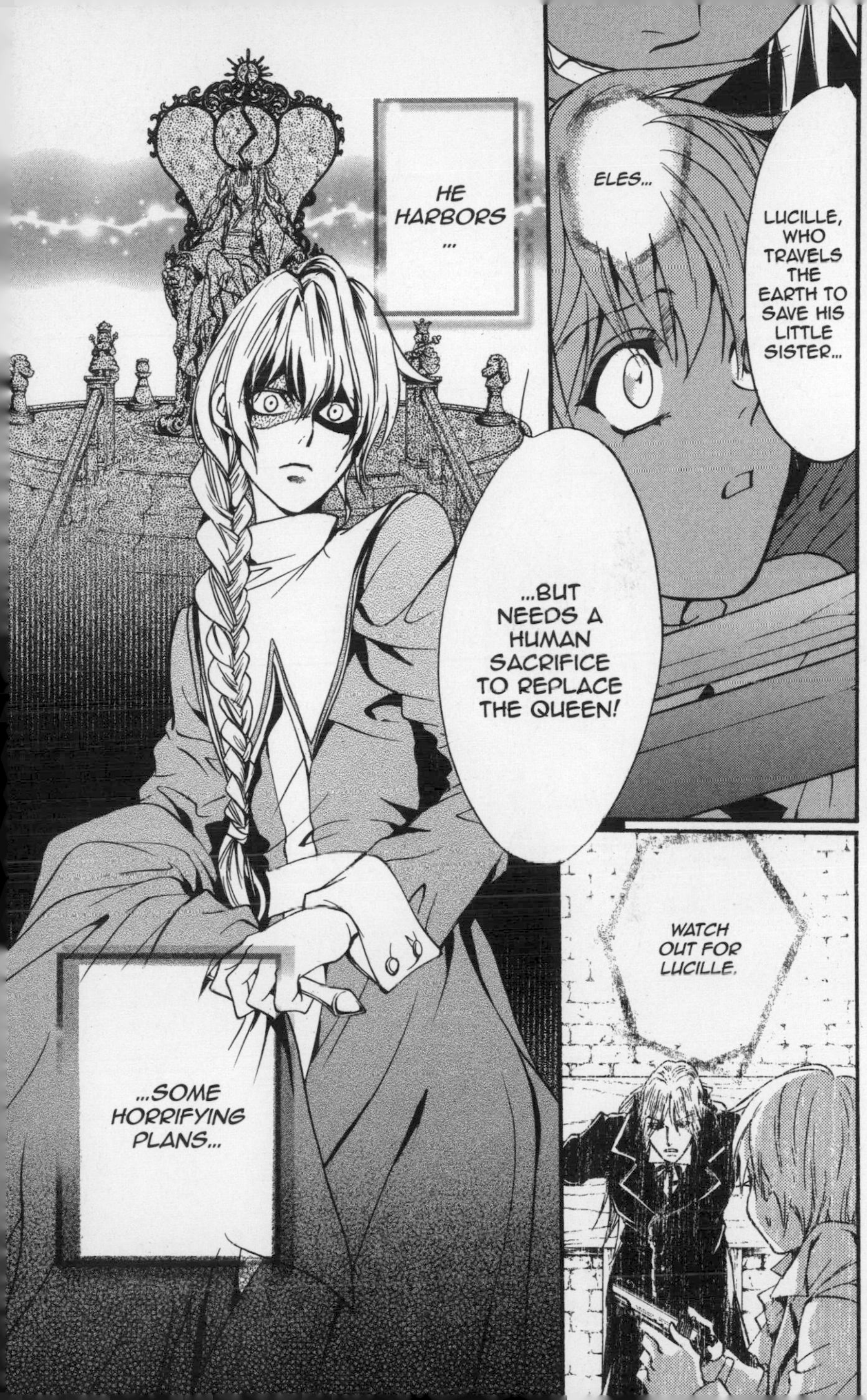
ELES...
LUCILLE, WHO TRAVELS THE EARTH TO SAVE HIS LITTLE SISTER...
...BUT NEEDS A HUMAN SACRIFICE TO REPLACE THE QUEEN!
WATCH OUT FOR LUCILLE.
HE HARBORS ...
...SOME HORRIFYING PLANS...

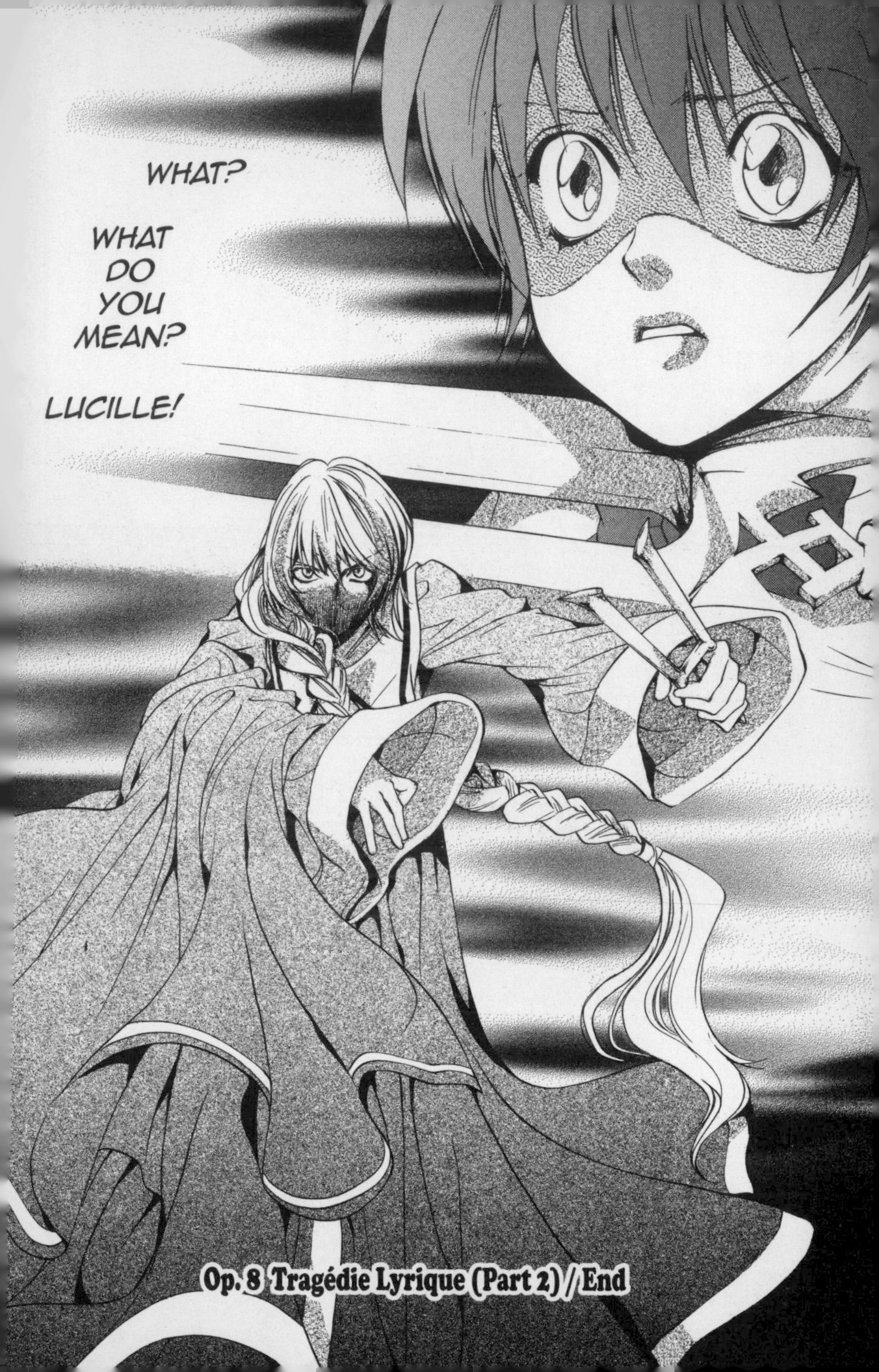
WHAT?
WHAT DO YOU MEAN?
LUCILLE!
Op. 8 Tragédie Lyrique (Part 2) / End

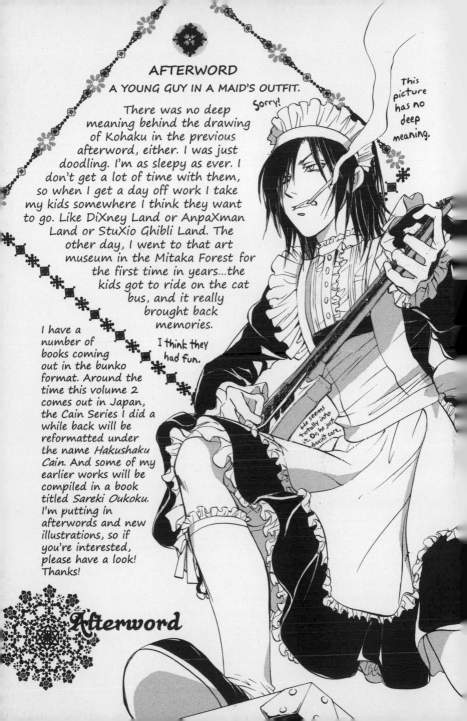

AFTERWORD
A YOUNG GUY IN A MAID'S OUTFIT.

Sorry!

This picture has no deep meaning.

There was no deep meaning behind the drawing of Kohaku in the previous afterword, either. I was just doodling. I'm as sleepy as ever. I don't get a lot of time with them, so when I get a day off work I take my kids somewhere I think they want to go. Like DiXney Land or AnpaXman Land or StuXio Ghibli Land. The other day, I went to that art museum in the Mitaka Forest for the first time in years...the kids got to ride on the cat bus, and it really brought back memories.

I think they had fun.

I have a number of books coming out in the bunko format. Around the time this volume 2 comes out in Japan, the Cain Series I did a while back will be reformatted under the name *Hakushaku Cain*. And some of my earlier works will be compiled in a book titled *Sareki Oukoku*. I'm putting in afterwords and new illustrations, so if you're interested, please have a look! Thanks!

He seems totally into it... Or, he just doesn't care.

Afterword

Creator:
Kaori Yuki

Date of Birth:
December 18

Blood Type:
B

Major Works:
Angel Sanctuary and The Cain Saga

 aori Yuki was born in Tokyo and started drawing at a very early age. Following her debut work, *Natsufuku no Erie* (Ellie in Summer Clothes), in the Japanese magazine *Bessatsu Hana to Yume*, she wrote a compelling series of short stories: *Zankoku na Douwatachi* (Cruel Fairy Tales), *Neji* (Screw) and *Sareki Ôkoku* (Gravel Kingdom).

As proven by her best-selling series *Angel Sanctuary*, *Godchild* and *Fairy Cube*, her celebrated body of work has etched an indelible mark on the Gothic comics genre. She likes mysteries and British films and is a fan of the movie *Dead Poets Society* and the show *Twin Peaks*.

GRAND GUIGNOL ORCHESTRA
Vol. 2
Shojo Beat Edition

STORY AND ART BY **KAORI YUKI**

Translation **Camellia Nieh**
Touch-up Art & Lettering **Eric Erbes**
Design **Fawn Lau**
Editors **Pancha Diaz, Joel Enos**

GUIGNOL KYUTEI GAKUDAN by Kaori Yuki
© Kaori Yuki 2009
All rights reserved.
First published in Japan in 2009 by HAKUSENSHA, Inc., Tokyo.
English language translation rights arranged with HAKUSENSHA, Inc., Tokyo.

The rights of the author(s) of the work(s) in this publication to be so identified
have been asserted in accordance with the Copyright, Designs and Patents Act 1988.
A CIP catalogue record for this book is available from the British Library.

Printed in the U.S.A.

Published by VIZ Media, LLC
P.O. Box 77010
San Francisco, CA 94107

10 9 8 7 6 5 4 3 2 1
First printing, February 2011

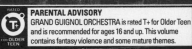

www.viz.com

www.shojobeat.com

Love Kaori Yuki?

Read the rest of VIZ Media's Kaori Yuki collection!

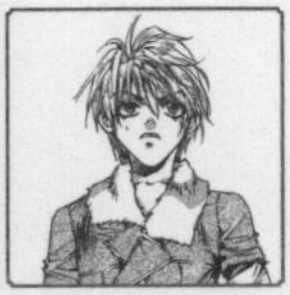

Angel Sanctuary • Rated T+ for Older Teen • 20 Volumes

The angel Alexiel loved God, but she rebelled against Heaven. As punishment, she is sent to Earth to live an endless series of tragic lives. She now inhabits the body of Setsuna Mudo, a troubled teen wrought with forbidden love.

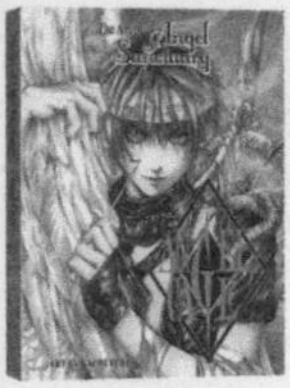

The Art of Angel Sanctuary: Angel Cage

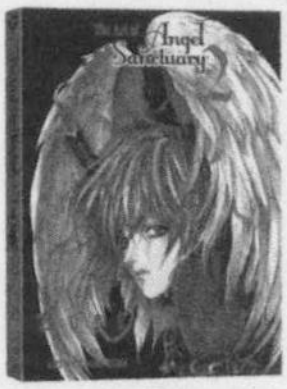

The Art of Angel Sanctuary 2: Lost Angel

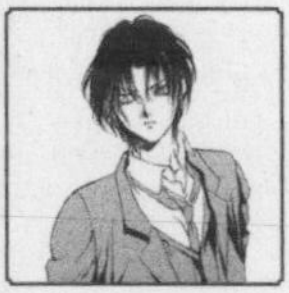

The Cain Saga • Rated M for Mature Readers • 5 Volumes

The prequel to the *Godchild* series, *The Cain Saga* follows the young Cain as he attempts to unravel the secrets of his birth. Delve into the tortured past of Earl Cain C. Hargreaves! Plus bonus short stories in each volume!

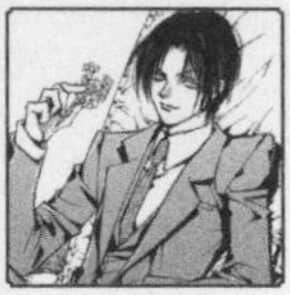

Godchild • Rated T+ for Older Teen • 8 Volumes

In 19th century London, dashing young nobleman Earl Cain Hargreaves weaves his way through the shadowy cobblestone streets that hide the dark secrets of aristocratic society. His mission is to solve the mystery of his shrouded lineage.

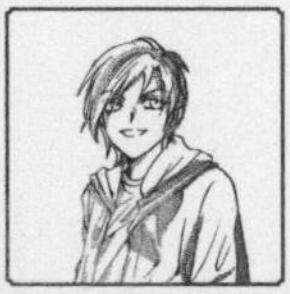

Fairy Cube • Rated T+ for Older Teen • 3 Volumes

Ian and Rin used to just *see* spirits. Now Ian *is* one. Using the Fairy Cube, Ian must figure out how to stop the lizard-spirit Tokage from taking over his life and destroying any chance he has of resurrection.

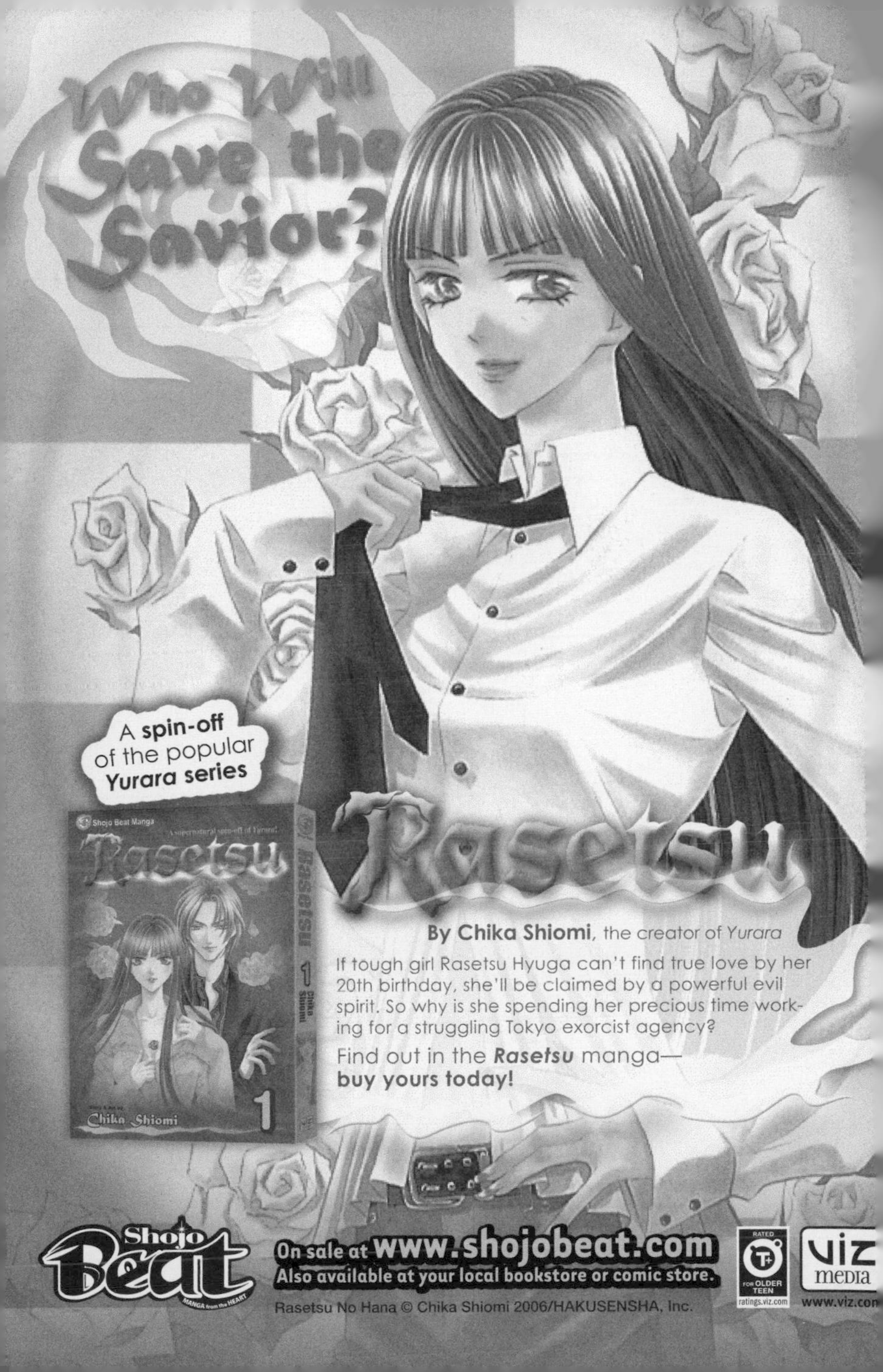
Who Will Save the Savior?
A spin-off of the popular Yurara series
Shojo Beat Manga
Rasetsu
Chika Shiomi
1
Rasetsu
By Chika Shiomi, the creator of Yurara
If tough girl Rasetsu Hyuga can't find true love by her 20th birthday, she'll be claimed by a powerful evil spirit. So why is she spending her precious time working for a struggling Tokyo exorcist agency?
Find out in the Rasetsu manga—buy yours today!
Shojo Beat
MANGA from the HEART
On sale at www.shojobeat.com
Also available at your local bookstore or comic store.
Rasetsu No Hana © Chika Shiomi 2006/HAKUSENSHA, Inc.
RATED T+ FOR OLDER TEEN
ratings.viz.com
VIZ media
www.viz.com

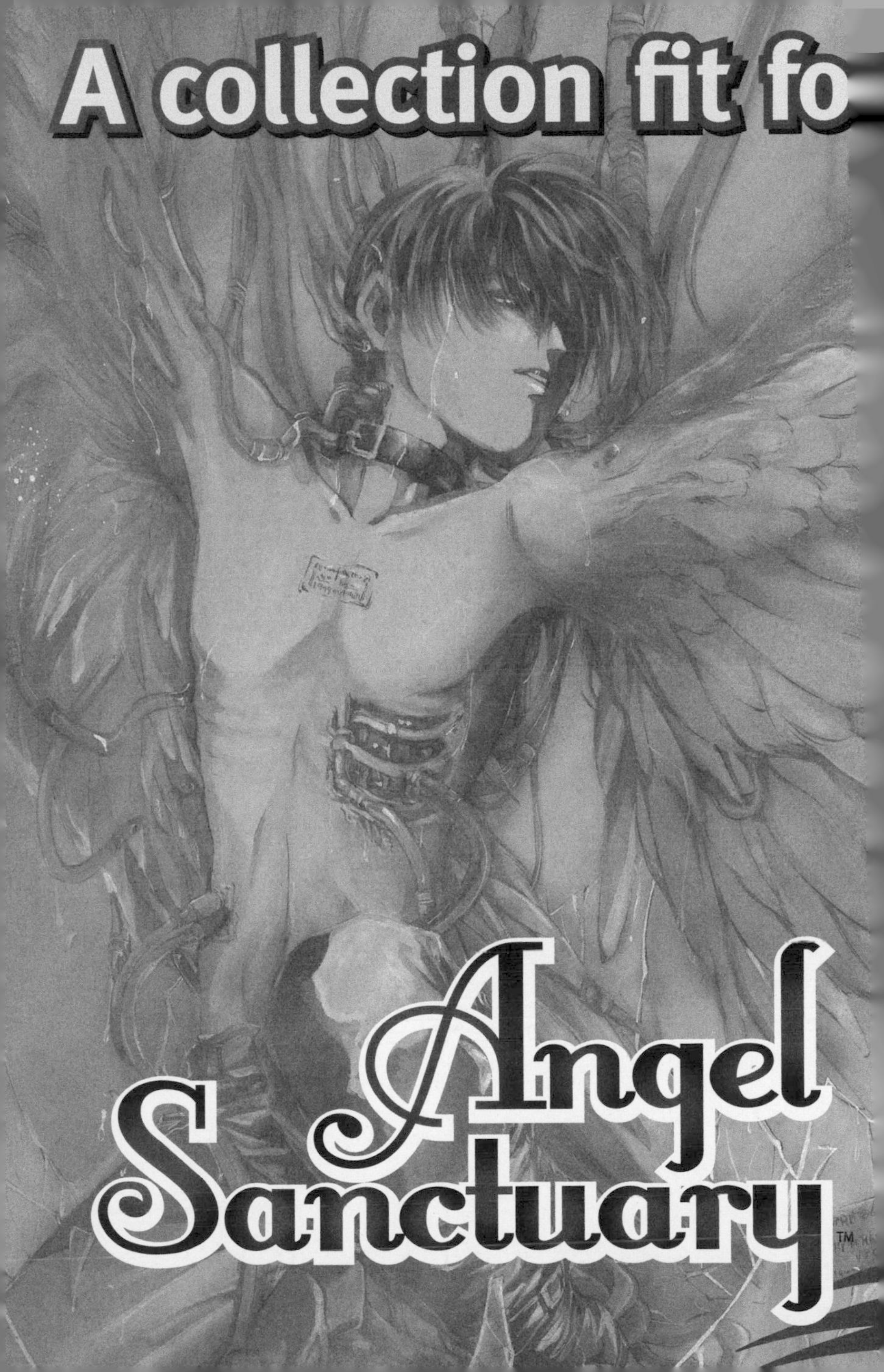

A collection fit fo
Angel Sanctuary™

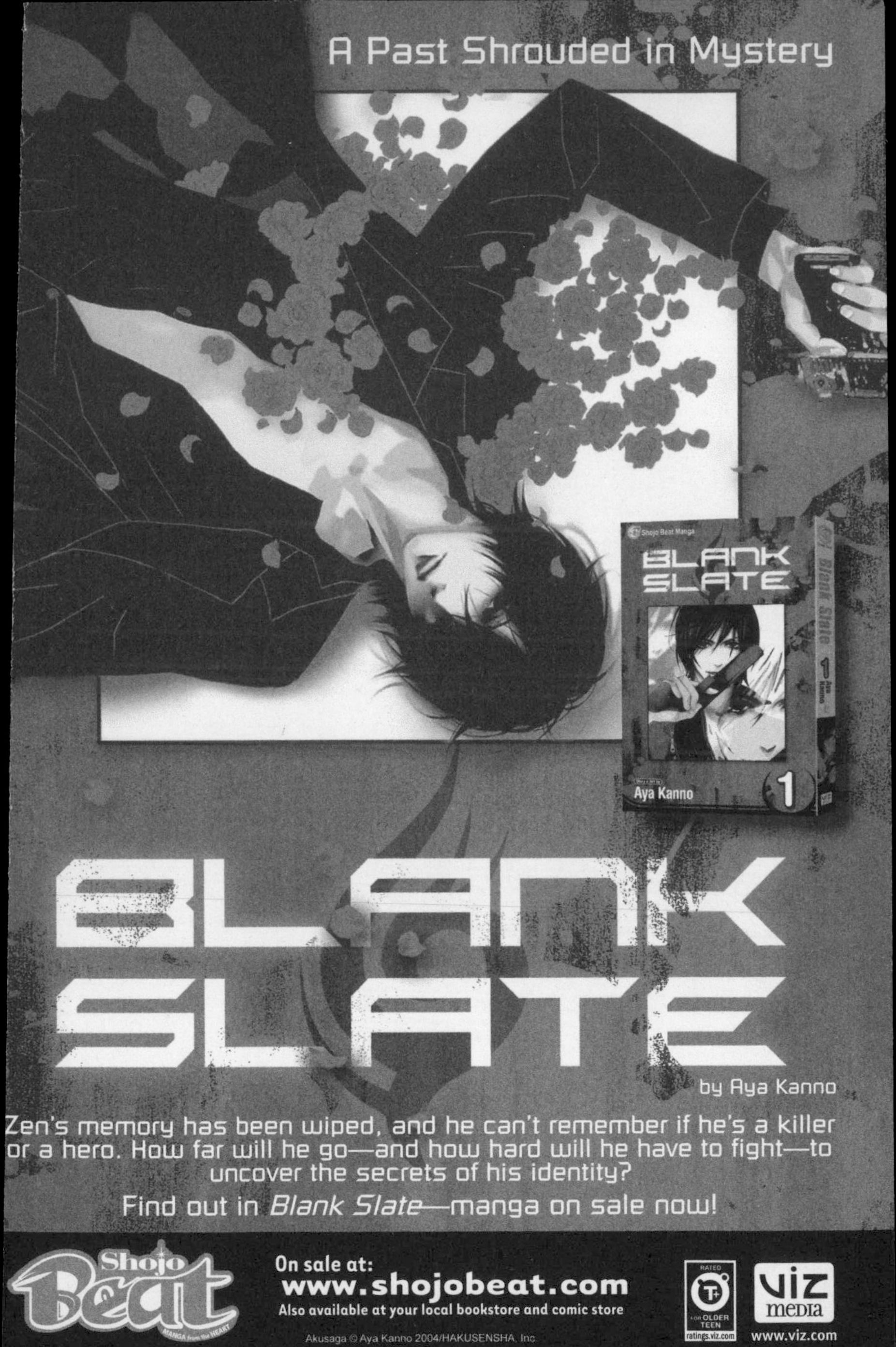
A Past Shrouded in Mystery
Shojo Beat Manga
BLANK SLATE
Aya Kanno
1
Blank Slate
BLANK SLATE
by Aya Kanno
Zen's memory has been wiped, and he can't remember if he's a killer or a hero. How far will he go—and how hard will he have to fight—to uncover the secrets of his identity?
Find out in *Blank Slate*—manga on sale now!
Shojo Beat
MANGA from the HEART
On sale at:
www.shojobeat.com
Also available at your local bookstore and comic store
RATED T+ FOR OLDER TEEN
ratings.viz.com
VIZ media
www.viz.com
Akusaga © Aya Kanno 2004/HAKUSENSHA, Inc.

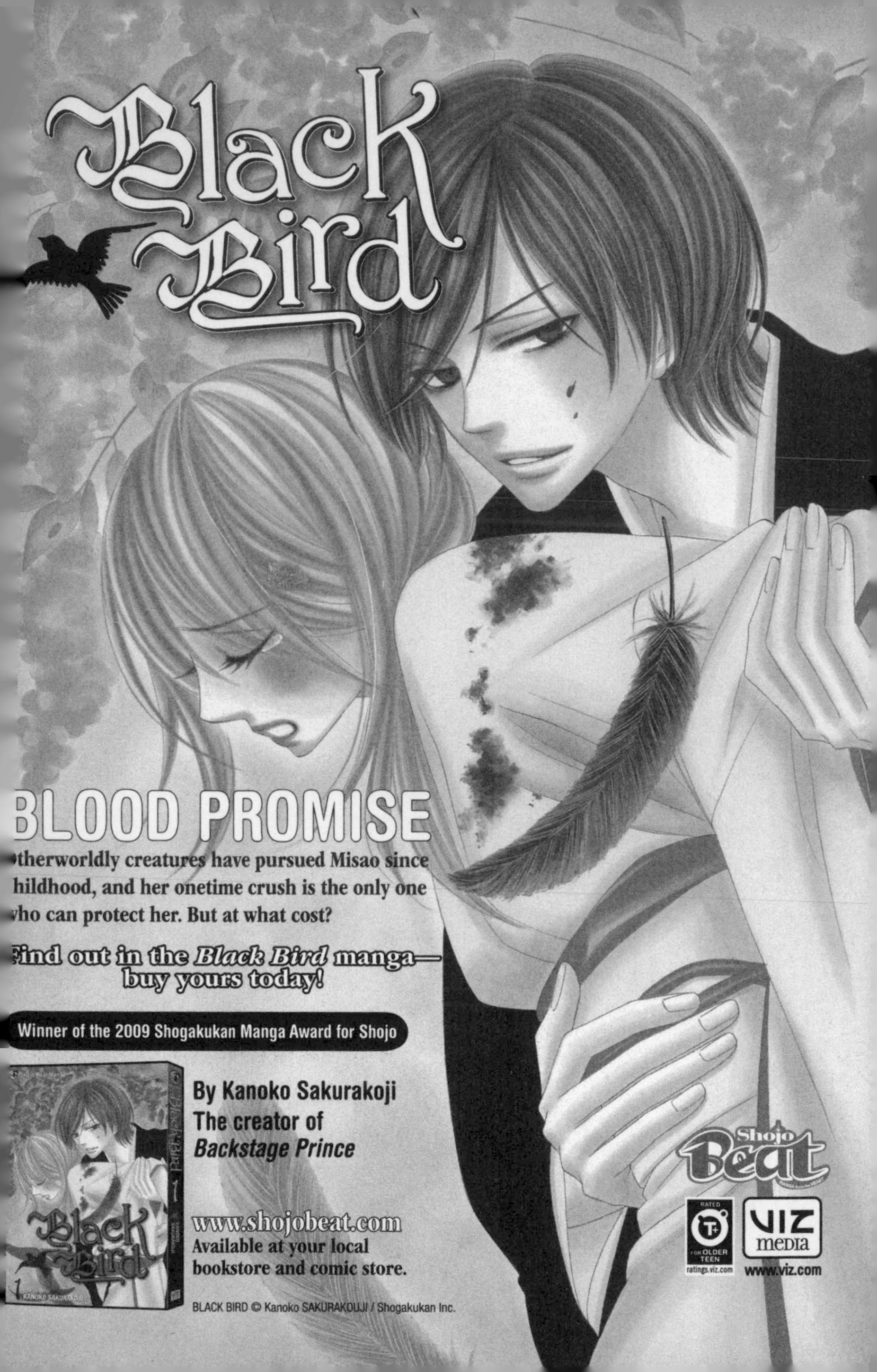
Black Bird
BLOOD PROMISE
Otherworldly creatures have pursued Misao since childhood, and her onetime crush is the only one who can protect her. But at what cost?
Find out in the Black Bird manga— buy yours today!
Winner of the 2009 Shogakukan Manga Award for Shojo
By Kanoko Sakurakoji
The creator of Backstage Prince
www.shojobeat.com
Available at your local bookstore and comic store.
Shojo Beat
RATED T+ FOR OLDER TEEN
ratings.viz.com
VIZ media
www.viz.com
BLACK BIRD © Kanoko SAKURAKOUJI / Shogakukan Inc.